SHADOW SCALE

Also by Rachel Hartman

Seraphina

Shadow Scale

RACHEL HARTMAN

DOUBLEDAY CANADA

Doubleday Canada and colophon are registered trademarks of
Random House of Canada Limited.

Library and Archives Canada Cataloguing in Publication

Hartman, Rachel, 1972-, author
Shadow scale / Rachel Hartman.

Sequel to: Seraphina.
Issued in print and electronic formats.
ISBN 978-0-385-66860-6 (bound) ISBN 978-0-385-66843-9 (epub)

I. Title.

PS8565.A6683S53 2015   jC813'.6   C2012-906582-X
                                                 C2012-907017-3

This book is a work of fiction. Names, characters, places and incidents are products of the
author's imagination or are used fictitiously. Any resemblance to actual events or locales or
persons, living or dead, is entirely coincidental.

Jacket design by Jason Zamajtuk

Printed and bound in the USA

Published in Canada by Doubleday Canada,
A division of Random House of Canada Limited,
A Penguin Random House Company

www.penguinrandomhouse.ca

10 9 8 7 6 5 4 3 2 1

Penguin
Random House
DOUBLEDAY CANADA

For Byron

Kerama

Lab 4

Porphyry

TANAMOOT

THE SOUTHLANDS

Lavondaville

N

W   E

S

GOREDD

Blystane

Ft. Oversea

SAMSAM

Segosh

NINYS

From Father Fargle's *Goredd*:

The Tangled Thicket of History

Let us first consider the role of Seraphina Dombegh in the events leading up to Queen Glisselda's reign.

Nearly forty years after Ardmagar Comonot and Queen Lavonda the Magnificent signed their historic treaty, the peace between dragons and humans was still dangerously fragile. In Lavondaville, the Sons of St. Ogdo preached anti-dragon rhetoric on street corners, fomented unrest, and committed violence against saarantrai. These dragons in human form were easily identified in those days by the bells they were forced to wear; for their own protection, saarantrai and their lizard-like cousins, the quigutl, were shut up in the neighborhood called Quighole every night, but this only served to single them out further. As the peace treaty's anniversary—and Ardmagar Comonot's state visit—neared, tensions mounted.

A fortnight before the Ardmagar was to arrive, tragedy struck. Queen Lavonda's only son, Prince Rufus, was murdered in classic draconic fashion: decapitation. His head, presumably eaten, was never found. Had a dragon truly killed him, though, or was it the Sons of St. Ogdo, hoping to inflame anti-dragon sentiment?

Into this thicket of politics and prejudice entered Seraphina Dombegh, newly hired assistant to the court composer, Viridius. The word *abomination* has fallen out of favor, but that is precisely what the people of Goredd would have considered Seraphina, for her mother was a dragon, her father a human. Had this secret been known, it could have meant Seraphina's death, so her father kept her isolated for her own safety. Silver dragon scales around her waist and left forearm might have given her away at any time. Whether it was loneliness or her musical talent that drove her, she took a terrible risk in leaving her father's house for Castle Orison.

Scales were not her only worry. Seraphina was also afflicted with maternal memories and visions of grotesque beings. Her maternal uncle, the dragon Orma, taught her to create within her mind a symbolic garden wherein she might house these curious beings; only by tending this garden of grotesques every night did she prevent visions from overtaking her.

Around the time of Prince Rufus's funeral, however, three denizens of Seraphina's mental garden overtook her in real life: Dame Okra Carmine, the Ninysh ambassador; a Samsamese piper called Lars; and Abdo, a young Porphyrian dancer. Seraphina eventually realized that these people were half-dragons like herself, that she was not alone in the world. They all had scales and peculiar abilities, mental or physical. It must have been both a relief and an additional worry. None of them were safe, after all. Lars, notably, was threatened on numerous occasions by Josef, Earl of Apsig, his dragon-hating half brother and a member of the Sons of St. Ogdo.

Seraphina might still have kept herself clear of politics and intrigue if not for her uncle Orma. For most of her life, he'd been her only friend, teaching her not merely how to control her visions but also music and draconic lore. Seraphina, in turn, had inspired in Orma an avuncular fondness, a depth of feeling deemed unacceptable by dragonkind. The draconic Censors, convinced that Orma was emotionally compromised, had hounded him for years, threatening to have him sent back to the dragons' homeland, the Tanamoot, for the surgical removal of his memories.

After Prince Rufus's funeral, Orma learned that his father, the banished ex-general Imlann, was in Goredd. Orma believed, and Seraphina's maternal memories confirmed, that Imlann was a threat to Ardmagar Comonot, part of a cabal of disgruntled generals who wished to destroy the peace with Goredd. Wary of the Censors, Orma did not trust himself to be impartial and unemotional about his own father. He asked Seraphina to report Imlann's presence to Prince Lucian Kiggs, Captain of the Queen's Guard. Though Seraphina would have liked to remain inconspicuous, she could not refuse her beloved uncle's request.

Did she approach Prince Lucian Kiggs with trepidation? Any sensible person would have. The prince had a reputation for being a perceptive and dogged investigator; if anyone at court was likely to uncover her secret, it was surely he. However, Seraphina had three unanticipated advantages. First, she had already come to his attention, favorably if unintentionally, as a patient harpsichord teacher to his cousin and fiancée, Princess Glisselda. Second, Seraphina had repeatedly found herself in a position to help people at court understand dragonkind, and the prince was grateful for her intercession. Finally, Prince Lucian, being the Queen's bastard grandson, had never felt quite comfortable at court; in Seraphina, he recognized a fellow outsider, even if he could not precisely identify why.

He believed her report about Imlann, even as he discerned that she was leaving certain things unsaid.

Two banished knights—Sir Cuthberte and Sir Karal—came

to the palace with news that they'd seen a rogue dragon in the countryside. Seraphina suspected it was Imlann. Prince Lucian Kiggs accompanied her to the knights' secret enclave to see if anyone could positively identify the rogue. Ancient Sir James recalled the dragon as "General Imlann" from an attack forty years prior. While they were there, Sir James's squire, Maurizio, demonstrated the dying martial art of dracomachia. Developed by St. Ogdo himself, dracomachia had once given Goredd the tools to battle dragons, but the art was now practiced by only a few. Seraphina realized how helpless humankind would be if the dragons broke the treaty.

Whether Imlann, in all his scaly, flaming horror, actually revealed himself to Seraphina and Prince Lucian on the road home or whether that episode is mere legend and embellishment is still a matter of scholarly debate. It is clear, however, that Seraphina and the prince became convinced that Imlann had killed Prince Rufus. They began to suspect that the wily old dragon was hiding at court in human form. Seraphina's warnings to Ardmagar Comonot, however, fell on deaf ears. The Ardmagar, though he had co-authored the peace, was arrogant and unsympathetic, not yet the dragon he would become in later years.

Imlann struck on Treaty Eve, giving poisoned wine to Princess Dionne, Princess Glisselda's mother. (Though the wine was also intended for Comonot, there is no evidence, contrary to some of my colleagues' assertions, that Princess Dionne and Comonot were engaged in an illicit love affair.) Seraphina and Prince Lucian prevented Princess Glisselda from drinking the wine, but Queen Lavonda was not so fortunate.

Let this be a lesson about the patience of dragons: Imlann had been at court for fifteen years, disguised as Princess Glisselda's governess, a trusted advisor and friend. Seraphina and Prince Lucian, realizing the truth at last, confronted Imlann, whereupon he seized Princess Glisselda and fled.

All the half-dragons had a role to play in Imlann's capture and death: Dame Okra Carmine's premonitions helped Seraphina and Prince Lucian find him; Lars distracted him with bagpipes so that Prince Lucian could rescue Princess Glisselda; and young Abdo squeezed Imlann's still-soft throat, preventing him from spitting fire. Seraphina delayed Imlann's escape by revealing the truth about herself, that she was his granddaughter, giving Orma time to transform. Orma was no match for Imlann, alas, and was badly injured. It was another dragon, Undersecretary Eskar of the dragon embassy, who finished Imlann off, high above the city.

History has shown that Imlann was indeed part of a cabal of dragon generals determined to overthrow Comonot and destroy the peace. While he wreaked havoc in Goredd, the others staged a coup in the Tanamoot, seizing control of the dragon government. The generals, who later styled themselves the "Old Ard," sent the Queen a letter declaring Comonot a criminal and demanding that Goredd turn him over at once. Queen Lavonda was incapacitated by poison, and Princess Dionne was dead. Princess Glisselda, in her first act as Queen, decided that Goredd would not return Comonot to face trumped-up charges and that, if necessary, Goredd would go to war for peace.

If your historian may be permitted a personal note: some forty years ago, when I was but a novice at St. Prue's, I served wine at a banquet our abbot gave in honor of Seraphina, herself a venerable lady of more than a hundred and ten. I had not yet discovered my historical vocation—in fact, I think something in her ignited my interests—but finding myself close to her at the end of the evening, I had the opportunity to ask exactly one question. Imagine, if you will, what question you would have asked. Alas, I was young and foolish, and I blurted out, "Is it true that you and Prince Lucian Kiggs, Heaven hold him, confessed your love for each other before the dragon civil war even began?"

Her dark eyes sparkled, and for a moment I felt I glimpsed a much younger woman inside the old. She took my plump young hand in her gnarled old one and squeezed it, saying, "Prince Lucian was the most honest and honorable man I have ever known, and that was a very long time ago."

Thus was the opportunity of a lifetime squandered by callow, romantic youth. And yet I felt and still feel that her twinkling eyes answered, even if her tongue would not.

I have but skimmed events that other historians have spent entire careers untangling. To my mind, Seraphina's story only really began when her uncle Orma, assisted by Undersecretary Eskar, went into hiding to escape the Censors, and when Seraphina, on the eve of war, decided the time had come to find the rest of the denizens of her mind's garden, the other half-dragons scattered throughout the Southlands and Porphyry. Those are the events I will examine here.

ᴄ∿Prologue∿ᴐ

I returned to myself.

I rubbed my eyes, forgetting that the left was bruised, and the pain snapped the world into focus. I was sitting on the splintery wooden floor of Uncle Orma's office, deep in the library of St. Ida's Music Conservatory, books piled around me like a nest of knowledge. A face looming above me resolved into Orma's beaky nose, black eyes, spectacles, and beard; his expression showed more curiosity than concern.

I was eleven years old. Orma had been teaching me meditation for months, but I'd never been so deep inside my head before, nor felt so disoriented emerging from it.

He thrust a mug of water under my nose. I grasped it shakily and drank. I wasn't thirsty, but any trace of kindness in my dragon uncle was a thing to encourage.

"Report, Seraphina," he said, straightening himself and

pushing up his spectacles. His voice held neither warmth nor impatience. Orma crossed the room in two strides and sat upon his desk, not bothering to clear the books off first.

I shifted on the hard floor. Providing me with a cushion would have required more empathy than a dragon—even in human form—could muster.

"It worked," I said in a voice like an elderly frog's. I gulped water and tried again. "I imagined a grove of fruit trees and pictured the little Porphyrian boy among them."

Orma tented his long fingers in front of his gray doublet and stared at me. "And were you able to induce a true vision of him?"

"Yes. I took his hands in mine, and then . . ." It was difficult to describe the next bit, a sickening swirl that had felt as if my consciousness were being sucked down a drain. I was too weary to explain. "I saw him in Porphyry, playing near a temple, chasing a puppy—"

"No headache or nausea?" interrupted Orma, whose draconic heart could not be plied with puppies.

I shook my head to make sure. "None."

"You exited the vision at will?" He might have been checking a list.

"I did."

"You seized the vision rather than it seizing you?" Check. "Did you give a name to the boy's symbolic representation in your head, the avatar?"

I felt the color rise in my cheeks, which was silly. Orma was incapable of laughing at me. "I named him Fruit Bat."

Orma nodded gravely, as if this were the most solemn and fitting name ever devised. "What did you name the rest?"

We stared at each other. Somewhere in the library outside Orma's office, a librarian monk was whistling off-key.

"W-was I supposed to have done the rest?" I said. "Shouldn't we give it some time? If Fruit Bat stays in his special garden and doesn't plague me with visions, we'll be certain—"

"How did you get that black eye?" Orma said, his gaze hawkish.

I pursed my lips. He knew perfectly well: I'd been overtaken by a vision during yesterday's music lesson, fallen out of my chair, and slammed my face against the corner of his desk.

At least I hadn't smashed my oud, he'd said then.

"It is only a matter of time before a vision fells you in the street and you are run over by a carriage," Orma said, leaning forward, elbows on his knees. "You don't have the luxury of time, unless you plan to stay in bed for the foreseeable future."

I carefully set the mug on the floor, away from his books. "I don't like inviting them all into my head at once," I said. "Some of the beings I see are quite horrifying. It's awful that they invade my mind without asking, but—"

"You misunderstand the mechanism," said Orma mildly. "If these grotesques were invading your consciousness, our other meditation strategies would have kept them out. *Your* mind is responsible: it reaches out compulsively. The avatars you create will be a real, permanent connection to these beings, so your mind won't have to lunge out clumsily anymore. If you want to see them, you need only reach inward."

I couldn't imagine wanting to visit any of these grotesques, ever. Suddenly it all seemed too much to bear. I'd started with my favorite, the friendliest one, and that had exhausted me. My eyes blurred again; I wiped the good one on my sleeve, ashamed to be leaking tears in front of my dragon uncle.

He watched me, his head cocked like a bird's. "You are not helpless, Seraphina. You are . . . Why is *helpful* not the antonym of *helpless*?"

He seemed so genuinely befuddled by this question that I laughed in spite of myself. "But how do I proceed?" I said. "Fruit Bat was obvious: he's always climbing trees. That dread swamp slug can loll in mud, I suppose, and I'll put the wild man in a cave. But the rest? What kind of garden do I build to contain them?"

Orma scratched his false beard; it often seemed to irritate him. He said, "Do you know what's wrong with your religion?"

I blinked at him, trying to parse the non sequitur.

"There's no proper creation myth," he said. "Your Saints appeared six, seven hundred years ago and kicked out the pagans—who had a perfectly serviceable myth involving the sun and a female aurochs, I might add. But for some reason your Saints didn't bother with an origin story." He cleaned his spectacles on the hem of his doublet. "Do you know the Porphyrian creation story?"

I stared at him pointedly. "My tutor woefully neglects Porphyrian theology." He was my tutor these days.

Orma ignored the jibe. "It's tolerably short. The twin gods, Necessity and Chance, walked among the stars. What needed to be, was; what might be, sometimes was."

I waited for the rest, but that seemed to be it. "I like that myth," he went on. "It corresponds to the laws of nature, except for the part where there are gods."

I frowned, trying to understand why he was telling me this. "Is that how you think I ought to create the rest of the garden?" I hazarded. "Walk through my mind like a god?"

"It's not blasphemy," he said, replacing his spectacles and peering owlishly at me. "It's a metaphor, like everything else you're building in your mind. It is permissible to be the god of your own metaphors."

"Gods aren't helpless," I said, with more bravado than I felt.

"Seraphina isn't helpless," said Orma solemnly. "This garden will be your bulwark. It will keep you safe."

"I wish I could believe that," I said, my voice frog-like again.

"It would probably help if you did. The human brain's capacity for belief produces interesting neurochemical effects in the . . ."

I ignored the lecture, adjusted my posture, and set my knees akimbo with my hands upon them. Closing my eyes, I made each breath successively deeper and slower.

I descended into my other world.

$\backsim$One$\sim$

Queen Glisselda spotted the dragon first. It was a swift-moving patch of darker darkness against the night sky, obliterating stars and birthing them again.

She pointed at it, shouting, "Singleton from the west, St. Ogdo save us!" in imitation of the knights of old. She spoiled the impression slightly by bouncing on her toes and laughing. The winter wind carried the cheerful sound away; far below us the city curled under a quilt of new snow, silent and thoughtful as a sleeping child.

Trained spotters had once scanned the skies for dragon battalions from this selfsame place, atop Castle Orison's Ard Tower. Tonight it was only the Queen and me, and the approaching "singleton" was a friend, thank Allsaints: the dragon Eskar, erstwhile undersecretary at our dragon embassy. She'd helped my uncle Orma evade the Censors almost three months ago, just as the dragon civil war was breaking out.

Ardmagar Comonot, the deposed leader of dragonkind, had expected Eskar to find Orma a safe haven and then return to us in Goredd, where Comonot had established his headquarters in exile. The Ardmagar had intended to make her one of his advisors, or even a general, but months had brought no Eskar and no explanation.

She had contacted Comonot, via quigutl device, earlier this evening. Over dinner, Comonot had informed Queen Glisselda that Eskar would fly in after midnight. Then he had taken himself off to bed, leaving the Queen to wait up or not, as she saw fit.

It was a very Comonot way of dealing with things. The Queen wearied of him.

He'd said nothing about why Eskar had suddenly decided to come back, or where she'd been. It was possible he didn't know. Glisselda and I had been speculating about it to distract ourselves from the cold. "Eskar has decided the dragon civil war is dragging on too long, and means to end it single-handedly," was Glisselda's final assessment. "Did she ever glare at you, Seraphina? She could stop the very planets in their spheres."

I hadn't experienced the glare, but I'd seen the way she looked at my uncle three months ago. Eskar had surely been with him this whole time.

Glisselda and I each held a torch, intending Eskar to understand that she should land on the tower top. This was Prince Lucian Kiggs's idea—something about updrafts and a fear that she'd take out a window trying to land in a courtyard. He had left unspoken the fact that she was less likely to alarm anyone way up here. Goredd had begun to see full-sized dragons in the sky, as

Comonot's allies came and went, but it would be an exaggeration to say people were used to it.

Now that Eskar was approaching, she looked too large to land on the tower top. Maybe she thought so, too; flapping dark leathery wings with a rush of hot wind, she veered south toward the far edge of town. Three city blocks still smoldered there, sending the new snow up as steam.

"What's she doing, checking out her countryman's handiwork? Some insomniac is going to see her," said Glisselda, pushing back the hood of her fur-lined cloak, her earlier merriment already dimming to fretfulness. Alas, this was her usual expression these days. Her golden curls gleamed incongruously in the torchlight.

Eskar soared into the spangled sky and then plummeted back out of the darkness, diving toward the heart of the city like a falcon after a wren. Glisselda gasped in alarm. At the last second, Eskar pulled up short—a black shadow against the new snow— and skimmed along the frozen Mews River, cracking the ice with her serpentine tail.

"And now she reveals how she might breach our defenses, flying so high our missiles and flaming pyria can't reach her. That's not how those houses were razed, Eskar!" called the young Queen into the wind, as if the dragon could hear her from such a distance. "He was already inside the walls!"

He had been the third dragon assassin Prince Lucian had flushed out, sent after Comonot by the Old Ard. The saarantras had transformed into a full-sized dragon to make his escape. Comonot had transformed in turn and killed his assailant before he could flee, but five people had died and fifty-six lost their homes in the resulting inferno.

All that destruction, caused by just two dragons. None of us dared to guess how awful the damage would be if Comonot's Loyalists failed to hold off the Old Ard and war came to Goredd in earnest.

"Lars is designing new war machines," I said, trying to inject some optimism. "And don't discount the dracomachists training at Fort Oversea." The elderly knights of the Southlands and their middle-aged squires, hastily promoted to knights, had joined together in this endeavor.

Glisselda snorted derisively, her eyes following Eskar's second circuit of the city. "Even when our knights were at full strength—and quickly trained dracomachists are not knights—this city was routinely burned to the ground. You and I have never seen the like, having been raised in peacetime."

The wind gusted, making it hard to forget how high up we were; my palms sweated in my gloves. "Comonot's Loyalists will defend us."

"I believe they will defend our people, but the city itself doesn't matter a jot to them. Lucian says we must focus on making the tunnels livable again. We survived there before, and we can always rebuild." She raised an arm and dropped it, as if she found it futile even to gesture. "This city is Grandmamma's legacy; it has blossomed in peacetime. I hate that I might have to let it go."

Eskar was returning, catching an updraft on the eastern side of Castle Hill. Glisselda and I pressed back against the parapet as the dragon came in to land. Her dark, laboring wings blasted sulfurous air, extinguishing our torches. I bent into the wind, terrified of being gusted over the edge. Eskar touched down on the tower top and paused with wings extended, a living shadow against the sky. I had dealt with dragons—I was half dragon—but the sight still raised hairs on the back of my neck. Before our eyes, the fangy, scaly darkness furled and contracted, cooled and condensed, folding in upon itself until all that remained on the icy tower top was a statuesque naked woman.

Glisselda gracefully swept off her fur cloak and approached the saarantras—the dragon in human form—holding out the warmed garment. Eskar bowed her head, and Glisselda draped the mantle gently across her bare shoulders.

"Welcome back, Undersecretary," said the young Queen.

"I'm not staying," said Eskar flatly.

"Indeed," said Glisselda, no trace of surprise in her voice. She'd only been Queen for three months, since her grandmother had fallen ill from poison and grief, but she'd already mastered the art of appearing unflappable. "Does Ardmagar Comonot know?"

"I'm more useful to him where I've been," Eskar said. "He will understand when I explain. Where is he?"

"Asleep, to be sure," said Glisselda. Her smile covered a spectacular annoyance that Comonot could not be bothered to stay up and greet Eskar himself. Glisselda saved her complaints about Comonot for her harpsichord lessons, so I routinely heard how inconsiderate he was; how she tired of apologizing to human allies for his boorish behavior; how ready she was for him to win his war and go home.

I understood dragons reasonably well, thanks to my uncle

Orma and to memories left me by my mother. Comonot could not offend Eskar, whatever he did. Indeed, the Undersecretary was probably wondering why we hadn't gone to bed ourselves. While Glisselda had felt propriety demanded a welcoming party, I was so thirsty for news of Uncle Orma that I'd leaped at the opportunity to greet Eskar myself.

I felt a little overcome, seeing her again. I'd last glimpsed her protectively holding my injured uncle's hand at St. Gobnait's Infirmary; it felt like an age ago. I reflexively extended a hand to her now and said, "Orma's well? You're not here with bad news, I hope."

Eskar looked at my hand and cocked an eyebrow. "He's fine, unless he's taking advantage of my absence to do something inadvisable."

"Please come inside, Undersecretary," Glisselda said. "It's a bitter night."

Eskar had brought a bundle of clothing clasped in her talons; she picked it out of the snow and followed us down the narrow stairs. Glisselda had cleverly left another torch burning below us in the belfry, and she collected it as we spiraled down the tower. We crossed a small courtyard, ghostly with snow. Most of Castle Orison was asleep, but night guards watched us pass through a back corridor into the palace proper. If they'd been alarmed by the late-night arrival of a dragon, they were too professional to show it.

A page boy, so sleepy he seemed not to register Eskar at all, held the door of the new Queen's study. Glisselda had left her grandmother's book-filled chamber alone, almost superstitiously, and had chosen another salon for herself, airier, more parlor than library. A broad desk loomed before the dark windows; rich tapestries cloaked the walls. At the hearth to our left, Prince Lucian Kiggs prodded the fire industriously.

Kiggs had arranged four high-backed chairs before the fire and started a kettle warming. He straightened to greet us, smoothing his crimson doublet, his expression neutral but his dark eyes keen. "Undersecretary," he said, giving the semi-naked saarantras full courtesy. Eskar ignored him, and I suppressed a smile. I'd hardly seen the prince these three months, but every gesture, every dark curl on his head, was still dear to me. He held my gaze briefly, then turned his attention to Glisselda. It would not do for him to address the second court composer before his cousin, fiancée, and Queen.

"Do sit, Selda," he said, brushing imaginary dust off one of the middle chairs and offering his hand. "I should think you're half frozen."

Glisselda took his proffered hand and let him seat her. There was snow around the hem of her woolen gown; she shook it onto the painted hearth tiles.

I took the chair nearest the door. I had been invited here for news of my uncle and should leave if the conversation turned to state secrets, but I was also, unofficially, a translator of sorts, helping smooth out dragon-human interactions. That Glisselda hadn't thrown Comonot out of the palace yet was due in part to my diplomacy.

Eskar dumped her bundle onto the seat between mine and Glisselda's and began untying it. Kiggs turned determinedly back to the fire, placing a new log with a cascade of sparks. "Have you come with good news about the war, Eskar?" he said.

"No," said Eskar, locating her trousers and turning them right side out. "I've been nowhere near the front. Nor do I intend to go there."

"Where have you been?" I blurted, entirely out of order but unable to contain myself. Kiggs met my eye, his brows bowed sympathetically.

Eskar tensed. "With Orma, as I'm sure you guessed. I don't like to say where. If the Censors learn his whereabouts, his mind is forfeit. They will strip his memories bare."

"Obviously none of us would tell them," said Glisselda, sounding affronted.

Eskar shoved her head and arms into her tunic. "Forgive me," she said as her head popped out. "Caution becomes a habit. We've been in Porphyry."

Relief rushed through me, as if I'd been underwater for three months and could finally take a breath. I was seized with an impulse to hug Eskar but knew better than to try. Dragons tend to bristle when embraced.

Glisselda was watching Eskar through narrowed eyes. "Your loyalty to Orma is admirable, but you owe even more to your Ardmagar. He could use a smart, strong fighter like you. I saw you bring down the dragon Imlann."

There was a long pause. Imlann, my dragon grandfather, had struck at midwinter, killing Glisselda's mother, poisoning her grandmother, and attempting to assassinate Ardmagar Comonot.

Orma had battled Imlann in the sky and been gravely injured; Eskar had arrived in time to finish Imlann off. Meanwhile, a cabal of dragon generals, the Old Ard, who deplored Comonot's Treaty with Goredd, had led a coup in the Tanamoot. They'd seized the capital and declared Comonot an outlaw.

If Comonot had been killed, the Old Ard might simply have swooped down upon Goredd, reigniting the war Comonot and Queen Lavonda had extinguished forty years ago. Comonot lived, however, and he had Loyalists willing to fight for him. The war had so far stayed in the mountains to the north, dragon against dragon, while Goredd watched warily. The Old Ard wanted Comonot, an end to peace with humankind, and their southern hunting grounds back; they were coming south eventually if the Loyalists couldn't hold them.

Eskar combed her fingers through her short black hair, making it stand on end, and sat down. "I cannot be Comonot's general," she said bluntly. "War is illogical."

Kiggs, who had taken the kettle off the fire and begun filling cups with tea, overfilled a cup and scalded his fingers. "Help me understand, Eskar," he said, shaking his hand and frowning. "Is it illogical for Comonot to want his country back, or to defend himself—and Goredd—from the Old Ard's aggression?"

"Neither," said Eskar, accepting a cup of tea from the prince. "Comonot is right to resist. But it's a reactive stance, answering aggression with aggression."

"War begets war," I said, quoting Pontheus, Kiggs's favorite philosopher. He met my eye and risked a quick smile.

Eskar turned her teacup in her hands but did not drink. "Reactivity makes him nearsighted. He focuses upon immediate threats and loses sight of the true goal."

"And this true goal is what, in your estimation?" said Kiggs, passing a cup to his cousin. Glisselda accepted it, never taking her eyes off Eskar.

"Ending this war," said Eskar, staring back at Glisselda. Neither of them blinked.

"That's what the Ardmagar is trying to do," said Kiggs, his eyes darting toward me with an unspoken question. I shrugged, having no insight into Eskar's argument.

"No, the Ardmagar is trying to win," said Eskar, glaring down her nose.

When we did not appear enlightened by this distinction, Eskar clarified: "Dragons lay one egg at a time, and we grow slowly. Each death is significant, and so we settle our differences with litigation, or with an individual combat at most.

"It has never been our way to fight on this scale; if the war continues, our whole species loses. Comonot should return to our capital, the Kerama, take up the Opal of Office, and argue his case, as is his right. If he can get there, our laws and traditions dictate that the Ker shall hear him out. The fighting would cease at once."

"You're certain the Old Ard would accept this?" asked Kiggs, handing me the final cup of tea.

"There are a surprising number of dragons in the Tanamoot who haven't taken sides," said Eskar. "They will come down on the side of order and tradition."

Glisselda tapped her foot on the hearth tiles. "How is Comonot to get there without fighting every ard along the way? There's a whole war's worth of enemies in his path."

"Not if he follows my sensible plan," said Eskar.

We all leaned in. Surely this was why she'd come back. But she scratched her chin and said nothing.

"Which is what, exactly?" I prompted, as designated dragonprodder.

"He should return with me to Porphyry," said Eskar, "and enter the Tanamoot from the other side, via the Omiga River valley. The Old Ard won't anticipate an incursion from that direction. Our treaty with the Porphyrians is so ancient that we forget it's not a law of nature but a document that can be changed or disregarded at need."

"The Porphyrians would allow this?" said Kiggs, swirling his tea.

"The Ardmagar would have to bargain," said Eskar. "And I expect that there might still be fighting along this route, so he can't go alone."

Queen Glisselda looked up at the shadowed ceiling, thinking. "Would he take an ard with him?"

"That would alarm the Porphyrians and make them uncooperative," said Eskar solemnly. "Porphyry has its own ard, a community of dragon exiles who've chosen a circumscribed life in human form over excision by the Censors. It's a provision of our treaty: Porphyry keeps an eye on these deviants in exchange for our leaving their precious valley alone. Some exiles might accompany Comonot if he'll pardon them and let them come home."

"How many is some?" asked Kiggs, spotting the weak link at once. "Enough?"

Eskar shrugged. "Leave that to me."

"And to Orma," I said, liking the thought of him helping the Ardmagar's cause.

At this mention of my uncle's name, Eskar lowered her gaze for a second and her lower lip twitched. I saw—or maybe felt—the smile lurking below the surface. I glanced at the royal cousins, but they seemed not to have registered the expression at all.

She was fond of Orma. I knew it. For a moment I missed him terribly.

Eskar fished in a deep pocket of her trousers and extracted a sealed letter. "For you," she said. "It isn't safe for Orma to send anything through the post, or use thniks. I enforce his safety tyrannically, he tells me."

The letter's wax seal, brittle from the cold, shattered under my fingers. I recognized the handwriting, and my heart beat faster. Leaning toward the wavering firelight, I read the dear, familiar scrawl:

Eskar will tell you where I am. You and I spoke of it often enough; I am pursuing the research I proposed. You will remember. I've been unexpectedly lucky, but I cannot put my findings here. I only risk writing you (despite Eskar's admonitions) because I have learned something potentially useful to your queen.

I have reason to think that you and other half-dragons can thread your minds together. "Like beads on a string," it has been described. In so doing, you will find you can make a barrier in the air, an unseen wall, strong enough to stop a dragon midflight. "Like a bird against a window," according to my source, who has more flair for description than I. You will be astonished to learn who it is.

The process will require practice. The more ityasaari on your string, the stronger the barrier. The uses should be obvious. I urge haste in finding your fellows before the war comes south. Unless you give up prematurely, your search will bring you here.

All in ard,

O

While I read, Eskar proclaimed herself tired. Glisselda escorted her to the anteroom and roused the dozy page boy, who led Eskar to her quarters. I was hazily aware of this, and of Lucian Kiggs watching me while I read. When I finished the letter, I looked up and met the prince's dark, questioning eyes.

I tried to smile reassuringly, but the letter had produced such a riot of emotions in me that I felt only the struggle between them. It was bittersweet hearing from Orma, all my love bound up in sorrow for his exile. His proposal, on the other hand, fascinated and horrified me. I had longed to find the others of my kind, but I'd had a frightening experience early on with another half-dragon invading my mind. Just the idea of another mind threaded to mine made me squirm.

"I'll be interested in what Comonot makes of her plan," said Queen Glisselda, returning to her seat. "Surely he's thought of this and rejected it. And there is still a great deal of risk to Goredd if he pleads his case and fails." Her blue eyes darted back and forth between Kiggs and me. "You're making strange faces. What did I miss?"

"Orma has had an idea," I said, handing her the letter. Glisselda held the page, and Kiggs read over her shoulder, their dark and golden heads together.

"What is he researching?" said Kiggs, looking at me over Glisselda's bowed head.

"Historical references to half-dragons," I said. "My strangeness, in part, got him obsessed with learning whether there had been others." I'd told them about my garden of grotesques; they had some idea what I meant by strangeness.

"In part?" asked Kiggs, catching the qualifier at once. He was too sharp by half; I had to look away, or my smile was going to reveal things it shouldn't.

"Orma also found it irritatingly illogical that there are no records of interbreeding in the dragon archives and no mention in Goreddi literature. The Saints mention 'abominations,' and there are laws forbidding cohabitation, but that's it. He thought surely someone, somewhere, would have tried the experiment and recorded the results."

Talk of dragon "experimentation" produces an odd facial expression in humans, halfway between amused and appalled. The Queen and prince were no exceptions.

I continued, "The Porphyrians have a word for what I am—ityasaari—and Orma had heard rumors that Porphyrians might be more open to the possibility of ..." I trailed off. Even now, when everyone knew about me, it was hard to talk about the practical mechanics of my parentage. "He hoped they might have some useful records."

"He seems to have been right," said Glisselda, scanning the letter again. She turned to me and smiled, patting Eskar's empty chair. I shifted one seat closer to the royal cousins. "What do you make of this 'unseen wall' idea?"

I shook my head. "I've never heard of such a thing. I can't picture it."

"It would be like St. Abaster's Trap," said Kiggs. I stared at him incredulously; he smiled, enjoying that. "Am I the only one who reads scripture? St. Abaster could harness the fires of Heaven to make a shining net with which he pulled dragons out of the sky."

I groaned. "I stopped reading St. Abaster when I got to 'Women of the South, take not the worm to thy beds, for thusly wilt thou bear thine own damnation.'"

Kiggs blinked slowly, as at a dawning realization. "That's not even the worst thing he says about dragons or . . . or . . ."

"And he's not alone," I said. "St. Ogdo, St. Vitt. Orma once extracted the worst parts and made me a pamphlet. Reading St. Abaster, in particular, is like being slapped."

"But will you attempt this mind-threading?" Queen Glisselda said with barely concealed hope. "If there's any chance it could spare our city . . ."

I shuddered, but covered it with exaggerated nodding. "I'll talk to the others." Abdo especially had some unique abilities. I'd start with him.

Glisselda took my hand and squeezed it. "Thank you, Seraphina. And not only for this." Her smile grew shy, or perhaps apologetic. "It's been a hard winter, with assassins burning down neighborhoods, Comonot being Comonot, and Grandmamma so ill. She never intended me to be Queen at fifteen."

"She may yet recover," said Kiggs gently. "And you're not much younger than she was when she and Comonot authored the peace."

Glisselda extended her other hand toward him; he took it. "Dear Lucian. Thank you, too." She took a deep breath, her eyes glittering in the firelight. "You've both been so important to me. The Crown consumes me, I sometimes feel, until I am only Queen. I don't get to be Glisselda except with you, Lucian, or"— she squeezed my hand again—"at my harpsichord lesson. I need that. I'm sorry I don't practice more."

"I'm surprised you've had time enough for the lessons," I said.

"I couldn't give them up!" she cried. "I have few enough chances to take off the mask."

I said, "If this invisible barrier works—if Abdo, Lars, Dame Okra, and I can thread our minds—then I want to search for the other half-dragons." Glisselda had proposed such a journey at midwinter, when she'd first learned there were others, but nothing had come of it.

Glisselda blushed furiously. "I've been reluctant to lose my music teacher."

I glanced at Orma's letter and knew just how she felt.

"Still," she continued stoutly, "I'll bear it if I must, for Goredd's sake."

I met Kiggs's eyes over the top of Glisselda's curly head. He nodded slightly at me and said, "I believe we all feel the same way, Selda. Our duties come first."

Glisselda laughed lightly and kissed his cheek. Then she kissed mine.

I left shortly thereafter, retrieving Orma's letter and bidding the cousins good night—or good morning. The sun was just rising. My mind was all abuzz; I might soon go in search of my people, and that eagerness had begun to triumph over every other feeling. Beside the door the page boy dozed, oblivious to all.

Two

I closed the shutters of my suite against the impending dawn. I'd told Viridius, the court composer and my employer, that I might be up till all hours and not to expect me until afternoon. He hadn't objected. Lars, my fellow ityasaari, lived with Viridius now and was effectively his assistant; I'd been promoted to second court composer, which gave me some autonomy.

I flopped down on my bed, exhausted but certain I wouldn't sleep. I was thinking of the ityasaari, how I would travel to exotic places to find them, how long it might take. What would I tell them? *Hello, friend. I have dreamed of this—*

No, that was stupid. *Have you felt deeply alone? Have you longed for a family?*

I made myself stop; it was too embarrassing. Anyway, I still had to visit my garden of grotesques; I had to settle the denizens before I slept. I would get terrible headaches or even a resumption of visions if I didn't.

It took some time to slow my breath, and longer to clear my mind, which kept insisting on holding imaginary conversations with Orma. *Are you sure this mind-threading is safe? You do remember what Jannoula did to me?* I wanted to ask. And: *Is the Porphyrian library as amazing as we always dreamed?*

Enough mind chatter. I imagined every thought encapsulated in a bubble; I exhaled them into the world. Gradually the noise ceased, and my mind was dark and still.

A wrought-iron gate appeared before me, the entrance to my other world. I grasped the bars with my imaginary hands and said the ritual words, as Orma had taught me: "This is my mind's garden. I tend it; I order it. I have nothing to fear."

The portal opened soundlessly. I crossed the threshold and felt something in me relax. I was home.

The garden had a different layout every time, but it was always familiar. Today I had entered at one of my favorite spots, the origin: Fruit Bat's grove. It was a stand of Porphyrian fruit trees—lemon, orange, fig, date, and gola nut—where a brown-skinned lad climbed and played and left fruit detritus everywhere.

All the denizens of my garden were half-dragons, although I'd only learned that a few months ago when three of them walked into my life. Fruit Bat was really a skinny twelve-year-old named Abdo. He claimed the sound of my flute had called him from afar; he'd sensed the connection between us and come looking for me. He and his dance troupe had arrived at midwinter and were still here in Lavondaville, waiting for the roads to thaw so they could travel again.

Fruit Bat was freer than some of my garden denizens, able to leave his designated area, perhaps because Abdo had unusual mental abilities of his own. He could talk to other ityasaari with his mind, for instance. Today Fruit Bat was in his grove, curled like a kitten in a nest of furry fig leaves, sound asleep. I smiled down at him, made a blanket appear, and tucked it around him. It wasn't a real blanket, and this wasn't really Abdo, but the symbol meant something to me. He was my favorite.

I moved on. Loud Lad's ravine opened up before me, and I yodeled down it. Loud Lad, blond and burly, yodeled back from below, where he seemed to be building a boat with wings. I waved; that was all the settling he ever required.

Loud Lad was Lars, the Samsamese bagpiper who now lived with Viridius; he had appeared at midwinter just like Abdo. I had envisioned each grotesque to look like the person I'd seen in my visions. Beyond that, each avatar had developed quirks, traits I hadn't consciously given them but that corresponded to their real-life counterparts. It was as if my mind had intuited these qualities and given an analogous trait to their avatars. Loud Lad was a noisy putterer; real-world Lars designed and built strange instruments and machines.

I wondered whether this would hold true for the ones I hadn't met yet, if the oddities they displayed in my garden would translate into life. The fat, bald Librarian, for example, sat in a shale quarry, squinting at fossil ferns through square spectacles and then tracing the same shape in the air with his finger. The fern lingered in the air, drawn in smoke. Glimmerghost, pale and ethereal, folded butterflies out of paper, and they fluttered in huge flocks around her garden. Bluey, her red hair standing straight up like a hedge, waded in a stream, eddies of green and purple swirling in her wake. How would these characteristics translate into real life?

I chatted soothingly to each one, squeezed shoulders, kissed foreheads. I had never met them but felt we were old friends. They were as familiar as family.

I reached the sundial lawn, ringed by a rose garden, where Miss Fusspots presided. She was the third and final half-dragon I'd met so far, the Ninysh ambassadress to Goredd, Dame Okra Carmine. In my garden, her double crawled on hands and knees between the roses, digging up weeds before they had a chance to sprout. In life, Dame Okra had an idiosyncratic talent for premonition.

In life, she could also be a cranky, unpleasant person. That would be a potential hazard of gathering everyone together, I supposed. Some were surely difficult people, or had been hurt just struggling to survive. I passed the golden nest of Finch, an old man with a beaked face; he must have been stared at, scorned, threatened with harm. Would he be bitter? Would he be relieved to find a safe place at long last, a place where half-dragons could support each other and be free from fear?

I passed several Porphyrians in a row—the dark, slender, athletic twins, Nag and Nagini, who raced each other over three sand dunes; dignified, elderly Pelican Man, who I was convinced was a philosopher or an astronomer; winged Miserere, circling in the sky. Abdo had hinted that in Porphyry, ityasaari were considered children of Chakhon, a god, and were revered. Maybe the Porphyrians wouldn't want to come?

Some of them might not, but I had a hunch some would. Abdo did not seem keen on the reverence, wrinkling his nose when he spoke of it, and I had firsthand knowledge that Master Smasher had not always had it easy.

I was approaching Master Smasher's statuary meadow now, where eighty-four marble statues jutted out of the grass like crooked teeth. Most were missing parts—arms, heads, toes. Master Smasher, tall and statuesque himself, picked through the weeds, collecting broken pieces and reassembling them. He'd made a woman out of hands and a bull entirely of ears.

"That finger-swan is new, isn't it?" I said, picking my way toward him. He didn't answer; I'd have been alarmed if he had. Just being this close to him brought it back, though, the memory of the terrible day I'd first seen him, when I had still been seized by involuntary visions, before I'd built this garden and gotten them under control.

My vision-eye had opened upon a craggy mountaintop, high above the city of Porphyry, where a man pulled an oxcart loaded with crates up a stony track too steep for any sensible ox. His wiry shoulders strained, but he was stronger than he looked. Dust frosted his knotted hair; sweat soaked through his embroidered tunic. Through brush and bramble, around brutal lumps of rock, he labored up the rutted path. When the wagon would budge no further, he lifted the crates and carried them to the ruins of an ancient tower that ringed the summit like a crown. It took three trips to move six large crates; he balanced them upon the crumbling wall.

He wrenched each crate open with his bare hands and hurled them, one by one, into the open sky. The boxes tumbled end over end through the emptiness, shedding straw and glassware into the sunlight. I heard the gritty crush of glass, the sickening crack of shattering wood, and this handsome young man, behind it all, shouting in a language I didn't know, with a rage and despair I knew too well.

When he'd finished breaking everything he'd brought, he stood upon the low wall and looked out over the city toward the horizon, where the sky kissed the violet sea. His lips moved, as if he were reciting a prayer. He stood unsteadily, lashed by the wind, and stared down the sheer mountain face at the glass shards winking invitingly in the sun.

In that instant, impossibly, I knew what he was thinking. He would throw himself down the mountain. His despair washed over me and led to desperation on my part. I was a floating vision-eye; he didn't know I was there; I had no way to reach him; it couldn't be done.

I tried because I had to. I reached toward him—with what?— and touched his face and said, *Please live. Please.*

He blinked like one waking from a dream and stepped back from the edge. He ran his hands over his hair, staggered to a corner of the old fort, and vomited. Then, his shoulders bent like an old man's, he stumbled back down the mountain toward his cart.

Master Smasher looked so serene now, reconfiguring statues in my garden. I could have taken both his hands and induced a vision, peered down upon whatever he was up to in the real world, but I didn't like to do it. It felt like spying.

I had never understood what had happened that day, how I'd been able to reach out, and it had never happened again. I could use my garden connection to speak to ityasaari I'd met in the real world, but not to the ones I hadn't. I could only peer at them, as through a spyglass.

Weariness hit me. I hurried on, ready to get to the end and go to bed. I tended short-limbed, elderly Newt, who rolled contentedly in his muddy wallow among the bluebells; I said good night to widemouthed, shark-toothed Gargoyella, who sat by the Faceless Lady fountain, gargling the waters. I paused at the swamp to shake my head bemusedly at Pandowdy, the most monstrous of all, an armless, legless silver-scaled slug, big as a standing stone, who lurked under the muddy waters.

Pandowdy was one I wasn't sure I wanted to find. How would I bring him back if I did? Roll him up a ramp onto a cart? Did he have eyes or ears so we could communicate? It had been hard enough to create this avatar in the garden; I'd had to wade right into the filthy water and lay my hands on his scaly skin, in lieu of taking his nonexistent hands. He'd been ice-cold, and pulsed horribly.

Maybe I didn't have to gather every one to make the invisible barricade strong enough. I hoped so, because I had no plans to find Jannoula, either. Her Wee Cottage was next, abutting the wetland; its surrounding yard, once full of herbs and flowers, was all gone to nettles and bramble. I picked my way gingerly toward the cottage door, my heart full of mixed emotions—pity, regret, some lingering bitterness. I tugged at the padlock on the door; it felt reassuringly heavy in my hand, cold iron, unrusted, immovable. Relief entered the mix.

Jannoula's avatar had been different from the very beginning, not passive and benign like the others. She'd been actively aware of this place—of me—and had moved her entire consciousness into my head in an attempt to take me over. I had freed myself only by tricking her into entering this cottage and locking her inside.

I dreaded that happening again, not least because I wasn't sure how it had happened, why she was different. Abdo was different, too, but that active connection had grown slowly, over time, and he seemed disinclined to move in and stay.

This was my primary worry about Orma's plan. What did this mind-threading really involve? Was it the kind of link I'd experienced with Jannoula, or something shallower? What if we couldn't untangle our . . . our mind-stuff, whatever it was, afterward? What if we hurt each other? As much could go wrong as could go right.

I turned away from the Wee Cottage, preoccupied with these thoughts, and found myself face to face with an incongruous snowy mountaintop. I had one more grotesque to tend, Tiny Tom, who lived in a stony grotto under the miniature peak. He owed his name to an eleven-year-old's unsubtle sense of irony, alas: he was eight feet tall, strong as a bear (I'd glimpsed him wrestling one in the real world), and clad in ragged blankets, sewn together to make crude clothing.

He wasn't inside his grotto, however, but in the snow out

front, leaving enormous clawed footprints as he staggered around clutching his woolly head, extremely agitated.

Once this kind of behavior had meant I had a vision coming, but I knew how to circumvent that now. Thanks to my faithful tending, visions had become rare. I'd had only one in the last three years, the vision of Abdo at midwinter, and in that case Abdo had been actively looking for me. That wasn't the usual situation at all.

"Sweet Tom, merry Tom," I said quietly, circling the wild man, keeping clear of his swinging elbows. He was hard to look at without pity: his filthy clothing, his sun-bleached thatch of hair, his beard cluttered with twigs, his crumbling teeth. "You've been living on that mountain all alone," I said soothingly to his grotesque, drawing closer. "What has it taken to survive? What have you suffered?"

We had all suffered, from Tiny Tom to Master Smasher. By all the Saints in Heaven, and their dogs, we didn't need to suffer alone. Not anymore.

Tiny Tom was breathing raggedly, but calming. He lowered his hands; his rheumy eyes bugged out at me. I did not turn away or flinch, but took his elbow and gently led him back into his cave, to the nest of bones he had made himself. He let himself be seated, his gigantic head beginning to nod. I ran my hand over his matted locks and stayed by him until he was asleep.

We needed this place, this garden, in the real world. I was going to make it happen. I owed it to all of them.

The Queen's support for the project, however, depended more on whether we could get this mysterious barrier working than on my wish to find the others. I gathered the three ityasaari of my acquaintance that afternoon to see what we could do. Lars offered the use of Viridius's suite.

Viridius was home and, because he was having a good day gout-wise, sitting up at the harpsichord in his brocade dressing gown, caressing the keys with his gnarled fingers. "Don't mind me," he said when I arrived, waggling his bushy red eyebrows. "Lars tells me this is half-dragon business; I won't interfere. I just need to get the second theme of this concerto grosso down."

Lars entered from the other room, a delicate porcelain teapot held gingerly in one large hand. He paused by Viridius and squeezed the old composer's shoulder; Viridius leaned briefly into Lars's arm and then turned back to his work. Lars brought the tea around and filled the five cups on the ornate table by the gout couch. Dame Okra had claimed the couch, putting up her feet and spreading her stiff green skirts around her. Abdo, swathed in a long knit tunic against the cold, bounced on his upholstered chair as if he could barely be constrained to sit, his long sleeves flapping over his hands like flippers. I took the other couch, and Lars settled his bulk carefully beside me, trading me a cup of tea for Orma's letter, which the other two had just read.

"Have you heard of anything like this?" I said, glancing from Dame Okra's scowl to Abdo's wide brown eyes. "Mental connections have occurred with some of us. Abdo can speak in our heads; my mind used to reach out compulsively to other half-dragons." Jannoula had entered my mind and seized it, but I didn't like talking about that. "What kind of connection is this mind-threading?"

"I'll tell you right now, I won't participate in any mind-threading," said Dame Okra flatly, her eyes swimming behind her thick spectacles. "It sounds horrible."

It sounds interesting to me, said Abdo's voice in my head.

"Do you know whether the Porphyrian ityasaari have ever joined together this way, or used their . . . their mind-stuff for this kind of physical manifestation?" I asked aloud so Dame Okra and Lars could hear half the conversation, anyway. Abdo's mouth and tongue were shingled with silver dragon scales, and he could not speak aloud.

No. But we do know about mind-stuff. We call it soul-light. With practice, some of us can learn to see it around other ityasaari, like a second self made of sunlight. I can reach out with mine a little; that's how I talk to them. I send out a finger of fire, said Abdo, sending his real finger in a slow, dramatic arc to poke Lars in the stomach.

Lars, his lips moving as he read, swatted Abdo's hand away.

Abdo gestured at Dame Okra with his head. *Her light is spiny, like a hedgehog, but Lars's is gentle and friendly.*

I saw nothing around either of them, but I noted an omission. *What about mine?*

Abdo studied the air around my head, toying with one of his many hair knots. *I see strands of light sticking out of your head like snakes, or umbilical cords, where we three—and others—are connected to you. Cords of our light. I don't see your light, and I don't know why.*

Heat rose in my cheeks. My light was missing? What did that mean? Was I deficient? An anomaly even among anomalies?

Dame Okra interjected in a voice like a braying mule: "Might we all participate in this conversation? That requires it to be audible." She paused, her scowl deepening. "No, don't talk to me silently, you villain. I won't tolerate it." She glared at Abdo and waved a hand around her head as if fending off gnats.

"He says we've all got—" The word *soul-light* didn't sit well with me; it smacked of religion, which brought me quickly to judgmental Saints. "Mind-fire. He can see it."

Lars carefully folded Orma's letter and placed it on the couch between us, shrugging his bulky shoulders. "I can't do anythink special with my mindt, as far as I know, but I am heppy to be a bead if someone else is the string."

"I'm sure that will be fine, Lars," I said, nodding encouragingly. "Abdo or I will discover the way to thread through you."

I don't think you can reach out like that, Phina madamina, said Abdo.

"I've reached out with my mind before," I said, more waspishly than I meant to. I had reached back into Jannoula's mind; I suppressed that memory at once.

Recently? he said, pulling the neck of his tunic up over his mouth.

"Give me a minute to relax into it. I'll show you," I said, glaring at the little skeptic. I nestled into a corner of the couch, closed my eyes, and focused on my breathing. It took time, because Dame Okra snorted like a horse, and then Viridius kept tinkling away on the harpsichord until Lars stepped over and gently asked him to stop.

I finally found my garden, and then Loud Lad's ravine in the middle of it. Loud Lad sat upon the lip of the chasm, as if waiting for me, a beatific smile on his round face. I prodded him to standing, and then concentrated on myself. I always imagined myself bodily present in the garden; I liked feeling the dewy grass between my toes. When I had tried this before—with Jannoula—I had needed to imagine that the grotesque and I were immaterial.

With effort, Loud Lad began to blur around the edges, then turn translucent in the middle. I could make out shapes through him. My own hands grew transparent, and when I was insubstantial enough, I stepped into Loud Lad to join my mind-stuff with his.

I passed through him as if he were fog. A second try gave the same result.

"It's like trying to travel through a spyglass," said a voice behind me in the garden. "If we could do that, I'd step through and visit the moon."

I turned around to see Fruit Bat—Abdo's double—animated by Abdo's consciousness. He could speak in my garden, unhindered by his scaly throat; this was how he spoke in my mind.

"I've done this before," I said.

"Yes, but your mind may have changed since then," he said, his dark eyes solemn. "It has changed in the time I've known you. I walked out of this garden and into your wider mind once—do you remember?"

I did. I had been depressed, and then a door had appeared in the undifferentiated fog of . . . of the rest of my mind. He had stepped through to comfort me, but I'd taken him for a second Jannoula. "I made you promise to stay in the garden after that," I said.

He nodded. "That's not all you did. You took precautions. There used to be an Abdo-sized hole in the wall, but you bricked it up."

Not intentionally, if so. The garden's edge was in sight; I pointed crossly. "Bricked? It's a woven willow fence."

"Ah, madamina. I know you call this place a garden, but it doesn't look like one to me. I see us confined to a narrow gate-house, with no admittance to the castle of your larger mind."

I looked around at the lush vegetation, the soaring blue sky, Loud Lad's deep ravine. "That's absurd," I said, trying to laugh, but deeply confused. This place had been created by my imagination, of course, but was its appearance so subjective?

This wasn't solving our mind-threading problem. "Even if I can't reach out to Lars," I said, "can you reach out and thread your mind-fire to mine? Make me a bead on the string?"

Abdo bit his lip and darted his gaze about. "Maybe," he said slowly.

"Go ahead and try it," I said.

There was a pause and then a blinding flash of pain, as if my head would split in two. I screamed—in my head? in the real world?—and scrabbled around the garden, looking for the egression gate. I found it and returned to myself, my throbbing head cradled in someone's hands.

Abdo's. He was leaning over me, his brown eyes brimming with regret. *Did I hurt you, Phina madamina?*

I sat up straighter, shakily, blinking against the glare from Viridius's windows. "I'm all right now."

I should have listened to my instinct, he fretted, patting my cheek and then my hair. *I can enter Fruit Bat, but I can't go any further into your mind than that. I can't see, let alone touch, your soul-light, not even from your garden. I don't know what else to try.*

I took a juddering breath. "T-try with Lars. The Queen won't let me go looking for the others if we can't make this work."

Lars's sea-gray eyes had grown enormous, watching me; he ran a nervous hand through his bristly blond hair. Abdo must have spoken reassuringly in his head, because Lars joined him on the Zibou carpet, sitting cross-legged and joining hands. He nodded at intervals, then turned to us and said, "We are tryink one idea Abdo has. He doesn't know if it works. He asks thet Dame Okra tell him if she sees anything."

"What kind of anything?" said Dame Okra warily.

"Soul-light. Mind-fire. Whatever you like to call it," said Lars, smiling. "Abdo is curious whether you can see it when we weave ours together."

I was excluded from that hope, I noted sourly. Was it because I had no visible mind-fire? Did that make me more like an ordinary human? All my life I had longed to be ordinary; how ridiculous to be disgruntled when I finally was. It was no use being envious; we were all different.

Dame Okra emitted a skeptical grunt. Viridius, who'd resumed composing, did a quarter turn on the harpsichord bench, the better to see this mind-fire for himself. He'd been excluded from Abdo's hope as well; at least I wasn't alone.

Abdo and Lars closed their eyes; Lars's enormous pink hands almost engulfed Abdo's wiry brown ones. I studied their faces and was relieved—not envious—to see no pain there. Indeed, Lars's face went slack and sleepy. Abdo pursed his lips, concentrating.

"Blue St. Prue!" cried Dame Okra.

"Do you see it? Where is it?" said Viridius, his blue eyes darting sharply.

Dame Okra squinted at the empty space above Lars's and Abdo's heads, the lines beside her mouth deepening. "That wouldn't stop a dragon," she said. She tossed back the dregs of her tea and then threw the cup as hard as she could toward the space.

Viridius, in her line of fire, threw up his gout-swollen hands, but the cup never reached him. It stopped short, wobbling in midair as if caught in a giant spiderweb, and remained suspended for several seconds before dropping to the carpet between Abdo and Lars.

"Saints' dogs!" Viridius swore. He'd picked up that expression from me.

Dame Okra sneered. "That's not nothing, but is it really the best you can do?"

Abdo opened one eye, which twinkled mischievously, then closed it again. Dame Okra watched, arms folded. Suddenly she cried, "Duck!" and threw herself flat on the ground.

Viridius followed suit without questioning, flinging himself off the harpsichord stool. My pathetic reflexes, alas, were too slow off the mark. Harpsichord strings twanged and windows shattered as I was bowled over the back of the couch.

I came to on the daybed in Viridius's solarium; its windows, still intact, had been out of range. The sun had slipped behind the mountains, but the sky was still pink. Dame Okra sat beside me, adjusting the wick of a lamp in her lap, illuminating her froggy face from below. She noticed me stirring and said, "How do you feel?"

It was an unusually tender inquiry, coming from her. My ears were ringing and my head throbbed, but for her sake I bravely said, "Not too awful."

I'd have something good to report to the Queen, at least, whenever I could stand up again.

"Of course you're fine," Dame Okra snapped, setting the lamp on a side table. "Abdo has been nearly hysterical, thinking he'd hurt you."

I tried to sit up, but my head weighed a thousand pounds. "Where is he?"

Dame Okra waved off my question. "You'll see him soon. I want a word with you first." Her pink tongue darted over her lips. "This is ill advised, this whole endeavor."

I closed my eyes. "If you dislike the idea of linking minds, you don't have to—"

"Indeed, I never shall," she said impatiently. "But it's not just that. It's this plan of yours to bring the half-dragons together." My eyes popped open again; she leered at me. "Oh yes, I know what this is really about. You think you're going to find a family.

We shall come together under one roof—a warm communing of weird ones!—and all our problems will be solved." She grinned toothily and batted her eyes.

I bristled at her mockery. "I want to help the others," I said. "I've glimpsed their sorrows. You and I have had it easy compared with some."

It was her turn to chafe. "Easy? Oh yes, with my scaly tail and boyish figure, what could be simpler? I was never kicked out of my mother's house at fifteen, never had to live on the streets of Segosh or steal to eat." Her voice was rising to a teakettle shrill. "Bluffing my way into secretarial work was a snap; marrying the old ambassador was trivial, with my fabulous looks. Outliving him—well, no, that really was easy. But persuading our ruling count to let me take over as ambassador, when no female had ever held the post before, was as easy as wetting the bed." She was shouting now. "Or falling out a window. Why, anyone could do it, because it was *nothing*."

She glared at me, her eyes bulging fiercely.

"Peace, Dame Okra," I said. "You thought you were alone in all the world. Surely it has been a relief to discover others like yourself?"

"Abdo and Lars are good enough," she conceded. "And you're not so terrible."

"Thank you," I said, trying to mean it. "But would you begrudge the others? Some never got past your streets-of-Segosh stage and are still stealing to eat." She opened her mouth, but I anticipated her: "And not because they're stupid or less deserving than you."

She puffed air through her lips. "Maybe," she said. "But do not make the mistake, Seraphina, of supposing that suffering ennobles anyone. Some may be lovely, but most will be hurt beyond your skill to heal." She stood up, adjusting her false bosom. "You're going to bring back some genuinely unpleasant people. You know my gift involves prognostication, and I'm telling you, this will end unhappily. I have foreseen it."

"Noted," I said, a chill creeping up my spine. Could she see that far into the future?

She turned to go, but looked back superciliously. "When it all goes to the devil—and it will—at least I shall have the pleasure of saying I told you so."

On that optimistic note, she left me to my headache.

ℭℋᵣℯℯ

By the next morning, the headache had dissipated and my enthusiasm restored itself. Maybe it didn't matter whether my mind-fire was hidden away, or if I could participate in the invisible wall; I was connected to our far-flung brethren in a way that Abdo, Dame Okra, and Lars were not. It would be my job—my honor, truly—to find them and bring them home.

Before bed, I had written to Glisselda about Abdo and Lars's success. A page boy interrupted my breakfast with an invitation to the Queen's suite. I put on a nicer gown than I would have otherwise and went to the royal family's wing of the palace. The guard, who was expecting me, let me into an airy sitting room with high ceilings, salon couches around a tiled hearth, and draperies of gold and white and blue. At the back of the room before the tall windows stood a round table set for breakfast, and behind it sat Glisselda's grandmother, Queen Lavonda, in a wheeled chair. Her spine was bent; her skin looked pale and fragile, like crumpled paper. Her grandchildren sat on either side, chatting encouragingly at her. Glisselda spooned porridge into her grandmother's mouth, open like a baby bird's, and then Kiggs tenderly wiped her chin.

The old Queen had never recovered from the events of midwinter. Imlann's poison had been neutralized, according to the best dragon physicians Comonot could procure. They saw no other cause for her continued illness, though one had hypothesized a series of small strokes, deep in her brain. Being dragons, they had rejected outright the notion that grief might be a cause, but the human population of Goredd believed otherwise. Queen Lavonda had lost all her children—Kiggs's mother, Princess Laurel, had died years before, but Prince Rufus and Princess Dionne had been murdered in short succession at midwinter, the latter killed by the same poison the Queen had survived.

The old Queen had nurses and servants in abundance, but I'd heard that Kiggs and Glisselda insisted upon feeding their grandmother breakfast each day. This was the first I'd seen of it, and I was filled with sorrow for them and awe at how much they loved and honored the old woman, even when she was no longer fully herself.

I approached and gave full courtesy.

"Seraphina!" cried Glisselda, handing the spoon over to her cousin and wiping her hands. "Your report was so encouraging that Lucian and I have started planning. You're to leave the day after the equinox, if this thaw persists."

I opened my mouth and closed it again. That was six days away.

"We've been trying to estimate how long your journey will take," said Kiggs, his eyes on his grandmother. She rolled her brown eyes toward him, her lips quivering anxiously. He patted her speckled hand. "If you took six weeks in Ninys and another six in Samsam, you might arrive in Porphyry just after midsummer."

"Officially, you'd be an emissary of the Goreddi Crown, authorized to solicit and acquire promises of supplies and troops for our defense," said Glisselda, retucking the napkin under her grandmother's chin. "Not that we don't trust dear Count Pesavolta and the Regent of Samsam to do their parts. But the personal touch is so much nicer."

"Your main objective is to find the ityasaari," said Kiggs.

"What if I can't?" I said. "Or can't find them quickly enough? Is it more important to stay on schedule or to bring them home?"

The royal cousins exchanged a look. "We must decide case by case," said Kiggs. "Selda, we need to ask Comonot to authorize the use of a thnik for Seraphina."

"And by 'we' you mean me," Glisselda said crossly, putting her hands on her hips. "That saar! After the argument we had yesterday over Eskar's—"

The old Queen began to weep softly. Glisselda was on her feet at once, her arms around her grandmother's frail shoulders. "Oh, Grandmamma, no!" she said, kissing her white hair. "I'm cross at that infuriating old dragon, not you. Not Lucian, either, see?" She went up behind Kiggs and hugged him, too.

"Honestly, Lucian, we should get married tomorrow," said

Glisselda out of the side of her mouth. "Let her have one happy thing in her life before she dies."

"Mm," said Kiggs, scraping the last porridge out of the bowl, scrupulously not looking at me.

Queen Lavonda, alas, was inconsolable. "We will continue this later, Seraphina," said Glisselda apologetically, ushering me toward the door. I gave full courtesy again, wishing there were something I could do.

I turned my mind to what they'd told me. Six days was sooner than I could have anticipated. I headed back toward my suite, mentally taking stock of my travel clothing. I had none. I hoped there was time to have some made.

I detoured to visit Glisselda's seamstress, who directed me to the seamstresses of the lower court. "There's eight of them, maidy, so they can stitch eight gowns at once."

I went down to the artisans' wing, but my feet slowed as I approached the seamstresses' workroom. I didn't want eight gowns, not if I was going to go careening all over the Southlands on a horse. I retraced my steps and, after some hesitation, knocked on a different door.

A slight, balding man answered, spectacles clamped to his narrow nose, a measuring ribbon around his neck like a scarf.

"The ladies'—" he began, but I didn't let him finish.

"How fast can you make riding breeches?" I asked. "I'll want them well padded."

The tailor smiled slightly and stood aside to let me in.

Abdo and Lars practiced linking minds outdoors over the next days, and they practiced a lot, fascinated by their own power. Queen Glisselda, Prince Lucian, and even Ardmagar Comonot would sometimes stand in the slushy courtyard, watching them. Abdo quickly learned to move the mind-net (as I had begun calling it) in a more controlled manner; for the Queen's amusement he made wide bowl-shaped impressions with it in the melting snow, knocked icicles from the eaves, and caused doves to fly off the roof in panic. He took care not to hit the doves, I noted.

Glisselda sidled up to me as I watched. "Even if you fail to find any of the other ityasaari," she said, taking my arm, "these two could do some good on their own."

"That mind-net couldn't protect this castle, let alone your city," scoffed Ardmagar Comonot, who stood several feet away from us. In his saarantras, he was a short, stocky man with an aquiline nose and heavy jowls. He wore his dark hair slicked back against his head. "I calculate from its print in the snow a spheroid no more than fifteen feet across. They'll be lucky to pull down one dragon at a time."

"Every bit will help," said Glisselda irritably. "They'll be practiced enough to move it effectively, and the dragons won't see it coming."

"I can't see it with these eyes, certainly," muttered Comonot, "but I can't vouch for my natural shape. Dragon eyesight is keener, and we can see into the ultraviolet—"

"Oh, for Heaven's sake!" said the Queen, turning her back on him. "If I say the sky is blue, he'll explain to me that it isn't!"

"I had meant to tell you, Your Majesty," I said, sensing that it was time to insert myself between the two of them. "I would like Abdo to travel with me. He can see the mind-fire of the other half-dragons, which would be immensely helpful in locating them."

Glisselda looked up at me; she was half a head shorter. "We're already sending Dame Okra so you can use her Ninysh house as a base of operations. She can't help?" Before I could answer, she gestured at Abdo and Lars, adding, "I'd feel better with these two here, in our arsenal."

"My Loyalists won't let the war come to Goredd," interjected Comonot. "Don't discount us."

Glisselda's face turned livid. "Ardmagar," she said, "forgive me, but I have lost some faith in you."

She turned on her heel and stalked back into the palace. Comonot watched her, his face inscrutable, his thick fingers absently toying with the gold medallions around his neck.

I shot a glance back at Abdo and Lars, still holding hands and laughing at discomfited doves. They wouldn't miss us. I took the Ardmagar's arm; he flinched, but didn't pull away. We walked into the palace together.

At midwinter, Ardmagar Comonot had named me his teacher, a title of tremendous honor among dragons. It meant he ceded me some authority over him—specifically, the understanding of humans. If I told him he was doing something wrong, he was supposed to take me seriously. He'd consulted me a few times during this long winter, but he sometimes couldn't see when he needed help. Sometimes I had to notice for him.

I didn't mind; I'd been an intermediary for my uncle Orma many times, and this duty reminded me of him.

Comonot must have had some idea of what I wanted to talk to him about, for he came quietly up the corridor, our footsteps echoing on the marble floor. I led him to the south solar, where I gave the Queen her harpsichord lessons. No one used the room for anything else, and the walk gave me time to overthink what I should say. I sat on a settee upholstered in green satin; Comonot planted himself before the windows, looking out.

He spoke first: "Yes, the Queen is more annoyed with me than usual."

I said, "Losing faith is well beyond annoyance. Do you know why?"

The old saar clasped his hands behind his back and wriggled his ringed fingers restlessly. "I sent Eskar and her mad scheme back to Porphyry," he said.

I felt a pang; I had hoped to speak to her about Orma. "It was a bad plan?"

He shifted his stance, folding his arms over his barrel chest. "Forget for the moment that there is an ancient treaty in question and that the Porphyrians are touchy about it. Eskar failed to consider that sneaking up the Omiga Valley would avail us nothing unless the bulk of the Old Ard were fighting elsewhere. Her plan requires a simultaneous feint south by my Loyalists to draw enemy troops away from the Kerama."

"South, as in all the way to Goredd?" I said.

"Correct. It is damned difficult to coordinate attacks at a distance, even with thniks." He jingled his medallions for emphasis. They were devices for communicating at a distance, created by the quigutl, a lesser species of dragon. "Goredd might have to hold out for weeks. You saw the damage a single, determined dragon did to this city."

There was still smoke rising from that quarter of town a week later. But Comonot's words didn't add up to Glisselda's reaction. I said, "If you merely pointed out a flaw in the plan with Goredd's safety in mind, that shouldn't have angered the Queen."

His shoulders sagged; his forehead rested against the glass. "Eskar, arguing with me, brought up some . . . defeats I had failed to mention to the Queen before now."

I inhaled sharply through my teeth. "Bad defeats?"

"Is there a good kind? The Old Ard have a new strategist, a General Laedi—some upstart I've never heard of—and he cheats most egregiously. He ambushes out of hatcheries, with no qualms about destroying the young. His ards pretend to surrender, then don't. Even our wins are almost losses; Laedi's forces keep fighting after they're beaten, to maximize casualties." Comonot turned to face me, looking baffled. "What kind of strategy is that?"

I was more perplexed by Comonot's strategy for dealing with Glisselda. "Why would you keep important information from the Queen?"

"She is bright and capable, but she is also very young. She gets . . ." He made a swirling gesture, like rising smoke.

"Upset?" I offered.

He nodded vigorously. "She's in over her head. That's not criticism; I am, too. But that's precisely it: I have enough to sort out without her emotions thrown into the mix."

He began pacing. I said, "You need to regain Glisselda's trust. May I make some suggestions, Ardmagar?"

He paused expectantly, his black eyes keen as a crow's.

I said, "Be more transparent, first of all. Maybe she'll be upset by your losses, but emotions pass. She will be more logical and clearheaded afterward, but she has to feel it first. It's like the order of operations in an equation."

Comonot pursed his thick lips. "She can't skip that step?"

"Just like you can't stop sleeping, even though it leaves you helpless and vulnerable for hours every day," I said.

"I'm not sure I accept that analogy," he said, but I could tell I'd gotten him thinking.

"The second thing you should do, and perhaps the more crucial: make a gesture of goodwill to reignite the Queen's trust. Preferably a large gesture."

Comonot's bushy eyebrows shot up. "An aurochs?"

I gaped at him for a couple of heartbeats before it dawned on me that he meant not merely an enormous cattlebeast but food. He would make it up to Glisselda with feasting. "That's a possibility," I said, nodding slowly, my mind racing. "I was thinking something still bigger. Your war policy is outside of my bailiwick, and I'd never presume to advise you, but I think your gesture should be on that scale. You might go to the front for a while, or . . . or dedicate an ard to the protection of Lavondaville, if you can spare one. Whatever might convince Queen Glisselda that you care for Goredd's safety."

He scratched his jowls. "*Care* is possibly too strong a—"

"Ardmagar!" I cried, annoyed with him now. "Pretend."

He sighed. "If I left the city, it would reduce the damage done by incompetent assassins. Certainly I wouldn't mind facing this

General Laedi myself and ripping his throat out." He gazed into the middle distance a moment, then focused on me again. "There is sense in what you say. I will consider what is best."

That was my dismissal. I rose and gave full courtesy. He watched me solemnly, then took my hand and placed it on the back of his neck. It was a show of submission; a real dragon teacher would have bitten him.

After his practice with Lars, I approached Abdo about accompanying me on my travels. He was enthusiastic, but cautioned, *You'll need to ask my family's permission. I'm three years away from my Day of Determination.* I nodded, trying to affect worldliness, but he spotted my confusion and added, *Adulthood. When you decide how people will address you, and you choose your path into the world.*

When I'd met Abdo at midwinter, he'd been traveling the south with his dance troupe, which included an aunt and his grandfather. His grandfather, as the senior family member, was the one I needed to ask. Abdo accompanied the old man to my suite the next morning, and I plied them with tea and cheese pastries and an impromptu oud concert. His grandfather, Tython, ate the pastry with one hand, holding Abdo's hand with the other.

"I promise to take good care of your grandson," I said, rising at last, and setting my oud in my seat.

Tython nodded gravely; his gray hair was plaited in clean lines, flush to his scalp. He patted Abdo's knotted hair and said in slow, careful Goreddi, "I must speak at you with Porphyrian.

Excuse me." He said something in Porphyrian to Abdo, who nodded.

I'll translate, said the lad, simultaneously signing at me with his eloquent fingers. I must have looked bemused, because Abdo clarified: *He doesn't know I can speak in your head. I think he would be envious; I can't speak in his.*

I understand some Porphyrian, I said. Abdo pulled a skeptical face.

Tython was clearing his throat. "Abdo belongs to the god Chakhon, not once but twice," he said, through Abdo's translation. "First, all ityasaari belong to Chakhon."

Even you foreign fools, said Abdo. My Porphyrian was rusty, but I knew his grandfather hadn't said that.

"Second, his mother is a priestess of Chakhon. Every fiber of him, body and soul, is owed to the god," said Tython. "Abdo was born to be the successor of Paulos Pende, our most revered ityasaari priest. However"—here the old man bent his head, as if ashamed—"Abdo chafed against his duties and would not take them seriously. He fought with Pende, scorned his mother, and ran away."

There's more to it than that, said Abdo, frowning at his grandfather.

Curious as I was to know Abdo's side of the story, I was even more curious about the fact that there were ityasaari priests in Porphyry. How different from the Southlands, where we'd had to hide ourselves away.

"I have kept Abdo safe, in hope of the day he takes up the

yoke he was born to bear," said Tython. "If you take him with you, understand what a solemn duty it is."

Ta-da, said Abdo, mushing his lips into a pout. *I'm a grave responsibility. Chakhon is watching.* His sarcasm made a thin veneer over his embarrassment.

"Chakhon is ... the god of chance?" I hedged, studying Abdo's expression.

The old man rose from his seat so abruptly that I feared I'd offended him. He reached out to me, however, and planted a kiss on each of my cheeks. I glanced at Abdo, who explained dully, *He's pleased you know Chakhon.*

It had been fifty-fifty, honestly, but it wouldn't do to admit that, nor to have said, *I'll take my chances,* as had immediately occurred to my troublemaking brain.

Tython stepped back, his creased face serious, and said in halting Goreddi, "Remember. A duty."

"Abdo is my friend," I said, giving Tython full courtesy. "I will keep him safe."

The old man watched my elaborate flourishes with vague amusement. He said something in Porphyrian; Abdo rose and followed him to the door. I padded after, saying "Thank you" and "Goodbye" in Porphyrian.

Abdo's astonished grimace gave me to understand that my pronunciation needed work. Tython's face crinkled into a smile, however, as if he found me charmingly absurd.

I closed the door behind them, baffled by all this talk of gods. A twelve-year-old boy was surely a handful, no matter his origins.

A twelve-year-old boy who was the property of a god . . . what did that mean, practically? If he wanted sweets for supper and I said no, would Chakhon hear of it? Was Chakhon the kind of god who smote people? We Goreddis had Saints like that.

A loud knock at the door made me jump. Abdo or Tython must have forgotten something. I pulled the door open.

There stood Prince Lucian Kiggs in his scarlet uniform doublet, a flat leather pouch under his arm. His dark hair curled angelically; my heart stuttered a little. I'd barely spoken to him since midwinter, when we had recognized a mutual attraction and decided, by mutual agreement, to avoid each other. He was Queen Glisselda's fiancé; I was her friend. That was not the only obstacle between us, but it overshadowed all others.

"Prince. Please, ah, come in," I said, startled into speaking without thinking.

Of course he wouldn't. I knew better than to ask, but he'd taken me by surprise.

He glanced up the deserted corridor and then turned his dark eyes back to me. "May I?" he asked, his brows contracted sadly. "Only for a minute."

I covered my fluster with a curtsy and ushered him into the sitting room, where tea things still languished on the table. This was his first time seeing my rooms; I wished I might have had a moment to tidy up. He surveyed my overflowing bookshelves, my eccentric collection of quigutl figurines, and my spinet piled with music. My oud still occupied the chair before the hearth, like some goose-necked gentleman caller.

"I hope I'm not interrupting," said Kiggs, smiling. "Do you often have your instruments to tea?"

"Only when I can get cheese pastries," I said, offering him one. He declined. I moved the oud and took another seat for myself, keeping the messy table respectably between us.

"I come bearing gifts," said Kiggs, fishing around in the front of his doublet. He pulled out a slender chain from which hung two pendant thniks—a round bronze medallion and a silver sweetheart knot—chiming softly against each other.

"We assumed we would have to arm-wrestle Comonot for these," said Kiggs, "but he's under the impression you recently did him a favor."

"Good," I said. "I mean, I hope I helped him. It's always so hard to tell."

The prince flashed me a rueful smile. "I've lived that. We must compare notes someday." He jingled the thniks, bringing us back to task. "The bronze links to one we've given Dame Okra, so the two of you can keep in touch while you're in Ninys. She intends for you to travel around while she valiantly stays at home in Segosh."

"Of course she does," I said. He smiled again. I felt a little guilty for cultivating those smiles; I wasn't allowed.

"The sweetheart knot"—he held up the intricate silver tangle—"connects with the master box in Selda's study. She wants to hear from you twice a week, whether you're having successes or not. She was adamant that if she doesn't hear from you, she shall fret, and her fretting has international consequences now."

I held out my hand, smiling at how he'd unconsciously copied her inflections. He laid the thniks in my palm and closed my fingers around them. My breath caught.

He quickly released me, clearing his throat and reaching for the leather pouch under his arm. "Next order of business: documents. You've got the Queen's scrip, should you need funds; a list of pyria ingredients to order on the Crown's behalf; another of Ninysh baronets and Samsamese earls of particular interest, with letters of introduction. Finding the ityasaari is your priority, but you'll be staying with local gentry as you travel. You may as well encourage them to commit aid."

"I'm to guilt everyone into helping us?" I teased.

"You're to gently remind them," he said, "of what Count Pesavolta and the Regent already promised on their behalf. Petty nobles are more likely to help if they believe we'll notice."

He held out the satchel; I took it and peeked in at the sheaf of parchments. "Nice to have legitimacy."

Kiggs laughed; I'd hoped he would. He was a bastard and had an odd sense of humor about it. His dark eyes gleamed in the firelight. "I shall miss you, Phina."

I fidgeted with the leather bag on my lap. "I already miss you," I said. "I've been missing you these last three months."

"You too?" he said. His hands tightened on the arms of his chair. "I'm so sorry."

I tried to smile. It felt thin on my lips.

Kiggs tapped his fingers on the arm of his chair. "I hadn't appreciated how hard it would be not to see you or speak to you. We cannot control our hearts, but I thought we might at least control our actions and minimize the lying—"

"You don't have to defend yourself to me," I said quietly. "I agreed with you."

"Agreed? Past tense?" he said, picking up on something I hadn't intended to reveal.

This prince was too astute. I loved him for it.

I swiftly crossed the room to my bookcase and found the book easily amid the clutter. I waved the slim volume of Pontheus's *Love and Work* that he'd given me.

"Is this a rebuke?" he said, leaning forward, his expression keen. "I know what you're going to quote: 'There is no pain in truth, no comfort in lies.' And that is all very well, except when you know the truth is going to hurt someone you love, and you know, furthermore, what pain she endures already: her mother dead, her grandmother dying, she herself thrown into the deep ocean of queenship and war before she's ready."

He rose animatedly and declared, "I will see her through this, Seraphina. I will bear this pain, suffer anything on her behalf until she's through this storm."

"It sounds so noble when you put it that way," I said, more snappishly than I meant to.

His shoulders slumped. "I'm not trying to be noble. I'm trying to be kind."

I stepped toward him until we were face to face, the breadth of a book between us. "I know you are," I said quietly. I tapped his chest with the volume of Pontheus. "The day will come."

He smiled sadly, then placed his hands around mine so we were clasping the book together. "I believe that—with everything I have," he said, holding my gaze. He kissed the edge of the book because he could not kiss me.

He released my hands—just as well, because I needed to breathe—and reached into his hidden doublet pocket again. "One last thing," he said, pulling out another medallion, gold this time. "Not a thnik," he said hastily, handing it over.

It was a Saint's medal, exquisitely engraved with an image of a woman holding her head on a platter: St. Capiti, my patroness.

My public patroness, that is. When I was an infant, the psalter had chosen St. Yirtrudis, the heretic. The quick-thinking priest had substituted St. Capiti. I was glad he had; I was scary enough without St. Yirtrudis tied to me. I had never been able to learn what her heresy consisted in, but the label *heretic* marred everything associated with her. Her shrines had been smashed and her images excised.

I had never told anyone about her, not even Kiggs.

"May Heaven smile upon your journey," Kiggs was saying. "I know you're not pious. It's for my peace of mind more than yours. And belief aside, I want to make sure you *know*." He swallowed hard, his throat bobbing. "Whatever you may find upon the road, you have a home and friends to come back to."

Words caught in my throat. I did have friends now, more than ever before in my life. I did feel at home here. What gap was I still trying to fill by gathering the ityasaari? When would that emptiness ever be filled?

Kiggs made for the door and I followed, silent as a shadow.

He paused with his hand on the latch, looked at me one more time, then turned and walked away.

I closed the door behind him and drifted toward my bedroom; the bed was piled with the clothes I meant to take and the bags they weren't quite fitting into. I held the volume of Pontheus to my heart, pressed the Saint's medallion to my lips, and then shoved them deep into one of my bags, underneath my linen shirts.

I would carry my home with me, out into the world, as I looked for others to bring into it.

Four

The epic journey Dame Okra, Abdo, and I made across the Goreddi countryside can be distilled to one word: miserable. It seems grossly unfair to our suffering that two weeks of mud, broken carriage wheels, and Dame Okra's swearing should be so reducible, but there are only so many Saints to swear by, and a carriage has only four wheels.

Mud, on the other hand, is infinite.

The roads improved once we crossed into Ninys. Four smooth-rolling days later, past cattle pastures, windmills, and the first inklings of spring wheat, Dame Okra's coachman delivered us safely to the capital, Segosh. Dame Okra had a house there, a narrow affair wedged between two others and sharing a gravel carriage yard at the back. Rusty diamond-shaped tiles shingled the roof above a jaundiced stucco facade; arched limestone cornices over shuttered windows gave the building a surprised expression, as if it couldn't believe we'd made it here without killing each other.

Every night of our journey, in every possible grade of roadside inn, I had cleaned and oiled the scales on my arm and midriff and tended to my garden of grotesques, focusing particularly on three ityasaari: Glimmerghost, Bluey, and Finch. They seemed most likely to be Ninysh, based on their pale complexions and fair or red hair, and the occasional spoken words I overheard during induced visions. Glimmerghost lived a hermetic existence in a pine forest; Bluey seemed to be a mural painter, which may have explained the colors swirling in her garden stream. I believed Finch lived in Segosh because I'd once spied him, in full plague-doctor gear, scuttling past the Cathedral Santi Wilibaio. Even Goreddi schoolchildren knew about its golden domes.

There were two other half-dragons in the Southlands: the Librarian, who spoke Samsamese and seemed to be a highland earl, and Tiny Tom, who haunted a cave in some mountains, I couldn't tell which. I suspected he was Goreddi, living on the borders of dragon country. I would look for him last, when I returned home.

Dame Okra had volunteered her house for the Ninysh ityasaari. Once the ityasaari were found, we would send them here, and she would put them up ("put up with them," she'd said; I pretended to believe she'd got the Goreddi idiom wrong). Later, she would escort the three back to Goredd while Abdo and I moved on to Samsam.

We had to be in the Samsamese town of Fnark by St. Abaster's Day, before midsummer. There was only one half-dragon in Samsam, a bald, fat fellow I called the Librarian, and our best chance of finding him was at the annual meeting of highland earls. We did not have time to waste in Ninys.

Upon our arrival, a phalanx of servants ferried my things to a sickly green guest room on the third floor and mercifully prepared me a bath. When I finally felt human again—insofar as I could, with silver dragon scales around my arm and torso—I went looking for Dame Okra. I found her on the ground floor, glaring up the center of her winding staircase at Abdo, who had climbed the banister to the top of the house. He slid back down in a slow circle, grinning impishly and crying, *The floor is full of sharks!*

Dame Okra seems unamused, I said, glancing at her reddening face.

Because she's a shark. Don't let her eat me! He scampered back up the railing.

"Ah, children," growled Dame Okra, watching him climb. "I forget what darlings they are. How I long for the opportunity to forget once more."

"I'll be taking him off your hands soon," I said soothingly.

"Not soon enough," she huffed. "Pesavolta will provide, have no fear, but—regrettably—it may be a few days before you can set out."

"That's fine," I said, my patience thinning. "Finch is here in Segosh. We'll look for him tomorrow."

Dame Okra peered up at me over her spectacles; her eyes were wide-set and watery like a spaniel's. "Finch? Is that what you call him in your head? I shudder to imagine what you once called me."

It was clearly an invitation to tell her, but I pretended not to understand. I foresaw only two ways she might react to the name

Miss Fusspots: amusement or incandescent anger. I was not so sure of the former that I cared to risk the latter.

"Does he have wings?" she continued. "Or chirp?"

"Finch?" I said, momentarily confused. "No, he's got a . . . a beak."

Dame Okra snorted sharply. "And he lives here in the city? Blue St. Prue, you'd think someone would have noticed."

The next morning, we walked to the heart of the city, Abdo bounding along like he was full of grasshoppers. *Hello, city! Hello, monuments!* he chattered as we navigated the busy streets, uphill toward the Palasho Pesavolta. We admired the great plaza with the palasho on one side, the golden domes of the Cathedral Santi Wilibaio on the other.

A Saint's day procession approached the cathedral, passing through the triumphal arch of King Moy. Abdo pranced excitedly and pestered me until I identified the Saint for him. It was St. Clare, the clear-seer, patron of truth-finding.

I decided to take it as a propitious sign.

Still, Finch was a needle in a city-sized haystack. From his mask and leather apron, I knew him for a plague doctor; in visions I usually glimpsed him in sickrooms or down alleys, trapping rats. My vision-eye couldn't stray far from the ityasaari I was observing; it was hard to know where those sickrooms were.

And it would be hard for me to ask. I didn't speak Ninysh, due to a peculiarity of my upbringing. My stepmother, Anne-Marie, came from the notorious Belgioso family, exiled from Ninys for a variety of crimes. My dragon mother had not been public knowledge, and Papa was anxious to keep it that way; his dastardly in-laws surely would have blackmailed him had they but known. My tutors were to teach me Samsamese and Porphyrian, but no Ninysh. I'm not sure what Papa thought—perhaps that a wily old Belgioso auntie could trick me more easily in her own tongue? My stepmother's generation were all native Goreddi speakers. Whatever Papa's motives, I had no Ninysh. I was not so enamored of grammar that I'd gone looking for it.

I hoped Abdo's ability to see mind-fire might make up for my language deficit—maybe he might spot Finch across a crowded plaza or down an alley. We skipped the shiny parts of town in favor of more workaday neighborhoods, where brewers' vats gusted hops-scented steam, wood turners swept sawdust into mounds, mules brayed, tanners scraped hair off stretched cowhides, and butchers washed blood off the abattoir floors, pushing it into the gutter with flat brooms. Neither Abdo nor I saw the first sign of Finch.

I did manage—through drawings and gestures—to find a hospital, but it was a facility for the well-to-do. An attendant nun who spoke some Goreddi turned up her nose when I asked about plague houses. "Not in the city," she said, looking scandalized.

It wasn't until the third morning that Abdo caught my arm and pointed out a space between two half-timbered shop fronts, a dark slit from which emanated a sigh of decay. *I saw a glimmer, very faint. Through the buildings. It's gone now, but we should follow it,* he said, his eyes bright, almost as excited as he'd been to see the cathedral. I stuck my head into the darkness, where a stair curled down into shadow. Hand in hand, we descended the slick steps and passed through a dank culvert, into the streets behind the streets, the grim warrens of the very poor.

The alley was narrow, unpaved, and dark. Chamber pots might be emptied onto streets all over town—that was part of city life in the Southlands—but the city didn't hire anyone to wash the streets in this neighborhood. Everything clumped together in an open sewer down the middle. I hesitated, worried about bringing Abdo here, but he seemed not frightened in the least. He walked ahead of me, prudently skirting puddles and piles of rags. The piles bestirred themselves and stretched gnarled hands toward him, palms up, wordlessly begging.

Abdo dug a hand into his shirt, where he kept his purse on a cord around his neck. *Does Goreddi coin spend here?* he asked. *That's all I've got.*

"I'm sure it will," I said, hastening after him. Needy hands plucked at my skirts. It surely wasn't safe to flash coins, even Goreddi copper, in a place like this. I let Abdo pass out a handful, and then shepherded him along. "Do you see the mind-fire down here?"

Abdo started forward again, craning his neck and squinting. At last he cried, *I do!* He pointed at a rickety timber structure. *Through that building.*

"He's inside the building?" I asked, incredulous. I'd had no idea this light, invisible to me, could shine so brightly.

Abdo shrugged. *Moving behind it, more like.*

We circled the building to the east, then Abdo said, *No, this way. He's moving west.* I followed him down a cluttered alley that reeked of old onions; it began westwardly but soon veered south.

This is wrong, he said. *I can see his light through walls, but not what road he's on. It's like a maze, and we're in the wrong part.*

Several dead ends later, we emerged into a broader dirt lane and saw, far ahead, a figure in a long leather apron and broad-brimmed hat, walking away from us. Abdo grabbed at my hand excitedly and pointed. *That's him!* We hurried, our feet splashing in the drainage ditch, skidding on filth. This was the very edge of the city, where the country began creeping in; we dodged a pig in the road and navigated a flock of complaining chickens. A mule, piled high with bundled twigs, obscured my view, but I cleared it in time to see our man duck down a stairwell and into the basement of a crumbling church.

Of course. No one would waste hospital beds on plague victims.

I reached the peeling door just as the latchstring was being pulled back through the hole. I grabbed at it, getting only a knot burn for my trouble.

His shimmer is directly behind the door, said Abdo, tracing an outline on the splintery wood.

I knocked, but there was no answer. I put my eye to the latch hole and peered into a dim crypt. Straw pallets littered the floor between the blocky priests' tombs and the thick support columns. Upon each pallet lay a wrecked being, neck and eyes swollen, fingers curled into gangrenous fists. Nuns—Sisters of St. Loola, by their yellow habits—picked their way gingerly among the dying, administering water or poppy tears.

Only now did the groans reach me, and the cadaverous stench.

Finch yanked open the door, and I nearly fell inside. A terrible beaked face glared at me with big glassy eyes; it was a sackcloth plague mask, the eyeholes set with lenses, the bulging leather beak stuffed with medicinal herbs to filter bad vapors. His leather apron was spattered and his gloves stained; his eyes, behind the glass lenses, were startlingly blue—and kind. He spoke in muffled Ninysh.

"D-do you speak Goreddi?" I asked.

"Must I ask you to leave in two languages?" he said, switching without apparent effort, his voice still muffled by the leather and by the real beak hidden under the mask's. "Is the stench, the neighborhood, your good sense not warning enough?"

"I need to speak with you," I said, putting my foot forward because he seemed about to close the door again. "Not now, clearly, but perhaps when you finish here?"

He laughed mirthlessly. "*Finish*, you say? When I leave this place, I have a leper colony to attend. Then I will be pulled in a dozen more directions. The poor need so much, and there are so few who care to give."

I fished my purse out of my bodice and pressed a silver coin upon him. He stared at it, lying forlornly in the worn palm of his glove. I gave him another.

The doctor cocked his head, like a bird listening for a worm. "Well, why didn't you say so?" he said, nodding slightly to Abdo.

I shot Abdo a glance, but Abdo was watching the doctor with imploring eyes. "I can find her house," said Finch, "but it will be evening before I have time." The masked doctor turned his eyes to me, gently pushed my foot aside with the grimy toe of his boot, and shut the door.

"So what did you tell Dr. Finch?" I asked Abdo as we turned to leave.

That we are of his kind, said Abdo dreamily, taking my hand. *He is curious by nature; he will come. I liked his mind. It's a humane color.*

I was delighted. We'd succeeded in finding a half-dragon after only three days' searching; he'd seemed cautiously receptive, at least. After weeks of mud, I finally had something substantive to report to Glisselda and Kiggs.

It was a most propitious start. I would enjoy telling Dame Okra as well.

We stopped briefly by Dame Okra's, but she wasn't home and we were too merry to stay indoors. I fetched my flute, and Abdo and I passed the afternoon performing in the cathedral plaza.

Once I could not have done this. I'd so feared exposure (and my father's wrath) that I would never have dared to play in public. It was still nerve-racking, but I'd discovered that playing in public was also tremendously gratifying, emblematic of my new life, new freedom, new openness. Once I had feared for my life; now my greatest fear was flubbing a note, and it seemed right to celebrate that shift as often as I could.

Abdo danced and tumbled while I played, and we drew an

appreciative crowd. The Ninysh are famous lovers of art, as the sculpture, fountains, and triumphal arches of Segosh will attest.

Of course, as every Goreddi knows, Ninysh public art was built on the back of Goredd: the Ninysh let us fight all those expensive, destructive dragon wars ourselves. It had rarely seemed worth Goreddi effort to create beautiful monuments or statuary, not when the dragons were going to raze it. Until Comonot's Treaty and the forty-year peace, only music had been able to flourish in Goredd, the one art we could pursue while surviving in tunnels underground.

Abdo and I returned to Dame Okra's near dusk in anticipation of Finch's arrival. I'd expected to find our dinner in the kitchen, since Dame Okra had stayed late at Palasho Pesavolta the last two evenings. Tonight, though, I heard her braying in the formal dining room, over an unfamiliar basso counterpoint.

Dame Okra sat at one end of the gleaming table, taking coffee with a much younger man, who leaped to his feet upon our arrival. He was a scrawny fellow, shorter than me, with lank red hair to his shoulders, a long face, and a wispy chin beard. He wore Count Pesavolta's orange and gold livery. I guessed he was past twenty, but not much.

"You deign to grace us with your presence at last, do you?" said Dame Okra, glaring at us. "Your armed escort is arranged. You leave tomorrow. Josquin here will prevent your getting too lost." She flapped a hand at him obscurely; he understood it as a command to sit. "He's my great-great-grand-cousin, or some nonsense."

"Pleased to finally meet you both," said Josquin, pulling out a chair for me. His voice was far deeper than his skinny build gave any hint of. "My cousin has told me—"

"Yes, shut up. My point is," said Dame Okra, bristling, "I trust him. For years he and his mother were the only people who knew what I was, and they never told. His mother sews my dresses and helps me look properly human." She adjusted her majestic—and false—bosom at this juncture, underscoring her point. Josquin politely found something deserving of attention in his coffee.

"He's been riding as a herald since he was ten," Dame Okra continued. "He knows every village and road."

"Most of them," said Josquin modestly. His blue eyes crinkled with amused affection for his old cousin, despite her surliness.

"The best roads," snapped Dame Okra. "The ones worth knowing. He'll translate. He's already engaged his fellow heralds to ride ahead and spread word of a reward for information leading to the hermit and the muralist. That will save you time, I should think. And he knows you've got to get to Samsam in time for—"

Dame Okra suddenly froze and took on a dyspeptic look, her eyes unfocused.

Abdo, who'd claimed a chair and cup of coffee for himself, looked first at Okra and then toward the front of the house. *I wish you could see this, Phina madamina. Dame Okra is having a premonition, her soul-light darting out like lightning. A big spiky finger from her mind to the front door.* He pointed to illustrate.

She reaches out with her mind, too? I asked. *She claims it's her stomach.*

Maybe she can't tell them apart, said Abdo cheekily.

Dame Okra jerked grotesquely, recovering herself. "Saints in Heaven!" she cried. "Who's this creature at the front door, then?" She leaped to her feet and rushed up the hall just as someone knocked.

I hurried after her. I had not yet had a chance to mention Finch. "Before you answer that—" I began, but it was too late.

"Augh!" she cried, her voice dripping disgust. "Seraphina, did you invite this person here, all plaguey and pestilent? No, sir, you may not track contagion into my house. Go around to the carriage yard and strip down."

The doctor had removed his grimy apron and gloves and changed his robes; he still wore the ominous beaked mask, and his boots were indeed too muddy for her fine floors. I squeezed by Dame Okra, who puffed up indignantly.

"Leave your boots here," I told the doctor. He hurriedly pried them off. I took his arm and said, "You are welcome. I failed to warn her you were coming."

I led our new guest to the dining room, Dame Okra squawking behind us. Josquin stood again, with a cry of "Buonarrive, Dotoro Basimo!" and offered the older man his seat.

Finch shuffled over in his stocking feet, shoulders hunched anxiously, and sat. Josquin took the seat beside him.

"You know this ghoul?" demanded Dame Okra, switching the conversation back to Goreddi. She lingered behind in the doorway with her arms folded skeptically.

"Dr. Basimo keeps Count Pesavolta apprised of plague cases," said Josquin brightly. "They're trying to prevent another epidemic year. It's a noble endeavor."

The doctor perched on the very edge of a chair, his hands clasped between his knees, eyeing us through his glass lenses with trepidation.

"He's one of us," I said to Dame Okra. "We found him this morning."

"Take your mask off, then. You're among friends, by St. Prue," Dame Okra called, coming no closer and sounding not the least bit friendly.

"You don't have to, if you're not comfortable," I said, belaying her demand.

Dr. Basimo considered a moment, then pulled off his bag-like mask. I knew what we would see. I'd warned Dame Okra, but still she gasped. Josquin averted his eyes and took a quick sip of coffee.

Under the mask's leather beak was a real one, thick and strong like a finch's. Unlike a finch's, it had serrated edges, reminiscent of a dragon's teeth. He had no separate nose, just avian nostrils atop the beak. His bald, liver-spotted head and scrawny old-man's neck made him look like a buzzard, but no buzzard ever gazed so intelligently through mournful eyes the color of a summer sky.

"Please call me Nedouard," said the doctor, taking pains to speak clearly. It was hard for him; I could see his black tongue laboring to make up for the stiffness of his beak, and he couldn't help the curious snapping sound where language required the lips he didn't have. "The little fellow said you were all half-dragons. I had believed there were none but me."

I sat down across from him and rolled up my left sleeve to show the silver dragon scales spiraling up my forearm. Nedouard hesitantly reached across and touched them. "I have a few of those as well," he said softly. "You are fortunate to have escaped this." He gestured toward his beak.

"It seems to manifest differently in everyone," I said. Abdo obligingly stuck out his scaly tongue.

Nedouard nodded thoughtfully. "That doesn't surprise me. The surprise is that humans and dragons can intermix at all. But what about—" He nodded at Josquin.

"Oh, not me," said the herald. He'd gone pale, but he tried valiantly to smile.

Dame Okra said grudgingly, "I have a tail. And no, I won't show you."

Nedouard accepted a cup of coffee from Abdo with an almost inaudible "Thank you," and then there was an awkward silence.

"Did you grow up in Segosh, Nedouard?" I asked gently.

"No, I was born in the village of Basimo," he said, stirring his coffee, though he'd put nothing in it. "My mother took refuge there, at the Convent of St. Loola. She'd fled her home; she told the nuns my father was a dragon, but they didn't believe it until they saw my face."

"You were born with . . . ?" I mimed the beak. "My scales didn't come in until I was eleven. Abdo's came in when he was . . . six?" I looked for confirmation; Abdo nodded.

"Oh, the scales came later," he said. "The face, alas, was always as you see it. My mother died in childbirth, but there was never any question of the sisters caring for me, however malformed— St. Loola is patroness to children and fools. They raised, educated, and loved me like a son. I wore a mask outside the convent. The villagers were fearful at first, but I was steady and peaceable. They came to accept me.

"Basimo was ravaged by plague when I was seventeen. The convent took in the sick, of course, and I learned to care for the victims, but ..." He picked up a spoon and set it down again, drummed agitated fingers. "In the end, there were only five of us left. There is no village of Basimo, not anymore. Only the name I brought with me."

"How do you manage here?" I asked, careful not to add, *With a face like that.*

He heard the omission, though, and looked up cannily. "I keep my mask on. Who would dare touch me to remove it?"

"Your patients don't find the mask ominous during years without plague?"

"My patients are so grateful that they don't mind what I look like." He cleared his throat and added, "And there are no years without plague. Some years it doesn't reach the rich, but it always lurks among the poor."

Nedouard attempted to sip his coffee at last, but his beak was too ungainly for the tiny cup. Dame Okra made a scoffing noise, and Nedouard set his cup down, clearly mortified.

I glared at Dame Okra and said doggedly: "We've had many plague-free years in Goredd. There hasn't been an epidemic in my lifetime."

"Goredd is different," said Nedouard, his grizzled eyebrows raised. "Quigutl eat your garbage, so you have fewer rats. It's rats that bring plague. I've done experiments, written treatises, but I'm a self-taught doctor with this . . ." He gestured at his face. "Who's going to listen?"

"We will listen. All Goredd will listen," I said firmly. "I am on a mission to find all our kind. Goredd requires our assistance with the dragon civil war, but once that's over, I hope we might form a community of half-dragons, supporting and valuing each other."

Dame Okra rolled her eyes so hard I feared she'd give herself an aneurysm.

Nedouard turned his cup in his fingers. "People rely on me here," he said.

"You might still help them," I said. "If your work were taken seriously, you might find a way to prevent these outbreaks, or cure the disease altogether."

His eyes shone. "It's tempting, I have to admit. May I think about it?"

"Of course," I said warmly. "How do we find you again?"

"I live . . . near where you found me," he said, looking at the floor.

"You may move your things here, to Dame Okra's house," I said. "She has room, and you might be more comfortable."

Dame Okra bristled, but held her tongue; she'd already agreed to house the Ninysh ityasaari before escorting them back to Goredd. I would hold her to that.

"Take your time and think it over," I added. "Abdo and I have to seek out two more of our kind in Ninys. It could be six weeks before we're back."

Nedouard looked up again, interested. "How many of us are there altogether?"

"Sixteen," I said, omitting Jannoula and Pandowdy.

His gaze sharpened, reminding me unexpectedly of Kiggs; there was a thinker behind that beak. "Interspecies fertility can't be high," he said. "There must be ten transgressing dragons for every one of us conceived. That suggests—"

"Are we quite finished?" cried Dame Okra, noisily piling coffee dishes onto the tray. "If I'm to see a lot of Dr. Basimo in the coming weeks, I shouldn't like to tire of him all at once."

Her unfriendliness embarrassed me, but Nedouard took the hint. He rose and shook hands all around; Abdo, who found this Southlander practice hilarious, pumped his arm with particular zeal. I saw the doctor out. "Dame Okra can be blunt," I said as he put his boots on, "but she has a . . . a kind heart." She didn't, particularly, but I could think of nothing else reassuring to say.

Nedouard bowed cordially, hunched his shoulders, and disappeared into the falling night. Maybe I couldn't see mind-fire, but I could see loneliness enshrouding him like a cloak. It was an old friend of mine. It weighed him down; he would surely join us.

When I returned to the dining room, I was surprised to see Abdo crawling under the table; Josquin was shifting the coffee set, moving napkins, and peering under plates. Dame Okra was exclaiming loudly to everyone: "Of course I didn't see him do it! You never catch a professional in the act."

"What's happened?" I asked.

Dame Okra whirled on me, pink with rage. "Your bird-man," she snarled, "has stolen three silver spoons."

Josquin declined to stay for dinner. "I'm meeting Captain Moy, the leader of your escort, for one last briefing," he said.

"Is he to know that we're half-dragons?" I said, more sharply than I intended.

Josquin's horsey face was well suited to looking serious. "He's already been told. Was I not supposed to?"

My face felt hot. Would I never get used to people knowing? "It's just . . . he won't be frightened of us, will he?" Fear was less awful than hate, but easier to ask about.

"Ah," said Josquin, growing thoughtful. "Our history differs from yours. Dragon incursions seldom made it this far south— thanks to Goredd. When Ninysh people learn what you are, I expect they'll be more curious than fearful."

"But the Saints themselves call half-dragons an abomination and a vile—"

"And we Ninysh are generally more relaxed about the Saints, too," he said, smiling apologetically. "We've needed less of their help. It's another lucky accident of history, a privilege afforded by peace."

Peace was a blessing indeed; the years since Comonot's Treaty had proved that.

Still, I wasn't sure I believed him. I'd noticed his horror at Nedouard's face; he'd tried valiantly to smile at my scales, but queasiness and unease had come first. If the Ninysh were so sanguine about differences, why had Dame Okra always gone to such lengths to conceal her tail?

Josquin seemed friendly enough, however. I would try to give our escort the benefit of the doubt.

Dame Okra was digging through the credenza as if Nedouard might magically have opened its doors without us noticing. Josquin smiled indulgently at her; he was fond of her, certainly, as baffling as that seemed. "Good evening, cousin," he said. "Seraphina, Abdo—I'll be here early. Be ready to leave."

He saw himself out. Dame Okra slammed the credenza doors, crying, "Why did I agree to house these monsters? I take it all back. They can sleep in the stable." She stomped off toward the kitchen, hissing and spitting. I sighed and rested my forehead against the cool, smooth table. Dame Okra made me tired.

"I only have so much patience," I mumbled to Abdo, "and she uses all of it."

He mused, *I wonder how hard it is to manipulate soul-light. The old priest, Paulos Pende, said it could be done. I already reach out with a finger of fire.* He jabbed the table with an index finger. *Could I mold hers with it? Could I make her kind, make her forget?*

I froze. *Forget what?* I asked, fearing to learn the answer.

Well, I could start with the spoons. Then she'd forget she hates Nedouard—

I sat up sharply. "Don't suggest it. Don't even think it."

He recoiled from my sudden vehemence, his eyes widening. *Oh, madamina, don't be angry. I only wished . . . Nedouard is kind and doesn't deserve her contempt. I only thought to help him.*

My mouth had gone dry, but I managed to say, "Dame Okra must have sovereignty over her own thoughts, Abdo, however noxious we may find them."

He studied my face. *There's a story you haven't told me. Is it about that lady you banished from your mind?*

Another time, I said wearily. He nodded and left me to my thoughts.

At bedtime, I still felt shaken by Abdo's blithe suggestion and how much it upset me. However many years in the past Jannoula lay, her shadow seemed to lurk below the surface like some dread behemoth.

I went to my room, hoping my bedtime routines would settle me. I washed and oiled the wide band of scales around my waist and the narrower one winding around my left forearm. I flopped onto the four-poster bed, breathed myself calm, and descended into my garden of grotesques.

Ever since Abdo had described my garden as a gatehouse, its surfaces had taken on an odd flatness when I arrived, as if the trees and statuary were a painted backdrop for a play. His suggestion had made me too aware that none of this was real, like a sleeper realizing she's dreaming. It's hard to stay asleep once you know.

I stood still a moment with my eyes closed, quietly breathing life back into my construct. When I opened my eyes, everything had righted itself: the sun warmed my face again; the grass individuated into blades, dewy and ticklish between my toes; I smelled roses and rosemary on the wafting breeze.

I checked Jannoula's cottage first, making sure the padlock on

the door still held, as if I might have summoned her just by thinking about her. I said good night to all the denizens I passed, and
when I reached his golden nest, I patted Finch—Nedouard—
upon his bald head, pleased to have found him, whatever his flaws.
I blew kisses toward Bluey, the painter, in her stream of swirling
colors and Glimmerghost, the hermit, in her butterfly garden; I
was coming for them next.

Settling the garden settled me somewhat. I returned to myself
in Dame Okra's green guest room. I had one last task to attend to
before I could sleep. I pulled the silver necklace out of my shirt
and felt for the sweetheart knot thnik.

I flipped the little switch. Upon Glisselda's desk in the study,
an ornamented box would be chirping like a cricket. Mine was not
the only device connected to that receiver. Comonot had one, as
did some of his generals, Count Pesavolta, the Regent of Samsam,
and the knights training at Fort Oversea. A page sat at the desk all
day, waiting to take calls.

"Castle Orison, identify yourself, if you please," droned a
bored young voice.

"Seraphina Dombegh," I said.

I thought the boy had made a rude sound, but it was his chair
scraping back as he stood, and then there was the thump of the
door closing. He knew whom he was to fetch if I called. I settled
down to wait. When two dear familiar voices cried, "Phina!" in
crackling unison over my quigutl device, I could not help smiling.

Five

Josquin had been serious about the early start. He met Abdo and me at Dame Okra's door before dawn, put us on horses, and led us through the dewy streets. Shopkeepers swept their stoops, the smell of first bread wafted enticingly, and traffic was light.

"All according to plan," Josquin said proudly. "Santi Wilibaio's market begins today. By noon the streets will be full of calves and capering kids."

Santi Wilibaio was our St. Willibald, called St. Villibaltus in Samsam. Whatever our differences, we Southlanders share the Saints.

At the city gates we met our escort, eight soldiers, half sporting blond beards, all with white plumes bobbing ostentatiously above their soup-bowl helmets. Their breastplates were engraved with martial scenes; their puffed sleeves, in Count Pesavolta's colors, were like great gold and orange cabbages. Their horses' harnesses—and those of our own mounts, I noticed—were studded with brass ornaments and tiny bells. Clearly, we weren't intending to sneak up on anyone.

Josquin hailed the leader, a man with broad shoulders, a big stomach, and a yellow beard like the blade of a shovel. He had no mustache; suddenly Josquin's chin beard seemed less idiosyncratic. This was some Ninysh fashion.

"Captain Moy," said Josquin. Moy bowed in the saddle, removing his helmet with a flourish. His blond hair was thinning on top; I guessed him to be about forty-five years old.

"Pleased to meet you," I said, using up all my Ninysh in one go and experiencing an anxious flutter at meeting an armed stranger who already knew what I was. It wasn't my secret anymore; that was out of my hands. It was still unsettling.

"The honor is ours," said Captain Moy in decent Goreddi. He flashed me a crooked smile full of square teeth, which I found oddly reassuring. "Our troop is called Des Osho—the Eight. We accompany visiting dignitaries."

Ha ha, we're dignitaries, said Abdo, watching Moy's plumes the way a cat watches a ball of wool.

Captain Moy barked an order, and the others rode into formation around us. None of them stared at Abdo or me; they were professionals. We left the city together, passing the growing line of carts coming to market. Farmers and teamsters gaped at our escort; we didn't look like the sort the Eight usually accompanied. Abdo waved at the farmers and grinned.

The nearest baronet's estate was Palasho do Lire, a day's ride away; we would stay the night there. The Ninysh countryside opened up into rolling pastureland, interspersed with acre strips of winter wheat; this early in spring, the stalks were a vibrant green, patches of black soil occasionally visible amid the thick growth.

The road cut straight for the horizon, running between low stone walls or hedgerows, curving around a village or vineyard; it bridged more than one river, swollen with spring runoff. Windmills, triangular sails spread to the brisk breeze, stood watch on distant rises; peasants looked up from mucky onion patches to gawp at us. Abdo blew them kisses.

Our escort started six ahead and two behind, but things soon shifted. Abdo, bored with the temperate pace, spurred himself to the front. Captain Moy dropped back and rode to my right; Josquin stayed on my left.

"We've all been looking forward to this assignment," said Moy jovially. "An interesting mission is worth its weight in gold."

"Are we interesting?" I asked, feeling my face go hot.

"Don't misunderstand me, maidy," said the captain, observing me sidelong. "It's not because of what you are, but what we are to do. Escorting fussy nobles gets old quickly, but searching for persons unknown? This is a challenge. We must discuss in more detail the women you seek. Josquin knows almost nothing."

Ahead of us, Abdo was engaged in elaborate hand signaling, holding his splayed hands above his head like a bird's crest. The soldier beside him removed his helmet—or *her* helmet, I should say. Bareheaded, she was clearly a woman, apple-cheeked and laughing, two golden braids wrapped around her scalp. She crowned Abdo with her plumed headgear, exclaiming delightedly.

"Excuse me," said Moy, spurring his horse. "I have some discipline to maintain."

"His daughter, Nan," Josquin muttered to me, indicating the woman. "They try each other's patience, but they're a good team. This honor guard isn't where they stick the lazy and incapable; it's a true honor for those who have earned it."

I wondered how they'd earned it; Ninys had seldom helped Goredd in wartime. I decided it would be rude to ask.

The Ninysh word *palasho* is generally translated "palace," but Palasho do Lire, its sandstone walls glowing orange with the sunset, looked more like a heavily fortified farmstead. Squat and square, the enclosure sulked atop a low hill, cattle pasture on all sides. A shallow ditch enclosed the pasture, more useful for keeping cattle in than anyone else out; our horses balked at the open-slatted bridge, but some cowherds rushed up and laid down planks to help our skittish steeds across.

The house steward, who knew Josquin, came out to greet us, shaking the herald's hand and directing a bevy of grooms to take our horses. The steward led us through a brick arch into a courtyard. Chickens eyed us from niches in the walls; an old nanny goat with crooked horns and distended udders bleated hoarse disapproval.

Most of the Eight went straight to quarters in a long outbuilding. Moy accompanied Josquin and me toward a hulking stone hall, like a barn with windows. Abdo grabbed Nan's hand

and towed her along. She grinned apologetica... same squared-off teeth as Moy.

She guesses my hand signs better than any of the oth...

Reason enough, I said, nodding cordially at Nan.

A stag-hunting scene, too fine for a barn, had... upon the double doors. My weary brain finally und... this was the great hall. I was to make my greeting an... tion to the local gentry straightaway, still dusty from t... breeches, doublet, broad-brimmed hat, and boots. I ball...

Josquin paused, hand on the door. "Nervous?"

"Shouldn't I change first?" I whispered, trying not t... panicky.

"Ah," he said, looking me up and down appraisingly... could, if it means that much to you. But may I make a su... tion?"

I shrugged assent, confusedly. The breeze brought with... whiff of pig.

He lowered his voice, his pale eyes intent. "Dame Okra sa... you're a musician, a performer. Well, we heralds are performer... too. We speak with the voices of counts, queens, sometimes even... Saints. Fine clothing may earn you the benefit of the doubt, but... authority still has to come from here." He jabbed a finger below his rib cage. "Stand up straight. Speak like you have every right, and they'll believe you. I'll be there with you, translating. All will be well."

That made sense, and I had performed enough now that I had a reservoir of confidence to draw from. I took a fortifying breath and entered a church-like space with columns holding up the

-blackened roof. I'd expected a receiving room or feasting hall.
...aps this chamber filled those purposes, too, but today it was
...of woolly yearling goats. Men and women vigorously brushed
...animals, collecting the sheddings in great baskets; other bas-
...s held the coarser shorn fleeces of older goats. Great bronze
...ldrons for washing or dyeing the wool rested above hearth fires
...the center of the room, circled in turn by drying racks. At the
...r end, women were setting up tapestry looms.

Josquin weaved through the busy hall toward a petite woman,
...er red hair streaked with silver, who was assembling a spinning
...vheel. She wore a blue kirtle over a linen blouse with riotous em-
...oroidery up the sleeves.

Josquin bowed low; I took my cue from him and, having no
skirts, bowed, too. I discerned the name Baroneta Do Lire in his
address, leaving no doubt that this was indeed the chatelaine.

She called Josquin by name; his was clearly a familiar face
here. He introduced me in mellifluent tones, and she looked impressed. The goats would have seemed magnificent, spoken of in
that voice. Under his breath Josquin said, "Go on. Read."

I drew Queen Glisselda's missive to the nobility of Ninys
from my satchel, lifted my chin, and smiled. Josquin gave a small,
approving nod. I ceremoniously unfolded the parchment and
read, Josquin translating my every word into fluid, grandiloquent
Ninysh:

> *Honorable lords* ["and ladies," I added hastily] *of Ninys,
> I bear the greetings and respectful good wishes of Queen
> Glisselda of Goredd.*

You have heard of the inter-draconic conflict in the north. It will inevitably spill south: the Old Ard want to hunt the Southlands again, not just Goredd but Ninys and Samsam as well. Goredd has often borne the brunt of dragon aggression alone. We hold no grudge for the past—indeed, we were honored to be a bulwark for the Southlands—but forty years of peace and the dissolution of the knightly orders have left us ill prepared for another onslaught.

Count Pesavolta has sent the last remaining Ninysh knights to Fort Oversea to train new dracomachists alongside ours. Goredd applauds his generous, cooperative spirit, but more is needed. We rely on the baronets of Ninys, heart and conscience of the south, to do your part.

Glisselda and Kiggs had agonized over this letter, trying to strike the right balance between urgency and desperation, flattery and guilt-mongering. It went on to list what aid Goredd could use—men, arms, grain, timber, the raw materials for St. Ogdo's fire, and more. Josquin polished my words in translation, laying them at Baroneta do Lire's feet like gleaming jewels.

The lady had been winding wool when I began; by the end, she'd dropped her distaff into her lap and placed her hand upon her heart. "Palasho do Lire would be honored to help," she said (per Josquin's translation). "We Ninysh know what we owe Goredd, that our beauteous, well-organized country was built upon Goreddi sacrifice. Marie"—this to a woman carrying a basket of wool—"fetch quill and ink. I'll put my promises in writing."

This was more than I had hoped for. We acquired the written

account and had dinner with the baroneta in a smaller, goat-free dining room—I could barely sit still, I was so pleased. As we filed out, led toward the guest wing by the steward, I whispered to Josquin, "You were right. There was nothing to fear."

He quirked a smile and said, "They won't all be this gracious."

Abdo and I were quartered together in a sparse guest room with a hearth and two curtained alcove beds. I felt a big-sisterly impulse to see that Abdo got a good night's sleep. His routines were as elaborate as mine: he cleaned his teeth with a wooden pick, changed into a long tunic he'd brought just for sleeping, wrapped his hair in a silk scarf, and bounced on the bed.

"Friend," I said after he'd been at it for several minutes, "that's not really necessary. Don't tell me your god demands it, either, because I'm not falling for it."

You only do necessary things before bed? he asked, still jumping.

"If I don't wash and oil my scales, they itch," I said crossly. My kettle was taking forever to boil on the hearth.

Not that. He stopped and stared owlishly. *You visit your "garden" every night.*

"Also necessary, or I am afflicted with involuntary visions of all you villains."

He cocked his head to one side. *When was the last time you had a vision?*

"Midwinter. It was a vision of you, if you recall. You were aware of me."

I was looking for you, he said. *I caused that vision, reaching out. But before that?*

I shook my head at him, perplexed. "I don't remember. Not for years. I tend my garden religiously."

Ha, he said, lying down at last, his face thoughtful. *I suspect you mean* superstitiously. *You should try ignoring it. See what happens.*

"Not while we're traveling," I said, taking my kettle off the fire. "What if a vision bowled me right off my horse?"

He didn't answer. I turned to look at him and saw that he'd fallen asleep.

Early the next morning, we were mostly dressed when our escort came to wake us. I was still lacing up my riding breeches—thank Allsaints I'd had them padded—and wore only my linen shirt up top, but Abdo answered the door anyway. In filed Josquin, Moy, and Nan, unconcerned about my state of disarray, bearing a hot loaf and crumbly goat cheese. They set up breakfast on the floor, since our room had no table; I put on my blue wool doublet and joined them.

Captain Moy moved the cheese to one side and spread a parchment map of Ninys before us on the floor. From a pouch at his waist, he fetched a pair of gold-rimmed spectacles and perched them incongruously on his nose. "Now," he said, accepting a hunk of bread from his daughter, who was hacking at the loaf with her dagger, "where do you expect to find these half-dragon ladies?"

Nan's eyes flashed briefly to my face when he said *half-dragon,* plainly curious.

"Unfortunately," I said, "I don't know Ninys at all. I see the others in visions, but only their immediate surroundings. That doesn't tell me much."

Moy seemed genuinely, absurdly delighted by my answer. "That's the challenge. Two women, one large country. If you're not back in Segosh in six weeks, Samsam will declare war on us—"

"No, they won't," said Josquin hastily, in case I couldn't tell Moy was exaggerating. "But my cousin will."

Moy shrugged and grinned. "We three know Ninys well. Describe what you've seen."

I knew most about Bluey, the painter whose avatar left colorful swirls in water. "One paints murals. She's doing a St. Jobertus now—I don't know where—but previously she painted an amazing St. Fionnuala at Meshi."

"Santi Fionani?" asked Nan. That was the Ninysh name for the Lady of Waters.

Moy jabbed a finger at a city along a river east of central Ninys. "How do you know it was Meshi?"

"I got lucky," I said. "I once saw her outdoors, and glimpsed the city banner."

"The one that says Meshi, under a pine," said Josquin around a lump of cheese.

"They're subtle in that part of the country," said Moy. His daughter unscrewed the lid from a pot of ink and carefully dabbed a red dot next to the city with a brush.

"The priest at Santi Fionani's may know where she went next," said Josquin. "And Meshi was on Dame Okra's list of strategically important lords, for the sulfur mine, no doubt. We would stop there in any case."

This was encouraging. I hazarded a description of the second ityasaari, Glimmerghost: "The other woman lives a hermetic existence in a great pine forest—"

"The Pinabra," said Moy, without blinking. "Meshi is at its western edge."

Josquin made a sweeping gesture at the map. "It's a large region, though. It rings the eastern mountains like a skirt."

"Zat is place to get lost," Nan said hesitantly. It was the first Goreddi I'd heard her speak. Her accent was poor, although she seemed to follow the conversation well enough.

"One thing at a time," said Moy. "Meshi is goal enough for now, with plenty of palashos for us to visit between here and there."

He got to his feet, Nan rolled up the map, and we were on the road in half an hour.

The palashos were numerous indeed; they dotted the countryside like carbuncles. Some days we stopped at two or three. Word got out that I played flute and Abdo danced, so we were often asked to perform. The Ninysh sometimes brought out dancers of their own. Abdo watched with rapt attention and then imitated the leaps and posturing all the way upstairs to bed. At some point Moy began to teach him the saltamunti and the voli-vola.

"Baronet Des Faiasho screamed in my face this evening," I reported, about a week into our journey, to Glisselda and Kiggs from one of Palasho Faiasho's guest rooms.

"Oh no!" cried Glisselda, simultaneously with Kiggs's "Are you all right?"

I was reclining upon a four-poster bed that was draped in silk and bulging with feather bolsters; Des Faiasho knew how to treat a guest, even one he'd screamed at. "I'm fine. As ever, Josquin was right: these lords aren't all gracious about what they owe Goredd. Some get defensive."

"Josquin sounds like he's quite often right," said Kiggs drily.

I wanted so badly to tease him for being jealous, but of course I couldn't. Luckily, Glisselda piped up: "Josquin this, Josquin that! Don't let the suave Ninysh rascal lure you away. We want you home after all this."

"Ah, Your Majesty, jealousy does not become you," I said to Glisselda, sending Kiggs an indirect message. I rolled onto my stomach and propped myself on my elbows. "In any case, after clarifying that Goredd can't push him around, Des Faiasho went on to commit fifteen hundred fighting men, armed and supplied, as well as grain, blacksmiths, carpenters—"

Glisselda listened no further than the number of men. She whooped in a most unqueenlike fashion. "An army! We're accreting a foreign army. Isn't it wonderful?"

Kiggs, I knew, would be jotting everything down conscientiously, so I continued listing supplies and specialists, finishing with the baronet's strangest offer of all: "Des Faiasho imports sabanewt oil from the southern archipelagoes. He insists it's a worthy substitute for naphtha in pyria." Pyria was a sticky, flammable substance the knights employed in their martial art, the dracomachia.

"Is he certain it works?" said Glisselda, attentive again.

"I'm certain he wants to sell us some," I said. "I can have samples sent."

"Have them sent to Sir Maurizio at Fort Oversea so the knights can test it," said Glisselda. "No one here can make St. Ogdo's fire."

"That's not entirely true," said Kiggs quietly. "The murder at that warehouse involved pyria. If our suspect in custody can't make it himself, he knows who can."

"Murder?" I asked, alarmed.

"I forget that things happen here that you don't hear about," said Glisselda. "Comonot established a dragon garrison shortly after you left. He called it 'a large gesture of good faith.' He said that several times, in case there was any mistaking."

I was glad he'd taken my advice and unsurprised by the ham-handed execution.

"It's gone over badly," said Kiggs. "The Sons of St. Ogdo are crawling out of their ratholes again. Protests, mostly, but also one violent riot, saarantrai assaulted, and a female dragon officer missing. We found her burned body in a warehouse by the river."

I closed my eyes, sickened. The Sons of St. Ogdo were a clandestine brotherhood of fanatical dragon-haters. Half the trouble at midwinter had been their fault; they so despised dragonkind that they were easily persuaded—by the dragon Imlann, in human form—to participate in the assassination attempts against Comonot. Lars's estranged brother, Josef, Earl of Apsig, had been in the thick of things; he'd returned to Samsam in the end, tail between his legs, humiliated to learn he'd done the bidding of a dragon.

"His large gesture of good faith has been a large headache for the city watch," said Kiggs.

"He meant well," said Glisselda. It was the first time I'd heard her defend Comonot's clumsy efforts. "Anyway, the Sons of St. Ogdo won't get away with murdering saarantrai. You know what a dogged investigator Lucian is. We'll take whatever steps are necessary to keep the peace."

"Comonot's Loyalists are our allies: that's the reality," said Kiggs. "Goredd must learn to adjust."

"Of course," I said weakly. "I know you have it well in hand."

When our conversation finished, however, I lay on the bed a long time with my arm over my eyes, feeling dully disappointed. I don't know what I had imagined would happen in Goredd after I told the truth about my origins and revealed my scales. Did I expect the Sons of St. Ogdo to dissolve into dust, or that Goreddis would learn in four months the kind of trust they hadn't learned in forty years?

Of course that was impossible. That didn't stop me from wishing I could change the attitudes of Goreddis single-handedly, reach in and make people see sense.

The members of our Ninysh escort, despite Josquin's protestations to the contrary, were not entirely sanguine about accompanying half-dragons. They concealed their feelings behind their professionalism, for the most part, but the longer we traveled, the more slips I began to notice. Once I noticed, I couldn't unsee.

Some of the Eight made St. Ogdo's sign if Abdo or I came too near. It was a subtle gesture intended to ward off the evil of dragons, just a circle made with thumb and finger. At first I thought I'd imagined it. The soldier saddling our horses seemed to make the sign over the beast's withers, but when I looked straight at him, he wasn't doing it. One soldier may have made it over her heart after I spoke to her, or did she have an itch?

Then there was the day Nan bought a bundle of barley twigs—slender, crunchy breadsticks, which Abdo loved—and Abdo reached right in and took three. Two of our soldiers, who had ridden up eagerly, now hesitated, reluctant to take any. Finally one of them made St. Ogdo's sign, as unobtrusively as he could. Abdo saw it and froze mid-chew; he'd spent enough time in Goredd to know the gesture.

Nan saw the sign and went incandescent. She flung the remaining barley twigs to the ground, leaped from her horse, and pulled her comrade headfirst off his. She went at him, fists flying. Moy had to break it up.

Nan ended up with a split lip, but she'd given the other fellow a black eye. Her father imposed some kind of discipline on them both; I didn't have enough Ninysh to understand, but Josquin paled. Nan seemed not to care. She returned to us, patted Abdo's horse, and said huskily, "Do not take zis to heart, *moush.*"

Moush, meaning "gnat," was her nickname for Abdo. Abdo nodded, his eyes wide.

I was the one who took it to heart.

I could not be completely comfortable now. It galled me to play my flute in the evenings. Josquin noticed the change, but if he fathomed the cause, he gave me no indication. "You're a herald, not a circus bear," he said one evening. "You can say no."

But I didn't say no. Playing flute was the one thing I knew could make people see a human, not a monster.

The eastern mountains came into view over the course of a week. I mistook them for a bank of clouds at first. As we traveled nearer, I discerned snowy peaks and a dark forest spreading at their feet like a stain. The legendary Pinabra.

We arrived in Meshi two days later. It stood at the border of the forest, along a river that divided the plains from the pines, western produce from eastern timber and ore. The crenellated turrets of Palasho Meshi rose at the center of town. The baronet was one of the more important Ninysh lordlings, supplying two crucial ingredients for pyria: sulfur and pine resin. We would be imposing on his hospitality for the night.

It was near noon, however, when we passed the city gates. Too early to call in at the palasho. "Let's go to St. Fionnuala's and ask the priest about his mural painter," I suggested to Josquin.

After a quick word with Moy, Josquin led us through the sunny streets toward the riverside, the likeliest place for a church dedicated to the Lady of Waters. The Eight quarreled merrily about whether to turn upstream or down, until Nan cried out and pointed. The church was north, upstream, in sight.

As we approached, I noted that the facade was like nothing I had ever seen, a cacophony of helical columns, curly stone acanthus leaves, Saints in carved niches, gilded shells, and twisted marble ribbons. It was too busy to be beautiful, at least by Goreddi standards.

This church has wiggly eyebrows, said Abdo, tracing the undulating cornices in the air. *And fish.*

St. Fionnuala brings rain, I said. *Hence the watery facade.*

The inside also dripped with ornamentation, made more bearable by semidarkness; candlelight reflected off gilt surfaces on the ceiling, columns, and statuary. Only Josquin, Abdo, and I entered, so as not to overwhelm the priest. Our boots upon the marble floor made the vaulted chamber ring with echoes.

My eyes adjusted, and then I saw, illuminated with indirect sunlight, the mural above the altar. Josquin caught his breath and whispered, "Santi Merdi!" St. Fionnuala gazed steadily back at us, her eyes clear and compassionate, her magnanimous face unearthly and yet solidly real. Her pale green hair flowed past her shoulders, becoming a river at her feet. Her gown was shimmering water flowing over abundant earth. She seemed about to speak; we stood stock-still, as if awaiting her utterance.

"Benevenedo des Celeshti, amini!" said a voice to our right, making us jump. A tall, stooped priest emerged from the shadows, his white beard and robe catching the light eerily. St. Fionnuala's waves in gold filigree adorned his mantle.

Josquin piously kissed a knuckle, like we do in Goredd. I

followed suit. Abdo didn't bother, but bounded up to examine the contents of a clay dish the priest held in his knobby hands.

"Yes, you should try those," said Josquin, smiling at Abdo's quizzical look. Abdo took what appeared to be a snail-shaped pastry, sticky with syrup. "Santi Fionani's shells," Josquin explained. "Quite a delicacy in the Pinabra."

Abdo took a bite, his eyes bulging. He swallowed and took another bite, his mouth puckering. *Phina madamina, you should try one,* he said. *No questions. Eat.* He plucked a sticky roll off the dish and shoved it into my hands. The priest beamed and said something in Ninysh. Josquin nodded, watching my face as I bit into the pastry.

It wasn't sweet. It tasted bitterly, fiercely, unmistakably of pine.

I didn't dare spit it out. Abdo gave up trying to hold in his silent laughter; Josquin and the priest exchanged a few amused words. "I told him you're Goreddi," said Josquin. "And he told me you have no cuisine worth eating in Goredd."

"Pine buns are cuisine?" I tried to scrape resin off my teeth with my tongue.

"Get used to that flavor. It's all over the Pinabra," said Josquin, grinning at me.

"Ask him about his muralist," I said crossly, gesturing at the painting.

Josquin conferred quietly with the priest. The last of my pine bun somehow ended up under the altar; I'm sure it made some church mice happy. I clasped my sticky hands behind my back and examined the mural closely. The painter had signed her name in the bottom corner: Od Fredricka des Uurne.

I waited for a lull in the conversation, then pointed out the signature to Josquin.

"*Od* is a title from the archipelagoes. It means 'great,'" said Josquin. "She's a modest sort, clearly. She's been commissioned to paint a Santi Jobirti next, as you thought. It's at Vaillou, quite deep in the forest. You'll be eating pine a long time."

I rolled my eyes at Josquin, bowed respectfully to the priest, and kissed my knuckle toward Heaven. Josquin left something in the offering box.

Outdoors, noon glared unbearably off the river and the plastered walls. There was only one step down from the church door, and we all stumbled over it, even Abdo.

Is Vaillou very far? Abdo asked.

Josquin said it's deep in the forest. I take that as a yes, I said. *Why?*

Abdo shielded his eyes with one hand and pointed east across the river with the other. *Because I see an ityasaari's mind just over there. Not far away at all.*

~Six~

We pursued this unexpected mind-fire, crossing the stone causeway over the wide, shallow river. Abdo rode ahead, the Eight close on his heels, chattering excitedly together. "They're intrigued by his ability to see minds," Josquin interpreted for me. "They think it would be useful."

It would be useful to me as well; I tried not to feel sour about it, but turned my own mind toward who this might be. Not the painter. Had we stumbled across hermetic Glimmerghost?

The neighborhoods across the river were more village than town, not as dense, well kept, or paved as those in western Meshi. The houses looked hastily built. "The miners live on this side," Josquin explained, pointing to men trudging homeward, coated head to toe in yellow sulfur dust. We passed the miners' taverns and grocers. Their dogs ran in semi-feral packs, chased by their wholly feral children.

Abdo led us past the village, off the main road, and up a sandy track into the pines. Between the tall trees and the low shrubs, there was no middle layer of foliage. I could see a long way through the endless colonnade of plumb-line-straight reddish brown tree trunks. The soil showed yellow between gnarled roots.

Abdo halted his steed, looked around in confusion, then pulled his feet from the stirrups and stood balanced on the saddle to gain a wider view. His horse shifted uncertainly, pawing the ground, but Abdo retained his footing.

Is something wrong? I asked.

No, he said, scratching between his hair knots and staring east of the road, toward a low ridge. *Her light is strange, that's all. I reached out to tell her we were coming, and it shrank to almost nothing, like that plant where the leaves curl up when you touch it.* He illustrated by making his hand close up like a flower. I'd never heard of such a plant.

Is she over that ridge, off the road? I asked.

Yes, but . . . He tapped a finger against his lips. *It might be best to give her a little time to see if she unfolds again. Maybe we could eat first?*

I conveyed this news to Josquin and Moy. Everyone seemed glad of a break; the Eight unpacked our simple provisions—bread from last night's palasho, cheese, apples—and settled in for the midday meal. Some, sitting with their backs to resin-caked pine trunks, looked ready for a nap.

I must have been very hungry, because it took longer than it should have to notice that Abdo had disappeared. At first I thought he'd wandered off to "talk to the birds"—as Josquin had explained the Ninysh euphemism—but then Nan started to complain that a whole loaf of bread was missing. I called with my mind, *Abdo? Where are you?*

I'm going the last mile alone, he replied. *She's very shy, I think. The Eight will scare her, and she'll scare them, and I don't want them hurting her spiders.*

Spiders? I said, looking around for any glimpse of him. Talking to him with my head gave me no sense of where he was, alas.

Josquin was watching me. "Are you well?" he asked.

I must have been making a face. "Abdo has gone on alone." I explained his reasons, and whom we'd found—the eerie pale hermit surrounded by butterflies in my mind's garden.

"We don't need the Eight," said Josquin, glancing over at our armed guards, some of whom were now napping heroically. "But I don't think Abdo should go alone, either."

I agreed. Josquin conveyed our intention to Moy, who frowned deeply and made Josquin take his dagger. I started up the ridge, Josquin at my heels. From the top, a barely perceptible track wound downhill between boulders; I couldn't see Abdo but guessed he would have followed a visible path rather than charging through the thickening underbrush. The path grew steeper, and then we were descending a little ravine with a gurgling stream at the bottom. The pines grew thicker here, and the rocks mossier. The path ran downstream and soon became bogged in yellow clay. We slipped and skidded along, managing not to fall in the mud or the stream, until we reached a massive fallen tree covered in mushrooms and moss.

It seemed to be the only bridge. We crossed to the other side, and the path veered away from the stream, winding into the forest again.

Fifty yards along, we reached a clearing, where a shaft of sunlight illuminated a ramshackle hut made of bark and ferns. Abdo was halfway across, stepping gingerly, ducking something I couldn't see. He'd mentioned spiders, and he looked like someone evading their webs, but I saw no silky threads gleaming in the sunshine.

Abdo looked back over his shoulder at us and said irritably, *Stop right there.*

Something in his tone made me freeze at once, but Josquin couldn't hear him. I snatched at the herald's sleeve as he passed, but missed. "Josquin!" I hissed.

Josquin looked back at me quizzically.

There was a sound of snapping twigs, and then Josquin disappeared down a hole.

Alarmed, I rushed forward. There was another snap, and Abdo cried, *Duck!*

I threw myself to the ground as an axe swung over my head and thudded into the trunk of a nearby tree.

"What is this?" I cried.

There are filaments of soul-light everywhere, like a giant spider-web, said Abdo. *Traps. You really should stay put.*

He waved the pilfered loaf at me. *I've been telling her about bread, and she's very interested. At least I think she is. I get images from her, but no words.*

He started picking his way forward again. I crawled through the ferns to the edge of Josquin's hole and looked down. He waved from the center of a nest of broken twigs. "No casualties but my dignity," called the herald, tugging on his chin beard. "Some might say that's no loss at all."

I explained about the filaments. "I'm not sure it's safe to breathe."

Oops, said Abdo. I looked up in time to see a cascade of small logs bowl his feet out from under him. He softened his landing with a diving roll, but some part of him must have grazed another mind-fire filament. Three mounds of pine needles began to rise from the forest floor, until each had grown to the height of a table. The nearest one twitched, shedding needles and revealing a woolly body the size of a human head connected to eight long, spindly legs.

I must have cried out, because Josquin shouted in alarm, "What is it?"

"Sp-spiders," I managed. Josquin reached up and handed me Moy's dagger. I took it, not sure what I could do with it. How could I reach the spiders—or Abdo—without snapping more invisible trigger threads?

Abdo, for his part, was gazing rapturously at the monsters with an openmouthed smile. *Oh, Phina madamina, I wish you could see this.*

I'm seeing plenty, I said. The spiders had begun taking shaky steps toward him.

These are machines, he said.

"What, like Lars builds?" I asked, disbelieving. I understood the mechanics of Lars's machines. They didn't look like creatures.

Not exactly. She's fixed her soul-light to them somehow. They're animated by clockwork and her mind, together. He shook his head, marveling. *This is her garden, Phina, but it's made of things, not people. Her mind reaches out to objects.*

He clambered to his feet and stepped toward the nearest spider, extending a hand to it as if it were a friendly dog.

"Don't!" I cried, on my feet again in a trice. I took a single step, heard an ominous click, and threw myself backward. A gout of flame burst from the ground where I'd been standing.

Stay still, Abdo scolded me. He was petting the spider now. It hadn't attacked.

Behind him, the hut's lichen-crusted door opened silently, and a pale, petite woman stepped into the sunlight.

I'd called her Glimmerghost for a reason. She seemed to float behind Abdo, ethereal and bone-thin, as if she had sought to become transparent in fact. She didn't seem old, but her hair was white, long, and so fine that it caught the slightest breeze and drifted around her head. Peeling blemishes—individual dragon scales—scarred her skin all over. From a distance they looked like graypox scars. Her dress was stained and mossy.

Her violet eyes gleamed with curiosity. She stepped toward Abdo with her slender hand outstretched, the way he'd approached the spider.

He turned to face her, and they stood a moment in silence, drenched in liquid sunlight. Abdo offered the loaf of bread, and she took it, the shade of a smile flickering across her face. She extended her other hand, and together they entered her earthy home.

This is going to take some time, Abdo told me after a quarter of an hour had passed. *If I speak too much to her, it gives her a headache. Her soul-light is strong and fragile all at once, like cobwebs.*

I rescued Josquin while we waited, although he insisted later—when I reported the incident to Captain Moy—that it was not so much rescuing as giving him a hand up.

An hour passed, and then two. I paced the edge of the clearing, where there seemed to be no filaments. Josquin went to update the Eight and returned.

Abdo said at last, *She'd like to come with us—she's curious—but she's also timid. She doesn't go among people. I don't want to bring her out before she's ready. I should stay here overnight.*

I began to protest, but he said, *I'm perfectly safe. Anyway, you can't reach me to protect me or bring me out. Go back to Meshi and call in at the palasho. I'll still be here in the morning, I promise.*

I didn't like it; the Eight, when Josquin and I returned to the main road and told them, liked it even less. After much discussion, we left a contingent of four—led by Nan—encamped at the edge of the clearing, out of range of Glimmerghost's defenses. The rest of us went back to town and called on Baronet Meshi as per our original intention. I checked in on Abdo so often that he began to get irritated with me, and I was so distracted that I failed to answer a direct question from the baronet about our old Queen's failing health. Josquin, with his usual aplomb, smoothed over my inadequacies and kicked me under the table.

Abdo interrupted my sleep early the next morning, saying, *Would you bring more bread with you when you come back? Blanche loves it, but she never got the hang of baking it herself.*

She had a name. That didn't quite soothe my crankiness at being awakened so early.

We brought bread that day—and the next. Baronet Meshi gave us a tour of his sulfur mines; I twitched with impatience all the way through. Finally, on the third morning, Abdo informed me that Blanche was willing and ready to travel, if we could find some way to transport her. She was frightened of horses.

Horses and humans. I stopped myself from suggesting that she ride one of her giant spiders back to Segosh.

Josquin visited his brother heralds at an inn west of Meshi, and returned to the palasho in an hour with a post carriage and an elderly herald named Folla, who would escort Blanche to Dame Okra's. I must have looked skeptical, because the old man took my hand between his palsied ones and said in heavily accented Goreddi, "I care for her like my own granddaughter. One week, fast coach, she is safe in Segosh. My promise."

We followed the coach on horseback and met Nan's party and Abdo at the point on the forest road where Abdo had gone in search of the mossy hut. I saw no sign of our hermit until Abdo sidled up to a pine and pointed. She was sitting on a branch, higher than I would have thought she could climb, watching us all carefully.

Don't worry, she'll come down, said Abdo. *She wanted to look everyone over first.*

She didn't look to me like she had any intention of descending, the way she clutched at the trunk with one arm, her other hand pressed to her mouth. Abdo, at the base of the tree, looked up at her and smiled, holding out a hand. Her face relaxed as she gazed at him, and she began to nod quaveringly. She took a deep breath, as if bracing herself, and climbed down the tree trunk like a squirrel.

Blanche carried a filthy leather satchel on a strap slung over her bony shoulder. *You should see the machines she's leaving behind, madamina,* said Abdo, his eyes following her admiringly. *She's brought only one of her spiders, bundled up in her bag.*

Only one spider. Dame Okra was going to be so pleased.

Blanche balked at the sight of the carriage, but Abdo took her hand in his and led her around the coach. They examined the wheels and springs. She whimpered at the horses, but Abdo patiently showed her how they were hitched up and couldn't get to her. He patted one horse's velvet nose. Blanche came no closer, but her suspicious squint eased a little.

She has to hold the carriage with her mind, Abdo explained to me. *She touches things with her soul-light and makes them a part of herself. I wish you could see how the whole thing glows. I bet she could move it without the horses.*

Old Folla popped his head out of the carriage, and Blanche gasped in surprise and clutched at Abdo. The lad smiled exaggeratedly, as if showing her a better way to react to Folla. She nodded, violet eyes solemn, and then spoke a laugh: "Ha. Ha."

Blanche stepped toward me, not meeting my eyes, and gave courtesy like a noblewoman. "Thank you," she said in carefully enunciated Goreddi.

Why is she thanking me? I asked Abdo in confusion.

She's been alone out here for thirty years, said Abdo, patting

Blanche's hand. *Since she was a child and her scales came in and her mother's husband—Lord Meshi himself—threw her out of the house.*

Blanche took one last, regretful look back toward the ridge, then leaned down and kissed Abdo's forehead. Abdo, never taking his eyes off her, handed her into the carriage.

I wish I could go with her, said Abdo fretfully as the carriage rolled away.

I need you here, I said.

Blanche's ghostly face appeared in the carriage's back window. Abdo waved. *She speaks five languages; she hid them down deep because she had no one to talk to. She was loved once, and educated, and then thrown away like garbage.*

I watched the carriage disappear around a bend in the road and felt a pang. There but for the grace of Allsaints went any of us, even here in Ninys. It was wonderful that we could help her; this was exactly what I had hoped to accomplish.

Abdo wriggled his hand into mine and smiled encouragingly up at me. *Come along, madamina. We still have a painter to find.*

I contacted Dame Okra over the thnik that night, for the first time, to let her know Blanche was coming. "Congratulations on finding another one," drawled Dame Okra. "I didn't think you could. Nedouard and I have a bet on. He wins only if you find both."

"You're getting along with him better now, I hope," I said.

She snorted. "I recovered my spoons, at least. Since he's under my roof now, I can steal everything back while he's out. He doesn't sell my silver, just magpies it away in the crannies of his room."

I rubbed my forehead in perplexity but inquired no further. She'd found a way to make peace with him; that would have to be good enough.

My companions and I plunged onward through the Pinabra and four days later reached Vaillou, a woodcutters' village on sandy bottomland. St. Jobertus's shrine, erected over a sacred spring, was the largest building. Across the chapel's pinewood ceiling, in purples and greens, a mural showed Jobertus healing the sick and aiding the poor. His compassionate eyes reminded me startlingly of Nedouard's.

She'd finished her work here and moved on.

A priest crept up silently and spoke to Josquin. I caught Count Pesavolta's name. The priest rummaged in his violet cassock and handed a scrap of palimpsest to Josquin.

"I wondered when the message I sent ahead would pay off," Josquin said, crossing the chapel toward me, "but I never anticipated this. Listen: 'I hear there's a reward for information leading to my whereabouts. I'm at Montesanti Monastery. Bring the money, or don't come at all.'" Josquin tapped the parchment against his hand. "That's a bit unfriendly."

"Do you know the monastery she mentions?" I asked.

"Indeed," he said, pursing his lips. "It's famous, although I've never been up there. The rock is a daunting climb, and they don't lower the ladder for just anyone."

I was thrilled to have such a definite lead, and feeling quite confident after Nedouard and Blanche, despite the tone of Od Fredricka's note. Three days passed quickly, over hilly, piney ground, until we arrived at the base of a weathered cliff.

"This is it," said Josquin, shading his eyes to look up. "The monastery was carved into the living rock. There's the entrance porch."

I made out what looked like a colonnaded cave entrance, halfway up the bluff.

Ye gods, said Abdo, standing on his horse. *I see her. She shines ferociously.*

Two ropes dangled from the entrance. Moy tugged on one, and a bell tinkled a long way off. From the other rope hung a slate and chalk; Josquin wrote in Ninysh, *We're here for Od Fredricka.* Two pale monks, summoned by the bell, peered down at us; they reeled up the slate, bumping it against limestone outcroppings, vines, and gnarled roots.

After several minutes, they sent the slate back down. *One may ascend. No more.*

"I should go," I said. Josquin frowned at this; Captain Moy muttered and shifted uneasily. "They're just monks," I said, folding my arms. "They're not going to hurt me."

"It's St. Abaster's Order, a Samsamese import," said Moy. "Stricter than our homegrown brothers. They won't welcome a woman, or a . . ." He gestured at my wrist. My scales were hidden under my long-sleeved doublet, but I rubbed my arm self-consciously.

He was right, of course. I could have quoted the relevant lines of scripture, and it was St. Abaster's dragon-killing trap we were trying to re-create. I had no illusions about this order's friendliness toward my kind.

"Just keep quiet and take care," said Josquin. "The Samsamese aren't as tolerant as we Ninysh."

As you Ninysh believe yourselves to be, said Abdo, echoing my thoughts.

Above us, something hurtled over the ledge. We stepped back reflexively, but it was a rope ladder, unrolling as it fell. The lowest rungs didn't touch the ground. Josquin handed me Count Pesavolta's scrip, the promised reward; I tucked it into my doublet and started to climb. The ladder swung, grinding against the limestone, making the rungs hard to grasp. My knuckles were thoroughly chafed by the time I reached the top. Two brown-robed monks grabbed my elbows and hauled me up.

The porch resembled a shallow, flat-bottomed cave with four decorative columns placed at intervals across its wide mouth. The monks had shaved their heads in a peculiar tonsure, bald but for a square patch at the crown. They wiped their gloved hands uneasily on their cassocks, as if I had contaminated them. I wordlessly followed them toward the back of the cave, through an oaken door reinforced with iron bands, and up a torch-lit corridor into the rocky heart of the cliff. The arched doors along the corridor were closed; it was eerily quiet. Perhaps St. Abaster's was a silent order.

At the end of the corridor, a stone staircase spiraled up into darkness. One monk took a torch from its wall sconce, handed it over, and pointed. These two clearly did not intend to accompany me any further. I hesitated, then mounted the steep stairs.

I climbed five or six stories at least, and was dizzy and lightly winded when I reached a heavy door at the end. A light push didn't budge it. I leaned into it with all my weight, and it groaned open into an airy and painfully bright chamber. I blinked and squinted until I discerned tall, glazed windows, a tile floor, wrought-iron candelabra, scaffolding. This was a freestanding octagonal chapel at the top of the bluffs.

I set my torch in a sconce beside the door and looked around for Od Fredricka. Upon the scaffolding perched a woman sketching on the bare plaster, a chunk of charcoal in her hand. She had already drawn an oval as tall as she was, a bulbous nose with flaring nostrils, a curving mouth, and long-lobed ears. I watched her add a pair of cruel eyes.

Oh, those eyes. I could tell I would be seeing them in uncomfortable dreams. They seemed to bore into me and find me wanting.

The artist took a step back and scrutinized her work, wiping her hands on her smock, leaving distinct charcoal handprints on her backside. A light shawl covered her head, hiding her most distinctive half-dragon feature, but I knew she must be Od Fredricka. Even in this bare-bones sketch, I could see the shadow of the realism and power to come, an echo of her other paintings.

Without turning around, she began speaking in a clear, light voice, apparently to me. She would have heard the door complain as I opened it. Alas for my dreadful Ninysh. I could tell she was saying something about St. Abaster, but nothing more.

"*Pallez-dit Goreliano?*" I called, asking if she spoke my language and undoubtedly butchering the pronunciation.

She glanced over her shoulder, a sneer on her freckled face. *"Nen. Samsamya?"*

My Samsamese was passable. "What were you saying?" I asked.

She began climbing down the scaffolding, stiffly, like an arthritic old woman. "That I always read the scriptures before I draw a Saint."

"Oh," I said. "That sounds sensible."

"History has become smudged over six hundred years. Only the Saints' own words have come down to us," she said, still climbing. "Edicts, precepts, philosophies. Lies. None of them wrote as much as St. Abaster, and what a *monstruoigo* he was."

That lone word of Ninysh was easy to guess.

"Look at him," she said, pausing to gaze back up at her drawing. "He hates you."

His eyes certainly seemed to. I shuddered.

"He hates us all," she continued, resuming her labored descent. "He pulled dragons out of the sky with his mind and killed five of his fellow Saints. Samsam hopes he will return someday. Should this worry us?"

She reached the ground at last and pulled off her head covering. I knew what I would see, but it was still a shock: her scalp was shingled with silver scales, like some horrifying case of cradle cap. Her violently red hair tufted through the gaps wherever it could, standing straight up like a hedge.

She was tall and stout, her smock flecked in blues and greens and just enough red to make you wonder. Her round baby face contradicted her matronly bosom, making it hard to guess her age, but I believed she was about thirty. She sauntered toward me, casually drawing a knife from her pocket and cleaning her grimy nails with it.

"So," said Od Fredricka, "why would Count Pesavolta send a Goreddi? What is his devilish scheme?" I opened my mouth to reassure her, but she cut me off. "It doesn't matter. I have fulfilled his condition. Now give me my money."

I handed over the promissory note Josquin had given me. She gave it a cursory glance, crumpled it, and tossed it onto the floor. "I would have to go into a large town to exchange that."

I stooped to retrieve the note. She kicked it out of reach.

"Why is Count Pesavolta looking for me?" she said, stepping around me in a circle, still holding the knife. "Not for a neighborly glass of pine brandy. He wants something. If I spend his note, his men will seize me."

"There's been a misunderstanding," I began, trying to emulate Josquin's tone, soothing and authoritative at once.

"I doubt that," she said. "The very wording of that message was suspicious: 'information leading to the whereabouts.' As if I were a criminal. You're not removing me from this place without violence."

"Count Pesavolta doesn't want you," I said. "Goredd does."

"Goredd?" she cried, her mouth buckling into a deeper scowl. "Liar. Pesavolta offered the reward."

"Look," I said, turning back my sleeve to show my scales. "I'm your sister."

She goggled at me, speechless.

"My name is Seraphina Dombegh. I'm Goreddi; I don't even

speak Ninysh. Goredd is gathering half-dragons to help her when the dragon war spills south. You mentioned St. Abaster's Trap. We can create something similar with our minds, an unseen barrier in the air."

Her face had gone weird and blue, as if she were holding her breath.

I continued hastily, "That's why I'm gathering our kind together, officially. But I also know that we have each felt alone, even rejected. I hope we might be family to each other, supporting—"

"You only get more ridiculous," Od Fredricka said with sharp finality, like a cleaver coming down on bone. "I should come to Goredd to be your *family*—devils take us all—because we both have scales? Shall we be the best of friends?" She clasped her hands to her breast. "All our problems magically solved, if only we were together!"

I stared, appalled, not knowing what to say. She glared back with cruel eyes, and it suddenly struck me that the eyes she'd sketched upon the wall were her own.

"You're an idiot and an ass," she said, leaning in. Her breath was rank. "Leave now, and never let me see you again."

"Think it over," I said, fighting to keep from trembling. "If you change your mind, go to the home of Dame Okra Carmine in Segosh. She's one of us—"

"One of us!" Od Fredricka repeated in a singsong voice. Then she opened her mouth frightfully wide and screamed in my face, a wordless, piercing shrill. I staggered back. She raised her knife and screamed again. I snatched the crumpled scrip off the floor and bolted down the spiral stairs without the torch, scrabbling in darkness until I reached the bottom.

The abbot was waiting for me, scowling. He must have heard the scream.

"I'm sorry"—I was breathing hard—"Father." I hastily smoothed the promissory note against my doublet. "Here. For your trouble. Forgive me."

He took the money but did not apparently forgive me. He pushed me toward the egress, poking me between the shoulder blades to urge me along, until I was out on the windy cliff porch again. He slammed the door behind me—or rather, closed it quietly so as not to further disrupt his order, but I knew that stern click for a slam. The single monk out on the porch seemed to have just finished winding up the rope ladder and was not entirely pleased to see me.

He cast the ladder back down, but I was so shaky I feared to climb it. I would lose my footing. The cliff would crumble at my touch.

Everything felt like it was crumbling. I leaned against one of the pillars and tried to catch my breath.

How dare she? I had come so far, at considerable trouble to myself, to do her this immeasurable favor, and she threw it back in my face. Monstrous ingratitude! She cared nothing for my heartache, my loneliness, my selfless efforts to bring us together. For a single, weightless moment, I hated her.

I couldn't sustain it, though, not when I was so much better at hating myself.

At the back of my mind, questions niggled. What had I

expected? I'd set myself up as the rescuer of someone who didn't want rescuing—or need it, to be brutally honest. Who was I to butt into this woman's life and tell her I knew better than she did what she had suffered and how she should fix it?

Might I have approached her differently? She was an artist; I was a musician. Surely there were things we might have discussed, ways we could have been friends?

I had framed my quest, this gathering of ityasaari, as an act of compassion, but it wasn't, really. Not if I set myself apart, as some hero to save them. It was impossible to see someone else's pain from that distance. Maybe I hadn't wanted to see it. Maybe I'd wanted them to see mine, or to reflect and affirm it like a mirror.

I wasn't here to help Od Fredricka so much as to heal myself. Dame Okra had implied that I wanted such a thing, and I'd ignored her.

I dreaded telling Glisselda and Kiggs how I'd spoiled my chance with Od Fredricka, although I felt certain they'd be nice about it. The mind barrier would still work, surely; there would be enough ityasaari. We had Nedouard and Blanche, and there were more to find.

I wasn't certain about any of them now, though. This had shaken my confidence.

I rubbed my watering eyes with a finger and thumb and took a breath to gather myself. I raised my eyes for a moment, taking in the spreading gorge below and the eastern mountains rising behind it.

One mountain, its peak snowy and crooked, loomed over the others. I knew that mountain; there was a miniature version of it in my garden of grotesques. I hadn't known where we might find it. I stared with a mixture of joy and dread.

Goredd still needed the ityasaari, whatever doubts I'd begun to have about myself. I climbed down the rope ladder as fast as I could manage.

Below, everyone had settled in for a light supper. Josquin sprang up to hold the bottom of the ladder steady; I took his hand and leaped down onto the carpet of pine needles. "She's not coming," I said loudly, preempting the inevitable questions.

"Sit. Eat," said Josquin gently, directing me toward Abdo. "You look shattered."

Nan handed me bread and cheese, her brows drawn in concern.

"That crooked mountain to the east," I said, nodding thanks. "How long would it take to get there?"

"Three days' ride," said Moy, sitting up straighter. "It's called Pashiagol, the Mad Goat's Horn. I grew up in its shadow."

"There isn't time for a detour," said Josquin, darting his gaze between us. "Dame Okra said six weeks; you have a tight schedule in Samsam."

"I know, but there's an ityasaari on that mountain," I said. "I hadn't realized he was Ninysh."

"If we ride hard, we might make it in two," Moy piped up. "Then you're only four days behind schedule. You can make that up in Samsam, I should think."

Josquin threw up his hands. "As long as you don't leave me to bear my cousin's wrath alone," he said, "I am at everyone's service. Let us detour through Donques."

I started in on my bread, surprised at how hungry I was. Abdo sidled closer and leaned his cheek against my shoulder. I met his canny gaze.

You're disappointed, he said.

Chastened, more like, I said, picking a pine needle off my cheese. *I see where I was lying to myself.*

He nodded gravely and shifted his eyes toward the monastery. *She's going to be all right. Her soul-light is strong and prickly as a hedgehog, like Dame Okra's. Perhaps this couldn't be helped. Anyway, one Dame Okra at a time is enough, don't you think?*

He was trying to make me laugh, but in truth, I would gladly have gathered a thousand Dame Okras, had they but consented to come.

↶Seven↷

After two days' hard riding over increasingly steep terrain, we finally reached the village of Donques, on the flank of the crooked mountain. My garden's wild man, Tiny Tom, lived in a cave somewhere nearby. He was eight feet tall with clawed talons for toes; surely he didn't come near the village. We would stay at the local palasho and spend a couple days combing the surrounding mountainside.

When I'd reported my failure with Od Fredricka, I'd mentioned the proximity of Tiny Tom. "You should go after him," Glisselda had said, "but don't forget that you're due in Fnark, in Samsam, by St. Abaster's Day. Can you still make it if you detour through Donques?"

"Josquin says so," I replied, but I was a little disconcerted. There was St. Abaster again, as if he were following me.

Of course, there was no guarantee of finding the Samsamese

ityasaari even if I made it to Fnark in time. If an extra day in Donques ensured that I could bring an ityasaari home, I would insist that we stay. Tiny Tom seemed like a bird in the hand.

As we rounded the last turn of the switchback trail, we saw the villagers of Donques out en masse. The men wore fine embroidered smocks and hats; the women had braided ribbons into their fair hair and given the children a quick spit polish. The whole village was resplendent; the gold, orange, and crimson flag of Ninys flapped from every peaked rooftop, and the window boxes overflowed with pink and yellow blooms.

The crowd was following an ox-drawn wagon far ahead of us, festooned with bright ribbons and garlands of flowers, carrying a statue draped in gauzy fabrics. Beside me, Moy grinned. "It's Santi Agniesti. She's our patroness here. Makes good cheese."

The citizenry were following the statue up the road at a funereal pace. At the sound of our horses, the crowd parted to let us pass. *Are we part of the procession?* asked Abdo. Without waiting for my answer, he stood upon his saddle, holding the reins one-handed with confident subtlety. He smiled down at the gaping villagers, waving his skinny arm and blowing kisses. He did a standing backflip on the saddle; the crowd gasped and then applauded lightly.

"Is this all right?" I asked Moy, but I could tell by his grin he was loving it.

"My cousins are all here somewhere; they'll enjoy this show. But be careful, *moush!*" he called, using Nan's nickname for Abdo. "Don't fall on your head."

Abdo batted his eyes like innocence incarnate, then gripped the front of his saddle and lifted his legs into a handstand.

"Santi Merdi!" boomed Moy, laughing. "I should tie you to your horse."

Abdo made it a one-handed handstand.

The village's market square was packed with people. Santi Agniesti's cart veered off toward her rosy chapel, painted with murals of birds, cows, and alpine flowers, but the crowds lingered among food stalls, merchants' booths, and puppet shows. "The palasho is up the road to our left," Josquin called, but our party had come to a grinding halt. Moy exclaimed joyously, dismounted, and was mobbed by people clasping his hands and slapping his back. Moy tossed small children into the air and kissed their foreheads.

Nan rode up to where Josquin and I were waiting. "Cousin, cousin, cousin *segonde*," she said, pointing at villagers as if counting off. "How you say . . . *oncle*."

"You're not leaping off your horse to greet them?" I asked.

"I am raised in Segosh." Nan haughtily lifted her chin. "Not to be milkmaid."

Josquin drummed his fingers on his saddle horn, squinted at the sky, and sighed. "The sun sets soon. We weren't going to find your ityasaari in the dark, in any case."

I opened my mouth to reassure him, but Abdo interrupted: *Phina madamina, Tiny Tom is close.* Abdo was staring eastward, craning his neck as if that would help him see through buildings. *His mind is a strange color. All swirly.*

Noted. I wondered whether to leave Moy here and pursue Tom with a smaller group. This ityasaari was strong and scary, but he'd never struck me as dangerous.

Moy strode toward us through the crowd, shouting in Ninysh. From his tone and her frown, I guessed he was teasing Nan for snubbing her cousins. "Would you play your flute, Seraphina?" he cried, switching languages. "A show for my cousins. Abdo and I could dance the saltamunti."

I hesitated, but Abdo was already leaping off his horse enthusiastically. *Yes, let's! It would be perfect. Tiny Tom will hear your flute and come to us.*

You do realize he's not tiny, I said, wondering what my garden denizens looked like to Abdo, if the garden didn't look like a garden. *People might be alarmed.*

The Eight can protect everyone, he insisted, taking Moy's hand and leading him to the center of the square.

I dismounted and rummaged for my flute in my saddle pack. Josquin, realizing Moy was serious, climbed off his horse, tugged at the hem of his doublet, and addressed the crowd, introducing us in grandiloquent tones. The villagers cleared the center of the square, chatting excitedly among themselves, pink faces eager.

Moy tossed his helmet to Nan and posed opposite Abdo, arms raised. They were amusingly mismatched: short and tall, skinny and burly, dark and blond. I lingered over my warm-ups. Abdo tapped a foot, melodramatically impatient with me. I took a deep breath, silently wished us luck, and lit into a furious saltamunti.

It was a dance for soldiers and muscular farmhands, full of athletic feats and manly posturing. Moy grinned ferociously, boots and breastplate gleaming, gifted with enthusiasm if not elegance.

Abdo, on the other hand, executed moves gracefully but didn't have the presence to carry off the posing. Together they made a surprisingly good team. Moy leaped and stamped while Abdo did barrel turns around him. The crowd shouted and whistled approvingly.

Tiny Tom likes this music, said Abdo. *He's coming.*

I looked around; Tiny Tom's great woolly head would be visible above the crowd if he got close.

Moy knelt, and Abdo leapfrogged over him; Moy made a stirrup of his hands, lifted Abdo into the air, and flipped him. The crowd roared. Moy lifted Abdo onto his shoulders, and then Abdo did a handstand atop Moy's upraised palms. The Eight clanged their swords against their shields in cacophonous applause.

Above the din, I heard a terrible, marrow-freezing scream.

I cut off mid-note, looking around wildly. Everyone stared at me, and I realized with a start that only I had heard the sound: Abdo had screamed inside my mind.

He was still in a handstand, held up by Moy, but a knife handle protruded from Abdo's left forearm. He crumpled. Moy caught him, thank Heaven, before he hit the ground. "Des Osho!" Moy barked, and the Eight were at his side at once, looking frantically searching for Abdo's attacker. Moy cradled Abdo, who curled up in agony, his blue tunic soaked with blood.

Josquin shouted, "There!" and pointed at a figure on a balcony of an inn across the square, scrambling to the roof. The man wore the habit and tonsure of St. Abaster's Order. His cassock hindered his climbing, but if he made it across the roof, we would quickly lose him.

As the monk rushed up the pitched slate roof, a pale shaggy head with leaves matted into its beard rose above the ridgeline in front of him like a full moon. The head was followed by a great hairy body, eight feet tall, inadequately clothed in scraps of blankets stitched together. The wild man had dragon talons for toes and patchy silver scales up to his ankles; his claws screeched against the slates as he walked down the steep roof toward the monk, who stood frozen, a second knife falling from his stunned fingers.

Tiny Tom picked the man up like a rag doll, snapped his neck, and tossed him off the roof into the crowd.

For a moment, the world seemed frozen. Then someone screamed, "Gianni Patto!" and the square erupted in pandemonium, some fleeing, some trying to recover the monk's body, some hurling stones at the monster on the roof.

Moy rushed back toward Josquin and Nan, clutching Abdo to his chest. Abdo stared at nothing, too shocked even to weep. Nan ripped the Ninysh flag off the front of a tavern while Josquin took Abdo from her father; together they extracted the knife and bound Abdo's arm in the colorful fabric. Moy turned back to join the Eight, who were shooting arrows at the monster on the roof. I caught up to the captain, grabbed his arm, and cried over the din, "Tell them to stop shooting! He's the one we're looking for!"

"You said he was tiny!" Moy shouted back. He shouldered his way through the panicking crowd toward his troops.

Across the square, Gianni Patto jumped from the roof onto the inn's balcony. He grinned as the Eight's arrows bounced futilely off his leathery skin. His terrible mouth was full of broken and decaying teeth. He leaped into the crowd below, villagers scattering around him like ripples in a pond. The Eight, now directed by Moy, encircled the wild man, swords drawn. Gianni Patto made no threatening move, but held out his hands, crossed at the wrists, as if asking to be bound. It took a couple of tries, but Moy did just that. Gianni offered no resistance.

Gianni Patto stared at me across the square. I stared back. He did not look like he had in my visions. That is, he was physically the same, but there was an intelligence in his eyes, something I knew but could not name, a cat-like deviousness.

The wild man roared inarticulately, then roared again, saying words this time and turning my insides to ice: "Sera! Feee-nah!"

How could he know my name? I asked Abdo, but he did not respond. I glanced over in alarm; Nan was on horseback, holding the wilting boy before her on the saddle.

Josquin plucked at my sleeve; he'd been speaking, but I hadn't been listening. ". . . Abdo to the palasho," he repeated, his voice a balm to my frantic heart. "The baronet will have the best physician. We need to hurry."

I nodded numbly and mounted my horse. Our guard rode ahead, two soldiers carrying the bundled body of the monk between them, two pulling Gianni by his bound wrists, and two flanking him with their swords drawn. Nan carried Abdo, and Captain Moy took up the rear with me. Gianni Patto docilely allowed himself to be led, his taloned toes scrabbling at the cobbles of the square, but he never took his eyes off me. I lagged as far behind as I dared; he twisted halfway around just to stare at me.

"I wish you had told me it was Gianni Patto you were after," said Moy, sighing heavily. "We could have done this differently."

"I didn't know he was famous," I said.

Moy tugged on his beard. "I wasn't sure he really existed, but he's the bogeyman at this altitude. My mother used to say, 'Behave, or we'll tie you in a tree for Gianni Patto.' They'll tell tales of him killing that monk for generations, you may be sure."

"The monk tried to kill Abdo first," I said, my throat tightening.

A monk of St. Abaster's Order. Had he followed us from the monastery? Did he know what we were?

The track to the palasho was steep and rugged, winding around boulders and stunted trees. Josquin galloped ahead, spurring his horse hard up the track. By the time we arrived, he had talked the portcullis open and was directing people this way and that. Two burly smiths helped wrangle Gianni toward a round tower as servants bore the monk's body to the chapel. Nan carried Abdo to the barracks infirmary. Grooms took our horses.

I stared at nothing, unfocused. Josquin touched my arm and said, "I've arranged a privy meeting with Lord Donques, since I expect you aren't up to the usual—" I met his eye and he stopped short. "No. Of course, Abdo first. Let's make sure he's all right."

We hurried across the courtyard and into the barracks. Nan blocked the infirmary doorway, her helmet under her arm, strands of blond hair stuck to her cheeks with sweat. "You don' want to see zis," she said.

"Seraphina can decide for herself," said Josquin. He clapped a hand on my shoulder and said in a lowered voice, "Find me in the keep when you're done here. I'll speak to Lord Donques myself. He's going to want to try your wild man for murder, I don't doubt. Do you still want the creature brought back with us to Segosh?"

"I do," I said. "That monk was here with murder on his mind. He had a second knife. Gianni Patto killed him to save Abdo's life—or maybe mine."

"Agreed. I will make that argument." Josquin bowed gravely and departed.

Nan moved to let me pass. Abdo lay upon a simple straw pallet on the floor; a middle-aged woman in a kerchief had unwrapped his arm and was washing it in a basin. The wash water had turned pink with blood. "How bad is it, Doctor?" I asked in Goreddi.

The woman turned serious eyes upon me and said something in Ninysh. Nan translated: "She not a doctor. Ze garrison is hunting bear. Ze doctor goes to zem. She is palasho's ... eh ..." Nan snapped her fingers, but the Goreddi word didn't come.

"Midwife," boomed a voice behind Nan. Moy squeezed past her in the doorway.

I met Abdo's eyes. He reached for me wordlessly, and I sat on the floor beside him. The midwife glanced over but didn't shoo me away. She carefully palpated Abdo's wrist; he gritted his teeth and cringed. I held his good hand, and he squeezed painfully. The midwife spoke and Nan translated again: "Move fingers, sweet apple. One by a time, starting from ..." She wriggled her thumb illustratively.

Abdo curled his left thumb. He curled it again.

"Now ze rest," said Nan, but Abdo burst into tears. The midwife's eyes welled up in sympathy.

"Tendons are cut." It was Moy translating this time. "She can't fix them. She's gonna stitch you up and give you good poultices to prevent infection."

Nan muttered something in an uncharitable tone.

"The baronet's doctor could do no better," said her father grimly. "Maybe Count Pesavolta has a surgeon who can repair tendons, maybe not. It's delicate work."

"He need zat hand," growled Nan.

The midwife mixed a draft of herbs and wine for Abdo; I helped him sit up to drink it. As it took effect, some of his shock dissipated and he began to speak groggily to me. *That monk tried to kill me. It's chance that he missed. I'm alive by chance.*

I held his good hand. *That's your god, isn't it? Chance?*

But what chance sent him after me? Abdo said, his voice slower and looser.

I don't know, I said. I could hardly grasp it myself. Could Od Fredricka have sent him after us? The abbot? If it was the abbot, was Od Fredricka in danger, too? Had she given up our secret to save herself? Alas, the monk was dead and we couldn't ask.

Thank the gods for Gianni Patto, said Abdo blearily, and then he was out.

I continued to hold his hand while the midwife stitched him up, slathered his arm with ointments, and bandaged the wound. I would have stayed by him all night if Nan had not hauled me to my feet and made me go to supper.

I wanted this day to be over so badly, but sleep fled, leaving me nothing but self-recrimination. I should have let Abdo go back to Segosh with Blanche. I should have skipped the monastery altogether and left Od Fredricka alone. I should never have come after Gianni Patto, who had even less language than Blanche and liked to wrestle bears. I hadn't believed him dangerous; that seemed so foolish now. He'd snapped the monk's neck with his bare hands. I revisited that moment as I tossed and turned, the monk flopping grotesquely off the rooftop over and over in my mind's eye.

I recalled Gianni speaking my name, and shuddered. That cat-like expression . . .

I sat bolt upright, horrified. It was well past midnight, but I leaped out of bed, put my breeches and boots back on, and crept out of my room.

Outside Josquin's door, I hesitated, wanting to wake him and fearing what he would witness if I did, and what he would think of me after. He'd become a friend, I realized.

I could not bear to lose his regard. I let him lie.

I found my way out of the keep and crossed the moonlit courtyard to the round tower. The outer door was guarded. My Ninysh was too poor to bluff my way in, but the guardsman must have had some idea of who I was. He gestured me to wait while he went indoors; to my surprise, he came back out with Moy. "We're guarding the wild man in shifts," said the captain, smiling. "You want a turn? We were rude not to offer."

"I want to talk to him—alone," I said. "He's not still being violent, is he?"

Moy shrugged. "He's been quiet as a lamb behind that solid oak door. You can talk through the grating, though I'm not sure he talks."

Gianni Patto shouldn't have had any language. When he'd said my name, that should have clued me in right away. I'd been too upset about Abdo to notice.

Moy held the tower door open and closed it behind me. I was in a short, high-ceilinged corridor, lit by a single torch in a sconce. There was a knife and whittled stick upon a stool; Moy apparently passed his time carving. The only occupied cell was on the left at the end. The fetid stench of unwashed wild man made the air heavy.

"Gianni?" I said, looking through the door's grating. A barred window across the cell let in a trickle of moonlight, but not enough for me to see the prisoner. I called his name again, and suddenly his eye was at the grating, pale and rheumy and wild.

He startled me into taking a step back; I forced myself not to look away. "You spoke my name," I said quietly. "Someone must have taught it to you. Who was it?"

His eye reeled, unfocused. He'd understood nothing; if he'd known any language at all—and I still believed he shouldn't—it could only have been Ninysh. He'd clearly been living alone on the mountainside for decades, probably from a younger age than Blanche. I could picture his villager mother, once she understood what sort of creature she had borne, tearfully leading him into a winter storm to be respectably lost for good.

I couldn't communicate with him; it had been foolish to try. I turned to go, but heard scrabbling behind me. I looked back and saw his fingers, the nails cracked and yellow, poking through the grating.

"Fee," he said, his voice ragged with phlegm. He spat. "Fee. Na."

I had wanted and dreaded his words. I cleared my throat. "That's right."

"Thisss voooice," said Gianni slowly, exaggerating consonants, dragging out the vowels. He was speaking Goreddi. My blood froze in my veins. "Decadesss of disssuse," he croaked. "Hard to mek the tongue dooo what I . . . ge-huhrrgh!" There was a splat upon the floor as he spat again. "What a terrible-tasting mouth I have!"

My heart pounded painfully. The voice dispelled any remaining doubts. I knew its inflections, even channeled through Gianni's disused voice box and recalcitrant mouth. How she'd accomplished this, I couldn't imagine. I said, "What do you want, Jannoula?"

Gianni's eye reappeared on the other side of the grate, now focused and shrewd. "Seraphina," he said—or *she* said, using his moist, breathy voice. "You're all grown up."

"What do you want?" I repeated.

Gianni's tongue clicked, scolding. "No 'Hello.' No 'How have you been, Jannoula? I hope you're not still languishing in prison.' I suppose that horrid uncle of yours continues to poison you against me."

The mention of Orma hurt, but I kept my face implacable. "The uncle who saved me, you mean? As I recall, it was *you* who poisoned things."

Gianni's pale brow came down; his crusty eye narrowed. "It has come to my attention that you are gathering our kind together."

"How could you possibly have learned that?" I said.

Laughter gurgled from the cell. "A mutual friend told me. I could help you, you know. My mind reaches out to our kind, just like yours does."

Or like it used to, said Jannoula/Gianni in my head, the way Abdo might have.

I had been backing away without realizing it; now I hit the dank stone wall opposite the cell door.

She could not have broken free of her cottage; she could not be loose in my mind!

I squeezed my eyes shut, searching wildly in my own head for the entrance to the garden of grotesques. This was not the way to find my garden; I needed to relax. I could still hear the voice echoing somewhere in my head, Gianni's gruff fundamental with overtones of Jannoula: *Is this where you keep the others now? This narrow trough? It used to be a garden, open to your wider mind.*

In an angry rush, I was there: Tiny Tom in front of me, the garden indeed looking strangely shrunken, but there was no time to consider that. Jannoula's mind filled Gianni's shape like a hand inside a puppet, but she had not broken through him to enter my mind herself. She was trying, pushing and clawing inside him; I could see her glowing at his core. Tiny Tom glowed, too, with a light of his own, a different color. I had never noticed until his fire was pitted against an alien light from within.

"Tiny Tom" was a piece of Gianni Patto's mind-fire. Abdo had told me that, but I'd never been able to see it until this moment, under duress.

Jannoula stretched and strained, distorting Tiny Tom's appearance, and I feared she would burst through. I saw how to release Gianni's mind-fire: it would be like undoing a button. I hesitated—would the uncontrollable visions return if I severed this connection?—but Jannoula writhed inside him again, and I panicked. With a thought, I unfastened Gianni Patto from my mind. The buttonhole sealed up at once behind him, as if it had never been.

I felt the release not as relief but as bereavement. A stab of grief. My eyes popped open in the real world and I stared into Gianni's eye through the grating in his cell door.

"What an appalling overreaction," said Giann-oula. "A great brute of a baby tossed out in half a bowl of bathwater. What could I possibly have done, locked in that cluttered broom closet with the others?"

I did not answer; my jaw was trembling. How had she found him? How had she entered his mind, what did she want from me, and why was I still not free of her after all these years?

I fled the room. She called after me. My only consolation was that her voice could not come with me in my head.

↬Eight↬

When I was eleven years old, before the creation of my garden, I had a vision while walking through the fish market with my stepmother, Anne-Marie. I collapsed face-first into a table, knocking over baskets, sending cascades of river eels writhing onto the flagstones. I came to drenched and stinking, red-armed fishwives cursing at my stepmother and me. Anne-Marie had said nothing, but paid for the fish and cooked them all week. I still dread eel pie.

The vision I'd had was of a woman curled upon the rough stone floor of a cell. Iron bars crisscrossed a tiny window; the bed was boards and straw. She was a prisoner, or maybe an anchorite— a holy sister in solitary confinement—but her clothing resembled no habit I had ever seen: a fitted one-piece suit, with a trapdoor between the legs, stitched together from a motley assortment of animal skins, fur side out. Except for her shaved head and bare feet, she resembled a large, mangy otter. I could not guess her age beyond that she was an adult, older than me.

My vision-eye hovered silently by the ceiling. The people in my visions never saw me; only one had ever seemed to hear me speak, and I wasn't certain of that. But this woman startled, stared, and reached up, feeling around for me; she had long, dirty nails. I couldn't quit an involuntary vision, no matter how it frightened me. I had to wait it out.

The vision began to fade. As if she sensed that, too, the woman cried out. I did not understand her words, but I glimpsed a keen intelligence in her eyes.

The fur-suited prisoner was the seventeenth and final peculiar person I had seen in my visions. I nicknamed her Otter.

I would blame my uncle Orma, and his barren, draconic imagination, for failing to guess that the people in my visions were half-dragons, but in truth we were both at fault. So strong was the taboo among both our peoples, and so complete my self-revulsion, that neither of us could countenance the idea that my parents' awful experiment had been replicated multiple times. Besides, none of them looked like me. Some, like Master Smasher, Nag, and Nagini, were quite good-looking; I had no reason to believe they weren't ordinary humans. Tiny Tom and the great slug, Pandowdy, on the other hand, were far more monstrous than I. I didn't recognize myself in any of these beings and had no idea why I was doomed to see them again and again.

Orma had intended to teach me music, but in the months after my scales came in, we spent most of our time trying to keep my visions at bay. I meditated; I visualized; I vomited a lot because the visions wreaked havoc on my equilibrium.

The garden of grotesques was the strategy that finally worked. Under Orma's instruction, I deliberately reached out to each of the seventeen beings I had seen, fixing permanent connections to them with the grotesques as anchors so my mind would stop lunging out at them. I did not quite understand what I was doing, only that it worked. I named the grotesque avatars and placed them in their particular parts of the garden—Fruit Bat in his grove, Pelican Man on the topiary lawn, Master Smasher in the statuary meadow.

I saved the creation of Otter's cottage garden for last. Her plight had sparked such pity in me that I wanted her space to be special, a peaceful, bucolic scene of herbs and flowers around an ornamental thatched cottage, which was not a functional residence; the other grotesques lived outdoors, and it seemed important to be consistent. I gave her a birdbath, a bench, and a little table where she might have tea.

I visualized Otter as I had done with each of the others. Her image materialized before me in the garden. I looked it over to see that I'd gotten the details right, but her strange clothing bothered me. That fur suit could not be of her choosing, surely. I changed it, envisioning her in a sturdy green gown, like a young wife from a good house in town, and with blond hair, like my stepmother's. I hoped real-world Otter would have approved, but of course she would never know. These grotesques in my head were symbols; they were not self-aware. I spoke ritual words, preparing the ground of my mind, and took Otter's hands in mine.

I whirled out into a vision, and again saw the fur-suited woman on the low bed of her cell, hugging her knees. My presence caught her attention; she leaped to her feet. This time, however, the vision was under my control. I pulled back to my mind's garden—taking something with me, but I could not have said what—and affixed this last connection so that unruly visions would ambush me no more.

"All in ard," I said to Otter, and released her hands. Or tried to.

She gripped me tightly. "All in ard," she repeated, her vocal inflections strangely flat but her sharp face alert. "Who are you? What is this place?"

"Saints' bones!" I cried. What was this? How was she able to talk to me?

She released my hands and stared at me with eyes as green as her gown. "How did you bring me here?" she asked. "Why did you?"

"I—I didn't," I stammered stupidly. She was mentally present. None of the others were. "I mean, I didn't try to ... it shouldn't have worked this way—"

"You tried something," she said, her eyes narrowing. She glanced around at the hollyhocks and foxgloves, the bench and table. Her expression softened; she reached out to touch a flower. "It's beautiful here," she said, her voice hushed and awed. She took a few tentative steps up the flagstone path, noticed the un-accustomed hang of clothing on her body, and twirled, watching her skirt flare. "You gave me an elegant gown!" She looked back at me, almost in tears. "What have I done to deserve your kind-ness?"

"You seemed miserable where you were," I said, still trying to understand. Her consciousness had followed me back into my mind somehow. "I wanted to make things a little easier for you."

She looked about ten years my senior, but she didn't act it. She tiptoed up the path like a child, sniffing flowers, fingering the ser-rated edges of leaves, exclaiming at the shadows under plants. "I love it here!" she announced. "I want to stay here forever. But where are we?"

She'd already asked once; I was being a bad host. I said, "I'm Seraphina, and this is my . . . my garden. Um, what's your name?"

"My name?" She spread her hand upon her heart, looking deeply moved that I had asked. "That's so important. Everyone should have a name, and mine is, of course . . ." She bunched her lips, thinking. "Jannoula. Is that a poetic name?"

I couldn't stop myself from smiling. "It's beautiful," I as-sured her.

"We shall be sisters," she declared. "Oh, how I have longed for a place like this!"

She hugged me. I stood stiffly at first, the way Orma might have, but then she said, "You've saved me from despair. Thank you, Seraphina," and I pitied her again. Strange as this was, maybe it wasn't so terrible. I really seemed to have helped her. Cautiously I hugged her back.

I left her twirling her new skirt among the flowers while I circled the greater garden's perimeter, chanting, *This is my garden, complete and contained,* and establishing the final boundary. At last, I returned to myself on the floor of Orma's office. Night had fallen; it had taken six hours to create the whole thing.

"The connections all feel stable and secure?" Orma asked as he walked me home through rain-slick streets. "Nothing's chafing you, or likely to jar you into a vision? You're still going to have to tend them every night to make sure nothing's come loose."

He had given me so much time and support that I didn't like to voice any doubts, but he had to know: "One of them was different. She spoke to me."

He stopped walking. "Tell me all," he demanded, folding his arms and looming so ominously that I feared I'd done something wrong. I reminded myself it was his way to be serious. When I had finished, he shook his head and said, "I never know enough to help you, Seraphina. I don't know how Jannoula talks to you, if the others don't. Be cautious. Watch her. If she frightens or harms you, tell me at once. Promise you will."

"Of course," I said, my alarm rising again. I didn't know what he could do if something went wrong, but his vehemence was a measure of his caring. That meant a lot.

Over the next days and weeks, I paid particular attention to Jannoula's part of the garden, but in fact she wasn't always mentally present when I put my grotesques to bed. Sometimes her avatar sat quietly among the poppies, as vacant as the rest. When she was present, she chased butterflies or sipped tea at her little table. I would stop and ask, "How are you?"

Usually she smiled and nodded and went back to what she was doing, but one day she sighed and said, "My real life is all sorrow. I feel so lucky to have a respite from it. I only wish I understood where we are."

"Inside my mind," I said, sitting down at the tea table with her. "I built a garden here because . . ." I was suddenly unsure what to tell her. I didn't like to say I was half dragon and my mind did peculiar things; I was too ashamed, I did not know how she would react, and surely Orma would consider it incautious. "I was lonely," I said at last. It was true. Papa had kept me on such a short lead that I'd never had friends. My uncle didn't count.

Jannoula nodded eagerly. "Me too. I'm a prisoner. I see no one but my captors."

"Why are you imprisoned?" I asked.

She just smiled sadly and poured me some tea.

Once, when she wasn't present, I took her avatar's hands and induced a vision. I was trying to be a friend; I wanted to understand what her life was really like, because I worried about her. Jannoula was in her dingy cell, as ever. Her shaved head and mangy fur suit were jarring enough, but then I saw something even worse. The sleeves of her suit had been pulled up, exposing her forearms. The skin was blistered, cracked, blackened, and burned from wrist to elbow. It looked freshly done to me, and her face . . . she seemed stunned. She wasn't even weeping.

She looked up at my vision-eye, and then her face filled with rage.

I pulled out of the vision in alarm. Jannoula followed me back to my garden, and for a moment I thought she might hit me. She raised her arms and then dropped them futilely, pacing back and forth before me. "Don't look at me without asking!" she cried.

She looked like her usual self in my garden, green gown and fair hair, but I couldn't get the image of her burned arms out of my mind. "Who's done this to you?" I asked. "And why?"

She looked away. "Please don't ask. I am ashamed that you saw me like that. You are my only shelter, Seraphina. My only escape. Don't poison it with your pity."

But I did pity her. I looked for ways to make her life more bearable, for things to interest and distract her. I observed Lavondaville closely as I walked to and from my music lesson, the limit of my circumscribed existence. At night I described things I'd seen, to her great delight. I left gifts in her garden—a puzzle, a tortoise, roses—and she exclaimed happily over every one. It took so little to please her.

One evening, as we sat sipping tea and watching a glorious sunset I'd dreamed up, she said, "Please don't be angry, but I heard you thinking today."

I froze, tea halfway to my lips. I'd grown so used to her that I'd forgotten she wasn't separate from me as other people were. Her consciousness was inside my head. How entangled with mine could it become? How entangled was it already?

"I don't hear your every thought," she said hastily. "Or else you think very little. But you seemed to have spoken to me intentionally when you looked at barges on the river."

In fact, I had been imagining how I would describe them to

her. The green water between red and blue barges made a striking image.

"I only mean to ask," she said, blushing charmingly, "if you would describe the city again while you're walking. I would love to hear it."

I relaxed a little. As spooky as it was to be reminded of our uncanny link, she didn't mean me any harm. "Of course," I said. "I'd be happy to."

As I walked to my music lesson the next day, I thought at Jannoula, describing everything I passed: the stone curlicues in the balustrade of Cathedral Bridge; the lizard-like quigutl climbing upside down along a clothesline between houses; the shouting pie vendors and their savory-smelling wares.

I wasn't completely sure she was hearing my descriptions until she replied: *You should eat a pie for me, since I can't taste one myself.*

It is generally inadvisable to obey voices in your head, and indeed I froze when I heard her, downright spooked that she could talk to me when I wasn't visiting my garden. Still, it wasn't much stranger than the fact that she'd heard me, and what a sweet request. I smiled in spite of myself and said, *Well, if you really insist . . .*

I had hoped she could taste the pie while I did, but she couldn't. I described the sweet apples and flaky pastry until she laughingly cried, *Enough! I'm envious now.*

We started conversing during the day as I walked around, and for the first time I began to feel I truly had a friend. She wasn't always there; her own life—her captors? I could only imagine— sometimes demanded her attention and, she explained, she couldn't be in two places at once. When she was gone, I saved up details for her: the legless beggar singing in St. Loola's Square; the way falling red maple leaves gavotted in the autumn breeze.

What does gavotted *mean?* she asked when I shared these things later. *Or* singing, *for that matter?*

"Have you never heard music before?" I exclaimed aloud, forgetting in my astonishment that I was eating dinner with my family. My father and stepmother stared; my little half sisters giggled. I stuffed a forkful of jellied eel into my mouth.

Poor Jannoula, though. If she was truly deprived of music, I had to correct this.

It wasn't as easy as it sounded. Jannoula could hear thoughts directed at her, but she could not sense through my senses. My daily music lessons with Orma could not enlighten her; she didn't hear me playing my instruments. I tried thinking at her while I played, but that just made my playing suffer. I sang to her in the garden after I'd settled the other grotesques for the night, but I was a self-conscious and indifferent singer even in my own head. I imagined an oud and played that, but it was only a pale shadow of the real thing. She remained unfailingly polite, but I could tell she didn't see the point.

Then one day I was practicing flute, thinking not about Jannoula but about some beastly arpeggios that kept tripping me up. I tensed every time they approached, overthought and overshot them. Orma's suggestion—that I play them extremely slowly until I had the technique down—was good as far as it went, but it didn't solve the way I cringed, or how the cringe itself tightened my timbre into an excruciating shrill.

Solving the notes was the easy part; I had to solve the dread, and I couldn't.

I took a break, stretched, tried again, failed, kicked over the music stand (I am not proud of that), and wondered whether I had reached the limits of my musical ability. Maybe I'd never had any. Surely someone with a modicum of talent wouldn't have to work this hard.

The music stand had hit my table and knocked a cascade of books and parchments onto the floor; I had my uncle's proclivity for filing by piling, alas. I picked everything up, leafing through to see whether I couldn't relocate this mountain to the bottom of my wardrobe and forget it. The avalanche consisted mostly of scores that I needed to study, but then my eyes lit upon Orma's scrawled handwriting: *On Emptiness.* It was a short treatise he'd written for me, back when we'd hoped to quell the visions through meditation. I drifted over to my bed and read the whole thing again.

And had an idea.

I needed to get out of my own way, release this anxiety and relax into the arpeggios. I had gotten good at vacating my mind; the obvious jokes aside, meditation practice had enabled me to create my garden, and to visit it. I lay back on my bed and imagined myself empty, pictured doors in my heart and how I would fling them open. I was a hollow channel; I would be my own instrument, reverberating.

I didn't sit up or open my eyes, just put my flute to my lips and began to play.

Oh! cried Jannoula in my mind. There was such anguish in her voice that I broke off in alarm. *No, don't stop!*

It took me a moment to understand that she had finally heard me—through my ears, or some other method? I wasn't sure. I only knew that I had found a way to open myself to her. I laughed, long and loud, while she continued to grouse. "Yes, Your Majesty," I said, grinning. I took a deep breath, filling and emptying myself together, and let my whole being ring with music once again.

Orma, unexpectedly, heard a difference in my playing at our next lesson. "That rondo is much improved," he said from his perch on his desk. "It's nothing I taught you, though. You've found some way to give it greater depth. It feels—" He cut himself short.

I waited. I had never heard him begin a sentence that way.

"That is," said Orma, scratching his false beard, "you're playing as humans do at their best. Filling the music with some discernible—" He waved his hands; this was hard for him. "Emotion? Self? Someday perhaps you'll be my teacher and explain it to me."

"But you did teach me," I said eagerly. "Your meditation treatise gave me the key. I cleared out all the detritus, or something, and now she can hear me play."

There was an uncomfortable silence. "She?" said Orma evenly.

I had not been keeping him apprised of Jannoula's actions, even as she'd begun to hear my thoughts and my music. Now it came out, how we talked every day, how she could hear my music and some of my thoughts. Orma listened silently, his black eyes inscrutable behind his spectacles; a defensive warmth rose in my chest against his studied neutrality. "She's humble and kind," I said, folding my arms. "Her life is a misery, and I'm pleased to give her some relief from it."

Orma licked his thin lips. "Has she told you where she is imprisoned, or why?"

"No," I said. "And she doesn't need to. She's my friend and I trust her."

My *friend.* She really was. The first I'd ever had.

"Monitor that trust," said Orma, cool as autumn. "Mind where it wavers."

"It will not waver," I said stoutly, and packed up my instruments to go home.

I heard not a peep from Jannoula for the rest of the afternoon and thought she had left me, recalled to her real life in her cell. She was present that evening when I put the other grotesques to bed, however, following me on my rounds and sulkily kicking flowers.

Her table, when we returned to her cottage garden, was set for tea. Jannoula did not touch her cup, but sat with her arms crossed, staring toward the distant trees of Fruit Bat's grove. Had she overheard my conversation with Orma somehow? I hadn't narrated it to her, or consciously opened myself. Surely that wasn't it. I said, "What's the matter, friend?"

She stuck out her lower lip. "I don't like your music teacher. 'Has she told you where she is imprisoned, or why?'" jeered Jannoula, quoting Orma exactly.

She'd heard it all. Suddenly I felt very exposed. What else could she hear that she wasn't bothering to inform me of? Could she hear my every thought, beyond the things I intentionally told her?

That was an alarming line of inquiry. I tried to focus instead on soothing her hurt. "You must excuse Orma," I said, laying a hand gently on her arm. "He's a saar; it's his way. He can sound unkind until you get to know him."

"You called him Uncle," she said, flicking my hand off.

"I—he—that's just what I call him," I said, a knot tightening in my gut. I had not yet told her I was half dragon, but I'd hoped to someday. It would have been a relief to have a friend who knew. She looked utterly revolted by the thought of Orma being my uncle, though. It broke my heart a little. I changed the subject: "I thought you could only hear through my ears if I deliberately opened to you."

Her lip curled disdainfully. "Don't tell me your trust is wavering."

"It's not," I said, shoving down my anxiety, bending the truth to match my words.

Within days I had reframed her new ability as an asset and forgotten why I'd found it alarming. Whenever my father scolded me—a constant of my life, what with his ceaseless worrying that my half-dragon heritage would be found out—Jannoula heard him and would retort sharply in my head: *So why don't you lock us up, then, you monster?* Whenever Anne-Marie gave me chores to do, Jannoula groaned, *Oh, making up the beds is exactly like torture!*

Each time I had to bite my lip, partly to keep from laughing, partly to make sure that I had not uttered those very words myself.

She said everything I wished I could say, and I loved her for it. We were sisters again, a stronger team than ever, our moment of Orma-induced friction forgotten.

But Orma had planted a seed in my mind.

One morning, after chores, I looked for her in the garden, but she wasn't there. That is, her grotesque sat primly under a giant chrysanthemum (a fancy of hers I'd indulged), with no light in its eyes. Jannoula's attention was elsewhere.

I hesitated. What was she going through in the real world? Every time I'd asked, she'd changed the subject; she wouldn't let me watch her in her cell. I believed she suffered, and I wanted to understand what was happening. I wanted to help. Could I reverse our strange connection and see for myself without alerting her to my presence? This grotesque was merely a metaphor, after all, a way to make sense of the truth, not the truth itself.

If I took Otter's hands, I'd have my usual floating vision; she'd sense me right away and be angry. Could I enter her mind the way she entered mine?

I had a harebrained notion that if I could enter her avatar, I might enter Jannoula herself. How, though? I thought of splitting her down the middle, but rejected that as disgusting. What if I were immaterial, like a ghost? I imagined myself so. I pressed my immaterial palms together like a river diver and pushed them into her grotesque's face. They passed through her nose like it was mist. I was up to my elbows; my hands didn't reappear out the back of her head. I bent my head and pressed on until—

I landed hard on the floor of a dim, narrow corridor lined with featureless gray doors. Rising shakily to my feet, I looked both directions; there was no obvious way back to myself.

Without warning, the air seemed to compress around me, a terrible pressure that nearly brought me to my knees. The pain eased up momentarily before rushing over me again in an agonizing undulation. I prayed it would recede before it broke me.

It did. I panted like a dog and trembled all over.

Voices echoed down the corridor. I pressed forward, walking when I could, waiting out more waves of pain. I could make no sound when the crush was upon me, only lean against the wall, panicked and paralyzed. Cries built up in me, unuttered.

I tried doors, which all opened into a darkness I dared not enter. One lightless room emitted a blast of icy wind; one smelled of acrid alchemical fumes; one was stuffed full of screams. I closed that one quickly, but the hallway's strange acoustics wouldn't let the sound die. It echoed on, a second wave amplifying the roll of pain. I plowed ahead, buffeted about, not daring to open any more doors.

Was this the inside of Jannoula's mind? Did she live with these constant waves of pain?

The corridor grew darker; I couldn't see. I felt my way, a hand on each wall, until the walls abruptly ended. I could no longer feel a floor under my feet. I looked back for the hallway I'd just come down, but I couldn't see it. There was nothing. Nothingness. My saved-up screams burst forth inaudibly, swallowed by the dense, anechoic emptiness. This void could not be filled.

A violent force bowled into me, shoving me back. The

corridor reappeared, doors whizzing by on either side as I was pushed backward, faster and faster—

I landed flat on the ground, all the air knocked out of me, in the dirt of my own garden. Jannoula stood over me, gasping, her hair disordered, her fists clenched as if she had punched me in the stomach. Maybe she had. Pain—my own—radiated from my core.

"What did you see?" she shouted, her face contorting.

"I'm so sorry." I coughed. My head lolled back onto the ground.

"Don't you . . . ever . . ." Her breath came as raggedly as my own. "That's none of your business. . . ."

I wrapped my arms around my head. She sat down beside me with a rustle and thump. "That was your mind," I said bleakly. "All that pain. Those were your screams."

I looked up; she was absently ripping a marigold, picking its orange petals apart. "Promise me you won't go back," she said, her lower lip trembling. "It's hard enough that I must go."

I studied her profile, the decisive nose, the subtle chin. "What would happen to your body in the real world if you stayed here?"

Jannoula looked at me sidelong. "I'm no good to them dead; they'd force-feed me, I suppose. Perhaps my catatonia would amuse them." She dug out the heart of the flower with her nails.

"Then stay," I said firmly, impulsively. "Don't go back to that pain, or go as little as you can." Orma would disapprove of this scheme, but Orma didn't have to know.

"Oh, Seraphina!" Jannoula grabbed my hand and kissed it.

Her lashes were bright with tears. "If we are to live as sisters, then let us have no more secrets. You asked who imprisoned me. It was my father's enemies."

I let out a low whistle. "But why?"

"They hope he will pay a usurious ransom. But he won't. He doesn't love me. He's ashamed of me."

"I'm so sorry," I said, thinking of my own father. I wasn't imprisoned, but . . . I wasn't free, either.

"Is it not a terrible fate to be robbed of a father's love?" she said.

"It is," I whispered, my heart aching for her.

A cat-like smile slowly crept across her lips.

How happy we were from then on!

Having Jannoula around all the time took some adjustment, of course, for both of us. She began to find the garden confining. "I don't like to complain, when you've been so generous," she said, "but I miss being able to see and taste and feel."

I tried to accommodate her by opening myself to sights and tastes, the way I'd done with music, but I couldn't make it work. Maybe I didn't have a strong enough emotional connection to my other senses, something that could permeate the garden's boundaries and pull the experience through.

"What if you left the garden gates ajar?" she suggested one evening. "I tried opening them, but they're locked."

"I wish you'd asked me first," I said, frowning. We were in her garden eating cakes, which were not as delicious as the real thing. She was right to be frustrated.

Her green eyes widened. "I didn't realize there were places I wasn't allowed. Since I live here now, I assumed . . ." She trailed off, downcast.

I left the gates open the next evening, experimentally. She reported back that some things trickled in—stray emotions, sensations, and thoughts—but it was all rather muted. Timidly, politely, she asked, "May I step out into your wider mind?"

I hesitated, feeling instinctively that this was a very big favor to ask. I said, "I don't want you digging around. Even sisters need some privacy."

"I would never pry that way," she said, so warmly that I felt silly for doubting. I took her hand in my garden and guided her through the gate myself.

She was rapturous, as if she'd been freed from her real prison, out in the world. Her happiness was contagious; I'd never felt the like myself. I decided to leave the gates open all the time—at least I think I did.

She began wandering my mind at will, discreet and unobtrusive, but sometimes she had accidents. Once she knocked over whatever sluice gate held back my anger, and I raged for hours until she figured out how to close it again. We laughed about it later, how I had screamed at my half sisters and smacked my father's balding pate with a tea tray.

"You know what's interesting?" she told me. "Anger tastes like cabbage rolls."

"What?" I yelped between gales of giggling. "That's ridiculous."

"It's true," she insisted. "And your laughter tastes like marzipan. But best of all is love, which smacks of blackberries."

I'd eaten a marzipan torte with blackberries just the evening before; apparently it had made a profound impression on her. She was always making these kinds of unexpected associations, and I enjoyed them. They painted the world a different color.

What does this do? Jannoula once asked while I was walking home from my lesson, and suddenly I couldn't remember my way. I found the river, though it flowed a strange direction. North was surely to my right, but when I turned, my inner compass reeled, too, and north was still to my right, always just out of reach. I kept turning until I grew dizzy and fell in the river. A barge woman fished me out and took me home, drenched but laughing. Anne-Marie was not subtle about sniffing my breath.

"Who would give me unwatered wine?" I laughed. "I'm only eleven!"

"You are twelve," said my stepmother sharply. "Go to your room."

I remembered with a start: the marzipan torte with blackberries. That had been for my birthday. Such an odd thing to forget.

Sometimes I would lose control of one of my eyes, or an arm or leg, which frightened me, until Jannoula explained. *I wanted to see the cathedral for myself,* she said, or *Just let me feel your velvet bodice.* It was perfectly understandable. She lived with such deprivation, and it was but a small sacrifice to give her tremendous joy.

Then one night I was awakened by Orma sitting on the edge of my bed. I yelped in alarm. "Don't wake the house," he said, shushing me. "Your father is always looking for reasons to be angry with me. Last month he was accusing me of sending you home drunk."

"Last month?" I whispered. I'd fallen in the river only . . . what day had that been?

His face was in shadow, but I could discern the whites of his eyes. "Is this Jannoula present and awake in your mind right now?" he whispered back. "Make no assumptions. Go to your garden and check."

His intensity frightened me a little. I descended to my mind's garden and found Jannoula's avatar, sleeping among snapdragons.

Orma nodded curtly when I told him. "I assumed she sleeps when you do. Do nothing to wake her. What do you remember of our lesson today?"

I rubbed my eyes and thought. I had retained very little, it seemed. I looked at him sheepishly. "I played harpsichord and oud, and we talked about modes and intervals. We argued over a volume of Thoric's *Polyphonic Transgressions* . . . didn't we?"

"At the end. What happened prior to that?"

I racked my brains. I remembered one other thing, but it made no sense. "I scratched the cover of the book with my oud's plectrum. Why did I do that?"

"You were angry with me. Or someone was." His mouth flattened into a stern line. "Someone who didn't like being rebuffed."

"Rebuffed for what?" I said, a slow-burning dread in the pit of my stomach.

"You kissed me," he said evenly. "On the mouth, to be precise. It wasn't like you. In fact, I'm quite certain it wasn't you."

My throat had gone completely dry. "That's not possible. I'd remember."

He removed his spectacles and cleaned them with the edge of his sleeve. "How long has she been moving you around, using your body as if it were her own? Or did you not realize she could do such a thing? She apparently makes you forget afterward."

I ran a hand over my face. "I'll talk to her. I'm sure she didn't mean to—"

"She meant to," he said. "She would not have stolen your memories if it were innocent. What happens when she usurps your body and decides not to give it back?"

"She wouldn't do that!" I whispered vehemently. "She's my friend. My only—"

"No," said Orma with surprising gentleness. "She is no friend to you at all. Could she make you kill your father, or hurt your little sisters?"

"She would never—" I began, then remembered hitting my father with the tea tray. It had seemed good fun at the time.

"You don't know what she might do, or what she really wants," said Orma. "I suspect she wants to be you. While her body is trapped in prison, you're her chance for a better life. You have to evict her."

"I've seen how she suffers," I said, pleading with him now. "It would be cruel to kick her out. And I don't think I could, even if—"

"You are not helpless," said Orma.

He'd spoken those words to me before. They hit me hard, and for a moment I hated him. Some quiet, sensible part of me, though—a part I had been paying very little heed to for quite some time—knew he was right. Now that I knew how far she had gone, I could not keep letting her do what she liked with me. I buried my face in my pillow, mortified by how easily I'd handed over the reins.

He made no move to console me, but waited until I showed my face again. "We need to free you from her," he said, "and we need to do it soon, lest she glean your intentions. Can she hear all your thoughts?"

"I think so, when the garden gates are open." They'd been open a long time. If I closed them, she'd know something was wrong. Could I use my thoughts to fool her?

The lines by Orma's mouth deepened. "You can't simply release her, I suppose?"

I took a shaky breath. "I think she's holding on to me as tightly as I'm holding on to her. If I let go, she wouldn't return the favor."

"Could you wall her off in some sort of prison?" he asked.

"Maybe," I said, feeling a sick, regretful pang. The irony was not lost on me.

We spent more than an hour planning; after he finally left, I stayed awake a few hours more, preparing. I knew I had to act now, while my resolve held and before she figured out what I was doing. I crept through my own mind, into Jannoula's part of the garden, and opened the door of the ornamental cottage, which I now named the Wee Cottage, because my garden's functional places must be named. I created a space inside it, then reinforced the walls and door, imagining them impenetrable, incorruptible. I circled the cottage seven times, chanting ritual words of my own invention. All the while, her avatar slept nearby.

Jannoula would surely wake soon. I hastily tidied up my mind and put a big padlock on the cottage door.

She was certain to notice it; I was counting on that.

I gazed down at her sleeping form among the flowers, curled up the way she'd been when I'd first met her, and my heart brimmed with pity. With a thought, I caused a toadstool the size of a table to grow beside her head and give her shade. She awoke, stretching sleepily, and smiled to see me there. "Good morning, sister," she said, sitting up. "You don't usually visit this time of day."

"Look," I said, pointing at the distraction I'd created. "I made you a toadstool."

"It's our favorite color!" She beamed with a childish innocence that reminded me painfully of early days. "I'd like a whole garden of them."

"Why not?" I said, a purposeful note of desperation beneath my cheer. Speckled toadstools began popping up all over.

She picked up on my anxious undertone at once; her green eyes darted, quick as minnows, to my face. "You're misdirecting me. What's going on?" She flicked her tongue out quickly, like a snake. I wondered what guilt tasted like.

"Don't be silly," I protested too vehemently. My nerves sang with tension.

She stepped closer, her brow furrowed, cocking an ear as if listening to my rapidly knocking pulse. "What have you done?"

The padlock on the Wee Cottage popped into my thoughts,

as if by accident. I struggled to suppress the thought, and the struggle itself drew her attention. She was at the cottage door in five strides, her gown swirling around her ankles. I hurried after.

"I can't see what's in here. What are you hiding from me?" she asked.

"Nothing."

"You're lying." She whirled on me. "Why would you do this? We are sisters: we share everything." She brought her face so close that I could see fine wrinkles around her eyes, like hairline cracks in an antique vase. Her hard life was written in those lines, along with an unexpected fragility. I steeled my heart against it.

Her eyes shone, bright and dangerous. "Do you know what else I perceive? You've been talking with your uncle."

"What?" I had not anticipated this. She perceived more than I'd realized she could in so short a time. My heartbeat quickened like a panicked rabbit. "You're mistaken."

"Never. No one else leaves such a blackberry residue in the air." She stuck out her tongue as if she were tasting it. "All I have ever wanted," she said, her voice strained, "is for you to love me exactly as you love him, and you won't. Am I not your dearest sister? Am I not more deserving than some wicked, heartless dragon, uncle or not?"

I had lost control of this conversation; the wind blew cold over the garden.

She tasted my fear and smiled ruthlessly. "You're half dragon. Were you going to tell me that? I had to learn it from your memories as I walked through your larger mind. You have not been honest with me at all, and now you're hiding something in that cottage. Open the door."

"No," I said.

She raised her arms over her head and slowly splayed her fingers. Her hands elongated grotesquely, like spindly tree branches or scalpel-sharp claws. They became forked lightning hurled at the sky, and their terrible touch raked the inside of my skull, scraping and shocking and shattering. I collapsed, scream-ing, clutching wildly at my head in the real world, and in my mind, and in my mind's mind, there was an infinite regression to the very center of myself.

Then the pain stopped, and for a high, shining moment, I saw Heaven.

Jannoula bent over my prone form. She held out her hand, now humanly proportioned, and I grasped it gratefully. She pulled me to my feet; I threw my arms around her, weeping.

She was my dearest sister. I loved her more than anything. I was overflowing with love. Words could not. I had never felt.

"There we go," she said, her voice a melody. She smiled like the fond sun and patted my head like the kiss of springtime. "All I need now," she said, "is for you to unlock that door."

How could I not? She was my sister. The key was already in my hand; if I trembled, it was because I could barely contain my joy at being useful.

I had the padlock off in a trice; I held it up to show her. She smiled as the Saints smile on all of us from Heaven, full of good-ness and light, overawing me. "Come," she said, taking my hand. "Let's see what this silly fuss was all about."

She opened the door upon darkness. "I don't see anything," she said, elegantly confused. "What's in here?"

"Nothing," I said, which was all I was sure of anymore.

"It can't be *nothing*," she said. Even her irritation carried a rich resonance, like a deeply peeved viola.

I stopped short at the threshold. I remembered being inside earlier; I'd circled the cottage and said ritual words. My own voice came to me, that very chant, telling myself, *Go into the cottage, go out of my mind.*

What had that meant? Would I go mad—out of my mind—if I entered?

Jannoula still held my hand. No matter how much I loved her, I dared not enter the cottage. It was probably bad for *her* to go into that eerie, dense darkness. I said, "Sister, neither of us should go in there. Please."

"Fie!" she cried, violently yanking my hand. "There's something that you don't want me to find, but I am going to find it!"

"Sister, please don't. I built this place to trick you. I see how wrong that was now. I can build anything, a palace worthy of you, just please don't—"

She let go of my hand, crossed the threshold, and slammed the door in my face.

My feeling for her went out like a candle in a puff of wind.

I quickly locked the padlock and sank to my knees, shaking uncontrollably. I was myself again—surely nothing could mean more than that—and yet I felt more bereaved than relieved. I had lost my friend forever.

I wept. I had loved her, in fact, before she forced me to.

I had seen sweetness in her, and fragility. It could not all have been a lie. She was in pain every day. What was it doing to her?

My head rang hollow without her presence, an aching emptiness like the void I'd seen at Jannoula's core—and yet not like. I used to fill this entire space myself. I would relearn the trick of it, or fill it with music. I would find the way.

Exhausted, I slept, waking in time to rush to St. Ida's Conservatory for my lesson. Orma listened to my breathless explanation: I'd tricked her; she was gone.

He said, "I'm astonished at this mantra you devised. When you were yourself, you knew it as a command for Jannoula: *Go into the cottage, go out of my mind.* But when she seized control—as you anticipated she might—you took it as a warning against following her into the cottage yourself. And it worked."

In truth, it had come far too close to failure. I didn't care to dwell on that. "What will happen to her?" I asked, a weight of guilt still on my heart.

He considered. "I presume she can enter your mind no further than the cottage door. Unless she likes sitting alone in darkness, she'll lose interest and keep herself to herself."

Herself seemed a terrible place to be; I still wished I could have saved her from it. This guilt was going to rankle a long time.

I tapped my flute thoughtfully against my chin, grateful to Orma for helping me. I wished I might have embraced him, or told him I really did love him, but that was not his way. Not our way. I contented myself with saying, "If you hadn't noticed—and cared enough to warn me when you did—I don't know what would have happened."

He snorted, pushed up his spectacles, and said, "Give yourself some credit. You heeded my warning; I wasn't sure you would. Now let's start with the suite by Tertius."

∾Nine∾

Jannoula's voice from Gianni's mouth brought everything back. I fled Gianni's cell, pushing past a confused Moy, and rushed up to my room at Palasho Donques. I buried myself under blankets and spent the whole night reliving it all: the violation, the horror, the guilt, the sorrow.

At first light, I pounded on Josquin's door. It took him some minutes to answer, bleary-eyed and tucking his shirt into breeches he'd evidently just put on. "I've been thinking," I said, my words pouring out in a miserable rush. "We shouldn't take the wild man back to Segosh."

"What are you proposing?" said Josquin hoarsely. I really had awakened him, it seemed. "Release him back into the wild?"

If Jannoula could make him talk, she could propel his taloned feet after us, the way she'd walked me through the world.

Whatever she was after, I wanted her nowhere near me. "Shouldn't Lord Donques incarcerate him here, where the murder happened?"

"He would have preferred that, yes," said Josquin, folding his arms. "I burned through rather a lot of his goodwill yesterday, convincing him to let us take the creature back to Segosh."

"Then he'll be happy you've changed your mind."

"And the next time I have to negotiate with him or anyone else?" said Josquin sharply. I recoiled at the rebuke; I had never seen him cross before. "I speak on Count Pesavolta's authority," he said, "but I have to be circumspect with it. He's no hereditary monarch, ordained by Heaven, whose caprices none may question. He rules by the goodwill of his baronets. I've spent enough of Count Pesavolta's capital here to make myself uncomfortable. If I throw it back in Lord Donques's face, suddenly my credibility—and the count's—would be in question. It would unbalance the whole economy of rule."

I could see no argument to make; he understood the peculiar politics of Ninys, and I did not. I acquiesced with a little bow and set off toward the infirmary to see Abdo. Josquin, perhaps sensing that he'd been hard on me, called after: "If you're worried about our safety, Seraphina, we'll have him bound. The Eight know what they're doing."

I turned to face him, walking backward a few steps while I bowed again, smiling to cover the unnameable dread in my heart. The Eight might bind Gianni's limbs, but it was the person who'd bound his mind who scared me.

We reached the capital in half the time it had taken us to reach the mountains, thanks to good Ninysh roads, a guide who knew them all, and the fact that we were no longer actively searching for anyone. Josquin knew where to change horses and where it was safe to ride after dark. Gianni Patto, his hands bound and a lead line tied securely around his torso like a harness, kept up with the horses easily. He made no aggressive move toward anyone, and his ice-blue eyes remained benignly unfocused.

I watched him like a hawk, but Jannoula did not speak through him again. At night, in my garden of grotesques, there was an ache where Tiny Tom had been.

Abdo was in pain and barely spoke. The monk's blade seemed to have severed more than just the tendons of his wrist; it had pierced his buoyant spirit somehow. How would the injury affect his dancing? Being robbed of music would have been a mortal blow to me; dancing surely meant as much to him. The Eight took turns riding with him, even the ones who'd made St. Ogdo's sign. He was a child, first and foremost, and that brought out their empathy. He sat curled on the saddle horn, resting his head upon a gleaming breastplate.

Darkness had fallen and mist was rising over the lowland farms when the torches of Segosh finally winked into sight ahead of us. The two youngest of our guards gave cries of joy and spurred their tired horses onward, racing for the city gates.

"Youth is wasted on the young," laughed Moy, who was carrying Abdo.

Shouts of alarm rang out from the gatehouse ahead; our bravos replied with something vaguely obscene. Seven weeks' travel, and my Ninysh had increased by only the rudest words. The gate-house guard returned the compliment, and there was laughter all round.

The city gates opened, iron hinges complaining shrilly. Upon a tiny pale donkey, swearing heartily herself, Dame Okra Carmine rode out, followed by a man in dark robes. Reflected torchlight danced upon her spectacles; a smirk played on her lips. "Don't look so astonished," she called, spurring her wee steed forward. "My premonitions of you, Seraphina, give me a very particular stomachache, like eating bad beets."

"I think of myself as more of a turnip," I said, parrying insult with absurdity.

She emitted a short laugh, then shouted something in Ninysh to the severe-looking man who'd ridden out behind her. "This is Dr. Belestros, Count Pesavolta's physician," Dame Okra explained. "If you want to keep doing handsprings, Abdo, you'd better let this fellow take you to the palace."

I don't like her premonitions, fretted Abdo. *She prods without permission.*

I'm not sure she can help it, I said.

She's just had one about Moy, said Abdo.

"Moy," called Dame Okra, "don't hand the child across; you'll drop him. Follow Dr. Belestros to Palasho Pesavolta."

"Of course, Ambassadress," said Moy, bowing his head to Dame Okra and letting Dr. Belestros ride ahead. Abdo met my gaze as they rode away; I couldn't read his expression in the darkness.

They'll take good care of you. I'll see you tomorrow, I said, relieved that Abdo's wrist, at least, might find healing. Abdo made no reply.

Dame Okra, having settled the matter of Abdo's arm, turned her donkey toward our remaining guard. Gianni Patto stood docilely behind the horses, his crooked mouth agape. Dame Okra gave an exaggerated sniff and said, "Is this the newest member of our big ugly family, then? He's whiffier than you mentioned."

"I couldn't find words to describe it," I said.

"Well, he's not staying at my house," said the old woman flatly.

"Technically, he's under arrest," said Josquin, reining his horse alongside mine.

Dame Okra wrinkled her snub nose and scowled. "I don't know where you think the count can keep him. You!" she called to the remains of our escort. "Take this hideous beast-thing up to the palace and quarter it in the count's third stable, the empty one. No point traumatizing Pesavolta's racehorses on top of everything else."

Our soldiers cheered; once Gianni was put away, they'd be free to go home. I felt a pang of homesickness myself, but the bulk of my mission was still ahead of me. I couldn't linger here if I was to reach the Samsamese highlands by St. Abaster's Day, and beyond that was Porphyry. Would Abdo have to stay behind while his arm healed?

It felt overwhelming just then, especially if I had to face it alone.

Josquin lingered beside me while the others rode toward the gates. I glanced at him, then looked again because he was staring back at me, his gingery eyebrows raised. "It was a good journey,

Seraphina," he said, bowing slightly in the saddle. "I feel privileged to have traveled with you."

"I feel the same," I said, surprised at the lump in my throat. Josquin had become a dear friend; I was going to miss him.

"Best of luck on your road ahead," he said, winding a finger in his scraggly beard, "and the blessings of St. Nola, who watches our steps. I hope that when you're finished, when you've found all of your kind and the war is over and you have leisure to do so, you will come back and visit us and tell us what adventures you have passed."

"Saints in Heaven. Breathe, boy!" cried Dame Okra crossly. "And then get gone with your fellows. This one's not for you, as you well know."

Josquin stiffened, mortified; it was too dark to tell whether he turned red, but the speed with which he spurred his horse toward the city gate suggested an affirmative.

I may have blushed as well. Who can say? It was dark.

His fellows had not yet entered the city. Gianni Patto had balked before the gate, agitated for the first time since Donques. He dug in with his clawed feet and would not take another step; he roared and tore at his bindings. The guards surrounded him, sensibly dismounting so as not to be yanked off their horses.

As Josquin rode up to help, I said to Dame Okra, "Did you have to be so mean?"

She sneered. "To my weedy great-great-grand-cousin? I'm astonished you care. He was going to lean in and kiss you next."

She was exaggerating, although my heated face didn't seem to think so. I waved her off impatiently. "Don't tell me you had a premonition."

She said, "There are things one can foresee without a pre . . . mo . . ."

I squinted at her. If she hadn't had a premonition before, she was having an enormous one now: one hand clutched her stomach, and her eyes were glassy.

"Dame Okra?" I said.

She snapped out of her trance, swaying disorientedly in the saddle, and screamed, "Josquin, hold on!"

Josquin turned toward us in confusion, as if he couldn't make sense of her words. Gianni Patto threw his head back and roared, the loudest, most nightmarish sound I had ever heard a living creature produce. All the horses startled, but Josquin's bucked and reared. Josquin flailed wildly, but couldn't grasp the saddle horn in time. He was thrown, landing on the flagstones with a sickening thud.

I leaped from my horse and was running before I had time to think. Josquin's legs lay crumpled at a gruesomely wrong angle; his face glistened, sweaty and greenish in the torchlight. I knelt beside the herald and took his hand, my throat clenched too tightly to speak.

"Can't feel my legs," gasped Josquin, trying awfully to smile. "I know that's bad, but . . . feeling them might be . . . worse."

The gatehouse guards rushed up with a field stretcher, shooing me away. Josquin smiled bravely one last time as they transferred and lifted him. They carried him away, and I stared after in a mute haze, a buzzing like wasps in my ears.

Gianni Patto had gone slack and stupid and docile again. The Eight, who had swarmed him, shouted blue murder and waved their blades in his face; Gianni didn't flinch or defend himself. He made no squeak of protest when they knocked him down and began to kick him.

"Stop," I said, too feebly to be effective. "Stop!" I shouted louder, rushing up to Nan and tugging on her arm. She glanced at me, and my face was enough. She pulled the woman next to her off Gianni, and then the pair put a quick halt to the kicking. The soldiers stepped back, breathing heavily; tears streaked more faces than just mine.

Gianni Patto raised his face from the paving stones; his icy eyes met mine with a gaze of such piercing lucidity that I staggered back as if struck. He smiled eerily.

For a moment I feared I might vomit.

"Fee-naaaah!" Gianni's voice rumbled like thunder.

"Take him away," I said, averting my eyes. "And for Heaven's sake, be careful."

They hobbled his ankles and strapped his arms to his sides; he rose, awkward and unresisting, and followed them into the city, his taloned feet scratching and chattering on the stones.

Dame Okra, strangely, had neither dismounted nor moved; she stared intently into the darkness, breathing hard. Her forehead glistened with sweat and her eyes bulged.

I shakily mounted my horse, trying to slow my jittering heart. It had happened so fast. "He isn't usually like this," I said numbly, as if that might reassure Dame Okra or myself. I knew what must have happened. Jannoula had surely been present in him again. Had she made Gianni scream? Had she hurt him? What was she up to? I couldn't begin to think; dread clung to me like a wet blanket.

"Eh?" said Dame Okra abruptly, as if startling awake. "Did you say something?"

I opened my mouth and closed it again, out of words. Dame Okra hadn't even reacted to Josquin's injury; she was mean, but not usually that mean.

"Then let's get back to the house. I have a most fearsome headache, and it's late," she snapped accusingly, as if I were the one keeping her out past her bedtime.

She spurred her donkey forward, not bothering to see whether I followed.

I didn't sleep. I couldn't. I paced Dame Okra's green guest room until the sun came up.

It had never occurred to me, not once, that in seeking out the ityasaari there might be a price to pay beyond the time, effort, and resources spent finding them. The death of the monk, even if he deserved it, was too high a price. Abdo's wrist was too high a price. Josquin's spine . . . I could barely think about that. It filled me with despair.

On top of all that, my search had attracted Jannoula's notice. Had she provoked Gianni to kill the monk? Had Gianni been screaming for my attention when he spooked Josquin's horse? She'd said she could help me search; I didn't need this kind of help.

I didn't know what to do. The thought of continuing the search made me nauseated. I wanted to give it up, go home, hide away from everyone. But then this terrible toll really would have been exacted in vain. Surely it was up to me to make these sacrifices mean something.

I flopped back on the bed, the weight of my thoughts pinning me down. The birds were singing as I fell asleep.

It was noon, at least, by the time I awoke; I could tell by the sun through the windows. I washed and dressed, a resolution growing in my mind: we couldn't take Gianni Patto back to Goredd. Maybe he would have been violent and unpredictable even if he hadn't been riddled with Jannoula, but I couldn't help believing she'd influenced him. I did not want Gianni Patto carrying her anywhere near my home or the people I loved. I had felt that way in Donques; I never should have let Josquin persuade me otherwise. I was going to tell Dame Okra, and she would tell Count Pesavolta to keep the creature—and thereby Jannoula—locked up.

The creature. That was unfair. I knew it, but I couldn't bear to think of him any other way just now.

I had accidentally neglected my garden the night before; Abdo had suggested I try such a thing. It hurt to think about Abdo. I considered tending to it now, but the grotesques weren't riled up, clearly, or I would have had a headache.

If they didn't need me, I didn't feel like visiting. I'd only have been there to soothe myself, and it niggled at me that maybe that was what I'd been doing all along. Maybe the garden had always been about me.

I staggered downstairs. Nedouard and Blanche sat in Dame Okra's formal dining room, side by side in comradely silence. Surgical tools, metal scraps, and dirty dishes were spread before them across the pristine white tablecloth between two incongruous bouquets of lilacs. Blanche, who had been coiling copper wire around an iron rod, smiled enormously when she saw me and leaped to her feet. She looked healthier; there was some pink in her cheeks, and her scales looked shinier and less like scabs. She'd acquired a pale green gown, and even it seemed more solid than what she'd worn before. "Hey hey you wanting it breakfast I can to make it at you," she said in an astonishing deluge of Goreddi. "Kitchen is all food."

I was overwhelmed by her sweetness and joy, and had to swallow hard before I could answer. Maybe we'd done a few things worth doing after all. "I'm not hungry, thank you," I managed to say. Blanche looked dumbfounded by the notion of "not hungry," but she plopped back down and resumed winding wire.

"She's remembering her words," said Nedouard. Even he seemed happier without his mask or leather apron; he wore a sensible wool doublet and linen shirt, like any other man of modest means. His eyes smiled, even if his beak could not, and he was polishing a wicked-looking saw. "Welcome back," he added, testing the blade by paring a delicate curl off the edge of his thumbnail.

"Is Dame Okra here?" I asked, wanting to talk about Gianni and get it over with.

"She's in the library," said Nedouard, setting aside the saw and absently reaching for a tiny silver bowl, a saltcellar. He stirred the salt with the tiny spoon.

"She is to talk on herself with ghosts!" cried Blanche, her violet eyes wide.

The old plague doctor laid a hand upon Blanche's arm and spoke in low tones. She nodded, whimpering, and refocused on her wires. "Dame Okra was up all night," said Nedouard. "Talking, apparently. It kept Blanche awake."

"Talking to whom?" I said, watching him empty the salt into a vase of flowers.

He raised his gentle blue eyes to my face. "Herself, I believe. It's not an unusual trait in someone so old, although I haven't observed her doing it before. I find it much more disturbing that she's so cheerful this morning."

"That is rather alarming," I said, and couldn't help smiling. "I'll need to see for myself before I believe it, but I promise to get to the bottom of things."

As I spoke, Nedouard matter-of-factly tucked the tiny silver salt bowl into the front of his shirt. I stared at him pointedly; it took him a moment to grasp why, and then he shamefacedly extracted the dish and set it back on the table. "Many of my patients are too poor to pay," he said. "I fear I have developed rather a habit of taking payment where I find it, from those who won't miss it. It's a difficult custom to break."

I suspected that wasn't the entire truth, and that the saltcellar would disappear back down his shirt the moment I left the room. I did him the honor of nodding, however, before I went looking for Dame Okra, who was rumored to be cheerful.

It was generally easy to find Dame Okra in her own house; her brassy voice was like a premonition itself, preceding her wherever she went. I could hear her talking as I approached the library. I pressed my ear against the door, and her voice carried clearly: "... more than a hundred years, thinking I was unique in all the world. You can imagine how alone I felt. Well, no, you wouldn't need to imagine, would you. You *know*."

That was quite an elaborate conversation for her to be having aloud with herself. I opened the door cautiously. Dame Okra sat behind an ornate mahogany desk at the far end of the library, papers spread around her, quill in hand. She looked up at the sound of the door opening and smiled gloriously.

I may have staggered back a step from shock. It was not just the smile: there was no one else in the room.

"Seraphina, come in! I'm so pleased you're finally awake," she said, gesturing toward a seat facing the desk. I darted my gaze across her desk, noting parchment, ink, books, pen, sealing wax. No thnik that I could see. Whom had she been speaking to?

"I'm making a full accounting of your journey and expenses for Count Pesavolta," said Dame Okra, seeming not to register my perplexity. "Don't worry, you needn't deal with him. You could sign this thank-you note, though." She waved me nearer so she might hand over a letter and pen.

I sat in a leather chair facing her desk and scanned the page. She'd written effusively about all the good he'd done, letting me travel through Ninys; it said Goredd was in his debt, but didn't make any specific promises. It seemed safe enough to sign.

"We need to talk about Gianni Patto," I said as I handed back the letter and quill.

"Not to worry," she said. "I went this morning and secured his release."

I goggled at her. "I—I'm sorry, you . . . what?"

Dame Okra nodded eagerly. "As soon as he's all cleaned up, he's coming here."

"Here, as in *here*?" I said, pointing at the floor beside my chair.

"I have room, and the count would keep him in the stables, not bring him indoors and start the long road to civilizing him," she said. She sounded so reasonable.

"You shouldn't bring him into your house," I said, shaking off my shock and recovering my purpose. "It was a mistake to bring him down from the mountains. He's violent, unpredictable, and not entirely in control of himself." He was also full to the brim with Jannoula; I had intended to say as much, but something made me hesitate.

Who *had* she been talking to? The back of my neck prickled.

"*You* shouldn't mind if he's here or not," said Dame Okra, her protuberant eyes narrowing. "You're to leave for Samsam tomorrow at dawn. Your guides have been at the palasho a week, waiting for you, and Pesavolta wants them off."

So soon. Of course there was no time to waste. "Will Abdo be well enough to come with me?" I'd said I'd visit him this morning, I recalled with a pang, but I'd slept straight through.

"Absolutely not," said Dame Okra, looking scandalized at the suggestion. "Abdo needs to rest for a few weeks. I'll take him to Goredd with Gianni, Blanche, and Ned."

"Can I see him before I go?"

"He's in surgery now to reconnect the tendons of his hand," she said. "Don't worry, Dr. Belestros is the best dragon physician the count could buy."

I wouldn't even get to say goodbye. "What about Josquin?" I said.

"Belestros has him sedated. He was in terrible pain all night," said Dame Okra mournfully. It was the first inkling of sadness she'd shown for her distant cousin, but it didn't last. Her smile reasserted itself. "You can't see him, either, but you could write him a letter. I know he's your friend."

She'd delivered a terrible amount of difficult news at once, but underneath my shock and sorrow, something else bothered me. I tried to untangle my feelings and see it clearly, to no avail until Dame Okra said, "All this struggle is going to be worth it in the end, Seraphina, when we're all together as we were meant to be."

That didn't sound like Dame Okra at all.

The cheerfulness. The turnaround on Gianni. The conversation she'd been having with herself . . .

I had been so preoccupied with Josquin's injury last night that I hadn't seen what had happened right in front of me. Before Gianni had screamed or Josquin had fallen off his horse, Dame Okra had had a premonition.

Her mind had reached out to Gianni and found Jannoula.

I studied Dame Okra's froggy face. The blissful expression wasn't Jannoula's; Dame Okra didn't look the way Gianni did when Jannoula spoke through him. Blanche had said Dame Okra hadn't slept; might Jannoula have spent all night talking to her? Persuading, manipulating . . . even changing?

If Dame Okra had been contacted by Jannoula, how did that work? Was it like hearing Abdo's voice, or could Jannoula have wormed into her more deeply, as she'd done to Gianni and to me? I remembered how she'd altered my thoughts and emotions, but also how they had snapped back into place when she was completely gone.

I remembered how she could linger in my head and listen to my conversations.

I said, "Show yourself, Jannoula."

Dame Okra's expression sharpened at once, her bulgy eyes narrowing to feline cunning. "Hello, Seraphina," she said with Jannoula's flat inflection. "I don't suppose this really counts as a surprise, but it is pleasant nonetheless."

Surprise or not, I felt sickened. "Release Dame Okra. Leave her at once."

Jann-Okra shook her head, tsking. "And you immediately turn things unpleasant. Why, Seraphina? Dear Okra's mind reached out to me. I'd tried knocking—it worked with Gianni, and other unsuspecting innocents—but she wouldn't answer. She was very closed off; I couldn't reach her any other way."

Dame Okra had been so adamant about not letting anyone into her mind. She must have heard Jannoula's "knock," but her suspicious nature kept her from answering. Gianni would not have had the wit, but who were these others? Someone had told her about my search.

"I've made an old woman a little less lonely," Jann-Okra was saying. "You overheard her talking to me, surely. How could you not? She has a voice like a mule."

I glowered. "I heard."

"Why begrudge her my company if she enjoys it?" She leered nastily, an expression Dame Okra's face was already quite good at. "I'm tempted to teach you a lesson. I could speak to you in your head again, through Miss Fusspots, and make you unfasten her, like you did Gianni. I could make you eject everyone from your garden, one by one, until you are truly, utterly alone."

She smiled bitterly. "You've never appreciated how lucky you are. Your mind reached for the rest spontaneously. I had to go looking, but my diligence reaps a good harvest at last. I have sought and I have found. Seeing them all in your head helped me. You were my map."

"Why?" I asked. "Why are you doing this?"

She looked mildly surprised. "I want exactly what you want, Seraphina: the half-dragons together at last. We're on the same quest; I consider you my helpmate."

"I'm not doing this for you!" I cried.

She wasn't listening; her eyes had suddenly gone glassy. Her wrinkled cheeks paled, and a sheen of sweat glistened on her forehead. I leaned forward, holding my breath, hoping that this was the opening salvo in some internal war, that Dame Okra was fighting back. The old woman was so pugnacious that I couldn't imagine her not battling Jannoula. If anyone could hope to defeat her, surely—

Her eyes refocused and Jannoula's voice said: "So that's her famous sense of premonition. Intriguing, and surprisingly painful." She rubbed Dame Okra's padded belly and swallowed like one fighting nausea. "The vision pleased me, however. Seraphina, you have helped me whether you meant to or not, and in mere moments you will learn how I've helped you."

There was a knock at the front door.

One of Dame Okra's maids scurried past the library to answer it; after a hushed and hurried exchange of words, the visitor came clumping down the corridor toward us. Jann-Okra pursed her thick lips into a coy smile. I turned to face the door, bracing myself, not sure whom or what we were expecting.

It was Od Fredricka. Her red hair had tangled into an even wilder mane; mud caked her shoes. She stared with wild eyes, as if she hadn't slept in days. She stumbled into the library, clasped her hands to her heart, and fell on her knees at my feet.

"Seraphina. Sister. Thank Allsaints I got here in time," said Od Fredricka, huskily, in Samsamese. "I don't know how to ask your forgiveness. I was awful. I mocked and abused you. I told the monks you were a monster, and they had you followed."

I put a hand to my mouth, horrified. Here was the author of Abdo's heartache.

"I have been alone all my life," she pleaded, cupping her hands as if I might pour forgiveness into them. "I raised a palisade against the world. It kept hurt at bay, but it gave me no option to let kindness in. I did not—could not—believe in your friendship.

"I see now what a lonely life that was," said the painter, groveling at my feet. "I don't want to die alone. I want us all to be together. Forgive me my unjust hostility."

I looked quickly back at Dame Okra, who raised her hands innocently and said in Jannoula's voice, "It's not me animating her. I can't occupy more than one mind at a time. I can't even attend to myself while I'm in Dame Okra's head. For all I know, my body is being eaten by wolves right now."

I ignored her melodrama. "You did something to her. You changed her mind."

"I merely opened a few doors and showed her a truth she had hidden from herself. Her loneliness is her own."

"You did that against her will."

Jannoula shrugged Dame Okra's shoulders. "If it was Od Fredricka's will to be a miserable crank, then her will is an ass. I have no qualms about overriding it."

Od Fredricka did not understand our Goreddi, but she heard her name spoken. She raised her forehead from the floor and said, "What?"

Dame Okra's face went momentarily slack, and then she blinked rapidly, clutching the arms of her chair as if she'd grown weak and dizzy. I watched her intently, wondering if this signaled the end of Jannoula's active possession. It seemed to, but I knew Jannoula's awareness might still be coiled passively in Dame Okra's head, observing everything through her eyes and ears.

Dame Okra rose with dignity and strode around the desk. "My dear, dear friend," she said, taking Od Fredricka's hands and gently urging her to her feet. "I am so pleased we are together at last."

They embraced each other like long-lost sisters. I turned away, a nauseous admixture of emotions stewing in my gut.

This is what I'd wanted, the garden, the half-dragons loving each other like family. But how could I possibly want it now?

Ten

I quit the library, only to find Blanche and Nedouard haunting
the corridor outside, their eyes wide and worried.

"We eavesdropped," whispered Nedouard.

"She have it voice like donkey!" said Blanche. "How is it ghost
in her mind?"

I put my arms around them and walked us back toward the
dining room. "Another half-dragon, called Jannoula, has found a
way to infest the minds of others," I said quietly. "Have either of
you heard her calling?"

Nedouard shook his head vigorously, but Blanche squeaked
in alarm. She reached up and rapped her knuckles on my head. I
understood; Jannoula had said she knocked.

Nedouard said, "Is keeping her out as simple as not answering
the door?"

"Perhaps," I said, although I feared not. Jannoula had tricked

Dame Okra into reaching out. Could all ityasaari reach out with their mind-fire? How many of us did so without realizing it?

Blanche nestled her head against my shoulder and whimpered. Nedouard said, "What does this Jannoula hope to accomplish by invading people's minds?"

"She claims she wants to bring us all together," I said. "Just like me. Beyond that, I'm not sure." I tried to smile, but didn't have the stomach for it. I left the pair of them whispering together, and climbed despondently to my room. I had Samsam to prepare for.

I was to leave the next morning; I saw no way out of it. I went through the motions, helping the housemaids wash my clothes and hang them on a line across the carriage yard, but my mind and heart weren't in it. I fretted.

It seemed futile to protest further against Gianni going to Goredd; Dame Okra was the Ninysh ambassadress, and I couldn't stop her returning to Goredd with Jannoula in her cranium. Kiggs and Glisselda needed to know what was coming. After hanging the laundry, I returned to my room, pulled out my charm necklace, and flipped the tiny switch on the sweetheart knot.

"Castle Orison, identify yourself, if you please," said Glisselda seconds later. She must have been sitting at her desk; this was earlier in the day than I usually called.

"Sera—" I began.

"Phina!" she cried. "How lovely to hear your voice. You're in Segosh? Is Abdo going to be all right?"

Not only had I forgotten to tend my garden, but I'd failed to report to the Queen last night. "He's having surgery. Dame Okra thinks his hand will be restored, but he'll need rest. He'll stay here and return to Goredd in a few weeks."

Glisselda said, "I'm so sorry. We'll take good care of him, I promise."

I was standing at the window, staring down into the street. A troop of Count Pesavolta's men rode past; I changed the subject. "Is Prince Lucian with you?"

"He's out making arrests," she said. "We gave the Sons of St. Ogdo two days to leave town. Most went peaceably, thank Heaven, but a few have decided to make things nasty for our Burrowers—the citizens making our tunnels livable again. The Sons sabotaged some supports and caused a cave-in. A sinkhole swallowed half the apse of St. Jobertus's Church."

"Sweet Heavenly Home!" I cried. "Was anyone hurt? The dragon scholars—"

She laughed unexpectedly. "*New* St. Jobertus's, which was empty at the time. The Sons wouldn't dare crawl around under the old one in Quighole. It's full of quigs," she chirped. "Lucian knows whom he's looking for, but I can't say more over this device. It's not secure enough, although I can't envision a Son of St. Ogdo listening in with a quigutl device of his own. I'd think he would die of irony poisoning."

I emitted a short chuckle. "I would hope so, but fear not."

"There you go," said Glisselda. "That made you laugh. You sounded so grim I'd have thought you were the one slogging through tunnels in darkness."

I felt like I had been, at that. "I have more news," I said, leaning my forehead against the windowpane. I took a deep breath and told her about Jannoula, all of it, from my own struggle to her possession of Gianni Patto. How Jannoula had walked Od Fredricka here from the Pinabra and altered Dame Okra's personality. How she meant to gather all the half-dragons together.

Glisselda was quiet a long time. "Phina, you should have told us," she said at last.

"I'm sorry. I didn't know she'd be back," I said hopelessly. "I didn't know she could find the others, or that she'd want to gather them, or—"

"Of course not," said Glisselda, sounding cross with me now. "That's not what I meant. You should have told us how she hurt you."

"Why?" I asked, my throat tightening.

"Because we're your friends, and we might have helped you bear it," said the Queen. "I know Lucian feels just the same, and if he were here, he'd say so."

It was never my first instinct to tell anyone anything personal. Uncle Orma, my only confidant for years, had been the one person who knew about Jannoula, and he hadn't truly known. He couldn't have understood how it felt.

I forgot that other people might care what went on inside my heart.

Glisselda's words were a comfort, but I'd been more comfortable before she uttered them, when I'd had everything tidily tucked away. Sympathy seemed only to bring all the pain I carried—all the feelings it couldn't address—to the fore.

She was a sharp little Queen; she gleaned something from my

silence. "Tell me," she said, artfully changing tack, "can Jannoula affect everyone's mind like this, or is it limited to ityasaari?"

I stepped back from the window, rubbing my eyes with one hand. "Um. Only ityasaari, as far as I know, or else surely she'd have forced her captors to let her out of prison." I assumed she was still in prison; I hadn't looked in on her for five years.

"What does she want?" asked Glisselda. "However delightful it must be to occupy Gianni Patto's mind, I can't imagine that being an end in itself, can you? She can't mean to spend all her time being other people."

"She meant to occupy me and never leave," I said, my voice quivering.

"But for what? Merely to escape prison, or to use you to some evil purpose? I mean, was she selfish and uncaring, or was she actively malevolent?"

It was the kind of question Lucian Kiggs would have asked. I paced in front of the window, thinking. Was there a difference between doing evil and being evil? I still pitied Jannoula's imprisonment, her pain and torment, and felt guilt for having sent her back to it. If the misery she experienced every day had been warping her sense of right and wrong even during the time I knew her, how much further had it bent her by now?

"I can't believe she's irredeemably bad," I said slowly, "but she'd stop at nothing to escape her imprisonment. Maybe Gianni's mind wasn't ideal for the long term, but she's got Dame Okra now. That's real power. The ambassadress has Count Pesavolta's confidence—and yours."

"Not mine anymore," said Glisselda, "but I see. She's coming back to Goredd."

"They all are—even Od Fredricka—if you still intend to pursue St. Abaster's Trap," I said, sitting on the edge of the bed.

"Do you think we shouldn't?" she asked.

I closed my eyes. I wanted to say, *No, we absolutely shouldn't. We don't know what she'll do.* I didn't trust myself to be fair, however; the problem needed a clearer, more objective set of eyes. I said, "I leave for Samsam tomorrow. I'll keep searching until you call me home. Tell Prince Lucian everything. He'll have ideas. He always does."

"Of course," she said, her voice brightening. "And I charge you not to fret unduly."

"I hear and obey." I smiled in spite of myself; *unduly* gave me room to maneuver.

"I kiss your cheeks," she said, "and Lucian would, too, if he were here."

I switched off the thnik and flopped back onto the bed, trying to gather all my scattered pieces: gladness at Glisselda's stouthearted, unflinching friendship; regret that Kiggs was going to hear my history from someone else; and that particular flavor of sorrow that came over me when I pitied Jannoula. I remembered her burned and blistered arms. To some degree, she could not help what she was, any more than Gianni Patto could. Our history—and my fear—got in the way of my trying to reason with her, but what if Kiggs or Glisselda could earn her trust and cooperation? There had to be some way to make this work.

Unsatisfied, I wrested myself out of bed and went to gather my clothes.

Gianni Patto arrived at Dame Okra's house just after dinner in a doublet and trunk hose fashioned from a tent and with his hair, beard, and eyebrows shaved off. He breathed noisily through his enormous red mouth, and his pale eyes drifted, unfocused. Dame Okra served him a late supper, cooing as she made a lake of gravy in his turnip mash. He was so tall that he sat on the floor, his clawed feet tucked under him, to eat off the table; he had no concept of utensils. Dame Okra spit on a napkin and dabbed at his pasty face. I could watch no more. I went to bed early, citing tomorrow's departure as an excuse, and no one minded that I went.

I washed my scales and tended my garden; I had barely fallen asleep when I was awakened by my window rattling. I opened my eyes blearily, closed them again, and then sat bolt upright as I realized what I'd seen.

Someone was climbing in my window.

Don't be alarmed, said a familiar voice in my head. *It's only me.*

I was on my feet in an instant, rushing to help Abdo climb inside. For a moment we hugged each other tightly, saying nothing; I could feel that his left hand, at the small of my back, was stiffly bandaged. I finally let him go and closed the window. Abdo bounded over and flopped across the end of the bed, grinning enormously.

"I deduce from your unorthodox entry that you made a similarly unauthorized exit from the palasho's infirmary," I said, sitting beside him.

They need more guards in that palasho, said Abdo merrily,

toying with one of his hair knots. *Any determined rascal could get in or out.*

I suspected most rascals would find the palasho walls a more serious impediment.

"I don't like to dampen your enthusiasm," I said, injecting a sisterly sternness into my voice and pointing at his bound wrist, "but I was told that after surgery you're supposed to rest for a few weeks. As much as I want to take you with me, I can't in good conscience drag you to Samsam if your arm—"

Dr. Belestros didn't do the surgery yet, said Abdo, sounding surprised. *He was to do it tomorrow.*

I opened my mouth and then closed it again. Dame Okra had lied to me.

Why? So I would leave without him? So she—or Jannoula—could take him to Goredd and keep an eye on him? Seize his mind at leisure?

Abdo was holding up the limb in question, wrapped from forearm to fingertips. *It doesn't hurt. Anyway, it was fifty-fifty that the surgery would even work. I read his notes.*

"You should give it a chance," I said. "How will you do handstands now?"

One-handed, he said archly. *I want to stay with you, Phina madamina. How will you find your Samsamese ityasaari without me? Who will introduce you to the ityasaari in Porphyry, or persuade them to come south? You can't walk in and order them around.*

I caught a rough note in his voice. "Are you homesick?" I asked. "Because you can have this surgery and then go home on your own."

Not until after I've been dragged back to Goredd by Dame Grumpus. Not until your war is over. His voice grew tearful. *I do miss Porphyry. I miss Auntie Naia, and the sea, and my bed, and eggplant, and . . . That's not even the point. I want to stay with you.*

I took his bandaged hand between mine. "Let's ask Nedouard how hard it will be to care for your wrist while traveling. If he says you can go—"

Abdo pulled away and rushed toward the door. "Quietly!" I whispered loudly, following right on his heels. "I don't want Dame Okra to know you're here." She, or Jannoula, didn't want Abdo coming with me to Samsam.

Nedouard's room was in the attic. Climbing the banisters one-handed barely slowed Abdo down. A light still shone under the doctor's door, and Nedouard answered Abdo's knock at once. The ghostly pale face behind him was Blanche's; her eyes lit up at the sight of Abdo.

"More insomniacs!" cried the doctor. "Come in, come in."

The ceiling sloped under the eaves, making the room feel smaller than it was. Nedouard had moved all his belongings here: bottles, crucibles, stretched glass vessels, apothecary ingredients, and—squirreled away in crannies—a collection of shiny objects.

One of Blanche's mechanical spiders was splayed open on the floor, as if they'd been dissecting it. She noticed me staring at the gears and said, "I am sad to hearing it Josquin be broken. He must to want a spider, need it legs, no? Legs on him."

I nodded tentatively, not sure I understood. Nedouard, his blue eyes gentle above his hooked beak, said, "You are kind to think of him, sister." Blanche smiled minutely and gathered her spider into a sack. Abdo helped her, and she kissed his forehead before quitting the room.

"She's a shy little thing," said Nedouard, rubbing his liver-spotted scalp. "Don't take it personally. How may I help you?"

"We need to know if Abdo is well enough to travel," I said.

Of course I am, Abdo grumped in my head, but Nedouard, not privy to our conversation, pulled up a chair for Abdo and then seated himself on a facing stool. Abdo grudgingly sat and held out his arm.

Nedouard unwrapped the bandages and said, "Lovely."

"Lovely?" I said, bracing myself to look. The midwife at Donques had done her best; Dr. Belestros had removed the stitches, leaving a raised and knotted scar.

"Is it still causing you pain?" said Nedouard. There was a long pause while Abdo spoke in his head. "You're past the danger of infection, but it's going to be stiff." A very long pause. "Your tendons will have formed adhesions in all the wrong places. They'll be the devil to untangle. I'm not sure what Belestros thought he could do, the arrogant dragon." Pause. "Maybe in the Tanamoot. In their own country, the dragons have superior equipment."

Nedouard rose, opened a cabinet, and pulled out ointment and soap. "Above all, keep it clean," he said. "We underestimate the importance of hygiene in the Southlands, and we pay for it dearly." He handed the supplies to Abdo. "Pack these, and then get some sleep. Seraphina, may I speak with you alone?"

"Of course," I said. Abdo looked irritated but did as Nedouard asked. The doctor motioned me to take Abdo's empty seat.

"Blanche didn't need help with her machine—as if I could

have helped. She's scared," said Nedouard in a low voice. "I am, too, and horrified for Dame Okra. Is there nothing we can do for her?"

The question bespoke his kindness. "I don't see how," I said, despairing. "Dame Okra could surely push back against Jannoula, but she seems disinclined to try."

"Is it possible to evict Jannoula from your mind once she's in?" asked the old doctor.

"I did it," I said, "but it was difficult. I had to trick her and build a place to contain her. I'm not sure it would work again; she'd be on guard against it."

"It's reassuring to know it's possible," he said, fidgeting with a button of his doublet. "When I hear Abdo's voice in my mind, there's no way not to hear him. I despair of being able to keep her out when she gets around to me."

"Abdo's voice must be like her knocking," I said, thinking fast. I had not reasoned this out until now. "Abdo can't manipulate your body or hear any thoughts except the ones you direct toward him in answer."

"He doesn't hear thoughts I direct toward him in answer," said Nedouard, sitting up straighter. "I always have to reply aloud."

That had been true of Lars and Dame Okra as well, I suddenly realized. I hadn't thought about it; I'd assumed they'd been answering aloud for my benefit.

Abdo could hear me reply in my head, but then, he was arguably in my mind already. "That's encouraging," I said. "Truly. Maybe Jannoula won't be able to enter any further than that unless you let her in."

Dame Okra hadn't even liked to hear Abdo's voice; she'd found it invasive. I remembered suddenly how Abdo had speculated about altering Dame Okra's memory—did that mean he could enter minds more completely if he chose to, whether he'd been invited in or not? I wasn't sure.

"If you hear Jannoula's voice, don't answer," I said, hoping that would be enough.

"That sounds easy," said Nedouard grimly. "But how was Dame Okra caught out?"

"Her mind reaches out involuntarily," I said. "It gives her prognostications; apparently it also makes her vulnerable. Jannoula was able to seize her."

"Dame Okra never reached out to anyone—in the friendly sense, I mean. She disliked even that much vulnerability," said Nedouard, shaking his bald head. "I confess, I find this intriguing. What makes us the way we are?"

"Dame Okra's prickliness, you mean?" I asked as he stood and crossed the attic room toward his bed. "Or Jannoula's desire to possess other people's minds?"

"Both," said Nedouard. He knelt by his bed and began feeling around under the mattress. "As well as that peculiar fellow who steals things that don't belong to him." He found what he was searching for: a sealed, folded parchment and a small, shiny object. He gazed at them tenderly. "Are we irretrievably broken, Seraphina, or can we be made whole again?"

With trembling hands, he placed the letter and a silver ring set with a tiny pearl in my lap. My heart leaped at the angular handwriting; it was Orma's. I took Nedouard's hands in my own—to still them, to thank him. He pulled away, saying only, "Those arrived while you were traveling. Forgive me."

I enfolded the ring in my hand, and his eyes unlocked from it. "Safe travels," he said.

I kissed his liver-spotted forehead and left. Stars shone through the little window at the bottom of the stairs.

Abdo, asleep, had usurped my bed entirely. It was remarkable how such a small person could require all the blankets.

I lit a lantern with an ember from the hearth and opened the letter. I had barely enough light to read by, but I didn't care. I worked for each word, and the work was a joy.

Eskar reports that you were well when she left, and that you took my suggestion to seek out the ityasaari. I do not know your exact route, but I assume if I send this care of Dame Okra, it will reach you eventually.

I have little news. Eskar has begun courting the exiles here, recruiting them to Comonot's cause. She believes he will change his mind, and she wants to be ready when he does. I don't point out her irrationality, though it gives me a certain satisfaction.

My research continues apace. I am impatient for you to be here. Some things can only be told in person. Eskar thinks I shouldn't write at all, that it is far too risky and impulsive.

I smiled, trying to imagine Uncle Orma being impulsive by any but dragon standards. Orma went on:

I am writing you anyway, because I must chance it. I send along an object. Keep it. It is of the utmost importance. The thing itself plus nothing equals everything.

That was all. I turned the page over; he hadn't even signed his name.

I examined the ring in the lamplight. Was it a quigutl device? If so, I'd have to agree with Eskar about being needlessly risky. He was hiding from the Censors; thniks could be traced. The ring had a single tiny pearl embedded in the silver, but no switch that I could see. The inside was inscribed with nothing but the silversmith's mark. The pearl itself might be the switch. I dared not pinch or press it. I slid the ring onto my index finger, where it jammed at the second knuckle. It fit the pinkie of my right hand. The pearl winked at me.

I would keep it, of course. The reason would surely become clear in time, and the thing itself—plus or minus anything—was lovely.

Abdo gave a fluttering snore. I flopped down beside him gently, or so I thought, but it was enough to disturb him. *Stop,* he muttered, rolling over.

"I need to start reviewing my Porphyrian," I whispered to him. "My tutor taught me a little, but—"

Southlanders can't speak it, said Abdo sleepily. *Too hard for your flimsy foreign minds. There are six genders and seven cases.*

That sounded familiar. I stretched out on the blanketless half of the bed and tried to remember: naive masculine, naive feminine, emergent masculine, emergent feminine, cosmic neuter, point neuter. Nominative, accusative, genitive, dative . . . locative? Evocative? Saints' dogs, I was never any good at this.

Still. Orma was in Porphyry. That was worth all the grammar in the world.

We just had to get through Samsam first.

ᕙᕦ Eleven ᕥᕤ

Abdo and I, in traveling clothes, waited atop the townhouse
steps, shivering in the predawn mist. I'd gathered our baggage as silently as possible; I hadn't seen Dame Okra and hoped
to keep it that way.

Between Nedouard and sleepiness, I hadn't told Abdo about
Jannoula last night. I was trying to explain now. "You remember
how Gianni Patto's mind was a strange color? It was mixed up
with a second ityasaari's—Jannoula's. She possessed him and
made him do her bidding."

I know that name, said Abdo, twisting his mouth as he considered.

"The lady I banished from my garden," I reminded him.

His eyes widened. *That was Jannoula? Back home, in Porphyry,
she gets into other ityasaari's minds, and the old priest, Paulos Pende,
pulls her back out.*

I gaped at him, stunned. "H-how long has this been going on?"

Abdo made a rude sound through his lips, like a snorting horse. *I don't know. She's a nuisance, really. Pende grabs her, like plucking off a tick. He showed me how.*

Before I could question him further, a cacophony of thudding hooves interrupted us. Around the corner rode our Samsamese escort: an old hunter in stained leathers with an evil-looking knife strapped to his leg and a grizzled braid down his back; behind him, leading four more horses, came a dark-haired bravo in crisp Samsamese black, a rapier at his side and a smirk on his lips.

The Regent of Samsam, famously stingy, had sent us only two men. I hoped they would be enough to protect us from the famously intolerant Samsamese.

The younger man waved and called loudly enough to make me cringe: "Goodt day, *grausleine*! Our Regent sends us to bring you—and your little boy—to Samsam."

You're a little boy, said Abdo, folding his skinny arms.

The men pulled up in front of the house. "I am Rodya," said the young swordsman jovially, impervious to Abdo's glare. "My comrade, Hanse, is the quiet one—ha!—but be assuredt, we are men of ability and reliability." He seemed unduly pleased with this wording. "The Regent toldt us to get you to the Erlmyt by St. Abaster's Day, and so we will, swift and safe." He tapped a fist against his heart. "Thet is our promise."

St. Abaster's Day was only a fortnight off. I hoped he was right.

Hanse, the old hunter, had silently dismounted and was

strapping our small luggage to the packhorse; he nodded his promise. I nodded back.

Rodya tried to help Abdo onto a horse. Abdo ducked under the horse, mounted from the other side, and grinned down at Rodya's befuddlement. Rodya wasn't the only one confused; the horse seemed spooked by the maneuver, snorting and circling, but Abdo stroked its mane and laid his cheek upon its neck to calm it.

"Eh, you know horses already! Goodt!" said Rodya, laughing it off. He turned to help me onto my horse, and I let him, out of pity.

"So you had no intention of saying goodbye?" shrilled a voice behind us. Dame Okra loomed at the top of the steps, glaring vitriol, arms akimbo. "Abdo can't go with you. He's hurt."

Oh yes, it's much clearer on her than it was on the wild man, said Abdo sagely, pursing his lips. *His soul-light was hazy, but she's got two colors, twisted around each other. It should just be a matter of—*

"Abdo, don't!" I cried, but it was too late. He'd been talking and reaching out to her at the same time, and now he clutched at his head with both hands, as if in pain. I wished I had his mindsight, or any glimpse of what passed, unspoken, between him and Dame Okra. Her expression, always volatile, ran from horror to pain to triumph to horror again in seconds. She staggered back, her spaniel eyes bulging, her mouth a terrible crooked line.

"All right, then," she gasped, staring at nothing, her face a pale green. "Travel. Good. It is well." She limped back into the house.

I looked at Abdo. His face was ashen. One of his hair knots had come undone, as if he'd had a physical altercation; the incongruous corkscrew flopped across his forehead.

Abdo, speak to me! I cried, my heart pounding. *Did Jannoula seize you?*

He turned his head sideways and shook it, like a swimmer with water in his ear, or like he was trying to hear Jannoula rattling around in there. He said, *No. I fought her off.*

I exhaled shakily. What little training the temple had given Abdo had put him far ahead of any Southlander ityasaari, as far as I could tell. No one else could see mind-fire or speak in people's heads; he'd worked out how to create St. Abaster's Trap essentially on his own. If anyone could fend off Jannoula, surely it was he.

Still, I couldn't help feeling he'd been extremely lucky just now.

His gaze had turned sheepish. *I couldn't unhook her from Dame Okra, though. I don't see why not. The principle is sound.*

Maybe you can ask this priest when we get to Porphyry, I said.

No thanks, said Abdo sourly. *He'd only tell me I need more training.*

"All right," I said aloud, trying to gather myself. "It's time we departed."

Hanse, the old hunter, had been watching without expression, scratching his stubbly chin, waiting for us to finish messing around. Young Rodya translated my words, and the older man nodded, turned his horse west, and led us out the city gates, across country toward Samsam.

Barring another surprise like Gianni Patto, I believed there was only one ityasaari in Samsam: a middle-aged man, bald, stout, and square-spectacled. With his clothes on, he looked hunchbacked; I'd had the dubious privilege of looking in on him while he was bathing, and knew he had a pair of vestigial wings, membranous like a bat's, carefully folded against his back. In my garden, I called him the Librarian because I'd never seen him without a book in his hand—not even in the bath. He lived in a crumbling mansion in a dismal valley where it always seemed to be raining.

"Thet is the Samsamese highlands," Lars had said when I'd described it to him, two days before our journey began.

"The highlands are enormous," I'd said, looking at the map spread on Viridius's worktable. "Can you narrow it down if I give you more details? There's a village within walking distance, and a river, and—"

Lars laughed, slapping the table with a beefy hand. "All great houses are near a village and a river. We have a proverb: 'In high-landts, every man is earl of his own valley.' Thet means a lot of valleys. Also, means a rude joke in Samsamese."

"I don't think I need that one spelled out," I said.

"Even the valleys have valleys, Phina. You couldt be looking for months." He jabbed a finger at the southern edge of the up-lands. "Thet is why you need to come here, to Fnark, where is St. Abaster's tomb. On St. Abaster's Day all the earls come down for their council, the Erlmyt."

"Just the one day?" With the vagaries of travel, it might be hard to arrive so promptly.

"It can last a week, or a few weeks, but thet is not guaranteed.

On St. Abaster's Day it begins. Then you see all the earls together, and find the one you're looking for."

"How are you so sure he's an earl?"

His gray eyes twinkled. "Who else in highlandts can afford so many books?"

"What if he doesn't come to this meeting?" I said. "He seems a solitary sort."

Lars shrugged his bulky shoulders. "Then perheps another earl will know him. It still saves you months of looking. It is your best chance."

I hadn't had the nerve to ask Lars the other question that immediately came to mind: *What if your half brother, Josef, Earl of Apsig, is at the meeting?* Josef and I had not parted on good terms after the events of midwinter; he despised half-dragons, and I was none too fond of would-be assassins.

If Earl Josef was at the Erlmyt, if he learned that the Librarian was my fellow half-dragon . . . I hardly dared contemplate the trouble that might cause.

It would be an exaggeration to say that the sky clouded over the moment we crossed the Samsamese border—but not by much.

Over the next fortnight, as we hastened toward Fnark past muddy pastures and rocky fields of rye, I tried not to think about Earl Josef at all, although my experience with him surely tempered my treatment of our Samsamese guides. I didn't trust them. The Eight, from relatively tolerant Ninys, had had enough unease about traveling with two half-dragons. There was no question in my mind that Hanse and Rodya, hailing from St. Abaster's homeland, should be kept in the dark about us. The Regent apparently had not told them we were seeking a half-dragon; they only knew that we needed to make it to the Erlmyt on time. I wasn't going to tell them otherwise.

I didn't admit I spoke Samsamese, erring ruthlessly on the side of caution.

It rained each night and misted every morning; in the afternoons, it poured. We stayed at inns, when there were inns, but half the time we camped. Everything we owned grew steadily damper. The ends of our fingers were wrinkled as a matter of course; I could hardly bear to examine my toes. At least it wasn't cold; St. Abaster's Day falls at the point where spring has its first inklings of summer.

Rodya, in an oiled cloak and broad hat rimmed with dangling droplets, was a ceaseless font of drippy cheer. "In Samsam we hev two seasons: rain and snow. Is better along the coast. One week sunshine every summer!"

If he tells one more joke about rain, I'm going to drown myself in it, said Abdo, slumping in the saddle. I wasn't enjoying the weather, but it seemed to affect him even more. *All it would take, surely, is to look up with my mouth open—*

How do you say "He talks too much" in Porphyrian? I asked hastily, trying to distract Abdo from his misery. I hazarded a guess, no doubt butchering the pronunciation.

Abdo gave me the expected fish-eye, but for an unexpected reason: *Wrong gender. You use cosmic neuter for a stranger.*

I glanced at Rodya; he leaned to one side and spat on the ground. *He's not a stranger anymore. If ever anyone embodied naive masculine, surely Rodya—*

You use cosmic neuter for a stranger, Abdo insisted. *And he's a stranger until you've asked, "How may I pronoun you?"*

But you told me cosmic neuter was the gender of gods and eggplant, I protested, unsure why I was arguing with a native speaker about his own language.

People may choose it, said Abdo. *But it's polite for strangers. You may be almost sure he's not an eggplant, but he might still be some agent of the gods.*

Abdo enjoyed correcting my grammar, but distraction only went so far, and I began to wonder whether the rain was really the problem. For hours each day he stared into the gray and rubbed the dark, knotty scar on his wrist. He didn't eat properly—not that I blamed him. The Samsamese are overly fond of cabbage and lumpy gravy. I berated myself for letting him come; after the first week, I was convinced he was unwell. When I asked him, he just shrugged listlessly.

I was keeping scrupulous track of the days. St. Siucre's Day, St. Munn's, and Scaladora, our day for remembering fallen knights, all passed with abundant drizzle and little fanfare. St. Abaster's Day dawned sunny, which seemed portentous, and soon after breakfast we crested a hill and got our first look at the Samsamese highlands. They rose abruptly out of the plain ahead, an imposing green tableland speckled with sturdy sheep and scrubby yellow gorse. The rain, over centuries, had battered the plateau and carved great grooves in its face; outcroppings of rock jutted forth like exposed bones. The clouds above loomed darker; gray streaks of rain trailed beneath them like an old woman's hair.

Hanse pointed to the southern end of the formation. "Fnark is beyond those bluffs," he said in Samsamese. "We should arrive the day after tomorrow."

Rodya needlessly translated this into Goreddi for me. I replied, "We're late."

"Oh, is not a worry," said Rodya, waving off my irritation. "The earls do not meet for only one day. Most of the earls might not even be there yet. Nobody comes on time."

I clamped my mouth shut, knowing that railing at him wasn't going to get us there any faster, but I surely wanted to. I tried to catch Abdo's eye, to share my pique with him at least, but he stared into the middle distance at nothing.

Fnark, two days later, was larger than I'd imagined, large enough to have streets and visible industry—a pottery and warehouses along the river. The houses abutted each other, end to end, sharing roof tiles; church spires punctured the sky. We crossed the river on an arched stone bridge and passed the market square, where intrepid merchants clustered together under the thatched shelter like cattle under a pasture tree.

In this climate, I supposed, if you wouldn't shop in the rain, you didn't shop at all.

Along the river road north, toward the rising tablelands, stood a walled complex resembling a Ninysh-style palasho. As we passed its iron gates, I saw that it was a shrine—and no small roadside shrine, but an enormous complex. Within its walls was everything a pilgrim could want: dormitories, souvenir stalls, chapels, and eateries. Rain fell on empty tables outside.

The place looked abandoned; I felt my irritation rising again. "You said the earls would be here all week," I said quietly to Rodya.

He shrugged. "They must be inside. We Samsamese are hardy, but thet don't mean we stand around in the rain."

Or maybe the earls had already gone home. If the meeting was of no fixed length, surely it sometimes ran short. I gritted my teeth and followed Hanse up the cobbled road toward the hulking church at the top of the hill.

We tied our horses and entered. The great church was empty but for a cluster of bedraggled pilgrims at the front, led in song by a priest. I knew the tune, a drinking song in Goredd, but it had very different lyrics here:

> *O faithless ignoramus, denier of Heaven*
> *Sitting smugly upon a disbelieving bottom*
> *O blatant person who disregards the scriptures*
> *Standing confidently in a puddle of sin*
> *There shall be smiting with lightning*
> *And blood-soaked retribution*
> *And heads kicked about like footballs*
> *And much worse upon your wretched person*
> *When Golden Abaster returns with judgment for you*
> *And salvation in the form of flowers for the rest of us*

Rodya was humming along; Hanse gravely removed his hat and placed it over his heart. Abdo leaned against a smooth pillar and closed his eyes.

The priest was surely the person to ask about whether we'd missed the earls. While he finished the service and administered St. Abaster's blessing to the crowd, I drifted around the church. After Ninys, where the churches had been frothing with architectural froufrou, this plain church came almost as a shock. The Samsamese called their own doctrine austere, but I hadn't realized doctrine could be reflected in decor. There were no statues, no pictures, no ornaments of any kind, only stone inscriptions in severe square lettering.

I read a few. *Under this plate lie the mortal remains of St. Abaster, who will return in glory and . . .* Ugh. More smiting. I didn't care to be this near St. Abaster, even dead. *Thus said St. Abaster: "Tolerate not the infidel, the unchaste woman, the permissive man, the dragon and his hideous spawn . . ."* I didn't read to the end of that one, but counted fifty-three intolerables in all.

There was one plaque I did read to the end, however, because it was short and the names—easily translated—caught my eye. *The blessed are not exempt from judgment. St. Abaster righteously smote: St. Masha, St. Daan, St. Tarkus, St. Pandowdy, St. Yirtrudis.*

St. Yirtrudis, my heretical psalter Saint, struck me first, but they weren't all heretics in this list. St. Masha and St. Daan were known and commonly invoked in Goredd; they'd been lovers, two men, martyred by other Saints, but they'd retained their blessed status. St. Tarkus and St. Pandowdy, on the other hand, I had never heard of—although I'd named my most monstrous grotesque, the one I'd decided not to look for, Pandowdy.

Pandowdy was also a pudding my Ninysh stepmother made. An ugly, mushy, steamed monstrosity, all suet and raisins. Those raisins, slimy and swollen with brandy, had inspired me to name the monster after the dessert. How odd to think of a Saint with the same name.

Yirtrudis, though. Her inclusion here was strange to me. I knew so little about her that any new detail was interesting. I'd never heard Goreddis claim that St. Abaster had smote her, but then, we weren't as into smiting as our neighbors, it seemed.

The last of the pilgrims received her portion of charcoal, another curious practice—these Samsamese were mysterious to me, for all that we prayed to the same Saints. Then the priest finally turned to us, his faint brows raised in mild surprise. Rodya and Hanse both knelt for and received his blessing. I held back, my arms folded.

"I had understood the Erlmyt would be held here," I said in Goreddi, letting Rodya translate into Samsamese.

The priest grunted. "Not this year."

I'd expected to hear *You just missed them,* although I'd fervently hoped for *They're here, but you didn't look in the right place.* I did not know what to make of this news at all. I blurted out, "Why not?"

He scowled deeply. "Do you want a blessing or not?"

Rodya leaped to his feet and actually drew his sword. In a church. I goggled at him.

"Answer her question," he drawled. "She represents the Gorshya Queen."

"I don't care if she represents Heaven itself," said the priest. "I have nothing to tell, except that half our yearly tithe comes from the Erlmyt, and we were given no notice and no explanation."

My heart sank. Now how would I find the Librarian? Lars had suggested it could take months to scour the highlands, but we were due in Porphyry by midsummer. I couldn't justify taking that much time to look for one man when there were seven ityasaari more easily found in Porphyry. We gathered Abdo, who had curled up in a ball at the base of the column, resting his head upon his folded arms, and stepped back out into the rain.

We stayed the night at the shrine's dormitories, which were strictly separated by sex. Abdo was clearly unwell. I argued with the monks, insisting that he was a child and I was his guardian and had to stay close and take care of him. After much grumbling, the monks finally conceded, allowing us both to stay in the infirmary. We were the only ones there, or I'd have complained a great deal more.

Abdo flopped onto a cot with his clothes on, like a Goreddi would have. He didn't change into his sleep tunic or wrap his sleep scarf around his head, like he normally did. I sat on the next cot, elbows on my knees, and watched him, worrying. His breathing evened out, and I thought he was asleep.

I closed my eyes, weary in my very soul.

I had never particularly felt like the Saints watched over me, but St. Abaster did seem to be dogging my footsteps on this journey, to my dismay. I was no great hand at scripture—I avoided most of it—but I knew every line written about my kind, thanks to the pamphlet Orma had made me. "Half human, all malevolence" was one of Abaster's best. Or: "If a woman hath lain with the beast, beat her with a mallet until she miscarries or dies. Let it be both, lest her horrifying issue live to claw its way out, or the woman live to conceive evil again."

"Darling old St. Abaster," I muttered into my hands. "I love you, too."

He smote people for that kind of sarcasm, said a voice in my head. It wasn't Abdo's voice, although I could feel, distinctly, that it came from Abdo's avatar in my garden.

I looked up. Abdo's eyes were open; his mouth quirked into a sly, familiar smile.

I gripped the edge of my cot, wrestling visceral horror. "Abdo said he'd escaped you," I said, working to keep my voice steady.

Of course I let him think that, said Jannoula, making Abdo sit up. She stuck his scaly tongue in and out of his mouth. *Feh. He really can't talk. I thought he was exaggerating.*

"He hasn't been completely unaware of you," I said, suddenly making sense of his ongoing preoccupation. He had been struggling with her.

Struggling alone. Why hadn't he told me?

His mind is entirely different, she said. *He has such facility with mind-fire. More than the others.* She flexed his fingers and toes experimentally, frowning at the fingers that wouldn't bend. *A mighty mind trapped in a small, inadequate body.*

"If he's so mighty, how did your consciousness gain ascendancy?" I asked.

He has to sleep sometime. I've just been rifling through his memories, and it looks like you've reached a dead end today. You could use my help, said Jannoula.

"You've possessed him while he's defenseless," I said, my voice rising. "I don't want this kind of help."

Careful, he'll wake up if you shout, or if I move him too violently. Abdo's dark eyes looked at me sidelong as if to underscore that last word. Was that a threat?

I only want to help you find the others, dear sweet Seraphina, she said, her voice syrupy. *You're looking for Ingar, Earl of Gasten—the one you call the Librarian. You'd know his name if you could reach out to him properly. All you can do is watch, alas. It's rather feeble.*

I plastered on a smile. "I'm lucky to have you, then."

Quite right, she said. *He's in Blystane, at the court of the Regent.*

"What's he doing there?" I asked. "And how do I know you're not sending me on some wild-goose chase?"

Jann-Abdo scowled. *Always so suspicious. Our goal is one and the same, Seraphina. Waste your time combing the bald hills, if you prefer, or else have the courtesy to take me at my word.*

I saw her melt from Abdo's face, replaced by a look of repugnance and horror. *Oh no,* he said, and it was him, wide awake. *Oh gods, no.*

I was at his side in an instant, sitting by him on the cot, my arms around him while he sobbed into my shoulder. *I couldn't . . . I didn't . . .*

"Why didn't you tell me you were struggling with her?" I asked into his hair.

Because it was my own stupid fault, and because I thought I could get rid of her myself, and you'd never need to know.

There was nothing I could say to comfort him. I held him in silence as long as he would let me, my own tears falling on his dear head.

Twelve

I waited until the next morning to report our change of course to Glisselda and Kiggs. "We're heading to Blystane," I said into the sweetheart knot thnik. Abdo, who clearly had not slept well, lay listlessly on the cot opposite. "Our ityasaari has gone to the capital to visit the Regent, I'm told."

"You trust this intelligence?" Kiggs's voice crackled.

Abdo straightened quickly in alarm. *Don't tell them, madamina. Please!*

He was ashamed that Jannoula had invaded his mind; I knew what that was like. I tried to be reassuring. *I won't mention you, but they need to know she's interfering.*

"It was Jannoula who told me," I said. "And no, I don't trust her. This is the only lead I have right now, however."

There was a long silence from the royal cousins. I kept my eye on Abdo, who had flopped back on the cot and wrapped his arms around his head. Kiggs and Selda were no doubt asking themselves, *How could Phina have heard from Jannoula out there in gloomy Samsam with only Abdo and two Samsamese for company?*

I hoped they'd conclude that Abdo had been taken and trust that I had good reason not to say so aloud. Jannoula could be coiled passively in his head, listening to everything we were saying. "That's all my news at present," I added, trying to emphasize the unspoken point.

Glisselda cleared her throat. "In *similar* news, Dame Okra and the others arrived from Ninys yesterday. They seem well. Dame Okra is in her usual good mood."

"We've arranged for the ityasaari to stay together in the south wing, where they will be comfortably secure," said Kiggs. "If they need anything, we can attend to them at once."

So they were keeping the ityasaari under guard and carefully watched. I supposed, short of canceling the whole project and sending everyone home, that was the safest way to proceed. I said, "It sounds like you're accounting for all contingencies."

"It's just as well that you're going to Blystane. We've heard nothing from the Regent in ten days," said Glisselda. "Maybe his thnik stopped working, or ... I scarcely dare think what. The knights at Fort Oversea have heard nothing from the capital, either."

"If something has happened, we need eyes on the ground," said Kiggs. "Report back at once."

"I will," I said. I wanted to ask for more detail—didn't they have spies in the capital?—but couldn't with Abdo within hearing. Saints' bones, this was going to be a problem. How could I talk to them—or him—openly?

"We need to go, Seraphina," said Glisselda abruptly.

"Grandmother has taken a significant turn for the worse," said Kiggs.

"I'm so sorry," I said. And then they were gone.

Abdo and I gathered our bags and headed for the stables. Abdo lagged behind, his feet dragging. The air was full of fine mist; buildings and trees hulked in the gloom.

"Has she troubled you this morning?" I asked Abdo quietly, waving at Rodya, who stood in the stable's entrance, arms akimbo.

She's not active right now, Abdo said, *but she's never entirely gone, either. I'm like a fish caught on a line; her hook is in me, and I can't get it out.*

We were too near Rodya to continue this discussion aloud. *There must be a way to unhook you,* I said. *We'll find it.*

Abdo took my hand and squeezed it hard.

The road to Blystane was straight and well maintained compared with others we'd traveled in Samsam, but halfway there we lost half our escort.

We were camping. I was alone in the tent, naked from the waist up, washing the scales around my midriff, when the tent flap rustled behind me. I assumed it was Abdo coming in before I'd finished my nightly ablutions. I turned, intending to ask for a few more minutes to myself, and met a different pair of black eyes behind me.

It was Rodya, staring in horror at the silver dragon scales across my back.

He screamed and scrambled backward away from me, knocking over the tent pole. The tent collapsed. My wash water spilled all over the bedrolls as I thrashed around. I kicked over the lantern, causing a brief flare-up, but the damp canvas smothered the flame. It seemed likely to smother me as well. Outside, Rodya screamed hysterically. Finally, a pair of calm, strong hands began pulling one end of the tent, dragging it off me. I rolled onto the wet ground.

I folded my arms, covering what I could, but my wide girdle of silver scales encircled me all the way around. Hanse stood over me, his creased face inscrutable, the canvas flung over his shoulder. Behind him, Rodya was practically dancing in the firelight. "There! See? What is she? A demon? A saar?"

"What are you, *grausleine*?" said Hanse in surprisingly clear Goreddi.

"My mother was a dragon," I said, my teeth chattering.

Hanse raised his eyebrows. "And the boy?"

I nodded. "Is also half dragon."

Then Rodya screamed again. Abdo had pulled a smoldering branch out of the fire and whacked him one-handed across the back of the knees with it. Rodya collapsed.

I saw him wander away from the fire. I should have hit him then, Abdo said grimly, hitting Rodya again while he was down.

I scrambled to put on my shirt, which had fallen on the damp, muddy ground. Rodya hadn't brought his weapon into my tent, which was lucky; by the time I looked up again, he'd scrambled to his feet and was chasing Abdo around the fire. Abdo wouldn't have stood a chance against the sword. Even now, Rodya came perilously close to catching him. Abdo dodged and rolled, trying to keep the fire between them.

Hanse watched in silence, sucking in his cheeks, coming to some conclusion of his own. As Rodya ran past, trying to catch Abdo, Hanse grabbed him by the shirt collar, wheeled him around, and punched him in the mouth.

"You saw her!" shrieked Rodya in Samsamese. "How can you take her part?"

"No, you saw her when you shouldn't have," said Hanse. "Did you not listen to your mother's stories, boy? Never spy on strange maidies bathing." He belted Rodya again. "They're always the ones who turn out to be other than they seem."

Rodya, his horse, and his things were gone by morning. Hanse would barely speak to me; that wasn't new, but in light of recent events and without Rodya to fill the awkward silences, it was hard to take. It seemed we had one or two things we might have spoken about. *I just pray we don't miss Rodya's sword*, I told Abdo as we packed to go.

Rodya's lucky to have a sword after last night, he said, mounting his horse.

Hanse guided us toward the coastal plain, and the rain grew less constant. The drama with Rodya and the occasional appearance of the sun perked Abdo up for a few days, but it didn't last. He wasn't sleeping well; his eyes looked sunken. Around us the landscape flattened into broad farms, cultivated with barley and flax; columnar poplars lined both sides of the road, their round leaves shivering anxiously in the breeze.

The crenellated walls of Blystane finally came into sight one afternoon. The cathedral spire rose above all, but I also discerned a fortress, bristling with towers, which I took to be the seat of government. The city had leaked out of its walls and puddled upon the surrounding plain. There was even a tent village to the north, which struck me as curious—and uncomfortable in soggy weather.

Hanse reined in his horse; I pulled up alongside and gave him a questioning look.

"Your destination," said Hanse, his eyes unaccountably sad. "You'll arrive within three hours, if you don't dawdle. Well before sunset."

"You're not coming with us?" I asked.

He scratched his bristly chin. "I can tell you are a decent person, *grausleine*, and I could not abandon you in the middle of nowhere, with no idea of your way forward. But I also cannot . . ." He paused so long I wasn't sure he was going to continue.

In fact, he wasn't. He turned his horse around and motioned us to be on our way. Abdo and I rode on, incredulous, turning to watch him over our shoulders. He did not look back as he rode away.

So he took Rodya's part after all, said Abdo.

"He followed his conscience," I said slowly, considering, "even when it went against his conscience."

We spurred our steeds forward in somber silence.

The closer we drew, the less haphazard the tent village looked. The tents were laid out in an orderly fashion, many with identical blue and black stripes, many flying banners; there were horses and armed men and cook fires. *Abdo,* I said silently, *what's going on here?*

It looks like an army, he said.

I thought so, too, but why was an army camped outside Blystane? I scanned the sky for smoke and strained my ears for cries, but there were none. A steady stream of farmers, merchants, and drovers passed us. The city seemed to be in no distress.

We were stopped at the city gate by guards in somber attire and questioned about our business. "We are envoys from Queen Glisselda of Goredd to His Grace the Regent of Samsam," I said, fully expecting that to suffice. I had papers—only slightly damp—if he required more proof.

The guard, a mustachioed fellow with a distractingly pointy helmet, pursed his lips prissily. "Do you mean His Grace the Honored and Honorable Steadfast Servant of St. Abaster, Heaven's Regent Until the Return, Harald Erstwhile Earl of Plimpi?"

"I suppose so," I said. In Goredd, we never used his full title. I began to see why.

"You suppose wrong," said the guardsman nastily. "He is no more—Saints judge him justly. Goredd won't have heard that yet, it seems."

The worst was confirmed. It took all my years of lying practice, plus the reserves of heraldic nerve I'd gained in Ninys, to appear unfazed. I looked down my nose at him and arched an eye-brow superciliously. "I'll trot home and tell our Queen then, shall I? See how she wants me to proceed?"

"I'm only telling you for your own good," he said, backtracking on his nastiness now that I'd shown myself uncowed. "You wouldn't want to exhibit unseemly surprise when you meet our new ruler, His Grace the Honored and Honorable Steadfast Servant of St. Abaster, Heaven's Regent Until the Return, Josef Erstwhile Earl of Apsig."

That news almost knocked me off my horse.

Two gatehouse guards escorted us through the city to the castle—for our protection, they said. It was just as well, because I was too shocked to listen to directions. It took me half the length of the city to regain my wits. We passed half-timbered shop fronts and brick houses, all reassuringly solid. The cobbled streets were mostly empty, but I saw no sign that violence had occurred, or that the people were afraid.

So why was there an army outside? Had it been a peaceful succession? Had the old Regent died of anything resembling natural causes? I remembered Josef's words the last time I'd seen him, that he was going to "make the Regent see sense . . . the kind that puts humans first over animals." I should've told Kiggs or Glisselda what he'd said to me that day. I'd been so intimidated that I'd inadvertently kept a secret. I hoped we weren't about to pay for my silence.

Goredd had had an ally in the old Regent. Josef was not nearly so predictable.

Our pointy-helmeted gatehouse guards accompanied us into the castle, all the way to the throne room, obviously keeping an eye on us.

The throne room, like St. Abaster's Church in Fnark, reflected a Samsamese sensibility: dark wood paneling, tall glazed windows, perpendicular lines. What decor there was consisted of hunting trophies, including a grand chandelier of interwoven antlers, like the nest of some unfathomable eagle. At the far end of the hall, upon a dais, stood an alabaster throne, reserved for the blessed bottom of St. Abaster, should he make good on his threat to return. Beside it squatted the Regent's modest chair of burnished wood, and before that was Josef, erstwhile Earl of Apsig, St. Abaster's current deputy in this world.

I recognized him at once, dressed in his usual austere black doublet and white ruff. His blond hair was longer than he used to keep it; he tucked an itinerant lock behind his ear while I watched. He stood facing a long side bench, intended for counselors but mostly empty now, speaking quietly with the two people seated there.

The guards did not traverse the room but positioned themselves on each side of the door, breastplates clanking noisily, and waved us along. They would be blocking our exit. My heart quailed, but I took Abdo's hand and led him the length of the hall, toward Josef and the others.

One of the people sitting on the bench was a bald, paunchy hunchback, dressed in a short brown houppelande cut to fit his odd figure. He glanced at us; I knew those square spectacles. It was the Librarian, whom Jannoula had called Ingar. That was fortuitous.

The second figure was a woman in a plain green surplice. Her head, perched on a swan-like neck, looked strangely small because of her short brown hair. Her fine-boned frame and porcelain complexion made her look fragile.

She looked up, directly into my eyes.

It was Jannoula.

Impossible. My mind rejected the notion outright—she was in prison, she couldn't be here.

I glanced at Abdo, who had let go of me and was waving a hand in front of his face, as if shooing away invisible flies. He noticed me looking and said sheepishly, *This close to her, I can see the line she's caught me with. It doesn't dissipate if I put my hand through it, though.* He gestured toward Ingar with his bandaged hand. *She's got a line connecting him as well.*

What comfort denial might have given me turned cold. How was this possible? What was she doing here? Had she been imprisoned in Samsam, and Josef let her out?

Josef followed Jannoula's gaze and saw me. His handsome face broke into a sneer. "Seraphina! Now this is a surprise," he said in flawless Goreddi.

I gave long, slow courtesy, stalling. It was hard enough to face Josef again, but Jannoula's presence rattled me even more. "I come as Queen Glisselda's envoy," I said.

"She must be terribly hard up if she's sending you," he said, sauntering toward us. Josef had the same pointed nose as his half brother, but Lars never flared his nostrils so disdainfully.

"What have you done?" I asked Josef, my eyes involuntarily darting toward Jannoula. Perhaps the question was for her, too;

I couldn't get over the fact that she was here. I forced myself to focus on the new Regent. "Is that your army outside?"

"It is," said Josef, smiling tightly. "And what I've done is very simple. I marched on the capital. The Regent, believing my troops were intended to help fulfill our promises to Goredd, let me walk right in. And now he is dead."

"The capital, the court . . . had nothing to say about this?" I said.

"My brother earls might have been a thorn in my side, had they demanded consensus, but their Erlmyt was canceled due to rumors of plague in Fnark." Josef exchanged a significant look with Jannoula. "By the time they learn what has happened, it will be a history lesson, not news."

I stared hard at Jannoula, wondering what that look had meant. Had the rumor of plague been her idea? Was she advising Josef?

She stared back brazenly.

"I've sent messengers to the earls," Josef was saying. "They'll know in two days, and they'll have no choice but to accept it. I can't inform Ninys yet, since Count Pesavolta is bound to tell Goredd. Queen Glisselda is not to know until the time of my choosing."

"Which is when?" I asked, tearing my gaze away from Jannoula. "When she needs Samsam's aid and you're not there?"

"Goredd has allied itself with dragons," said Josef, tossing his hair out of his eyes. "A true follower of the Saints, any real Samsamese, cannot countenance that. I have Heaven on my side,

Seraphina. Not only the valedictions of St. Ogdo and the strictures of St. Abaster, but the endorsement of a holy hermit."

I glanced at Ingar in some confusion. Josef noticed where I looked and said, "Not him. He's her disciple. Allow me to introduce Sister Jannoula." He held out an arm toward her. She lowered her gaze and rose with a bashful curtsy.

We came to it at last. I folded my arms, unimpressed by Jannoula's bashful act. By the look in Josef's eyes, he was clearly smitten—though religiously or romantically, I wasn't sure. Maybe it was too fine a distinction to make.

She was no holy anything. I couldn't fathom how this charade of hers connected to her gathering of the ityasaari.

"Well, you've thoroughly fooled the new Regent," I said aloud, addressing her as if it were just the two of us, still in my head. As if we were old acquaintances. Josef would surely wonder about that. "Does a prison cell count as a hermitage now?"

"How dare you?" cried Josef, stepping between us.

Jannoula lay a hand on his elbow. "Please, Your Grace. I can defend myself from unbelievers."

"I've seen miracles," said Josef stoutly. "I've glimpsed the light of Heaven blazing around her, you soulless fiend."

I met Jannoula's eye and held it; she hadn't told the new Regent that she was my fellow soulless fiend, it seemed. I had the advantage. I said, "It's true that one of my parents was a dragon." I pointed at Josef's holy hermit and her walleyed sidekick, Ingar the Librarian. "It's true of them as well."

"You lie!" cried Josef.

I held my tongue, waiting to see how Jannoula would play this, trying to glean something of her purpose from how she treated the new Regent. Her face was inscrutable, a mask.

It was Ingar who broke the silence. "Is this not glorious, Blessed?" he said in Samsamese, clasping his fat hands together. "This is what we've been waiting for, the others of our kind."

Josef turned the tiniest bit green. He swiveled slowly to face Jannoula and said, "Explain yourself."

Her face became the picture of mournful contrition. I knew that face well; my heart hardened against it. She bowed her head and said, "Seraphina tells the truth, my lord. I . . . I did not wish you to know. I feared you would reject me, as so many have before. I was imprisoned for what I am, by people who could not see beyond it."

She undid the silver buttons along the sides of her sleeves and then rolled the material back from her forearms. Even though I knew what I would see, the pity and horror of that day came back to me in a rush; apparently my heart was not as hard as I'd believed. Josef stared at the knotted, scarred skin where she'd been burned.

"They peeled off my scales," she said softly, "and sealed the wounds with white-hot iron."

I clapped a hand to my mouth. She'd never told me that part.

Her eyes glittered with unshed tears. "Heaven pitied me, and I lost consciousness. That's when I saw the Saints, who spoke to me and blessed me."

Josef's sharp face had softened into sorrow. He was moved by her story and looked more sympathetic—dare I say human?—

than I'd ever seen him. As I watched, his expression changed again; his eyes widened in awe and his mouth fell open. He gasped and dropped to his knees, his gaze transfixed on the air around and above Jannoula.

Ye gods, said Abdo, plainly awed. *Her mind-fire is . . . it's a conflagration.*

Of course I could see nothing. *Is she manipulating his mind?*

Abdo tilted his head sideways, studying the situation. *Not the way you mean; she's not hooked into him the way she's hooked into Ingar or me. It's something else.*

"Forgive me, Blessed," said Josef, touching the hem of her gown. "Clearly, the Saints chose you in spite of your heritage."

"Or because of it," she said, eyeing him narrowly. "To teach you a lesson."

"Then I will endeavor to be humble and learn it," he said. He bowed his head and clasped his hands. "As St. Kathanda wrote, 'Even the most grotesque insect may have divine purpose; gauge not Heaven's favor by appearance alone.'"

This had passed beyond ridiculous. "St. Daan in a pan!" I cried. "You can't possibly believe she's—"

"Enough of your doubting and misdirection, Seraphina," said Josef, getting to his feet and glowering. "Don't imagine I consider you blessed through association."

"Heaven forbid," I said, folding my arms.

"It still remains what to do with you," he said. "I can't let you report back to your Queen. You will hand over every quigutl device you have." When I balked, he added, "I won't hesitate to have my guards strip you."

I fished out my charm necklace. To my regret, the St. Capiti medallion Kiggs had given me was strung there with the two thniks. Josef took the chain, his eye scanning my person for anything else. "Your ring," he said. I handed over Orma's pinkie ring. He examined it, pinching and prodding the pearl, and I cringed, expecting Orma's voice to crackle forth at any moment.

Nothing happened, which was both a relief and a disappointment.

Josef handed the ring back. A search of Abdo turned up nothing. "You're my prisoners," said the Regent. "Any attempt to contact your Queen or her spies will result in severe—"

"Forgive me, Lord Regent," said Jannoula, raising her eyebrows mildly, "but you cannot keep Seraphina prisoner. She needs to go to Porphyry."

Josef stared incredulously. I'm sure I looked no less flabbergasted.

"It's holy work," Jannoula insisted. "The Saints tell me not to detain her."

Josef stood straighter, indignation written in his eyes, and I found myself hoping his truculent nature might prevail—not that I wished to stay locked up in Samsam, but I liked even less how powerful Jannoula's influence seemed to be. Surely there were lines she couldn't cross, however dazzlingly she glowed.

"We will discuss this in private, Blessed," said Josef. His voice held a warning, but I suspected he'd already lost. Jannoula's lips curled into her sly smile. Josef shouted, "Guards! Escort these two to rooms in the east corridor, for now, and keep them under watch." The two who'd accompanied Abdo and me through the city stepped up, and two more from the foyer, absurdly carrying halberds indoors, entered the throne room behind them. Josef gave us over to their supervision.

As Abdo and I were escorted out, I glanced at Jannoula. She stared back intently, a calculating light in her eyes.

Thirteen

Abdo and I were put in separate rooms. My accommodations were quite comfortable, except for the guard at the door. I paced the hearthrug for hours, wondering what would become of us and lamenting the loss of my thniks. Glisselda and Kiggs needed to know about Josef and Jannoula. I finally crawled into the four-poster bed and soothed myself by settling my garden. No sooner had I fallen asleep, or so it seemed, than Jannoula was shaking me awake. I thought I must be dreaming.

"Up," she said sharply, giving me a pinch. "You need to be on the ship to Porphyry before this headstrong Regent changes his mind again."

I stumbled into my clothes and followed her out. Ingar waited in the dim hallway, carrying a travel pack of his own, his gaze vague behind square spectacles. Beside him waited Abdo.

Jannoula took my arm; I cringed at her touch, but dared not

pull away. I let her lead me up the corridor and down a spiral stair, into the lower parts of the castle, stealing glances at her all the way. She was a little shorter than me, now that I'd grown to full height, but was no less intimidating for that; her very presence seemed to shrink me, the weight of our history pulling me into myself.

Was she angry with me? Her fine-featured face let nothing slip.

We exited the castle through the harborside gate, and the cold wind off the water woke me fully. Jannoula led us under the pale pink sky, along the harbor wall, down slippery stone steps toward a dinghy, tied to an enormous iron ring. A grizzled oarsman was already aboard, asleep with his oiled rain hat over his eyes; he startled at Jannoula's shout, knocking one of his oars overboard. "In, quickly, all of you," she said, handing Abdo aboard. Ingar leaped across the dark channel with surprising agility.

"Ingar's coming to Porphyry?" I asked.

"I'm sending him to help you," said Jannoula, rubbing her hands to warm them.

"Why don't you come, too?" I asked. Not that I wished her to, but it seemed preferable to leaving her here, persuading Josef to who knew what.

She didn't answer, but I suspected I knew why. Abdo had mentioned the ityasaari priest Paulos Pende untangling her mind-fire from the others. The Porphyrians already knew who she was, and didn't like her much.

I couldn't leave with this many unanswered questions. "What do you hope to accomplish by ingratiating yourself with Josef?"

Her nostrils flared. "I'm looking out for our interests, don't worry," she said, hugging herself against the stiff breeze. "This Regent is a little . . . unpredictable. I had no idea he'd want to detain you, but of course I can't allow it. You've got to finish gathering everyone. Ingar will help you stay on task and not let your awful uncle distract you."

I started, alarmed that she knew where Orma was; she smirked, then leaned in and whispered, "Abdo had an interesting and relevant memory when Josef was examining your pearl ring yesterday. I visited his mind while he was sleeping and found it."

She tried to shove me toward the dinghy. I resisted, crying, "What are you trying to accomplish here? Why Josef?"

She eased off pushing. "There is no end to your questions. Here I am, helping you along, and you still won't trust me. What will it take, Seraphina?"

"That's easy. Release Abdo, Dame Okra, and everyone else whose minds you've caught on your hooks, and I'll consider—"

She shoved me hard, and suddenly there was no embankment below my feet. I fell toward the sea, and her eyes widened as if she were surprised to have unbalanced me.

I landed hard in Ingar's lap, making the boat buck and violently throw up spray. Ingar, looking mildly astonished, squeaked, "Oh!" Abdo helped me right myself, but I pulled away from him and stood up in the tilting, rocking boat. I shouted at Jannoula, "I'm going to Porphyry for my Queen, not for you. I'm not helping you!"

Jannoula turned her back on me and stiffly climbed the stairs toward the castle, its spires dark against the lightening sky.

The ship was a two-masted Porphyrian merchanteer anchored far out in the water. Ingar had vouchers for our passage, all in order, and so the sailors hauled us up one by one in a sling chair. Abdo pushed off the side of the ship with his feet, so he spun as he ascended; Ingar bumped his way up like a lumpy sack of grain.

I hated to admit Jannoula was helping, but she had gotten us out of Blystane quickly, and at the Regent's expense. Regardless of her reasons—which I could not possibly trust—we were on our way. This was the final leg of our search. I would find the seven ityasaari in Porphyry, locate my awful uncle, as Jannoula called him, and return home at last.

Home. The word seemed to echo in my heart. I wanted nothing in the world so much as that. Even thoughts of Orma didn't buoy me the way they usually did.

Abdo missed his home, too, I knew. Simply being on a ship among Porphyrians, listening to them talk, seemed to cheer him immensely. He bounded around the deck, eager to explore; Ingar gamely followed him. I questioned a sailor in my shaky Porphyrian; he eventually understood and led me down a claustrophobic corridor beneath the forecastle to the single, cramped cabin where the three of us would board.

I thanked the man, who departed for his duties, and then I learned the crucial importance of ducking through doorways.

The cabin, I discovered once I'd managed to enter without braining myself, had three narrow bunks: an upper and lower built into the left-hand wall and one to the right atop a chest of drawers. I claimed the lower left bunk for myself, assuming Abdo would want the top. Ingar could sleep by himself across the room, all of two feet away. I peevishly kicked his empty bunk. I did not want him here; maybe he'd fall in the ocean. I sprawled crookedly, keeping my boots off the scratchy coverlet, and felt the ship roll beneath me.

A feeling rolled inside me, too. I didn't want to look at it.

My entire expedition seemed to have gone wrong. It had started so wonderfully, with Nedouard and Blanche; I felt they were kindred spirits, and that I'd truly done some good for them. Everything had slowly disintegrated since then. Casually lethal Gianni Patto. Mean Od Fredricka, forced into friendliness through Jannoula's manipulations. The seizing of Dame Okra and Abdo.

Jannoula, still barred from my head, was free from her old prison, walking the world, and entering the minds of others. She could do all kinds of damage now. Hateful Earl Josef, who'd partly credited her with his ascension, might be only the beginning.

I ground the heels of my hands into my eyes. She wanted me to bring the Porphyrian ityasaari back to Goredd to join the others. How in good conscience could I even ask them, not knowing what she had in mind? Even if Kiggs and Glisselda stopped her bodily at the Goreddi border and locked her up, did it matter where she was if she could reach everyone with her mind?

Ingar entered the cabin. "Oh, excuse. You were nepping?" His accent was as hard as cold butter.

I rolled onto my side, turning my back on him. I had no desire to talk to Jannoula's spy, but he kept talking to me. "I am, eh, so fery pleased to mit you. It is egzekly like she toldt me. Soon together we shell be!"

I looked at him over my shoulder. A vapid smile split Ingar's fat face. His bovine brown eyes drifted vacantly behind square lenses; his moony pale head reflected the blue gleam from the porthole. Perhaps this spy could cut both ways.

"What else does Jannoula say?" I asked, sitting up carefully.

"Wonderfool thingks about you, always!" he cried, his doughy hands gesticulating his enthusiasm. "You are her favorite, and thet is a great blessink upon you."

I was her favorite. My stomach turned. I said, "How long have you known her?"

"Four years," he said, looking shyly at his feet, as if I'd asked him how long he'd loved her. Maybe I had. He added, "But we only mit—*meet*? Is more correct?" I nodded, and he continued: "I hev *meet* her for the first time two months ago. Before thet . . . no, *that*. Before that, I only speak to her in my head. You understand."

"I do," I said, but I was silently calculating. Four years meant soon after I'd locked her avatar in the Wee Cottage and shut her out of my mind. She hadn't stayed lonely long. "How did she find you four years ago?"

Ingar hefted his bulky frame onto the bureau-top bed and beamed. "She sees me the way she sees us all: through the Eye of Heaven, with the helpink of the Saints."

That was uninformative. I tried to refine the question. "But what did she do once the Saints helped her find you? Did she just show up in your mind one day?"

He blinked. "I heared her voice. She saidt, 'My friendt, you are not alone. Let me to come in. I am of your kindt, and we are blessed.'" He kissed a knuckle toward Heaven.

He'd heard her voice, then, and answered her. Could he have ignored it? If he'd said, *No, don't come in,* would the reply itself have been enough to give her an opening? She'd implied that Dame Okra had been keeping her out successfully.

I said, "She said a mutual friend informed her of my travels. Who might that be?"

"One of the other helf-dragons? She holdts spiritual hands with six of us."

I did some quick addition and couldn't make it work. "Who?"

He counted off on his fingers. "Abdo, me—of course—eh, Gianni, Okra, Od Fredricka, and my countryman Lars."

I clapped a hand to my mouth. The room was suddenly too small. I couldn't breathe. "Excuse me," I muttered, pushing past Ingar's knees, heading for the cabin door.

"The ship is rocking too much," he said cheerfully, miming it. "I understand."

But he didn't. I slammed the door in his face.

I had to ask Abdo, even if it meant Jannoula would learn that I had asked. "Was she in Lars's head before we left Goredd?"

No, said Abdo definitively. *I never saw her mind hooked into anyone's until we met Gianni Patto. But it's been almost three months since we've seen Lars.*

We stood by the prow, gritting our teeth into the briny wind.

Sailors bustled around us, nautically occupied, knotting and climbing and swabbing and unfurling. We tried to keep out of their way.

"Well, if Ingar is to be believed, she hasn't taken Blanche or Nedouard yet," I said, trying to feel encouraged. Abdo leaned over the railing and got a faceful of spray, presumably on purpose.

She will, said Abdo matter-of-factly.

I looked at him sidelong and saw his unguarded expression of bleak resignation and despair. It broke my heart. I laid a hand on his arm. "We'll go to this Paulos Pende and have him unhook her from your mind the minute we land in Porphyry," I said firmly.

Abdo pulled away from me and said nothing.

All our talk about Lars had given me an idea. I could speak with my mind to the ityasaari I'd met in person; I had only to induce a vision. "Lars could get word of Josef's ascension to the Queen. I should contact him before it occurs to Jannoula that I can."

How do you know Jannoula won't be present in Lars's head while you're talking to him? said Abdo, hopping down from the railing to follow me belowdecks. *Or that she isn't listening through my ears this very instant? She could stop Lars from reporting to the Queen easily enough.*

"I don't," I said as we descended the narrow stairs, "but I have to try. Besides, my more immediate concern is Ingar. If he gleans that I'm contacting Lars, he'll surely bring Jannoula into it. I need you to distract him."

Ingar was still on the bureau-bed, now reading a book the size of his hand. His rucksack was open beside him, and it appeared, from this angle, to contain nothing but books. I wondered how many he had brought with him, and whether books were an angle one might take toward . . . what? Manipulating his loyalty? Buying his cooperation?

Abdo, at Ingar's knee, widened his eyes endearingly and smiled up at the turnip-headed older man. Abdo must have silently spoken, because Ingar looked up from his page and replied in Porphyrian: "What kind of fish? I'd love to see it."

His Porphyrian's better than yours, said Abdo. He slipped out of the room ahead of the old bookhound.

I flopped back onto the scratchy coverlet and tried to focus my mind. The ceaseless rocking of the ship bothered me, but I finally calmed myself enough to locate the garden of grotesques. After my unintentional experiments with neglecting it, I'd gone back to tending it religiously, even though there had been no unfortunate repercussions, as far as I could tell. It calmed me, even if the garden denizens didn't require quite such rigorous supervision.

But a parent who spends every day with a child can't see the child growing. Similarly, my constant presence had blinded me to my garden's incremental changes. When I went in looking for Loud Lad, I immediately found myself teetering on the lip of his ravine. It lay unusually, perilously close to the entrance today; there was barely space to stand between the gate and the chasm. I threw myself backward and avoided falling in; as I lay there in the dirt, I saw Loud Lad on the other edge. I waved at him, expecting he would build a peculiar bridge and cross over to me.

He didn't; he leaped across. It was a much longer leap than I could have attempted, and his black boots barely got any purchase when he landed. He had to grasp at the clinging shrubbery to keep from falling back, which was alarming. However, I was far more alarmed that he could jump the ravine at all.

It used to be wider than this, I was certain. It had shrunk. When? How?

Had the whole garden been shrinking? I glanced at the cloudless sky, the distant dunes and fruit trees. Everything looked the same as yesterday, but that was inconclusive. Was there some way to measure? I would consider how to do it.

Loud Lad dusted himself off and picked his way toward me along the ravine edge. I clasped his hands in mine and a whirling vision overtook me.

My consciousness emerged dizzily, hovering near the ceiling of a parlor in Castle Orison. I knew every detail of the room: the harpsichord with a sunburst inlaid on the lid; the satin curtains, opulent Zibou carpets, and overabundance of cushions; the wide gout couch where Master Viridius, my erstwhile employer, reclined with his feet up. He closed his eyes and dreamily waved one bandaged hand, conducting the earsplitting music that filled the room and surely threatened to break the windows again.

Opposite the old man, Lars gingerly balanced his muscular bulk on an ornate chair and played a double-reed instrument, a soprano shawm. It took a lot of air—his face reddened right to the roots of his hair—and was correspondingly loud.

A wave of homesickness bowled into me. I would have given anything to be in that firelit room improvising harmonies, sore ears notwithstanding.

Lars glanced toward my vision-eye, aware of me watching

him—or aware that I had taken hold of his mind-fire in the garden? How did it work, exactly? He played to the end of the piece. Viridius cried, "Bravo! My second theme needs polish, but it's coming."

"My dear," said Lars, examining the reeds of his instrument, "you remember I toldt you thet Seraphina can look upon me from far away? Well, she does so now."

"Indeed! Can she hear me?" Viridius looked up at the wrong corner of the room, drawing his bushy red brows together, and spoke with exaggerated slowness: "Hel-lo, Se-ra-phi-na, we all miss you here."

Lars smiled fondly at the older man. "I wantedt you to know so you don't think I am talking out loudt to myself. So, Phina! Goodt evening to you."

I didn't know you played shawm, I said, amused.

"I am picking it up again after a long time," he said, his big fingers fluttering on the finger holes, playing the shadow of a song. "But it is not exactly a shawm. It is the Samsamese bombarde."

It's loud, I said.

His round face split into a grin.

I continued: *Listen, I need you to take a message to the Queen and Prince Lucian.*

"Of course. But hev you lost your quigutl locket?"

It was stolen—this was awkward—*by your brother.*

Lars frowned. "My brother? He was at the Erlmyt?"

No one was at the Erlmyt, but Queen Glisselda knows that. I need you to tell her that the old Regent is dead, probably murdered in a coup. The new Regent is . . . is Josef.

Lars hung his head and sighed bleakly, his shoulders sagging. Any news of his brother was hard for him to bear. Until he had taken up with Viridius, Lars had never had an easy family life; his father had killed his mother upon learning Lars was half dragon, and then Josef had killed their father in revenge. Something had stopped Josef from killing Lars, but brotherly love had never seemed to be part of the equation.

"How did this happen?" he asked.

"What has your brother done now?" Viridius stage-whispered from across the room, ready to get indignant on his behalf. Lars waved him off irritably.

Please tell Viridius, I said. If Jannoula checked in on Lars before he could tell the Queen, she might stop him. Certainly, Josef did not want Glisselda to know; I assumed Jannoula agreed. Nothing would stop Viridius from passing the news along.

"But you haven't toldt me everything," snapped Lars. "Did my *ferdamdte* brother kill the Regent himself?" Viridius clapped a bandaged hand to his mouth. Lars pinched the bridge of his nose and continued, "Why wouldt the earls and bishops make him Regent after thet? It takes a consensus to invest a new Regent."

A consensus of everyone, or merely of those present?

"Those present," he conceded, shaking his head. "This is why the highland earls feel sometimes, eh, shut out."

Well, the highland earls don't know yet. As for the others . . . I hesitated. Ingar had been there; was a consensus of one enough? How would Lars react if I mentioned Jannoula? I dared not chance it. *Queen Glisselda needs to know this immediately.*

"We will tell the Queen at once," said Lars, meeting Viridius's eye. Viridius nodded vigorously and reached for his polished walking canes.

Tell her also that I won't be reporting in until I get a replacement thnik from the embassy in Porphyry. That could be two weeks or more.

Viridius was rising awkwardly to his feet, saying, "Phina, if you can hear me, come home soon. The choristers have gotten unruly without you. It isn't the same."

Tell Viridius I miss his grumping, I instructed Lars, but he wasn't listening.

I wished I could plant a consoling kiss on top of Lars's head, but of course I could not really reach him. Viridius did it for me.

I emerged from the vision, and another wave of homesickness hit me.

No, a different kind of sickness.

Abdo, I called with my mind, *come back. Quickly. Bring a bucket.*

He arrived in time, but only just.

For two ceaseless, churning days, my stomach tried to turn itself inside out. It raged and tempested. I couldn't stand up. Abdo and Ingar took shifts dabbing my head with a sponge and feeding me spoonfuls of honeyed water, half of which came back up.

You're green, Abdo informed me one night, his eyes wide. *Green as a lizard.*

On the third day, I slept at last and dreamed that I was alphabetizing an infinite library that turned out to be myself. When I awoke, I staggered up on deck, blinking in the wind and sunshine, and found that life had gone on without me. The sailors were allowing Abdo to climb the rigging, bandaged hand and all, and Ingar not only spoke better Porphyrian than me but had taken to the sailors' impenetrable patois like a second mother tongue.

"Nautical Porphyrian wasn't difficult to pick up," Ingar explained over dinner in the crowded sailors' mess. He, Abdo, and I were crammed together at a side table, eating salt cod and mushy lentils off square plates. "Once I realized they said *braixai* where standard Porphyrian has *brachas*, it was a matter of substituting diphthongs and—"

"You have a facility with languages," I said, impressed in spite of myself. His Goreddi had improved, his Samsamese accent melting away before my ears, even during our first conversation.

He turned pink to his scalp. "I've read a lot, in many languages. That gives me a basis for speaking, but I didn't have the phonemes until I heard them."

"But how did you learn to read so many languages?" I pressed.

He looked up from his lentils, his spectacles reflecting the lantern light. "I examined the words from all angles until they made sense. Isn't that the usual way?"

For the first time in days, I cracked a grin; my face felt like it had forgotten how. The usual way? It was the daft, steep, unscalable way, and yet I felt like I was glimpsing the real Ingar, not Jannoula's stooge. "Maybe you can help me with Porphyrian grammar," I said. "I'm hopeless at—"

Abdo kicked me under the table. *I'm teaching you Porphyrian! Of course you are,* I said, *but I need all the help I can get.*

Abdo crossed his arms and glared at me. Ingar, oblivious to

the tension between his tablemates, said: "Let me guess: you gender only the most obvious nouns correctly, you confuse the dative with the ablative, and you are completely thrown by the optative."

Abdo's mouth fell open. *It's like he knows you!* he cried, and then he was speaking in Ingar's head, where I couldn't hear. Ingar smiled benignly, occasionally answering aloud in Porphyrian. I could follow much of what he said; I was a good listener, if nothing else, and my vivid imagination helped fill the gaps in my comprehension.

Ingar's enthusiasm began to curdle, however. His eyes dulled and his speech slowed and slurred. Alarmed, I glanced at Abdo, only to see him staring in rapt fascination at a spot just above Ingar's head.

Ye gods, said Abdo. *She's pouring into his mind right now, filling him up like a jug. A big, empty jug.*

I pushed back from the table reflexively. Ingar's eyes unfocused and a docile smile rippled across his fleshy lips. I waited, tensed like a hare, but Ingar only blinked vaguely. *What's she doing? I asked Abdo. Is she not here to speak to me?*

Abdo frowned. *Not everything she does is about you. She's been visiting Ingar for years. They must have their own things to talk about.*

Ingar's head drifted a little to one side, like butter melting in a pan. He sighed.

Abdo and I helped Ingar to his feet, draping his heavy arms across our shoulders. Our mismatched heights meant we propped Ingar at an angle; his head lolled downhill, toward Abdo. The sailors grinned knowingly as we passed, as if we were helping our drunken comrade to bed.

Fourteen

Ten days later, Porphyry finally came into view, gleaming like a pearl. The city had been built into two enormous bowl-shaped depressions in the side of a double-peaked mountain. The twin branches of the river Omiga rushed out from behind it, plunging to the sea in a series of cataracts on the west side and a single, terrifying fall to the east. As our ship passed the lighthouses and entered the harbor, I began to see dark columnar trees sticking up like fingers from private gardens. Gilded statuary glinted atop the alabaster domes of temples; colonnades and porticoes, built from the purplish marble that gave the city its name, cast dramatic shadows in the afternoon sun. The city climbed vertically, terraced like the seats of an amphitheater, the eyes of the buildings fixed upon some captivating nautical comedy in the harbor below.

At least I hoped we were a comedy. That seemed preferable to the alternative.

Porphyry was not, strictly speaking, part of the Southlands, and Porphyrians would have been insulted by the suggestion. Abdo had told me more than once that his people considered Ninys, Samsam, and Goredd a backwater. Porphyry was the southernmost city-state in a vast trading network that extended to the far north and across the western ocean to countries we'd only heard the vaguest rumor of: Ziziba, Fior, Tagi.

Porphyry's twelve founding families—the Agogoi—had settled at the mouth of the Omiga River more than a thousand years ago, believing it a strategic position for controlling trade with the Southlands. They weren't wrong, exactly, but it took a few centuries before the Southlands were fit to trade with.

The Southlands in those days comprised dozens of chieftaincies, warring with each other and preyed upon by the dragons from the northern mountains. Eight hundred years ago, the legendary Queen Belondweg united Goredd under one banner and drove the dragons back for the first time. It didn't last; the dragons returned in force in the Great Wave.

That conflict ended with the Age of Saints, six hundred years ago, when Saints walked the Southlands and taught us to fight dragons more effectively. There followed a two-hundred-year lull, the Peace of St. Ogdo, during which Ninys and Samsam were established. The dragons, however, were only biding their time.

The last four centuries had cycled surges and restorations, war and incomplete peace. Comonot's Treaty had brought the first real peace since St. Ogdo's.

All that time, the Porphyrians had watched and waited, apart from our turmoil. They'd made peace with the dragons as soon as they'd landed and could not fathom why we did not do likewise—or why we had not sensibly settled somewhere dragons didn't care to hunt. The Porphyrians traded intermittently with the chaotic south and more steadily with the distant north and west, and while this hadn't made them wildly wealthy, they'd lived comfortably enough to dabble in philosophy and scholarship and culture.

Only in the last forty years, with the stability of Comonot's peace and the Southlands needing to rebuild, had Porphyry finally begun to see the trade its founders had hoped for. I'd seen Porphyrian merchants at Goreddi markets my entire life; many had settled in the Southlands to run that end of their import-export operations.

Porphyry's ancient treaty with the Tanamoot meant that the city had a very different relationship with dragonkind. The community of exiles that Eskar had been courting, trying to persuade them to Comonot's cause, could never have existed in Goredd. We liked our dragons transient and clearly marked with bells. Even Porphyrian attitudes toward ityasaari, if Abdo's upbringing in the temple was any indication, spoke of a very different dragon-human dynamic. I was eager to see it in action.

Abdo was just plain eager. The moment his city had drifted into sight, he had climbed onto the capstan and bounced with uncontainable joy.

Movement in the sky caught my eye. Dark shapes swooped and dove over the mountains behind the city. They darted in and out of sight, possibly dozens, too swift to count or keep track of. I tapped Abdo's shoulder and pointed. "Dragons!"

Abdo shaded his eyes with his good hand. *Those will be our exiles. They're permitted to fly at the four corners of the year, during our Games of the God and Goddess at the solstices and equinoxes.*

"Don't tell me we made it here by midsummer!" I cried. Somewhere in all my illness, I'd lost count of the days.

Ingar, with us at the prow, questioned a scurrying sailor. "Midsummer was five days ago, he says. This is the last day of the games."

We'd reached Porphyry only five days after Kiggs and Glisselda had planned that we should, months ago, in the comfort of Castle Orison. We'd had enough mishaps and unexpected detours that I could hardly believe we'd been so timely.

I just hoped other things the Queen and prince hadn't been able to plan for—the progress of the dragon civil war, and whether it would move south into Goredd—had not yet made our journey superfluous. I'd have to find the Goreddi embassy as soon as I could, contact the Queen, and learn what was happening.

Our ship put into the eastern harbor, at the cargo docks. I'd been shy about inflicting my Porphyrian on the crew, but as we waited for the gangway, I spoke to the young boatswain standing near us. "Have you the knowing for where we are able to find this desired thing, the Goreddi pigeon coop?"

The lad goggled at me.

What are you doing? asked Abdo, elbowing me with unnecessary severity.

I'm asking him where the Goreddi embassy is located, I said.

No, you're not, said Abdo. *Besides, I'm sure he doesn't know. You may have stupid-foreigner license, but that can be stretched only so far.*

Stupid-foreigner license? I asked.

Porphyrians expect you to speak badly and have the manners of a goat; we find it amusing when you do, and a little disappointing when you don't. The sailors are subtly leaning closer, even now, to hear what absurd thing you'll say next.

I glanced over my shoulder. An elderly sailor grinned toothlessly at me. Embarrassed, I turned back to the gangway, which was almost down.

"I do need to find the embassy," I told Abdo. "And we should get you to the temple of Chakhon and this priest, Paulos Pende."

Later, he said, looking ready to bolt off the ship as soon as he could. *I want to go home first and rest.*

Ever since he'd quit the temple—for reasons he still hadn't made clear to me—Abdo had lived with his aunt Naia, an accountant for a shipping firm. Her apartment was near the harbor market, in a neighborhood called Skondia. Abdo's grandfather, who would've returned to Porphyry months ago, was to have informed Naia we were coming.

The harborside was full of sailors, stevedores, cargo cranes, crab pots, and fishwives; gulls aggressively darted around, stealing scraps. Abdo slipped through the churning crowd, as skilled and nimble as the gulls. He was hard to follow, not least because I didn't know which way we were supposed to be going. I'd spot him beside a piled net, lose him, glimpse him near a guano-coated pylon, lose him again, and then see him materialize beside a musician playing some sort of miniature oud. We worked our way east, finally emerging into emptier, shadier, gently sloping streets lined with apartment blocks.

I had not been keeping track of Ingar, hoping maybe he'd trip over a fishing line and fall into the sea, but he'd doggedly kept up with us.

The bottom floor of Aunt Naia's apartment building held stores and businesses; Abdo led Ingar and me to the stairs, wedged between a bustling tavern and a net-repair shop. A waft of cardamom tea and frying greeted us; a baby's cry echoed down the stairwell. Neighbors, descending in the dimness, exclaimed happily at Abdo and stared at Ingar and me. His aunt's flat was at the top, four floors up.

A short, rounded woman, dressed in a practical yellow tunic and trousers, answered Abdo's knock. Her chin-length brown hair was divided into countless tiny twists tipped with blue and green ceramic beads. A pair of gold-rimmed spectacles perched upon her nose; a stylus protruded from behind her ear. She beamed at the sight of Abdo and held out her arms to him.

Abdo burst into tears and collapsed against her bosom. She staggered back a step in surprise, then held firm, kissing his head, holding him tightly, waiting out the tears. "Sweet bean," she muttered into his hair knots. "What's this, then?"

Abdo dried his eyes and held up his left hand. He did not, in fact, need bandages anymore—the wound had healed—but he still kept it wrapped. Aunt Naia's brow creased and she began speaking too rapidly for me to follow. Abdo tried to answer with hand signs—I'd seen him sign to his grandfather—but his injured hand hindered him.

Aunt Naia signed back. I wondered how long it would take Ingar, who watched intently, to work out this finger language.

"Forgive me," said Naia suddenly, addressing Ingar and myself in simpler Porphyrian. "You are Abdo's friends. Please come in. Guests are from the gods."

Ingar, at least, knew how to answer: "A generous heart is the truest temple."

Aunt Naia ushered us into the apartment's main room, modestly furnished with a backless couch, a low table piled with ledger books, a charcoal brazier, and a number of small carpets and cushions. A square window with a view of the harbor let in the lingering evening light; curtains closed off the entrances to three other rooms.

Abdo plopped himself on the couch and extended his bandaged hand. *Help me take this off, Phina madamina,* he urged. *And tell her what happened. I'm having trouble.*

I sat beside him, unwrapping the bandages, and told Aunt Naia—with Ingar's translation assistance—of our travels through the Southlands, how helpful Abdo had been, and of the attack that had led to this injury.

His hand lay inertly in my lap. "Show me, fig," said Aunt Naia, kneeling.

Abdo swallowed hard and wiggled his thumb. He wiggled it again. His other fingers splayed rigidly, as immobile as sticks.

The next morning Abdo pleaded illness and stayed in bed; he slept on a folding mat in an alcove full of ledger books, a curtain pulled across the doorway. Naia, Ingar, and I tiptoed around, quietly breakfasting on fish and eggplant fritters brought up from a restaurant downstairs. Naia checked in to see if Abdo would eat, then came out of the alcove shaking her head sadly.

"He mourns his hand," she said, rubbing her forehead with her thumb. "Let's give him some time."

I suspected it wasn't just his hand. He'd also been depressed about Jannoula invading his mind, but he'd had to keep moving or he never would've gotten home. Now that he was home, the full weight of it had landed on him.

After breakfast, Naia was adamant that Ingar and I attend the public baths. "I know you Southlanders are afraid of your souls being sucked down the drain," she said firmly, "but that's a myth. It is good to be clean."

Ingar seemed interested, which astonished me, considering that the hunch under his shirt was a pair of vestigial wings. My heart shrank from the prospect of revealing the scales on my arm and midriff to dozens—hundreds?—of strangers. I pleaded shyness fervently enough that I was off the hook for the morning, anyway. "I will take you this afternoon, at Old-Timers' Hour," said Naia decisively as she gathered her basket of bath things. She left Abdo a note and prodded Ingar out the door with one finger.

I left when they did, heading the opposite way per Naia's directions—west through handcart traffic along the cobbled seawall road—in search of the Goreddi embassy and a thnik with which to contact Queen Glisselda. The sky arched overhead, outrageously clear and blue; the sun on the back of my woolen doublet grew hot. Everyone I passed—from the lowliest gull-baiting harbor urchin to the bearded, perfumed merchant checking his inventory off a list—was dressed sensibly for this weather in light, drapey fabrics. I removed my outer layer, but the linen shirt beneath was already drenched with sweat.

Naia was right that I needed a bath. I needed some lighter clothing as well.

Such was my exaggerated sense of Goreddi importance that I'd expected to find the embassy among the monumental marble-faced buildings around the city's central square, the Zokalaa. After staring stupidly at the columned temples, the Vasilikon (a domed hall where the Assembly of Agogoi met), and the Grand Emporio (a busy covered market), I was forced to inflict my questionable Porphyrian on passersby. First I tried one of the couriers darting across the square like bees, but he wouldn't stop for the likes of me. Then I tried a young mother with two trailing servants, one with an enormous shopping basket, the other carrying the baby. She smiled indulgently and directed me up a side street so steep it had steps and so narrow I could touch the whitewashed walls to either side. There was no traffic here except a man driving a donkey laden with copperware. I had to duck into a doorway to let him pass.

At last, upon a plain wooden door in a shadowy alcove, I saw the bronze plaque that read *Embassy* in both Porphyrian and Goreddi. The knocker was shaped like a rabbit, Pau-Henoa, the Goreddi trickster hero.

A Porphyrian doorman opened a tiny peephole at eye level, took my name, and shut the portal again. I waited, shading my eyes against the strengthening sun. He popped out at last, like the cuckoo of this particular clock, handed me a folded parchment envelope, and disappeared again.

I hesitated, considering whether I should knock again and ask to see the ambassador, but surely if he'd wanted to see me, I'd have been asked inside. Maybe he wasn't even here, but petitioning for Goreddi interests at the Assembly of Agogoi.

I presumed that was how it worked. They had no royalty here in Porphyry.

I opened the envelope, and a thnik fell into my palm, gleaming dully, another sweetheart knot. I wouldn't have to share with the ambassador after all; apparently Glisselda had sent word that I was to have my own. I walked downhill, back toward the harbor, looking for a private place where I could talk to my Queen, since I couldn't just go back to Naia's. Jannoula might listen in through Abdo.

The western docks cradled travel and pleasure vessels, and on the far west side, a breakwater extended nearly half a mile across the mouth of the harbor. At its end rose a lighthouse, the mate of a second beacon on the other side. I set out for the breakwater.

It was a popular place to walk; one could take in the sea air without the bustle and stink of fishing boats. Couples young and old enjoyed the cool breezes; carts selling eggplant fritters and sardines-on-a-stick were set up at intervals, in case anyone had skipped breakfast. Most of the walkers wore gold circlets on their heads, meaning they were wealthy Agogoi. Servants sometimes followed a few steps behind, holding a sunshade or carrying a baby. Masters and servants alike watched me with a mixture of amusement and confusion. A foreign fool, pasty, overdressed, and sweating like a pig, made a quaint novelty this sunny morning.

The promenade split and circled the bottom of the lighthouse. The strollers turned around here but did not linger. Could one grow immune to the sight of sea meeting sky? The island of Laika, where the Porphyrians harbored their navy, slumbered to the southwest. Seabirds reeled giddily around it; when the wind was right, I could hear sea lions roaring, although I couldn't distinguish them from the rocks. I sat upon a block of stone, warmed by the sun and not too guano-covered, and called home for the first time in weeks.

"Castle Orison. Identify yourself, if you please," said a page boy.

"Seraphina Dom—" I began, but Glisselda was apparently standing right there.

"Phina!" she cried. "You made it to Porphyry. Everyone is well?"

I grinned at her enthusiasm. "Everyone is a lot of people to account for," I said. "But yes, I'm well. Abdo . . ."

Was not well. My voice snagged on that.

"We got the message you sent through Lars," she said. "It was clever of you to make sure Viridius knew what had happened. Lars seems to have been compromised."

The breeze turned colder; a gull screamed. "What happened?" I said.

"Lars came to tell us your news," she said. "Just as you'd expect. Big, loyal Lars, and Viridius with him, propped up on his canes. Lars told us you ran into trouble and lost your thnik, but you were on a ship to Porphyry now, and we could get a new thnik to you there. The whole time, Viridius was saying, 'Yes, but, my dear, tell them about—' But Lars kept talking over him. Finally Viridius got fed up and cried, 'See here, the most important news is that Lars's brother, Josef, has usurped—'

"Then, apparently, Viridius's cane slipped and he fell," said Glisselda gravely. "I didn't see what had happened, but Lucian misses nothing. Lars kicked it out from under him."

Below me, the sea churned. I gripped the edge of my stone perch, suddenly dizzy. Lars never would have done such a thing.

Not unless Jannoula, present in his mind and listening in, had taken over and moved his foot for him.

Glisselda's voice crackled: "Viridius hit his head and was unconscious for two days. Lars was utterly distraught, which I felt confirmed an accident, but Lucian insists it was guilt. The upshot is that the two are no longer together. Lars has moved into the south wing with Dame Okra and the Ninysh ityasaari. He's still working on our war machines, but he hardly speaks to anyone. Lucian is having him watched."

"Viridius recovered, though?" I asked, my throat dry. Cantankerous though he was, I was fond of the old composer.

"Physically, yes. He's upset with Lars, as you might imagine. He told us about the coup in Samsam. Lucian's theory is that Lars is ashamed of his brother and didn't want us to know, but that doesn't sound like Lars to me."

"No," I said grimly. "Lars would have told you, and he never would have—" My voice caught. I took a deep breath. "Jannoula is in Samsam; I saw her. I believe she has been helping Josef—maybe even with his ascension—and she's got hold of Lars."

There was a long silence. "That's rather a lot to take in at once," said Glisselda at last. "So anything we say in front of Lars might be heard in Samsam?"

"Lars, Dame Okra, Od Fredricka, Gianni Patto," I said. "For all I know, she's finally found her way into Nedouard and Blanche as well. Say nothing sensitive in front of any of them." I stared up at the sky. "On my end she's got Ingar and Abdo."

"St. Masha's stone," breathed the Queen. "We feared that you meant Abdo when you called from Fnark."

"I wish I understood what Jannoula's up to," I fretted.

Glisselda said grimly, "We know enough. This dalliance in Samsam, aiding and abetting an unsympathetic Regent, shows hostile intent. There's no chance that Jannoula has taken over Josef's mind, is there?"

"She preys on his piety," I said. "Abdo assured me she wasn't inside Josef's mind. However, she . . ." I was unsure how to explain. "She can make her mind-fire visible to humans. It's a trick to make herself look Heaven-touched. Be on your guard against it."

Was it possible to resist Jannoula's glamour? I fervently hoped so.

"Oh, I have no intention of letting her into Goredd if I can help it," said the Queen. "Alas, the person who would most enjoy meeting her at the border and arresting her for . . . oh, who knows what? He'd come up with something clever and entirely legal."

I couldn't help smiling; she knew her cousin well.

"Unfortunately, he won't be here," continued Glisselda.

"What?" I cried. "Where will he be?"

"Ah," she said. "I ought not to divulge too much over a thnik, but I believe I may say that the old general begins to think Eskar's plan has merit. He's coming to Porphyry, and dragging Lucian with him."

So Comonot had apparently gotten over his reservations about bringing the war south to Goredd. I tried to glean how Glisselda felt about that, but her voice gave me no hint. "I need you to finish in Porphyry, Seraphina," Glisselda was saying. "The Ardmagar will arrive in about two weeks; Eskar and the knights at Fort Oversea have been told to make ready. All your pieces must be in place, too. You and the ityasaari will travel home with Lucian."

"Indeed!" I squeaked. My heart had leaped at the mention of home.

Or of Prince Lucian.

Glisselda scolded lightly, "I'm jealous of you two."

"Y-you are?" I said cautiously, uncertain what she was implying.

"By Allsaints, yes. Here I am, Queen, stuck in one place, and you two get to go gallivanting all over in my name. It's terribly unfair."

I relaxed a little. "You're envious."

"That's what I said!" She sounded snippy now; I was trying her patience. Her innocent intention and my guilty conscience weren't meshing.

A voice in the background spoke quietly to Glisselda, and she said, "St. Daan in a pan, I've got to go. Keep me apprised of your progress."

"Of course," I said, but she had already switched off her device.

I walked back up the breakwater, my heart torn two ways. Along with my guilt, of course, came its opposite and cause: the joyful anticipation of seeing Prince Lucian Kiggs so soon.

ᴄᴏFifteen〜

I returned by way of the harbor market, where I bought some lighter clothes, some olive oil salve for my scales, and a large embroidered pillow as a gift for Naia.

Abdo's auntie loved the pillow, but she still made good on her threat to take me to the baths. I survived it by observing everything with an academic, dragon-like detachment: the nautical mosaics across the domed ceiling; the greenish, mildly musty water; my old-fashioned Goreddi shame at being naked; the elderly watching me closely with amusement; and the fact that I was the palest, scaliest person there.

It was all very curious. I might write some sort of treatise.

I had been happy to give Abdo a day to himself while I visited the embassy and the baths, but when he didn't get up the next day, I began to worry. I had two weeks to find the other ityasaari—and Orma—before Kiggs and Comonot arrived, and surely Abdo wanted Paulos Pende, the ityasaari priest, to free him from Jannoula as soon as possible?

Speaking in a low voice so Ingar wouldn't hear, I asked Naia after breakfast, "May I wake Abdo? He had hoped to visit the temple of Chakhon soonest."

Naia looked appalled. "I doubt that," she said. "You must have misunderstood."

I thought back to our last conversation on the subject, aboard the ship. In fact, he'd been unenthusiastic. "Why wouldn't he want to go?"

She pursed her lips, her eyes darting toward Abdo's curtain, as if she weren't sure how much he would want her to tell me. "He quarreled with Paulos Pende and parted on bad terms. I doubt the priest would want to see Abdo, either."

Ah. Abdo's reticence on the subject began to make sense. But if the old priest wouldn't see Abdo, surely he'd see me. Maybe I could broker enough of a peace that the old man would agree to unhook Jannoula. Besides, Paulos Pende was the logical place to start if I was to find the Porphyrian ityasaari. I'd glimpsed the temple of Chakhon yesterday as I'd passed through the Zokalaa.

Ingar had sidled up behind me while I talked to Aunt Naia. He was a problem. I didn't want him spying on my progress and keeping Jannoula apprised, but he would surely follow me around like a dog.

I decided to take the bald bookworm to Porphyry's renowned library, the Bibliagathon—where Orma had been researching half-dragons. I could lose Ingar there, and maybe take a quick look for my uncle. We set off before noon, toward the heights of the wealthy west side of town.

"I've heard . . . so much . . . ," puffed Ingar. I'd been climbing the hill too fast for him, but he wasn't one to let a little thing like lack of breath stop him from talking. "My own library is . . . not inconsiderable. . . ."

I paused so he could rest. His hairless head sweated rivulets and was alarmingly red. I looked away, at the city spread below us like a colorful bowl, the harbor a splash of violet soup at the bottom. Ingar leaned against a shady garden wall; vines vomited gaudy pink flowers through a crack above his head.

"I've had it sent to Goredd," he said when he could finally put together an entire sentence without panting.

"Had what sent?" I'd lost the thread of his thought.

"My library," he said. "Jannoula wants to build Heaven on earth, and what else can a paltry fellow like myself contribute? It wouldn't be much of a paradise without books, you must agree."

"Heaven on earth?" I said. This was new. "What is that supposed to be?"

"You know," he said, his bovine eyes wide. "When we're all together. We will live together in Goredd, with you, and be safe and happy."

I opened my mouth and closed it again. Was that what she was after, or was that what she told Ingar she was after, to manipulate him? For all I knew, it was what she'd told Ingar in an attempt to manipulate me, to show she shared my dream of recreating my garden in the world.

That dream tasted bitter to me now.

Besides, Heaven on earth didn't explain her actions in Samsam. Josef's regency surely portended the opposite of safety for half-dragons, no matter how smitten he might have been with Jannoula herself. She was up to more than Ingar knew.

"I have twenty-seven thousand books in my library, give or take," said Ingar, spontaneously setting off again, as if he heard the Bibliagathon calling his name. I followed in silence. "My mother collected books," he was saying. "That's how she met my father, the saarantras. He acquired rare books for her, and there are indeed marvels in my collection. I have the original testaments of St. Vitt, St. Nola, and St. Eustace."

"The original—meaning, written in the Saints' own hands?" I asked.

He shrugged modestly. "A savvier theologian than I would have to inspect them, but I believe so, yes. They're from the Age of Saints, certainly. The script of that era incorporates some idiosyncratic features—"

He broke off because just then the famed edifice came into view: the graceful columns and soaring dome, the porches and courtyards where philosophers had walked and argued. A repository of the knowledge of ages, the Bibliagathon occupied an entire city block, and more. Orma had told me half the books were divided among three additional outbuildings: one for the ancient and frangible, one for extremely obscure texts, and one for new acquisitions and the difficult to categorize.

Ingar hopped on his toes like a little boy; in that moment, I understood him. Here was his Heaven on earth, surely.

My plan to leave Ingar in the library had a significant flaw:

I was not immune to the siren call of books myself. I wandered, transfixed by the endless shelves and scroll niches, the colonnaded courtyards and burbling fountains, the scholars passionately scribbling treatises at long wooden tables, the gentle slant of sunlight along the open corridors.

That Orma might be here was all the excuse I needed to stay. If he were seeking out historical references to half-dragons, where would he be? I could read the inscriptions above the doors only with difficulty; Porphyrian script differs from Southlander, so I had to think about each letter. Luckily, the inscriptions came with bas-relief carvings. Some were obscure—how does a bullfrog represent philosophy?—but the carving of musical instruments seemed unambiguous.

Orma was a musicologist by training. It was a place to start.

The musicology room was unoccupied except for a bust of the poet-philosopher Necans at the far end. His bronze nose shone, polished by generations of scholars unable to resist the temptation to tweak it. I perused the shelves, noting with a certain pride that we had more music books at St. Ida's in Lavondaville. My uncle had had nearly as many texts in his office.

Some books were in Southlander script; some were even familiar from my student days. A fat volume of Thoric's *Polyphonic Transgressions*, bound in white calf, reminded me so vividly of Orma's old copy that I pulled the book down on a sentimental whim, looked at the cover, and nearly dropped it.

There was a gouge mark across the cover where I'd attacked it with my plectrum the day Jannoula had used my mouth to kiss Orma's.

This was Orma's copy, unquestionably. He'd left Goredd with as many books as he could carry—some of which, I'd learned from the librarian at St. Ida's, weren't even his. Had he gotten tired of carrying them? He was so possessive of his books that it was hard to imagine him willingly giving one up.

The book bulged strangely. There was a lectern—a reading desk—near the bust of Necans. I opened the volume of Thoric there and found a second book, a slender manuscript, tucked inside. Behind that was a sheaf of loose papers, which spilled across the desk, cascading over the edge and settling to the floor like falling leaves. I gathered them up, my excitement growing. I knew Orma's angular writing; these were his notes. If he'd left them, he must be coming back.

I tried to reorder the jumbled pages, but they weren't numbered. I began to read, and the first page, happily, soon became obvious. He'd written *THESIS* across the top in large letters. I read:

It is difficult to find confirmed historical cases of dragon-human interbreeding. Dragons barely acknowledge that such a thing is possible; if it has happened, they didn't record it. Human sources occasionally allude to the possibility, without documenting any instances (exception: Porphyrian sources). What if historical half-dragons did exist but their origins were obscured? I propose to search for accounts of people with unusual abilities or characteristics, look for patterns, and surmise from there.

A large, well-documented collection of such individuals has been under our noses all along: the Saints of the Southlands.

The Saints? "That's a crackpot theory, Uncle," I murmured.

Crackpot or not, I read on. The library around me faded and the sun crossed the sky unnoted. Orma had systematically researched Southlander Saints—including Saints I'd never heard of—and listed every inhuman characteristic: St. Prue's blue skin, St. Polypous's extra legs, St. Clare's visions. He'd drawn up a chart in which he rated their quirks as likely, plausible, metaphorical, or outright invention (he considered St. Capiti's detachable head the latter; he had a point).

I was fascinated and lightly horrified. This kind of thing could get you burned for heresy in Samsam, or so I'd heard. In Goredd . . . well, no one would believe him. He was a dragon. He admitted to guessing. His argument was a colossal house of cards, and I awaited the inevitable breeze that would knock it down. Instead, I found this:

> *The testament is more complete and revealing than I could*
> *have hoped. I see why the old priest would have sent it here*
> *once he saw what it contained. He didn't dare destroy a holy*
> *relic, but he couldn't let anyone else know it existed, let alone*
> *read it. There is no better hiding place than this library,*
> *I think.*

Did he mean the bound manuscript tucked in with his notes? I opened it roughly; the spine cracked, chiding me. Its antique pages were as brittle as leaf pastry, and I didn't dare touch them, but I saw that the booklet was written in an alphabet I didn't know.

A librarian circled the courtyard, banging a gong. I'd been here for hours; the Bibliagathon was closing in ten minutes. It seemed Orma wasn't coming today, and that the time I'd spent reading his notes might have been better spent seeking Paulos Pende at the temple. There was a bundle of charcoal pencils on the lectern for scholars; I used one to scrawl Naia's address and *Find me!* at the end of Orma's notes, then wedged the pages and testament back into the larger book. I could check back regularly while still seeking out the ityasaari. I drifted outside, preoccupied by my plans, and descended the marble steps.

Should I wait for Ingar? Eh. He could find his own way home.

At the bottom of the stairs, four liveried men set down a litter they were carrying. A jeweled hand parted the curtains, and a statuesque woman emerged, dressed in an exquisite saffron gown, pleated and high-waisted. Her strong shoulders were bared to the breeze; the hair piled high on her head was almost architecturally elaborate, with a gold circlet woven through it.

The circlet meant she was of the Agogoi. Abdo had said it was like the stripes on a bee: a warning. *This one has the power to sting you.*

The woman walked toward me, the wooden soles of her sandals clacking on the stairs. I judged her ten years my senior and, when she reached me, half a head taller. I'm not short. I tried not to stare up at her.

She said in crisp and resonant Goreddi: "You are Seraphina Dombegh."

My first instinct was to curtsy, but I wasn't even wearing a skirt; I was dressed like a workingwoman from the harborside, in the tunic and trousers I'd bought yesterday. Porphyrians did not shake hands. I bowed as my last resort. The woman did not smile.

"I am Zythia Perdixis Camba," she said solemnly. "You should call me—"

"Camba," I said, eager to show that Abdo had taught me correct address. Of course, I'd interrupted her with my good manners.

"Paulos Pende sent me to find you," she said.

"Indeed," I said, pleased to think my day had not been a waste after all, even if it was spooky that this priest knew I was in the city—knew my name, even.

Camba glanced toward the library doors. "I am to wait for your companion also."

"I'm not sure that's a good idea," I began, but then, as if on cue, Ingar appeared at the top of the stairs, a librarian at each of his elbows and a third gently prying books out of his hands.

Camba eyed Ingar's stout, hunchbacked form skeptically. "He is ityasaari, too?"

I nodded. It was so strange to hear someone speak casually of ityasaari, as if we were nothing unusual. I supposed that if she knew Pende well, she'd be accustomed to us.

But how did Pende know?

Ingar began descending the stairs with a smile on his moony face. His brows shot up at the sight of Camba. She addressed him in Goreddi: "Greetings, friend. I am to bring you to Paulos Pende."

Ingar stared at her bug-eyed, as if he'd forgotten every language he knew. Then he turned and scuttled back up the stairs. I called after him, confused, until I realized that maybe he wouldn't want to meet with Pende. Abdo had said Pende routinely pulled

Jannoula out of people's minds; I couldn't see Ingar submitting to that willingly.

Camba gestured a wordless order, and two of her litter-bearers rushed after Ingar.

Ingar, at the top of the steps, frantically ripped off his doublet and pulled his linen shirt over his head, revealing his pale, sagging torso. I saw he'd smuggled out a book between his vestigial wings, the rapscallion. The book thudded onto the steps behind him as he stretched his wings wide.

He stretched them wider.

Maybe they weren't so vestigial after all.

His pursuers stopped to stare at the silvery wings, membranous like a dragon's. Ingar took a running jump toward the wall of the library, flapping his wings as elegantly and effectively as a frightened chicken. Still, he gained enough elevation to scramble up the side of the building, grab the edge of the roof, and haul himself over.

Once on the roof, he stood huffing and puffing with his hands on his knees. Whatever else was true, he was still a fat old book-hound.

Camba kicked off her sandals and strode purposefully toward the high library wall. She studied the surface for handholds and then, agile as a cat, climbed up after him.

She was remarkably strong, and it crossed my mind that she might be an ityasaari herself. But I had never seen Camba in visions; she did not exist in my garden of grotesques. Did I not see them all?

Camba reached Ingar and then, heedless of her honeycombed

hair, threw him over her shoulder like a sack of sand and climbed back down with him. Ingar flopped around, shouting, but Camba hauled him back to the litter, as unconcerned as if this were her job every day.

As soon as we were all three crammed inside, the litter lurched into motion. Some thoughtful person had retrieved Ingar's shirt. He pulled it over his head, whining, "My lady warned me about Paulos Pende. He's dangerous."

"Paulos Pende is the kindest being who ever lived," said Camba lightly, straightening her skirts and smoothing her hair. "*I* am dangerous. I don't like to do it, but I can break your arms like pastry. Recollect that before you trying anything unwise."

Ingar, wide-eyed, nodded minutely. I wondered what kind of priest employed a ferocious woman who could break your arms. The same kind who mysteriously knew I was looking for him, apparently. It had been my plan to see him today, but I can't pretend I felt no apprehension as our overloaded conveyance jostled and joggled downhill.

Camba, on the other hand, retrieved a little scroll from behind the seat cushion and read silently, not bothered about us in the least.

~Sixteen~

The swaying litter, too reminiscent of a ship for my tastes, stopped at last, and we emerged, blinking and stretching, in the bustling Zokalaa. At its west end stood the temple of Lakhis of Autumn, grim goddess of relentless necessity, and to the east was a much more popular temple, gauging by the worshipers climbing up and down the steps: the temple of Chakhon of the Spring, the merry god of chance in his fertility aspect.

Camba turned toward the temple of Chakhon, steering Ingar up the marble steps through a descending crowd of young women. We crossed a columned peristyle and passed through a doorway into darkness, where I was hit by a heavy fog of incense and by thick, scratchy cords that dangled all around us, like a forest of vines. As we brushed them, the cords rang bells high in the ceiling, producing a clanging cacophony. It alarmed me initially, but then I grinned at the unexpectedness of it. This god of chance and

I had a similar sense of humor. I held out my arms as I passed through, causing more bells to ring. "That's impious," whispered Camba, elbowing me. "Go toward the light."

Big braziers flamed somewhere ahead. We emerged from the thicket of ropes into an airy space like a cathedral nave. Before us towered a statue of a beautiful blindfolded man sitting cross-legged, his open hands upturned upon his knees; worshipers lingered back near the ropes, approaching the altar whenever the god moved them.

Camba didn't wait for the prompting of the god, or else felt it at once. She knelt, fanned fragrant smoke from one of the braziers over her face, then rose and bowed.

"Listen, ridiculous foreigners," she said, keeping her eyes fixed upon Great Chakhon, "we will enter the holy precinct. I thought it unwise to bring you inside, but Pende is old and does not like to travel. Follow my lead in all things. Touch nothing. Avoid eye contact with the priestesses. Can I rely on you?"

The prospect of offending everyone was a bit intimidating, but I nodded. Ingar perked up a bit and said, "I've read about your holy precincts. I know that—"

"Whatever you have read is insufficient and incomplete," said Camba curtly.

She led us through a hidden door behind the statue of Chakhon, into an anteroom where we removed our shoes, then to a trickling fountain where we were to cleanse our hands, feet, and thoughts. I did not like to pull my sleeves up, but there was no way around it. Camba eyed my silver scales sidelong but made no comment. The purification of thoughts was achieved symbolically by taking water into the mouth and forcibly ejecting it through the nose. We inept Southlanders couldn't do this without precipitating a fit of coughing. Camba rolled her eyes, but finally proclaimed us clean enough.

As we moved from the anteroom to the cloister, a white-robed initiate presented us with a basket containing the Loaf of Chance. Ingar tried to take a slice, since it was on offer, but Camba slapped his hand away. Apparently this was not for us. Camba herself took as little as possible and seemed to be picking stones out of her mouth surreptitiously. She stowed them in a little pouch at her waist.

The Sisters of Chance walked the cloister with their eyes closed, pausing as their god commanded and opening their eyes with slow portentousness. We looked away as Camba had instructed us; Ingar whispered to me that if you met a priestess's eyes, you would sever her connection with her god. Camba overheard and muttered, "Incomplete."

We arrived at Pende's sparsely furnished cell, but he wasn't there. Camba asked a passing novice, who directed us deeper into the precinct. We emerged from the cloister into a walled garden full of lumpy topiaries, overgrown from their original shapes into looming, bulbous things.

Or were they supposed to look like that? Maybe they were the topiaries of chance.

Upon a stone bench sat an extremely old man draped in priestly white. He squinted at us myopically, one hand upon a red sack-like wattle at his throat.

I recognized him immediately. In my mind's garden, I called

him Pelican Man, and he sat on a bench, gazing at the stars. He'd always struck me as gentle and wise.

Camba knelt before him on the mossy lawn and indicated that we should do the same. When we had properly humbled ourselves, Pende spoke. His voice was gravelly; he wore false teeth of ivory that clacked when he spoke and made him hard to understand.

Camba translated Pende's words: "You shall not find the rest of our ityasaari, Seraphina Dombegh. I have told them to stay away from you. I warn you: I have mind gifts, too. I will defend my people. I am as formidable a foe as you have ever faced."

My face went hot. I had imagined conversations with gentle, mystical Pelican Man; none of them started like this. I swallowed hard. "There seems to be some misunderstanding," I said. "You and your fellow ityasaari have nothing to fear from me."

"Liar!" cried the old man. Wispy white hair stood up all over his head like pale fire. "The mind invader, Jannoula, told Brasidas to expect her agent, the one she sent to collect us. Don't feign surprise. Brasidas told me all after I unhooked Jannoula from his mind."

He knew something of Jannoula's purpose; then he also knew something of mine, but not quite enough. "I realize our goals may look the same from a distance," I said, trying to sound reassuring, "but I'm not working with Jannoula."

Pende grunted dismissively and looked away. Camba, on the other hand, watched me intently. "Jannoula invaded my mind against my will when I was a child," I said. "She has changed the minds and hearts of people I love, and moved them around like marionettes. I know what she can do, and she is no friend of mine."

Beside me, Ingar stared incredulously, openmouthed. Apparently he hadn't known how I felt about Jannoula; I could not meet his eye.

I found my words again. "She is no longer in my mind. I got rid of her."

Camba exchanged a glance with Pende, her fine brows arched skeptically. "It is not possible to unhook her yourself," she said. "You need the help of another."

"I didn't unhook her," I began, just as it occurred to me that I had hooked the others, including Pende, to myself via their avatars. Would he judge me harshly for that? I continued hastily: "I tricked her into leaving me and blocked her return."

Camba conferred quietly with the priest, then said to me, "May Paulos Pende place his hands upon your head? He can see something of your future, and something of your past, but he must touch you to do it."

I hesitated, but saw no other way to convince him to trust me. I waddled forward on my knees. Pende reached with palsied hands, his finger joints burled with arthritis. He placed the heel of his left hand on my forehead and the fingers of his right upon the nape of my neck. His deep brown eyes met mine.

It felt like a bird in my skull, fluttering its wings against the bony confinement. Pende's eyes widened in surprise, but he knit his grizzled brows determinedly, concentrating. I felt a more agitated bird this time. It pecked at the inside of my head, right between my eyes. I flinched.

Paulos Pende withdrew his hands and cocked his head to one side. "How strange. I can enter the tiny atrium where you keep pieces of other ityasaari—including myself." He glared sternly. "But I can go no further. The doors to the greater house are locked, and one door was most mysterious. I could not see where it led."

"Even I can't pass that door," I said, believing I knew which he meant. "That's how I shut Jannoula out."

He shook his head, faint admiration in his eyes. "I saw no trace of her. You are not her creature. And you have power, or you once did."

I gaped at him, heat blooming inexplicably in my chest. "I . . . I did?"

The lines beside his mouth deepened. "You still do, but you've bound it all up. You can't use it unless you release it and yourself. I can't see your soul-light at all, that's how entirely closed you are."

"Do you mean the wall I built around the garden?" I said, trying to understand. "My mind kept reaching out uncontrollably; I had no choice."

"Oh, there is always a choice," he said, his false teeth clacking. He straightened them with his tongue. "This piece of myself you are holding: you took it against my will. I require you to let it go."

"I can do that," I said hastily. Unfastening Gianni Patto had seemed to produce no ill effects besides my garden shrinking a little. I reached inside, focused on getting to the garden quickly, and unbuttoned Paulos Pende from the fabric of my mind. I bent double, letting the damp moss tickle my forehead, and waited out the wave of anguish. It hurt no less for being expected. When

I could finally bear to uncurl again, Pende was watching me curiously.

"That hurt you," said Pende, sounding surprised. "What are we to you?"

"For years you were my only friends," I said. But it was more than that, I was beginning to suspect. These pieces of others had become pieces of myself.

Camba heard and translated. Pende's dark eyes softened a little, and for a moment he almost smiled, but then he turned his hawkish gaze on Ingar and said, "It's your turn now, little man."

Ingar squirmed and shook his pale head vehemently.

Pende spoke to Camba, gesturing at the air around Ingar's head; my Porphyrian wasn't strong enough to make out all of it, but I understood Camba's reply: "I see two colors, but which is which?"

Camba could see mind-fire. Abdo had said that ityasaari could learn to see it with practice—Camba had to be a half-dragon. Was Pende teaching her to manipulate it? And if she was ityasaari, why had I never seen her? Had I bound up my mind—as Pende claimed—before finding all of them?

"Paulos Pende needs to touch your head, Batwing," said Camba flatly, rising and looming over him with folded arms, ready to resume the role of enforcer.

"His name is Ingar," I said, suddenly sorry for him. "What will you do to him?"

"We can't leave Jannoula in your head, Ingar," said Paulos Pende, speaking slowly, as to a child. Camba copied his inflection in her translation; neither of them realized Ingar didn't need it. "The more ityasaari Jannoula catches, the more powerful she grows. I must unhook you and deprive her of your strength."

Ingar, on his knees, tried to back away. Camba planted herself behind him.

"You don't understand," Ingar whispered shakily, his spectacles slightly askew. "I was lost and she found me. I was monstrous and she cared for me. I am nothing without her, and I will die if you remove her. I don't know how to live in this world."

Camba's brown eyes filled with an unexpected sympathy. "It only seems that way," she said, bending over Ingar protectively, like a tree.

Ingar bowed his head, muttering as if in prayer, slapping at his temples. Camba's voice sharpened again: "Don't summon her to you. Pende can't unhook her if she's fully present."

Camba wrenched Ingar's arms behind him and hauled him toward the bench. Ingar wailed; Camba whispered in his ear, which didn't seem to help. Paulos Pende grasped Ingar by the forehead and nape; the old priest's lips pressed together with effort and his hands slid right, as if he were straining to twist off the top of Ingar's bald scalp. Pende mimed lifting a heavy crown off Ingar's head and triumphantly held it high.

From the way Camba watched, I deduced that there was something to see between Pende's hands, some mind-fire perhaps. Then Pende brought his hands together with a thunderous crack, far louder than any mere handclap. The sound echoed off the garden walls and left my ears ringing.

Ingar collapsed against Camba, who did not let him fall.

Ingar's face was slack and vacant; his eyes rolled behind his spectacles.

"You're free, friend," said Camba, setting him upright. Ingar fell back inertly. Camba determinedly propped Ingar up again. Ingar balanced better this time, but Camba's strong hands hovered behind him just in case.

Pende stroked his red wattle and closed his eyes. His face had gone gray, and he swayed in his seat, as if the effort of unhooking Jannoula had exhausted him. I didn't like to pester him when he was tired, but a much dearer friend than Ingar was struggling far harder with Jannoula: "Camba, would you tell him Abdo has also been seized? I want to bring him, but he's anxious about facing Pende again."

"We should wait to discuss that," said Camba, glancing apprehensively at Pende.

Pende's sunken eyes had popped open at the sound of Abdo's name. He began to speak, quietly at first, then with growing vehemence. His Porphyrian was opaque to me, but his tone grew transparently angry. Was this about Abdo?

Camba left Ingar's side and sat at the old priest's feet. She touched his feet and spoke in low tones, but Pende would not let himself be calmed. His complaint reached a climax; his eyes reeled and spittle flecked his lips. Finally, he turned his baleful gaze on me and shouted in heavily accented Goreddi, "And you! You want to take the rest from me. I do not permit this."

I recoiled as if struck. He'd grown angry so quickly. What had I done?

Camba rose to her feet, cutting short a new tirade, I suspected;

she bowed deferentially, and the old priest lightly touched the crown of her towering hair. I wasn't sure what to do, if I should bow or say something, but Camba hauled Ingar to his feet and held out a strong arm to usher me away. "Don't speak," she whispered. "Follow me." I did as she asked, but kept my eyes on Pende as long as I could. He did not meet my gaze but closed his eyes and folded his limbs as if settling in to meditate.

"I should have warned you not to talk to him after the unhooking," muttered Camba as we made our way back through the priestesses' cloister. "He's two hundred years old; he can't keep his temper when he's tired, and Abdo is the sorest of subjects."

"What did Abdo—" I began, but Camba cut me off with a hiss and a finger on her lips. I followed her gaze toward one of the veiled priestesses. Could that be Abdo's priestess mother? I watched her pass, but the god did not open her eyes.

Camba, bearing Ingar on one arm, pulled me with her free hand. "He broke Pende's heart," she whispered. "Abdo was to be the priest's successor. Now Pende has no one."

"He has you," I hazarded, hoping I'd interpreted their relationship correctly.

She flashed a mournful look from under her lashes. We'd reached the anteroom, where our shoes waited; Camba slipped on her sandals and helped Ingar with his scuffed ankle boots before answering: "With luck, I can be a stopgap until the god grants us another, mightier mind. Which he may or may not do. Such is the nature of Chance, may he strike us softly."

I followed Camba through the dim, smoky sanctuary, occupied with my own thoughts. Pende clearly didn't want me to take the other ityasaari south. How much power did he have to enforce his wishes? If he said the word, would the ityasaari agree? Even if they didn't agree, were they bound to obey?

Camba had seemed deferential and protective, yet acutely aware of Pende's limitations as an irascible old man whose strength was failing. Besides, the ityasaari could return to Porphyry after assisting Goredd. Maybe I'd once hoped we'd all be together forever, but that seemed naive and foolish now.

I assumed Pende himself wouldn't come, that I'd found my second Od Fredricka, though with considerably more power to resist Jannoula's moving him by force.

We emerged onto the temple steps, facing a glorious sunset across the Zokalaa. The thinning crowds, rushing home to dinner, cast long shadows against the gold-glazed paving stones.

Camba had bent her long neck down to Ingar's level and was muttering in his ear. "Do you feel the breeze on your face?" I heard her say. "That's yours, and worth feeling. Look at those orange clouds. All the trials of a day may be endured if you know there's such a sky at the end of it. Some days I told my heart to wait, just wait, because the sunset would teach me again that my pain was nothing compared with the eternal, circling sky."

It was a dazzling sky, I had to admit, with clouds layered like wisps of pink and purple silk. Behind us, the blue deepened to black; the stars awakened.

"At last you see it with your eyes and no other's," said Camba, her own eyes shining. "It may feel overpowering and unbearable, but I am here to help you bear it."

I was touched by her words; I hoped Ingar was, too, but he

seemed too shocked to take in very much. I didn't like to interrupt, but I needed to get him back to Naia's. Camba spoke first,
however, looking across at me: "When do you return to the Southlands?"

"In about two weeks, when friends come to fetch us back." I
meant Kiggs and Comonot; I wasn't sure whether their coming
was a secret.

Ingar groaned and sagged, his knees buckling; Camba's circling arm kept him upright. "Two weeks isn't much time for re-
habilitation," she said, her voice thoughtful and low. "Ingar needs
help during these next days. He will feel lost without Jannoula at
first, and he may invite her in again."

I studied Ingar's vacant eyes. "Abdo said Jannoula puts a hook
in people; Pende phrased it the same way, 'unhooking her from his
mind.' So why is Ingar so . . . empty?"

Camba smiled unexpectedly and gazed at Ingar almost fondly.
"I've never seen such a deflated bladder; there's barely enough
Ingar-light to fill him up. Jannoula steals your mind, if you allow
it. Her hook can be the roots of a tree, or a tapeworm, winding
through you, sucking your soul-light away. She takes without giving, but she's convinced him that he likes it, or deserves it."

Camba's eyes turned sad in the dwindling light. "Would . . .
would you permit me to take him home and oversee his care?
You've never had Jannoula forcibly stripped from your mind. I
know what it's like."

I nodded solemnly, not wishing to seem too eager to be rid of
him. Something else had struck me, however, a familiar huskiness
in Camba's voice. I knew her voice, I suddenly realized, but from

where? Not from my visions. I said, "Camba, you're ityasaari, and yet I've never seen you."

With her free hand, Camba demurely raised the hem of her diaphanous dress, just enough to reveal a band of silver scales around each knee, distinctively half dragon.

That removed all doubts, if I'd had any. "In visions, I mean," I said. "My mind reached out to others—before I stopped it—but not to you."

Camba drew herself up to her full height; the gibbous moon was rising behind her towering hair. "You reached out to me. You even spoke. I recognize your voice."

"Now I know you're mistaken," I said. "Only two ityasaari ever heard me speak, Jannoula and—"

"A person on the mountaintop, throwing crates and screaming," she said, pointing north at the double peak looming over the city. "I looked different then. I was born into a masculine body, and I had misgendered myself."

I had known the voice and hadn't believed my ears. She was in my garden after all. I racked my brains for the Porphyrian verb Abdo had taught me, a polite inquiry that didn't even exist in the Southlands. "How may I pronoun you?" I hazarded.

Camba smiled warmly and inclined her stately head. "I pronoun myself emergent feminine," she said in Porphyrian, then added in my native tongue, "Or I do now, at last. On my Day of Determination, I declared myself naive masculine. I was already ityasaari; it embarrassed me to be even more complicated than that."

She led Ingar down the temple steps and bundled him into

her waiting litter. I studied her movements, looking for something that recalled that vision, the day she'd been ready to die. It was hard to see beyond the jewelry, hair, and saffron draperies, but suddenly the sunset glazed her bare shoulders a burnt orange, and I recognized in the strength and sureness of her limbs the echo of a person I'd once seen, a harmonic that I'd mistaken for the fundamental.

She was the one whose despair I'd felt, whom I'd reached out to in empathy. In my garden she lived in the statuary meadow, and I'd called her Master Smasher.

ᐸᔑeventeen᠕

I walked back to Naia's, lost in my memory of that vision, and then lost in fact. Porphyry became a labyrinth after sunset. It should have been a simple proposition to find Naia's again: the harbor was downhill, and east was to the right along the shoreline. Porphyry, alas, was all dead ends and cul-de-sacs and nonplanar geometries. Three rights didn't make a left. I began to fear that I would meet myself coming from the other direction.

I finally made it back, and up four flights of stairs. Naia had left a lamp burning. She was asleep on the couch, wrapped in a cobwebby shawl, her cheek pressed into the pillow I'd given her. I extinguished the lamp, and she didn't stir.

I quietly ventured a peek behind Abdo's curtain, just to check on him. Getting him together with Pende was going to be harder than I'd realized, and I did not like the idea of Abdo suffering in the meantime. I listened for steady breathing to tell me Abdo was asleep, but I heard nothing.

Once my eyes adjusted to the near darkness, I saw that Abdo had propped himself on an elbow and was staring back at me.

I hoped it was Abdo and not Jannoula. I approached cautiously.

"How are you feeling?" I whispered, drawing back the curtain on the window so the moonlight illuminated us. His sleeping mat took up half his alcove. I sat beside him on the wooden floor, my back against shelves of Naia's ledger books.

Abdo lay down and was silent for some moments. At last he said, *I feel awful. When we were on the ship, Jannoula ignored me most of the time. Maybe she was busy, maybe it was simpler to watch you through Ingar. For several days she's hounded me, though, and especially these last hours. She's come after me with such terrible force that I feel like my head might split open.*

I felt a rush of horror just under my ribs. She was taking revenge for Ingar's release, I had no doubt.

"I don't suppose you can let her through to talk to me?" I realized as I spoke the words that this was a terrible idea, but I was itching to pick a fight with Jannoula myself.

Abdo was shaking his head vehemently, the whites of his eyes reflecting the moonlight. *If I let her seize me while I'm awake, I'm sure she'll never let go. I have to push against her every minute.* He wrapped his arms around his head and began to weep soundlessly. *I'm scared to sleep. I'm scared to move. I have to concentrate.*

My heart was breaking for him. I said, "Pende pulled her out of Ingar's head; he could do the same for you. We could go to the temple of Chakhon first thing tomorrow morning."

He sobbed harder, his breath coming in ragged gulps. I didn't know what to do. I took his good hand between both of mine, sympathetic tears blurring my vision, and I hummed softly, a Southlander lullaby. His breathing slowly calmed; he wiped his eyes with the back of his useless hand.

I should go to the temple and let him fix me, he said. *But it feels so much like defeat.*

"What do you mean?" I asked, stroking his hand.

Pende invaded my mind, too, said Abdo. *Not literally, but I felt his expectations as creeping, strangling vines. He said my mind was the brightest in ten generations and that only I could be his successor. His hopes were going to swallow me right up, and . . . I had to push back. I would have disappeared otherwise.*

You needed to dance, I said silently, feeling I understood him. I'd left my father's house, despite the danger of exposure, because I needed to play music, to grow into myself and my own life away from him. I remembered how assertive Abdo's dance had been the first time I saw him, how it seemed to be a way of underlining his presence in the world.

He inhaled shakily. *I'll come with you to the temple. I hate it, but I'm in too much pain. I can't keep fighting her forever.*

"Pende can't keep you against your will," I said firmly, not sure whether that was true. Getting Jannoula out of Abdo's head was surely the first priority, though; we'd face the repercussions of letting Pende help after that was sorted out.

Abdo was soon asleep, in spite of himself. I hoped Jannoula would have mercy and let him stay that way. He still had a tight hold of my hand, and I couldn't disentangle myself without waking him. I lay upon the wooden floor beside his mat and somehow found my own portion of sleep.

A few hours later, I was startled awake by the realization that I'd forgotten to tend my garden again. I closed my eyes and quickly went to check on it. The denizens were all calm and quiet, as if nothing had happened; it was becoming more and more apparent that they didn't rely on my daily vigilance. I spent several minutes walking in circles before I realized I was looking for Pelican Man—Pende's grotesque—and that I wasn't going to find him or his topiary lawn.

Once again the garden seemed to have shrunk. The trees in Fruit Bat's grove were shorter; I could pick oranges that used to hang out of reach. Did the garden contract when I neglected it, or was it simply more apparent after a longer absence? I wanted a way to measure the change. I imagined two large standing stones, one on either side of Miss Fusspot's rose garden. I named them the Milestones, even though they weren't a mile apart, and I paced between them three times to be sure my count was accurate. They were forty-nine paces apart. I would remember that, and measure each time I was here.

I returned to myself and stretched, achy from sleeping on the floor. Abdo had released my hand, so I got up, closed his curtain, and tiptoed across the apartment to the narrow bed Naia had meant me to sleep in. I lay awake some hours longer, fretting over my garden's diminution. As hard as I tried, I could not figure out what it meant.

I was awakened again, after the sun was well up, by the sound of many voices speaking Porphyrian too rapidly for me to understand. I emerged from the guest room, blinking blearily, and found myself unexpectedly faced with a couple of dozen people packed into Naia's main room. They wore the bright tunics and trousers of the lower city, many with fish-gutting knives at their belts or their hair tied back with colorful fabric. A pile of children bounced and giggled on the couch; a pair of women unwrapped hot dishes of barley, eggplant, and fish, turning Naia's writing desk into a buffet table.

A hush fell the moment I appeared, two dozen pairs of dark, inquisitive eyes staring unabashedly at me. Finally, a woman who shared Naia's round cheeks and short stature spoke slowly enough for me to understand: "What is this foreigner doing here?"

Naia elbowed her way to my side and began introducing everyone—Aunt Mili, Uncle Marus, Cousin Mnesias—in such rapid succession that I felt certain she didn't intend me to remember any of them. They each nodded tersely, looking lightly affronted by my gall at popping out of nowhere. Naia's father, Tython, smiled at me, but we were off to the next cousin before I could even smile back. We worked our way across the apartment and then out to the stairwell, where nieces and nephews sat on the steps, passing a bowl of dates.

When we reached the lower landing, Naia whispered, "I told

one of my sisters that I was worried about Abdo, so now the entire family descends on us. We'll figure out how to help him, don't worry."

She didn't say so, but from the way she was patting my shoulder, I deduced that the family would find my presence extraneous. I was being dismissed.

"I know how to help Abdo," I said. "Another ityasaari has invaded his mind, and she's hurting him. I'd hoped to take him to the temple this morning."

And given how badly Paulos Pende had reacted when I'd mentioned Abdo, I thought it might be better for Abdo's family to take him.

Naia frowned skeptically. "Abdo wouldn't want to go to the temple."

"Last night he agreed to go," I said, hoping his resolution still held this morning. "He needs to go as soon as possible so Paulos Pende can remove this invasive ityasaari from Abdo's mind before she takes over completely. She could make Abdo do anything, against his will. She could make him kill Paulos Pende, or himself."

Naia glanced back over her shoulder; the sound of arguing filtered down from her apartment. "My family has a complicated history with Chakhon," she said, "but I will convince them this is urgent, even if I have to carry Abdo to the temple myself."

She retreated up the stairs, not looking back. Her nieces and nephews watched me, wide-eyed. I decided they needed to know their cousin was in trouble; surely the more people that knew, the better. "Abdo needs a temple of Chakhon like . . . like as if he flames with fire," I said in Porphyrian, hoping the sentiment, at least, made sense to them. The children nodded solemnly, their mouths puckered as if they were saving their laughter for later.

I heard it before I reached the bottom of the stairs.

I stepped out into the sunshine, thoroughly preoccupied. I needed something to do, or I'd spend the whole day fretting about Abdo. Luckily, I had an uncle and five more ityasaari to locate—without Paulos Pende's help and, I suspected, against his wishes.

I was contemplating where to start when I realized my name was being called. I turned and saw a pimply-faced youth in a pointed red cap standing near the door of Naia's building; I'd walked right past him when I came out. The lad flashed a grin and then spoke with exaggerated slowness, sticking his lips out like a horse's. "Are you the foreigner who's staying with Naia?" he asked. "Seraphina?"

"Yes, it is I, yes, Seraphina," I managed. He gave a curious bow, like an awkward paraphrase of Southlander courtesy, and handed me a hinged metal box the size of a small book. I turned it in my hands, uncertain what to do with it. The messenger pointed out an ornate latch, which opened the thing. The two flat interior surfaces were covered in smooth wax, and carved into the wax were words in Goreddi:

Seraphina, this letter greets you and begs your attention.
  Ingar is sleeping at last. I kept him awake most of the night,

asking him about himself, making him remember. The key is
to fortify him so he doesn't believe he needs her, and to exhaust
him so he sleeps. It is common to relapse, but we must guard
against it. Pende will hardly be pleased to unhook Jannoula a
second time.

I understand he left his luggage at Naia's, and that it was
mostly books. He will be in dire need of occupation—Gods
know I can't stay awake forever. Would you kindly gather his
books and bring them to me at House Perdixis? It would be a
great blessing.

Camba

The red-capped messenger grinned when I looked up. Was I supposed to pay him? It seemed he only wanted the box back. "Any reply?" he asked. I shook my head.

Ingar's belongings were all upstairs, of course, but I did not care to face Abdo's extended family again, not right after I'd been so unceremoniously ejected.

However, I knew where there was another book—a difficult, ciphered book—that might keep Ingar occupied for a while. I would fetch it from Orma's stash at the Bibliagathon, deliver it to Camba, learn where the other ityasaari could be found (for surely Camba knew), and start searching in earnest.

I stopped in the Zokalaa on the way to the library, found an everything-on-a-stick vendor, and bought two skewers of eggplant for breakfast. The sky was clear, and the breeze carried whiffs of charcoal smoke, fish, and unfamiliar flowers. A nuncio announced news from a pedestal in the Zokalaa at intervals each day; he was a portly gentleman whose booming voice made Josquin's sound like a feeble squeak. I stood and listened to him while I ate my eggplant, and was pleased with how much I understood. It helped that he spoke slowly and clearly. I walked on, smiling at shopkeepers stacking fruit into tidy pyramids and children skipping up the steep streets as if the slope were no obstacle.

At the Bibliagathon, I went straight to the musicology room, intent on retrieving the slim manuscript that had been tucked into Orma's notes. My ulterior motive, of course, was to check whether Orma had returned. He might even be here, hard at work. Alas, the little room was empty, and his notes were wedged into the volume of Thoric exactly as I'd replaced them. I glanced behind me as if he might walk around the corner, set his things on the table with apparent unconcern, look up slowly, and . . . not smile.

He did not appear. This was a silly way to look for him, like some shy suitor mooning about in front of the beloved's house, hoping for a glimpse. Orma had come to Porphyry with Eskar, and Eskar had been dealing with the exiles. Did the exiles live in a particular neighborhood? That would be the place to start.

Still, I filched the leather-bound, handwritten testament Orma had secreted in the book, not merely to give Ingar something to do—although it would work brilliantly for that—but in hopes that Orma would miss it and would contact me at the address I'd written in his notes.

The librarians had frisked Ingar last night; I couldn't walk out with this book under my arm. I shoved the ancient manuscript up under my tunic.

Of course, this unsubtle subterfuge made it awkward to talk

with librarians; I'd clearly done things in the wrong order. Keeping my arms folded across my even-flatter-than-usual chest, I approached a pair of librarians pushing a cart of scrolls up the corridor. They listened politely to my mangled questions, but neither remembered a tall, bushy-haired, bespectacled foreigner with a beaky nose and no manners.

"No manners by our standards, or by yours?" the younger librarian asked, sagely stroking his peach-fuzzed chin.

"By mine," I said.

"So, climbing shelves and drinking ink," said the other librarian, a stout woman with a charcoal pencil stuck into her curly hair. I was not quite convinced she knew it was there. "I'd remember such an unruly Southlander," she said.

"Ha ha," I said, trying to maintain a cheerful expression. "But where is it a neighborhood of saarantrai? Where part of the city?"

The younger man broke into a smile. "The exiles mostly live in Metasaari. That, we can help you find."

The woman knew exactly where her pencil was; she extracted it expertly and drew directions to Metasaari on a scrap of paper, and then another map (at my request) to House Perdixis, which turned out to be quite close. I thanked the librarians in the most formal way possible. The young man got a funny look on his face, then said in flawless Goreddi: "Sometimes simpler is better. If you say a casual *charimatizi* in a sweet voice, maybe batting your eyes, no one will fault you."

"Well then, *charimatizi*," I said, blinking aggressively. It wasn't quite the same as batting, but that was all he was going to get.

From the way the pair grinned at each other, I knew I'd

provided them with ridiculous-foreigner stories for a week. I hugged my chest and wandered off, knowing they weren't the only ones who'd gotten a laugh.

I went to Camba's first, since it was only three blocks north and two blocks east. The librarians had explained what I would see, or I would never have recognized the facade of the great house: the only part visible was an intricately carved wooden door between a wineshop and a pastry maker's. Plain marble columns flanked the door, their pediments inlaid with geometric figures in contrasting colors. Wealth was evident if you looked, but House Perdixis did not put on an ostentatious display.

I extracted the purloined manuscript from under my tunic and examined the battered leather cover. This unassuming text contained proof, according to Orma's notes, that the Saints had been half-dragons. That thought perturbed me. When it was merely Orma's crackpot fancy, I could laugh at the notion—indeed, I felt urgently that I needed to laugh. It was deeply unsettling to think that the Saints might have been something as prosaic as me.

What did it mean for all of us—human and ityasaari alike—if it was true? Why didn't any of our scriptures mention it? Had the Saints' few, negative allusions to interbreeding been a deliberate obfuscation of the truth, similar to the way I had always hidden?

There was no point tying myself in knots until I knew for sure what this testament said. I would want to read Ingar's translation when it was finished.

House Perdixis had a bronze knocker shaped like a hand, poised to beat insistently upon the door. An aged doorman answered almost at once but would not let me in. Camba wasn't home; she'd taken Ingar to some Mathematical Society meeting, as best I could discern. I left the manuscript for Ingar and retreated, disappointed. I would bring the rest of Ingar's belongings tomorrow, and ask Camba about the other ityasaari then.

As I turned to leave, I heard a scrabbling above me, claws against tile. I looked up and saw a woman in black squatting on the roof of the wineshop, watching me. She was tiny, barely Abdo's size, and in place of arms she had wings with clawed hands at the ends. Long silver scales plumed her wings like feathers. Her graying hair was braided tightly to her scalp in zigzagging lines; she had two swords strapped across her back.

I knew her. In my garden, I called her Miserere. In visions, I'd seen her nab pickpockets in the Grand Emporio and stop temple thieves, putting those swords to swift and skillful use. She was an officer of the law; her black-clad brethren patrolled the Zokalaa. What was she doing here? Had she followed me? It occurred to me that Pende might have asked her to. I hoped that wasn't the case; perhaps she was merely curious.

"Hello!" I called, and then more properly in Porphyrian, "I greet you as the ocean greets the morning sun."

Her eyes glittered with amusement, or possibly malice. Her mouth, a thin line, was hard to read. She spread her wings and launched herself into the sky.

She was so elegant in flight that she took my breath with her.

I reached Metasaari an hour later. A buttress jutted out of the mountain, separating the two halves of the city at the top, so I'd had to return to the harbor, go east, and then climb back uphill. The eastern heights, like the western, grew wealthier the higher one went. There were fewer apartment blocks here and more single dwellings, some with colorful marble facades or fluted columns. Trees lined the streets, dark cedars and pollarded sycamores with whitewashed trunks. I reached a large park with a public fountain where women were gossiping, water jugs on their hips. Fruit and nut vendors stalked the perimeter with carts; servants scurried past, feet slapping the flagstone street.

This park, according to the librarians' map, was the heart of Metasaari. It was a far cry from Quighole, our dismal saar ghetto back home.

But where were the dragons? I saw no one with my sallow complexion. The people here, conversing in the shade of the stunted sycamores, pushing handcarts up the hill, were all brown-skinned Porphyrians.

I stopped at a corner caupona, where food bubbled in great pots built right into the counter. They had eggplant stew and octopus balls in gravy—tastier than it sounds—but I wasn't there to eat. I lined up behind a thin and apparently hungry man who ordered a lot of everything; he finally shuffled off to an outdoor table, balancing a heaped bowl in each hand, and I stepped up to the counter.

"Excuse," I said to the shriveled proprietress. "Does your mouth speak Goreddi?"

She waved her ladle impatiently and said in Porphyrian, "What're you having?"

"One glass tea," I managed, fumbling for a coin in my little purse. "No Goreddi? It is fair. I try more. Do you see saarantrai in circle of this park?"

She shook her head and muttered, "Foreign fool," as she handed me my change. I turned, mortified, toward the patio tables. "You forgot your tea!" the woman called after me. I retrieved it; the cup rattled against the saucer.

"Excuse me," said a low, pleasant voice, the thin man who'd stood ahead of me in line. He was sitting at a patio table, waving a large hand in case I didn't see him. "I didn't mean to eavesdrop," he said in Goreddi, "but I speak your language. Can I help?"

I hesitated, then set my tea on his table and pulled up a chair. He hailed the caupona owner, who grumblingly brought him spiced wine. "She's rude to everyone," he stage-whispered. "It's part of her charm."

Small spectacles perched upon his long, straight nose, and he had pulled his long, straight hair into a Ninysh-style ponytail at the nape of his neck. He wore a short Goreddi houppelande over Porphyrian trousers. Clearly he was a man who traveled.

"Have you been to Goredd?" I asked, swallowing my rising homesickness.

"I lived there for years," said the man warmly. He held out a hand. "I'm Lalo."

"Seraphina," I said, shaking his hand, another curious memento of home.

"I heard you're looking for dragons?" he said, digging into his bowl of octopus.

I took a sip of scalding tea. It was unexpectedly minty. "I am. There's supposed to be a community of exiles here."

"That's right," said Lalo. "Metasaari. This is it."

I looked at the other caupona patrons, the women beside the fountain, the fruit vendors and pedestrians, and saw only Porphyrians. "Where are the saarantrai?"

He laughed. The sun glinted on his teeth. "All around you, hatchling. I am one."

I almost choked on my tea. I stared at Lalo's face, his easy grin, his dark skin. Saints in Heaven. He was like no dragon I'd ever met.

He leaned forward, elbows on the table. "I know what you're thinking. You've only ever seen saarantrai the color of cave fish, but brown is our default shade. Look." He splayed his large hand on the tiled tabletop. Before my very eyes, the skin of his hand lightened until it was almost as pale as my own, and then it darkened again.

I was too astonished to speak.

"Silver blood," he explained. "If we bring it to the surface, we pale. This sort of camouflage is useful in our natural habitat, where the biggest danger is other dragons, or in the Southlands, where we don't dare stand out too much."

Embarrassingly, I had noted the skin color of the people in this neighborhood and then considered the matter no further.

Looking out at Metasaari now, I saw what my assumptions had blinded me to: a subtle angularity, more muted colors of clothing, no ornaments, and short, practical hairstyles. The fruit vendors didn't shout or sing about their wares; the fountain's gurgling was louder than the women's gossiping. If these were saarantrai, they were more subdued than their Porphyrian counterparts.

Still, Lalo grinned. These were not quite saarantrai as I'd known them in Goredd, either.

Orma would likely be dark-skinned here. Could I have walked past without seeing him? I had asked the librarians whether they'd seen a foreigner, presumably pale like me.

"Are you looking for someone specific?" said Lalo, starting in on his eggplant.

I took another sip of tea. "His name is Orma."

"Son of Imlann and Eri? Brother of Linn?"

My heart leaped. "Yes! You've seen him?"

Lalo shook his head. "Not for years. I was at university with his sister."

Orma had surely been cautious, even of other dragons; that was no surprise. I tried a different angle. "He's with another dragon, called Eskar."

"Eskar, yes. She's been here for several months," he said, wagging his spoon at me. He added in a quieter voice, "She's trying to get us home to the Tanamoot. Not everyone thinks it wise. For my part, I'm no fighter, but I'll do what it takes to get back. I've found nothing but heartbreak here."

"Why were you exiled?" I said, instinctively matching his quietness.

Lalo sighed, disconcertingly melancholy, and scraped up the last of his octopus gravy with his spoon. "I wasn't. I fell in love with a Goreddi woman and went home for excision like a good little saar." He took a gulp of wine and gazed up at the cloudless sky. "In a fit of romantic stupidity, however, I made myself a mind-pearl before I went."

I knew a bit about mind-pearls, a way dragons had of encapsulating memories and hiding them; my mother had left some in my mind, which I'd never suspected until the sight of Orma in his natural shape had triggered them to open. The trigger could be anything.

I twisted the pearl ring on my pinkie, suddenly wondering what Orma had meant by *The thing itself plus nothing equals everything.* Had he made himself a mind-pearl? Was that what he was trying to tell me?

Lalo's gaze had grown distant. "I wanted to keep those days alive inside me even if I couldn't remember them. I purposefully forgot how to trigger my mind-pearl, because I never intended to do it. Alas, I tripped over that forgotten trigger, remembered all, found her again, and . . . she'd moved on. She's married, and here I am, stuck with my sorrow."

"I'm sorry," I said, finding this turn of conversation intense and awkward. I couldn't imagine such an admission from Orma or Eskar. "Um. Do you know where I can find Eskar?"

He stuffed his mouth with eggplant and rice and didn't look at me. "Eskar's gone. Two weeks now, not a word to anyone."

That was a surprise. Comonot's entire Porphyrian gambit was her idea; surely she wouldn't have left, not with Comonot due to arrive in less than two weeks. If she wasn't here, where would she have gone? "Was there another dragon with her?" I pressed.

Lalo shrugged irritably. "I don't know."

I wasn't put off by his brusqueness; that's what I was used to from dragons. He was clearly done talking to me. I rose to go, scraping the chair back. "Thank you for your time." He nodded, brushing crumbs off his table for the birds.

I walked back toward Naia's. The more I thought about it—Orma's cryptic riddle, his caginess in the letter—the more convinced I was that he'd made a mind-pearl, and that he'd wanted me to know. Had it been a precaution, or had he feared that the Censors were close on his trail?

Might he have left town with Eskar—or more accurately, might Eskar have left town with him? I could believe that she'd leave Porphyry, even with the Ardmagar's arrival imminent, to protect Orma.

I wished Orma's ring had been a thnik after all; I could have contacted him and put my mind at ease. Instead, I fretted all the way to the lower city, the afternoon sun beating on the crown of my head.

I had hopes, at the end of this day of dead ends, that at least Abdo's struggle might have come to its conclusion. Alas, the moment I stepped into Naia's building, I could tell something had gone terribly wrong. A few of Abdo's cousins still sat on the stairs, no longer laughing. Only the older women remained in Naia's apartment, lighting candles in a circle on the floor. I paused in the doorway, wondering whether I had come back too early, but Naia jumped up as soon as she spotted me. Without a word, she took my elbow, led me to Abdo's alcove, and drew back the curtain. Abdo lay on his mat, twitching fitfully, his eyes open but unseeing. An old woman dabbed his forehead with a wet sea sponge.

"We took him to Paulos Pende," Naia whispered. "Have no doubt. You were right. The old priest put aside his ire—how could he not, seeing Abdo like this?"

"Abdo was like this?" I asked, horrified.

"Worse. He fought us; he bit Uncle Fasias. He would have been screaming, if he could scream." She paused, and I saw that she was holding back tears. Her nostrils flattened as she inhaled; her lips trembled. "Pende could do nothing for him, not when Jannoula has got him and he's fighting her so hard. We need to wait until he prevails and she is dormant, or until he loses the fight and she is at rest."

I knelt by Abdo's aged auntie, held out my hand, and said, "May I take a turn?" She wordlessly handed me the sponge, but she didn't leave. We sat together and shared our sorrow.

ᴄᴦEiꞬHteenᴧᴐ

There followed a fortnight of frustration.

I took Ingar's things to Camba's the very next day, but the doorman said Camba was attending a performance of Necans's *Bitter Nothing* with her Tragedy Fanciers' Club. I said I'd come back another day.

Abdo's extended family cared for him in shifts. Naia was one of eight siblings, so every day it seemed I was meeting new aunts, uncles, and cousins. They came bearing hot food and took turns feeding him. The cousins brought amusements—dice, jacks, a snaking board game called sysix—but Abdo was in no condition to play. He tossed and turned as if with fever, or slept fitfully; sometimes he woke with Jannoula in his eyes, but she never had enough control to speak to me through him.

Morning and evening, I tried to talk to him. He replied only once: *I'm building a wall, Phina madamina. Like you did. I think I can keep her from—*

Then his struggle pulled him under again.

I went out every day with a tight, cold knot of worry under my ribs. Sometimes a dizziness would overtake me, an effervescent buzz of fear, but I steeled myself against it, putting one foot in front of the other and faithfully barking up all the wrong trees.

I went back to Camba's. She was washing her hair and couldn't see me.

I got better at identifying saarantrai in Metasaari; they were emotional for dragons, but their mannerisms were understated. They hadn't picked up the boisterous range of Porphyrian gestures one saw in the rest of the city; they kissed each other's cheeks in greeting, but with the utmost seriousness. I asked at saarantrai shops, doctors' offices, importing houses, and law firms, but everyone told the same story: Eskar had been and gone. No one had so much as glimpsed Orma; his notes at the Bibliagathon remained undisturbed.

After four or five days of writing Camba and receiving no reply, I resigned myself to finding the other ityasaari on my own. I still had a garden in my mind, for all that it was rapidly shrinking (forty-seven paces between the Milestones; forty-two; thirty-nine). I could induce visions of any of them.

Winged Miserere, whom I'd already glimpsed, didn't require even that much effort. I saw her almost every day, perched on rooftops or statuary, policing the city like some sinister vulture, her very presence a deterrent to crime. I couldn't get near her perch, alas, and she did not deign to approach me. It occurred to me that my best chance to meet her might be to commit a crime. Of course, I never seriously entertained the notion; Kiggs and Glisselda would have been mortified.

I located the tall, athletic twins of my visions—called Nag and Nagini in my garden—on the day they were to receive public honors for their victories during the city's Solstice Games. I rushed to the Zokalaa in time to catch most of the ceremony, watching from the back of the crowd, standing on tiptoe and craning my neck. They were fraternal twins, male and female, but they looked nearly identical with their close-cropped hair, white tunics, and skin the darkest shade on the Porphyrian spectrum. I guessed they were about my age, sixteen or seventeen. They stood atop the steps of the Vasilikon, holding hands, their eyes lowered modestly, while a great-voiced herald read out the Assembly's proclamation of honor and a priestess of Lakhis crowned them with lush green wreaths.

Beside me, a bearded man—but then, that described half the men of Porphyry—smiled at my interest and leaned in. "They're the best runners we've seen in a generation," he said in Samsamese, mistaking my ethnicity.

He nattered on about their speed and statistics, and the glory of the goddess. I listened, curious whether he'd tell me they were ityasaari, but he never mentioned it. Was it simply unremarkable, or did he not know?

The twins lived with the other consecrated athletes in a special precinct behind the temple of Lakhis. There was no entry for the likes of me.

In visions, I often saw the one called Gargoyella hurrying up the steps of the Vasilikon. She was an elderly woman with white braids wrapped around her golden Agogoi circlet; she always wore a red stole trimmed in blue, clearly some badge of office. I questioned citizens in the Zokalaa and learned that she was a lawyer, the Assembly's chief prosecutor, and her real name was Maaga Reges Phloxia.

I screwed up all my courage and stepped in front of her one evening as she was descending the steps. She was much shorter than me, and clearly did not like being stopped, because she smiled at me.

I'd seen that smile in visions, so I wasn't surprised, but it was still alarming. Her mouth, which she normally kept tightly pursed, spread unnaturally wide, almost to her ears, revealing pointed teeth like a shark's.

"Out of my way," she said in clear Goreddi.

"Forgive me, Phloxia," I said. "My name is Seraphina Dom—"

"I know who you are," Phloxia said sharply. "Paulos Pende has forbidden me to speak to you. Do you know the full legal implications of such a priestly injunction?"

She was so lawyerly, so reminiscent of my father, that I almost laughed. I could tell I was about to get an earful, so I raised my hands in surrender to her shark-like smile and backed away. "I don't know Porphyrian law at all," I said. "I'm going to have to take your word for it, whatever your argument may be."

Her gaze softened a little. "I think he's depriving us of a wonderful opportunity. I always suspected we had Southlander cousins. I've been looking for a loophole," she said quietly, her mouth wobbling grotesquely as she spoke. "I haven't found one yet."

Then she wrapped her stole around her and hurried away into the Zokalaa crowds.

The last ityasaari, Newt, was a singer. I enjoyed inducing visions of him; I could have listened forever. I knew he often performed in the harbor market, warbling behind a row of canvas booths, or joining in with singing fisherfolk as they unloaded their crab pots. I began stalking him with my flute, parking myself in the market to play. He didn't approach, but I'd hear him in the distance, singing the shadow of my song. We circled, shy of each other, never meeting, until one morning I spotted him, sitting on the edge of the fountain: a white-haired, freckled old man with an oddly elongated torso and stunted limbs.

He had cataracts in both eyes, but he looked up as if he sensed me and smiled beatifically, his wispy hair fluffing in the breeze like clouds upon the mountaintop. He closed his scaled eyes, raised his chin, and began to sing a low, droning note. The crowd around him quieted to a dull murmur, elbowing each other, as if they knew his singing and treasured it. Above his drone, as light and tremulous as flames dancing on water, keened an ephemeral overtone, a ghostly, whistling harmonic.

This singing technique was called sinus-song in Ziziba. I'd read about it, and speculated upon its mechanics with Orma, but I'd never heard it done. I didn't know the art was practiced in Porphyry.

After a couple of false starts, I found a way to accompany his ethereal song with my clumsy, earthbound flute. Together we wove a song of sky and sea and the mortals who must live between the two.

A trumpet blared, a brassy knife through the middle of our music, and we cut off abruptly. The crowd parted for a large palanquin draped in white, borne by muscular young men. Behind the gauzy curtains, I could make out three priests of Chakhon, Paulos Pende among them. Worried about the "priestly injunction" Phloxia had mentioned, I turned away reflexively so he wouldn't see me. I didn't want to get Newt in trouble for associating with me.

The litter passed and the marketplace resumed its bustle, but my music partner had disappeared into the maze of tables and tents.

⚔

Camba wrote back at long last, two weeks to the day after Pende had pulled Jannoula out of Ingar's mind:

> *Many thanks for the peculiar syphered journal. As you perhaps anticipated, Ingar can't stop himself from thinking about it, taking notes, and trying to translate it. He has asked to see you. Come at once, before the day heats up, and we'll sit out in the garden.*

The handwriting, blocky and stiff, was not Camba's, and for a moment I wondered if Ingar had written the note, pretending to be Camba. Ingar would not have misspelled *ciphered*, though, not with his language skills. It was most peculiar.

Still, I welcomed the distraction and, unexpectedly, looked forward to seeing Ingar again.

The doddering doorman of House Perdixis let me in; I was expected, it seemed, so the note must have been written with Camba's knowledge. I waited in her dim, faded atrium, where a cracked fountain trickled. An allegorical statue of Commerce gazed sternly into the pool; she was green in all her nooks and crannies. Camba, long-necked and stately, came out to meet me, kissed me solemnly upon both cheeks, and made me remove my shoes. Behind her, a petite white-haired woman, elegantly dressed, lingered in the doorway, watching me with crow-like eyes.

"My mother, Amalia Perdixis Lita," said Camba, gesturing graciously.

I was rifling through my memory, trying to recollect the proper way a foreigner should greet a woman who outranks her in age, class, and sheer Porphyrian-ness, when Camba's mother did the surprising. She approached and kissed my cheeks, then grabbed my head and planted a larger kiss on my brow. I'm sure I looked flabbergasted; her face crinkled into a smile.

"Camba tells me you're the one who spoke to her on the mountainside that terrible day," said the old woman in Porphyrian. "She thought she'd ruined the reputation of House Perdixis with that poisonous glassware, but you persuaded her to come back and face her brothers. As her mother, I must thank you for that."

I blinked, thinking my Porphyrian had failed me.

Camba took my arm and led me away, saying, "We'll be in the garden, Mother."

She took me up a dim corridor. "Poisonous glassware?" I asked in Goreddi.

Camba averted her eyes. "I imported it from Ziziba, my first solo business deal. It came extremely cheap; I never questioned why. We later learned it was coated with an iridescent glaze, pretty to look at but easily dissolved by liquids. A baby died."

That was why she'd wanted to kill herself. I'd assumed it was shame at being half dragon. I'd revised my guess after learning she'd misgendered herself, but that had also been wrong.

A single action could derive from many motivations. I should never assume.

We passed through a book-lined study, where two boys about Abdo's age worked complicated geometry problems. "Mestor, Paulos," said Camba, pausing to glance at their work. "Finish Eudema's theorem, and then you're dismissed."

"Yes, Aunt Camba," they droned.

"I leave the import business to my elder brothers these days," said Camba as we quit the room. She smiled shyly. "Now I tutor my nephews in mathematics and study with Paulos Pende."

We emerged into a manicured garden, a tidy square of lawn bordered by dark cedars and flanked by two long rectangular pools. A linen sunshade billowed gently in the breeze, and underneath it half a dozen people sat in wrought-iron chairs. It took a moment for my eyes to readjust to the sunlight and recognize Ingar, Phloxia the lawyer, winged Miserere, harbor-singing Newt, and the smiling twins.

"Phloxia found a loophole," said Camba beside me, her voice quiet and low, "and we can't be charged with impiety if we didn't know you were coming."

"You invited me!" I cried, astonished.

Her eyes twinkled deviously. "Indeed, I did not. My nephews took dictation to practice their Goreddi. It was never meant to be sent. Clearly, Chakhon's chancy hand was in it, to a degree even Pende couldn't dispute. By merciful Necessity, goddess of guests, we welcome you."

Seeing them all like this, gathered together in a garden, I felt a little overcome. This was what I had longed for, so exactly, down to the cool grass and tidily shaped shrubberies. I caught Ingar's eye across the yard; he smiled and nodded, but held back while the others lined up and kissed my cheeks in turn.

"Mina," said Miserere, introducing herself.

"So pleased," I croaked, clasping one of her clawed hands in mine.

Mina helped Newt forward, for he was nearly blind. "I'm called Brasidas," he said in Porphyrian, extending his short arm. I took his twisted hand and kissed his freckled cheeks; he beamed and added, "Did you bring your flute?"

"She couldn't know we would be here," snapped Phloxia in Goreddi.

"But now that I am here, is it legal for you to stay?" I asked, teasing Phloxia while she administered air-kisses near my ears.

"Oh, I'm here on an errand," said Phloxia, a devilish look in her eyes. She held up a gold filigree brooch. "I'm returning this to Camba. I can't trust the servants with it, and I certainly can't be expected to leave until she takes it from me."

"Maybe Seraphina sings," said Brasidas hopefully in Porphyrian.

"Shove over and let the twins have their turn," said the shark-toothed lawyer, pulling Brasidas aside.

The tall, graceful youngsters kissed both my cheeks at once. "Gaios, Gelina," they said, their voices nearly identical. Our dragon heritage had left so many ityasaari deformed, but these two had been born absurdly beautiful. Even their silver scales had the decency to manifest in tidy patches behind their ears. They dressed in simple tunics without ornament or ostentation, according to the dictates of Necessity, but that only seemed to underscore how naturally radiant they were.

Servants had set up a table to one side and laid it with figs, olives, and honeyed millet cakes. Camba poured from a sweating silver ewer a cold, thick concoction of lemon, honey, and snow. It froze my teeth.

We talked together in a mix of Goreddi and Porphyrian, Ingar or Phloxia translating when I needed it. I asked them for their stories; they told me how Pende had taken them under his wing as youngsters and they had served the temple of Chakhon for a time. Mina still acted as a guardian of sorts, and Brasidas sang there on holy days.

"Pende is our spiritual father," said Phloxia, smiling ruefully, "and each of us his disappointing child."

"He's happy with Camba," offered Brasidas, talking around a mouthful of figs.

"Yes, well, Camba came back to him, and Pende trained her to see the soul-light," said Phloxia. She leaned over her plate of millet cakes and whispered exaggeratedly, "The rest of us were failures. We saw no light. I'm not sure we all can."

"I can see Gelina's," said Gaios, his eyes wide and earnest.

"And I yours, brother," said Gelina, resting her shapely head on his shoulder.

"The twins are a walking solipsism: self-referential," said Phloxia, gazing at them fondly. She was like a sweeter Dame Okra. "Anyway, they broke the old man's heart in turn by leaving Chakhon for Lakhis."

"It was necessary," said Gelina, her brows buckling anxiously. Gaios nodded.

Winged Mina stuffed olives into her mouth at an alarming rate, never spitting out any pits. When she spoke, her voice was raspy and raw: "The god doesn't call us all. Pende understands why we leave."

"I told Pende I had to leave, by Chakhon's own logic," said Phloxia. "If I'm to serve the god of chance, my presence in the temple should also be a matter of chance."

Ingar chuckled at this, shaking his bald head; he seemed at home here. "Phloxia," said Camba, who was sitting beside him, "you twist logic to your own purposes."

"It's a lawyer's duty," sniffed Phloxia, bunching her wobbly mouth into a pout.

Camba's eyes twinkled fondly. "Didn't I hear you had a brooch for me?"

"That's hearsay!" cried Phloxia. "I can neither confirm nor deny . . ."

I rose and drifted over to the food table before the servants carried the last of the millet cakes away. Behind me the others laughed. They had so much history together and knew each other so well. I felt a bit overcome. This was what I had wanted to create in Goredd. Exactly this.

These ityasaari might be willing to bend Pende's rules enough to meet me here, but I doubted they would go so far as to travel to Goredd against his wishes—and why should they? To defend someone else's country? To re-create what they already had here?

I couldn't ask them to come to Goredd, not with Jannoula waiting to pounce on them as soon as they ventured south, not when the one who could free them of her was certain to stay behind.

"You look melancholy," said Ingar at my elbow, startling me. "I suspect I know why. I dreamed of this garden, too. So did Jannoula, but it can be accomplished without her."

This was a new Ingar. The intensity and focus of his gaze astonished me.

"You look well," I said.

He nodded gravely and pushed up his square spectacles. "Thank Camba. She believed in me when there wasn't much me to be found." Ingar's thick lips twitched; he took a deep breath. "But you know what else has helped? I'll show you."

Ingar led me toward the house, under a shady portico. Two iron-framed chairs stood like sentinels beside a pile of books. Ingar picked a slim volume off the top of the heap. I recognized it immediately.

"I deciphered this," said Ingar, gesturing me to a seat. "It's Goreddi transliterated into the Porphyrian alphabet and written in mirror-hand, with gaps inserted at intervals to make it look like a cipher. Not so difficult, honestly, and I'm not the first to have read it. Look here." He flipped to the last page, where someone had written in Goreddi:

To the librarians:
    This is a tome of some historical value, I believe. It cannot remain in Goredd, but neither can I destroy it. Please file it wherever you file apocryphal religious writings. Heaven keep you.
    Father Reynard of St. Vitt's, Bowstugh Wallow

Lower down the page, Father Reynard had added one more faint line: *St. Yirtrudis, if you are a Saint—if anyone is—forgive me for what I must do.*

"Is this book about Yirtrudis? She's a strange Saint to address otherwise," I said, an unexpected hope rising in my chest. I'd always felt a visceral kinship with the hidden patroness of my hidden heritage.

Suddenly the possibility that Orma's thesis might be true nearly overwhelmed me. My patroness, at least, might be truly, properly mine.

Ingar waggled his eyebrows. "It's the only known copy of St. Yirtrudis's testament. Perhaps even the original. How's your ecclesiastical history?"

"Utterly worthless," I said.

Ingar was relishing this. "Just two generations ago, this Father Reynard became Bishop Reynard of Blystane. From that seat of power, backed by my people, the aggressively devout Samsamese, he denounced St. Yirtrudis as a heretic."

"Because of something in this testament?" I asked, clamping my hands between my knees to still them.

"Because of everything in it!" cried Ingar. "Yirtrudis throws everything we think we know about the Saints into confusion."

I lowered my voice, as if the Porphyrians were going to care. "Does it say the Saints were half-dragons?"

Ingar leaned back to observe me with more distance. "That's one of many remarkable claims. But how did you guess?"

I explained about Orma's theories. "I found the book with his notes. He claimed to have read it, but he didn't leave his translation at the library."

"I'll write one out for you," said Ingar, nodding firmly. "I can read the text easily, of course, having cracked the cipher. You should hear the story in her own words. Everything is clear to me now."

I opened my mouth to ask what he meant, but something over my shoulder had caught his eye. I followed his gaze and saw Camba approaching, her sandals clacking on the flagstones.

"We've heard about Abdo," Camba said solemnly. "I'm sorry he's suffering. It's cold consolation, but Jannoula's struggle with Abdo may be preventing her from bringing other evils to fruition. Here." She handed me a bundle wrapped in a napkin. "Some cakes for Abdo and his family. Please take them our love and prayers." This was clearly my cue to go. I rose and glanced down at Ingar.

His eyes shone like hopeful stars as he looked at Camba. In that instant one thing became clear to me: Ingar wasn't coming to Goredd, either. I couldn't blame him, but my melancholy returned and followed me back to Naia's.

That night I entered my garden of grotesques with a new sense of purpose. I was not there merely to soothe the grotesques—or myself—but to change something that had been niggling at me. I'd been finding myself more and more embarrassed by the silly names I'd given these people I was connected to. Master Smasher was the wrong gender, even in Goreddi; Newt (for his stunted limbs) and Gargoyella (for her enormous mouth) were outright insulting.

It was bad enough that I had affixed everyone's mind-fire to myself without asking. The least I could do was call them by their right names.

I walked the winding paths, through meadows, over streams, among lush foliage, touching each upon the head and renaming them: Brasidas, Phloxia, Mina, Gaios, Gelina, Ingar, Camba, Blanche, Nedouard, Od Fredricka, Dame Okra, Lars, Abdo.

I'd expected to feel everyone's presence more keenly if I named them; maybe it wasn't just shame that drove me, but some hope of renewal (the Milestones were now but twenty-three paces apart). If my garden could never exist in the real world as I had imagined it, so be it, but I would shore it up here. I felt Pende's and Gianni's absence constantly, as if I'd lost two teeth and couldn't stop prodding my gums with my tongue.

Only when I reached Pandowdy, the single ityasaari I had not yet met in the real world, did I begin to realize my mistake. He rose out of the swamp, an enormous scaly slug, caked with grime, as big as ever. He loomed over me and touched the sky.

Literally.

His nose—or whatever you call the pointy tip of a featureless worm—jabbed the limpid blue as if it were the ceiling of a canvas tent. I gaped, disbelieving, whirled to face the rest of the garden, and bumped my head on another dollop of drooping sky.

I fell to my knees in a patch of moss—or not moss, but a tiny rose garden, with a tiny sundial in the center, and a tiny Dame Okra beside it, the size of a skittle-pin. I picked her up and stared at her. Beside the minuscule rose garden ran a narrow ditch, once an imposing ravine; jammed in this cranny was a skittle-pin Lars.

The sky, sagging further, touched the back of my neck. It was clammy.

The shrunken denizens of my garden were all within arm's reach, as were the border fences, the egression gate, and the peeling, full-sized door of Jannoula's cottage. That hadn't shrunk; it was the only thing holding up the sky.

I gathered my people like twigs and laid them side by side on the lawn. How had this happened? Had I done this by naming them? I had only intended good, had only meant to ... to acknowledge who they really were.

Was I finally seeing my own handiwork clearly? Abdo had called my garden a narrow gatehouse. I had imagined these human forms; maybe naming them had dispelled that illusion. All that was left was the mind-fire I had stolen. If I squinted, the row of doll-like avatars glowed faintly. I could finally see mind-fire; that was no comfort at all.

My formerly wide-open spaces were making me claustrophobic. I beat back the damp sky-fabric and crawled toward the egression gate. "This is my garden, all in ard," I said, the words catching in my throat. "I tend it faithfully. Let it keep faith with me."

I opened my eyes to the darkness of Naia's apartment. I lay still for some moments, breathing hard and listening to echoing footsteps in the street below, to the bump and creak of ships upon the ceaseless sea. My heartbeat slowed, but my racing thoughts did not.

ᴄᴧNineteen᷈ᴧᴊ

My thnik linked me to Glisselda; another connected her with Kiggs. During that fruitless fortnight, she kept me apprised of when his ship would arrive. I haunted the docks the morning it was due, getting underfoot of fishermen and stevedores. I had just bought myself lunch and was wholly occupied with keeping it away from the bold and saucy seagulls when I heard someone cry, "Garegia!" which is Porphyrian for Goredd.

A sloop had entered the harbor and was drifting slowly west in search of its berth. It flew a purple and green flag, adorned with a prancing rabbit, the emblem of the Royal House of Goredd.

I tossed my eggplant fritters to the gulls and was running toward the western docks in two heartbeats.

I followed the ship, dodging haggling merchants, crab pots, and heaped fishing nets, skirting cargo piles and gaggles of bearded sailors, trying to keep the mast and flag in sight. I reached the right berth, out of breath, just as the mariners lowered the gangway. I scanned the faces on deck and spotted the familiar hawkish nose and jowly chin of Ardmagar Comonot, deposed leader of all dragonkind.

He spotted me from the prow and cried out a greeting. He'd already relaxed into a darker complexion; his hair had been powerfully slicked down but was curling back up at the fringes. Comonot waved vigorously, with no thought for the safety of those around him. "Seraphina!" he called, elbowing seamen aside in his haste to maneuver down the gangway. He wore a long blue robe, pleated and embroidered in the style of a Porphyrian gentleman. As he drew nearer, I saw something new: a pale scar along his jawline.

Comonot kissed me effusively on both cheeks in the Porphyrian style, bizarrely grabbing my ears as he did so. I struggled not to laugh; he tried harder than most dragons, but there was always some nuance of human behavior that eluded him.

He stepped back, looked me over, and said in more typical draconic fashion, "Your nose is burned, but you look like you've been eating well."

I smiled, but I was craning my neck, looking for Kiggs in the crowd. I saw Goreddi sailors and the Ardmagar's retinue of saar secretaries and human bodyguards. "Where's Prince Lucian?" I asked, a nervous knot in my stomach.

"I'm sure I don't know," said Comonot, tapping a thick finger upon his lips. He turned to a sailor standing patiently behind him. "Did the prince disembark, or did we throw him overboard during that awful storm?"

I looked at the sailor and saw a stranger, his face framed by a thin travel beard, his hair a bit too long, his smile a bit too . . . No, I knew that smile. My heart knew it, even if my eyes were too stupid to understand what was right in front of them.

"I believe the prince considered throwing *himself* overboard during the storm," said Kiggs earnestly, his brown eyes laughing. "In the end, he decided it might be worth the effort to hang on."

All cleverness failed me. "I'm glad to see you, Prince."

Kiggs stepped up as Comonot had done and kissed my cheeks without the ear pulling. I managed air-kisses at the edge of his silly little beard. He smelled of salt and musty ship innards and himself.

I felt suddenly shy. The months had made strangers of us.

The Ardmagar inserted himself between us and took my arm. "I joked—did you notice? I said I didn't know, when in fact I did, and then I pretended to wonder—"

"Indeed, Ardmagar. Well done," I said.

"He's been testing jokes on me since we left Lavondaville," said Prince Lucian Kiggs, smiling over Comonot's head. "It only took me a week to notice they were jokes."

"Old saar, new tricks," I said, smiling back.

"Don't imagine I'm as slow to recognize mockery as I once was, either," said the Ardmagar, but he didn't seem angry. He was gazing wide-eyed at the harbor crowds, the ships, the warehouses. Months of close dealings with humans had done nothing to diminish his naked fascination with human variety.

Kiggs excused himself to have words with their retinue, who seemed to be in some confusion over baggage and porters.

Comonot, at my shoulder, said quietly, "So. After trying everything else, it's down to Eskar's plan after all. Sneaking in the back door while my Loyalists feint south. This is all assuming I can persuade the Porphyrians to let me break a centuries-old treaty and travel up the Omiga Valley."

"And that they'll let the exiles go," I said. "I've met a few already. Eskar has been preparing your way, it seems. Do you know where she is?"

"She's here," Comonot said. "You just said so."

"No, she *was* here. She's been missing for almost a month," I said, adding the last fortnight to Lalo's reported two weeks. "You don't keep better track of your operatives than that?"

"I don't worry about them, if that's what you're asking," said Comonot. He pulled a mass of gold chains out of the neck hole of his robe and sorted through their pendants for the right thnik.

Kiggs was returning to us through the harborside crowd. "We sent a runner ahead to House Malou," he called, "and they've hired some bearers to—" He cut himself short at the sight of the Ardmagar's jewelry. "Don't dangle your thniks," he said, hurrying to block Comonot from the prying eyes of passersby.

"Porphyrians aren't alarmed by dragons," I assured him.

The Ardmagar rolled his eyes at the pair of us. He'd found the communicator, a silver oblong, and spoke into it: "Eskar. Where are you? Report at once."

We all strained to hear over the milling crowd, the washing sea, the screams of two gulls fighting over a fritter—possibly one of mine—but the thnik didn't peep. Comonot shrugged. "Silence proves nothing. Maybe she can't answer at the moment. She'll get back to me as soon as she can."

I felt the dizzying rush of panic postponed. "Orma's gone, too."

"Ah. Well, in that case, I'd guess that the Censors got wind of them and they had to go deeper into hiding," said the Ardmagar, turning away. One of his secretaries came running up to lead the old general to the litter they'd hired for him.

"Doesn't the Tanamoot's treaty with Porphyry forbid the Censors from coming after exiles here?" I asked, dogging his steps. Kiggs followed right behind me.

"Only registered exiles," said Comonot over his shoulder as he reached the boxy conveyance. A bearer held open the purple-and-white-striped curtain as the Ardmagar clambered clumsily inside. "Your uncle would not have been registered."

Kiggs, at my elbow, said quietly, "Don't worry, we'll find out what's happened."

I nodded stupidly. The effervescent fear was back, the rush under my ribs. I had pushed down my worries about Orma, but Comonot's talk of Censors brought it gushing to the surface. I took a tight breath and gestured at the litter. "Where are you going now?"

"House Malou. They're expecting us," said the prince, making no move to get in after Comonot, but studying my expression. His own held a mix of concern and regret. The breeze tossed his hair around and blew through the gap between us.

The Ardmagar popped his head out of the striped curtains.

"Quit lollygagging, Prince. You have Agogoi to meet, and a nation to represent."

"Give me a minute," said Kiggs, waving a hand irritably at Comonot, his eyes never leaving my face. The Ardmagar snorted and pulled his head back inside the litter.

Kiggs leaned in; my breath caught foolishly. He said, "Selda has kept me apprised of your progress here. She's worried that you'll feel you've failed."

I looked down at the sea-beaten stone pier; his eyes were too much for me.

"And she told me," he continued doggedly, "'Lucian, you are to take good care of her, for she may be feeling fragile. Tell her we love her just the same, and we're so pleased she tried, and it's going to be all right.'"

I had not been aware of fragility, but his words brought a raging tide of emotion to my shores. I had failed to find Orma, to protect Abdo from Jannoula, to gather the ityasaari. The garden I'd longed for was here, and I couldn't have it; the prince I'd longed for was here, and the answer was exactly the same. For a moment it was too much. I waited until I trusted myself to answer. "She is very kind. Kinder than I deserve."

"We will discuss your deserving," he said, and though my eyes were still lowered, I could hear the smile in his voice. "We'll have plenty of time."

"Yes, you will!" cried Comonot behind us, popping his head out again like some impatient turtle. "Prince, now. Seraphina, come to House Malou tonight. There's to be a welcoming dinner;

they won't mind one more. Say whatever you need to say to each other then."

I met Kiggs's eyes at last, all full of hope and worry. He pulled himself away and climbed into the litter. The bearers hefted it up and trundled slowly away from me, up the hill, toward the colorful marble facades of the western heights.

I watched it go, wondering if Kiggs and I would indeed be able to say all we needed to say to each other, and how long that would take. High above me, a gull laughed.

I desperately needed a bath if I was going into high company this evening. I returned to Naia's apartment for my things, and to check on Abdo.

His extended family was there en masse today; I could tell from the solemn expressions that nothing had changed. I crossed the crowded flat to retrieve my bathing box from behind the curtain, which took some time. I had finally understood, after broad hints from the aunties and a straightforward talking-to from Naia, that it was rude to greet the room at large. I had to greet my elders individually, by name. After fetching my box, I crossed the room again, saying farewell to everyone individually. Abdo's aunties laughed and called after me, "We've almost civilized you!" and "Don't forget to tip the attendant!"

I'd been to the baths several times now, thrice on my own. I still went at Old-Timers' Hour; my bravery had limits. When the old people stared, at least I could pretend it was due to poor eyesight.

I left my clothes in a cubbyhole (not neglecting to tip the attendant), walked underneath a cold torrent rushing from a decorative dolphin's mouth (an excruciating procedure that Naia had insisted was crucial for sanitation), and climbed into the warm communal pool. Oldsters—of every gender Porphyry had to offer—lined the perimeter, seated upon a long underwater bench; their heads bobbed at the surface like cheerful cabbages. Some nodded at me in recognition. Some stared, but they seemed more agog at my ghostly pale body than at the scales shingling my middle.

"Do the people down south live in caves?" an old man had once asked loudly, unconcerned with whether I might understand what he was saying. "Like those spidery crickets, you know. You can almost see through her."

No one had ever commented on the scales, to my immeasurable relief. Today, however, a finger ran across my back, right along the line where my human skin gave way to dragon. The flesh there was often red and angry, as if it resented the sharp scales pushing through, and the unexpected touch hurt. I flinched, biting back a cry, and the toothless granny to my right grinned up at me, her eyes two crescents of mischief.

She mumbled something I had no hope of understanding. The woman on her other side, her body jiggling with giggles, spoke loudly and slowly: "Lend her your silver teeth, you stingy foreigner. You have too many, and she has none of her own."

I couldn't help it: I laughed, and the whole pool laughed with me. Naia had said that awe of an ityasaari would clash with be-musement at a foreigner. It looked like the two had finally re-solved into plain amusement.

But the most surprising thing was that I really didn't mind. These scales, my visible emblem of shame, which had so terrified Rodya, which I had hidden, suppressed, and even once tried to pry off with a knife—how was I now able to laugh about them with strangers? Something had changed in me. I was such a long way from where I had started.

After I dried myself, I changed into the nicest outfit I owned, a lapis-blue tunic embroidered with red and gold flowers and chips of mirror, its skirt longer and fuller than the usual, falling in crisp pleats past my knees. I had bought it at a harborside shop, thinking I might someday have to go into company and disliking the sort of filmy sleeveless gowns the highborn ladies wore.

Comonot had said evening, but I had no address for House Malou. I left my bath box with the attendant (overnight, for a more generous tip) and wandered along to the library, pausing halfway up the hill to admire the orange and lilac of the set-ting sun.

House Malou (the librarians informed me, eyeing my new tunic with interest) was four streets from Camba's, not hidden be-hind shops but unabashedly occupying an entire block. I found it easily. Its blue door had a shiny brass knocker shaped like an acanthus leaf. I worried the doorman wouldn't let me in, but ap-parently he'd been warned to expect me. He led me into a high-ceilinged atrium, newer and fancier than Camba's; mosaics of sea horses, octopuses, and mer-dogs covered the ceiling, glass and gilt tiles catching the light. There was a murmur of water and of voices from deeper inside the house. The fountain's statue was of a man balancing what looked like a pink cathedral on his head. A closer look revealed a miniature city, complete with temples and markets, carved of rosy coral. The allegorical name on the base of the statue was a word I didn't know.

"Duty," said a familiar baritone, startling me so I almost put a foot in the pool. Kiggs made a move to catch my elbow, but I regained my balance on my own.

"You have good Porphyrian," I said.

He smiled self-effacingly. "I asked the doorman."

He'd cleaned up and changed into his crimson dress doublet; his hair was still damp from the bath. I was pleased to note that he'd kept the beard, and then surprised that I was pleased. He noticed me staring and ran a self-conscious hand down his face. "I'm told the Agogoi take you more seriously if you have a beard," he said.

"I'll have to try that," I said.

His mouth twitched as he held in a laugh. I remembered why I liked this prince.

"Comonot's in the dining room with our hosts," said Kiggs, ushering me forth. "In *a* dining room, more accurately. I've found three so far; there may be more."

"This is just dinner?" I asked, following him up the corridor. "No politics?"

"Oh, it's all politics," said Kiggs, his eyes keen. "The kind Comonot sometimes unwittingly excels at, wherein he meets everyone and charms them with his, uh, charm. We should keep an eye on him."

We passed through the depths of the house, glimpsing a vast domed chamber, a private bath like an artificial lake, a library, and two formal gardens before arriving at an open courtyard paved in five colors of tessellated marble. Couches lined the perimeter; a fountain of wine burbled in the center amid tables of towering delicacies. Nearly a hundred people milled around, helping themselves to food and wine, lounging languidly on couches, eating and laughing.

"It's an egalitarian gathering," Kiggs whispered delightedly in my ear. "There's no hierarchy of seating; we may eat or sit where we like. I want to try this in Goredd."

I didn't wish to contradict his enthusiasm; maybe he didn't see all the servants maneuvering through the cracks and crannies of the crowd, refilling glasses and removing empty platters. Maybe I saw them only because I'd been staying harborside. Two of Abdo's aunties were servants in the great houses.

Kiggs steered me through the chattering guests toward a stout older woman with a face like a bulldog's. Her head was shaved, which meant she was a widow—there were several at Old-Timers' Hour—but she still wore the golden Agogoi circlet. It creased her bare scalp. She raised her eyebrows expectantly at Kiggs as if she knew him already.

"Madam Speaker," he said, bowing respectfully. "May I present Seraphina Dombegh, Queen Glisselda's emissary to your ityasaari. Seraphina, this is Her Honor, Phyllida Malou Melaye."

I wasn't sure how one greeted the Speaker of the Assembly; I tried Goreddi-style full courtesy, which surely looked a little strange in my harborside clothing. In fact, my clothing looked a little strange in this setting, I now realized. I wasn't underdressed, exactly; rather, I was from the entirely wrong class.

Speaker Melaye flared her nostrils skeptically. "I've heard of you," she said in Goreddi. "You would have done better to speak to me first if you were hoping to borrow our ityasaari. I could have arranged something; even priests have their price. Instead, you've outraged the temple of Chakhon. You'll never make any progress with them now."

I knew Pende was displeased, but outraged? And the whole temple, at that? I curtsied to cover my mortification and managed to say, "I live and learn, Your Honor."

She made a dismissive noise and waved me off. Her diaphanous full sleeves billowed as she moved, giving her the appearance of a cranky butterfly.

"It wouldn't have made a difference," said Kiggs softly as we turned away. "Selda said that ityasaari priest was set against you. Melaye couldn't have bought him off."

"Maybe, maybe not," I said, sighing. It hadn't occurred to me that the Assembly might have a say in whether the ityasaari could or should come south; I wished I'd had a chance to try that angle.

"Phina," said Kiggs, and I met his eye. His smile radiated warmth and sympathy. "I have strict orders not to let you brood about this. Selda will have my hide."

The evening rapidly became a blur of novelty meats—the most tentacled being octopus stuffed with squid stuffed with cuttlefish—and introductions I couldn't keep straight. A handful of people had traveled the Southlands (including an octogenarian who insisted that we Goreddis were poisoning ourselves by eating so much pine; Kiggs was confounded by this, but I thought of Josquin and Moy and laughed to myself). I met the heads of all the founding families, of whom I only remembered the one I'd already met, Amalia Perdixis Lita. Two of her sons, smiling, bearded fellows in their forties, accompanied her. Camba was evidently the baby of the family.

We kept glimpsing Comonot and losing him again. Halfway through the evening, he planted himself beside the fountain and began telling stories in a wine-ripe voice. Kiggs darted over to Comonot's side at once, and I followed. Drink rendered the Ardmagar talkative, and there were matters of state and strategy that the prince wouldn't wish him to reveal to the gathering crowd.

"I've seen war and carnage," the old saar was saying. "I've killed humans, burned villages, eaten their babies, and stepped on their dogs. I've killed other dragons—not often, but I've severed more than one jugular and been scalded by the steaming blood. Battling the Old Ard should have been nothing new."

His jowly face sweated in the evening heat. He took a swallow of wine. "Still, I had never seen anything like this. The sky-rending screams, the choking sulfurous smoke stinging your eyes even through nictitating eyelids. Below you spreads a valley of charred and oozing meat—meat you can't even eat, all nestmates and co-fliers. You recognize that flayed wing or this mangled head, the smells of a hundred individuals beneath the singular reek of death.

"How many did I kill? When they first charged us, fangs bared and gullets blazing, I hoped I might not have to kill at all. A bite on the back of the neck to establish dominance, and they'd back down. That was our way, once. But the moment comes when claws are tearing at your eyes and your wing is on fire and you have no other option.

"We won that battle, if you can call it winning. We were the only side with dragons still flying. They fought to the death, all of them." The Ardmagar paused, his eyes glazed, remembering.

"It was unconscionable," he said at last. "Eskar was right. I can't countenance the deaths of so many. We lay single eggs and incubate them for three years. We are a slow-maturing species. When I think of all the time and resources and education that lay wrecked on the floor of that valley, just to stop me from returning north . . ." He shook his head, his mouth bowed bleakly. "What a waste."

"Why did they fight to the death?" asked a tall man at the edge of the listening crowd. I recognized him as one of Camba's brothers; shadows flickered over his face in the lamplight. "The Old Ard are dragons, too. They value logic as much as you do. Where's the logic in dying?" Around him the crowd murmured in agreement.

Comonot considered. "Logic can lead to many ends, citizen. No one likes to admit that—not even your philosophers. Dragons revere its incorruptible purity, but logic will coldly lead you over a cliff. It all depends on where you begin, on first principles.

"The Old Ard have found a new ideology. Its endpoint is potentially the death of thousands, up to and including themselves. I can assure you that they have arrived there through ruthless, unflinching logic, from some very particular beginning. We could, in principle, reason backward to find out what it is. I'm not sure I care to."

"Why not?" asked someone else.

Comonot's eyebrows shot up in surprise. "Because what if it makes sense?"

The gathered Porphyrians laughed at his marvelous joke. Comonot blinked owlishly at them, and I suspected he hadn't been joking at all.

Our hostess, the Honorable Phyllida Malou Melaye, had quietly joined the circle of listeners. She raised her bulldog chin and spoke up: "It is generally in Porphyry's interest for the Old Ard to be quelled. They're bent on taking back the Southlands, where half our fortune is tied. However, as much as we'd like to support you, Ardmagar, you must acknowledge that we risk retribution if we help you and you lose. The Old Ard would not overlook it; they might even punish us before they take the south."

Comonot bowed cordially. "I hear and respect your caution, Madam Speaker."

"You must balance Porphyry's risk with adequate compensation," she said, refilling her wineglass at the fountain. "We have a panoply of ideologies here, but there's one we all agree on: flexibility is always possible, for the right price."

"I expected that," said Comonot. "I am prepared to negotiate for—"

Kiggs elbowed the Ardmagar, which caused the old saar to slop some wine onto the floor. Servants appeared as if out of nowhere to mop up; Comonot scowled as Kiggs whispered urgently in his ear. "I wasn't going to blurt it all out here," Comonot grumbled back. "Give me some credit, Prince."

Speaker Melaye raised her glass. "We will negotiate in committee over the coming days. Let us enjoy our dinner. Business makes a bitter sauce."

Comonot wordlessly raised his glass to her in turn and downed what remained of his wine.

Twenty

After dinner, all the guests retired to a large terrace on the southern side of the house, where two bright braziers burned. House Malou's resident artist, the poet Sherdil, gave a recitation while everyone drank fig wine and eagerly awaited the moonrise.

My Porphyrian was not quite equal to the metrics and metaphors of poetry. I was concentrating so hard that I jumped when Kiggs touched my shoulder. "Oh, excuse me," he whispered, lightly amused. "You're enjoying this."

I shrugged. "Poetry is difficult."

"So that's a yes." He smiled. "Don't pretend; I know you. You go haring after 'difficult' at every opportunity. But I don't like to interrupt if you're engrossed."

An unaccountable bubble of lightness rose in me. "If it were music, you wouldn't stand a chance, but I don't mind missing this."

Still, he hesitated; I took his arm encouragingly. We had the same intuition at once and looked around for Comonot, but the Ardmagar was pleasantly engaged with a glass at the far end of the terrace. We avoided his eye, ducking around merry guests and glazed pots bristling with ornamental grasses, climbing the terrace toward the silent house.

The corridors were cool and empty. Kiggs led me to a triangular garden, an irregular space left over by a new addition to the house. The air was drunk with lemon and jasmine; translucent windows glowed warmly with lamplight from indoors. The moon hovered below the roofline, but an oracular aura shone where it would soon rise. We sat upon a cool stone bench, leaving a gap wide enough for fat Propriety to squeeze between us.

Propriety. If Goreddis made allegorical statues, she'd be the first we'd carve.

"You didn't tell me Comonot had gone to the front," I said, adjusting the skirt of my tunic. "I pictured him moping around the castle all this time, driving Glisselda mad."

"Oh, he still managed that, even from a distance," said Kiggs, sitting cross-legged like a child. His sparse beard made a humane frame for his smile. "We couldn't tell you over the thnik, but he left shortly after you did. No more directing his war from afar. Now that he's seen what's really going on out there, he's at great pains to stop it. He agrees with Eskar that if he can find a way to get to the Kerama, the war at large will cease while succession is settled properly. He might still lose the succession argument—or combat, or whatever it comes down to—but the dragon civil war would be over."

"What about this new ideology?" I asked. "Will it drive them to keep fighting?"

Kiggs shook his head and sighed. "These are exactly the questions that keep me up at night. Comonot believes dragon law and custom will prevail. If we don't trust him, we've no one left to trust, but I can't pretend there's no risk."

Kiggs reached down the front of his doublet with one hand and drew out a bronze thnik in the shape of a St. Clare medallion. "Selda turns sixteen tomorrow," he said, weighing the device in his hand. "I am likely to be tied up with Comonot and the Assembly all day. It's after midnight back home, but surely it's better to wake her in the early hours of her birthday than in the early hours of the day after."

"Much better," I said, smiling ruefully at his conscientiousness.

He flipped the switch and we waited. No one answered. Kiggs gave it a minute, a furrow deepening between his brows. "That laggardly page boy is supposed to sleep in the study, under the desk."

"Maybe his stressful post has driven him to drink," I joked morosely.

Kiggs frowned, unamused. "I'll have to try again tomorrow, I suppose."

"L-Lucian?" crackled Glisselda's voice. "Is that you?"

A relieved smile broke over his face. "Indeed! And also—"

"Thank Allsaints in Heaven! But who got word to you so soon?" she cried, her voice creaking tearfully. "I was just coming in to tell you myself."

Kiggs met my gaze, his eyes wide and alarmed. "What do you

mean, who got word to me? It's been sixteen years since the happy event. That's plenty of time."

There was a pause while she made sense of his words. "You villain!" she cried. "You haven't heard anything. You're calling for my birthday."

"Of course I am, goose," he said.

"Would you believe," said Glisselda, her voice quavering, "I forgot all about it?"

Kiggs inhaled sharply. "What's happened?"

Glisselda burst out crying. "Oh, Lucian! St. Eustace has come for Grandmamma at last, rest she snugly in the arms of Heaven."

"M-may she dine at Heaven's table," said the prince, staring at nothing. He rubbed his beard, then his eyes with a finger and thumb.

I watched Kiggs, hand upon my heart. Queen Lavonda had been declining since the events at midwinter, but it was still shocking to think that she was dead.

"She went peacefully," Glisselda was saying. "I fed her breakfast, the nurse said she seemed sleepy at lunch, and then we could not rouse her for supper. She slipped away little by little this evening." Her voice broke; she gave a tiny cough. "She has climbed the Golden Stair. Mamma is surely waiting at the top to scold her for coming so soon."

"No," said Kiggs gently. "Uncle Rufus won't allow scolding. He'll be waiting, too, with St. Brandoll and a treacle tart."

"Grandmamma never liked treacle tarts," fretted Glisselda.

"Believe me, he's counting on that," said Kiggs.

They laughed a little and wept. I quietly pressed knuckles

against my lips. They'd lost Prince Rufus, Princess Dionne, and now their grandmother—their whole family in less than a year.

"Did you say someone was with you?" said Glisselda, suddenly self-conscious.

"Phina's here," said Kiggs.

"Hello," I said, absurdly waving as if she could see me.

"Phina!" cried Glisselda. "Now isn't that lucky? It does put my heart at ease, the pair of you there together, just knowing you're both well and whole and . . . and alive. You'll be home soon and then everything will be right again, or close enough."

Kiggs did not answer, but closed his eyes and lowered his head onto his hands. I cleared my throat and said, "I'm ready to come home, Your Majesty. I'm homesick—"

"Me too!" cried the young Queen. "Isn't that silly, since I *am* home? But it hasn't felt like home since Mamma died, and it's even grimmer with you and Lucian gone. Lucian, have you told her about Fort Oversea?"

Kiggs raised his head, as if to answer, but Glisselda cut him off, saying, "Fetch the knights with Lucian, Seraphina, and then come straight home." Background mumbling interrupted her momentarily. "I'm being summoned. I have to sit with St. Eustace for Grandmamma." Her voice caught again. "But thank you. You called at the right moment, making the unbearable somewhat more bearable. I'm so grateful for you both."

She disconnected. Kiggs put the thnik away and sat holding his head, elbows on his knees. His shoulders shook. I folded my hands in my lap, wishing I could draw him close and comfort him, thinking maybe I should do it anyway, even though we'd promised each other not to. He was so adamant about being fair to Glisselda—and I agreed, in principle—but sometimes surely it was better to err on the side of kindness?

Alas, I couldn't be sure it wasn't the side of selfishness. I clamped my hands between my knees.

Kiggs ran his fingers through his curling hair. "Forgive me, Phina. I thought we could wish her a happy birthday and then have a nice talk, or . . ." He gestured bleakly toward the full moon, now risen above the rooftop.

"There will be time," I said. "We'll talk all the way to Fort Oversea."

"Yes, we will," he said, an unexpected bitterness in his voice. "That's what I wanted. I didn't have to come along with Comonot, you realize. He can handle himself. You could've made your own way home; the knights can find Goredd on a map."

"You wanted to see me," I said quietly, my heart sinking.

"And for my selfishness, Selda has to bear our grandmother's death alone." Kiggs stood and paced restlessly. "Even when I'm with her, I'm not. I know it was my idea to . . . to lie, but even a lie of omission builds a wall between people. I'm trapped behind it, unable to give Selda the unconditional support she needs."

"You don't need to explain it to me," I said, folding my arms. "I've lived it. I'd half expected you to break and tell her the truth by now."

He laughed mirthlessly. "Oh, I've considered it. Would that tear down the wall, though, or build it higher?" He trailed off, wiping his eyes. "How did you stand lying about yourself for years? You must have felt cut off from the whole world."

I fought down the lump in my throat. "I did indeed. And then I met this prince who seemed able to see through me, to the truth behind the lies. He was terrifying and fascinating, but to my amazement, it was an immeasurable relief to be seen."

Kiggs's dark eyes softened. "What you'd hidden was not so awful. What I've hidden will hurt Selda, whom I love like my own sister."

There was a wall between Kiggs and me, too, built of propriety and promises. I could not reach out to him, could not kiss his sorrowing brow. Holding back was misery, but he'd surely use any lapse as a stick to beat himself with later.

I said, "Yes, it will hurt her. But—" I hesitated; the idea was forming, looking for words to clothe itself in. "Letting her bear her own pain can be a gesture of respect."

He sat down again, his eyes locked on my face. "What?"

"I mean," I said, still struggling for the right way to say it, "you're carrying all the weight of it yourself to protect her. You've decided she's too fragile to bear the truth, but is she? What if you let her be strong on her own behalf? It would honor her, in a way."

He snorted, but I could tell he was thinking now. That was what I loved most of all: Kiggs thinking. His eyes lit up. I clasped my hands between my knees again.

"That is the most convoluted piece of sophistry I've ever heard," he said, wagging a finger at me. "Shall I slap her across the face, if pain is such an honor?"

"Who's a sophist?" I said. "You know that's a specious argument."

He smiled mournfully. "I'm going to refute you, because you're wrong, but I don't have it in me now." He rubbed his eyes. "Tomorrow will be a long day of negotiations." He yawned.

I took the hint, although I didn't like to. "I should let you get some sleep," I said.

I rose to go, but Kiggs reached for my hand. In that moment the entire world bent toward that focal point; all we felt or understood, all matter and emptiness, compressed between two hands, one warm, one cold. I didn't know which was which.

He took a shaky breath and let me go. "I'll see you tomorrow," he said. "And I will refute you."

I bowed. "Good night, Prince," I said, fully believing he would hear the words behind my words, the things I couldn't say.

ᴄ᷉Twenty-One᷉ᴈ

I was not invited to Comonot's meeting with the heads of the Agogoi, nor did I expect to be. Surely Kiggs and I would be leaving Porphyry soon—how long could negotiations possibly take?—and I'd already decided not to spend my last few days trying to persuade the ityasaari to come south with me. They were happy here; let them remain so. I would return and see them in more peaceful times.

Instead, I spent the next morning with Abdo and his family. Abdo had been less feverish and more tranquil the last two days, but he slept all the time. I hoped this might mean Jannoula was relenting and that Naia could take him back to Paulos Pende whenever he opened his eyes. Around midday I wandered to the harbor market and played flute in the sunshine. Children skipped circles around me. I'd hoped Brasidas would find me, but he wasn't around.

When I returned to Naia's in the late afternoon, a note had arrived from Ardmagar Comonot: *Meet the prince and me at the Metasaari public garden at sunset.* That was it; no hint of how his meeting had gone.

I went early and ate at the little caupona where I'd met Saar Lalo. I'd come to love octopus balls in gravy; I would miss Porphyrian food in Goredd. I loitered at a table, nursing my mint tea and watching the sun go down.

Kiggs and Comonot appeared at last, two lengthening shadows in the descending dusk; I met them by the public fountain where water spewed from a mer-dog's snout. "This way," said the Ardmagar, in lieu of a greeting, and we set off toward a long, low colonnaded house on the north side of the square.

"How did the negotiations go?" I whispered to Kiggs.

The prince shook his head. "We're sworn to secrecy. These may not be my gods, but I don't relish meeting Dread Necessity down a dark alley," he said. "However, I believe I may hint obliquely that the jewel of our purpose is to be ransomed at a high price, and that the Ardmagar is a miserly villain."

"I can hear you," said Comonot over his shoulder as he knocked on the door.

I pinched my lips shut around a laugh, but found Kiggs's hint perplexing. Comonot was prepared to pay to end his war. What price had Porphyry demanded?

A middle-aged woman with short hair and a serious expression opened the door. "Ardmagar," she said, saluting the sky and revealing herself to be a saarantras.

"Lucian, Seraphina," said Comonot, "I introduce Ikat, civic

leader of the dragons in exile and—I'm given to understand—an excellent physician."

Ikat, in good saar fashion, didn't acknowledge the introduction, but she did hold the door for us. She was dressed in a plain tunic and trousers of undyed cotton, no ornaments, her brown feet bare. She led us silently through her atrium toward a central square garden. Chairs and benches had been set in a circle, and ten saarantrai sat under globular lanterns. I assumed they were all saarantrai; I recognized Lalo. Ikat snapped thrice and a slender serving girl fetched another wooden bench for Kiggs and me. We sat, and Comonot went around the circle, introducing himself to everyone.

"More exiles than this are willing to help, I hope," I whispered to Kiggs.

"That's part of what we're here to find out," he whispered back. "This is the 'Futile Council,' as Eskar calls it. Saarantrai have no voice in the Assembly, so they've created their own impotent ruling body, which occasionally sends petitions for the Agogoi to ignore."

"Has the Ardmagar located Eskar yet?" I asked, and the prince shook his head.

The serving girl offered us honeyed almond cakes. Kiggs took one, muttering under his breath, "I'll need you to translate if this meeting is held in Mootya."

"Soft-mouth Mootya, you mean," said the serving girl in Goreddi. Kiggs looked up at her. She had a pointy face reminiscent of a rat's, and her twig-like brown arms were bare to the shoulder. She was full grown in height, but her stance suggested a petulant ten-year-old. She sneered down at the prince and said, "If you expect us to roar at each other, you'll be disappointed. We've transposed Mootya into sounds our soft mouths can make, but it's the same language."

Kiggs was enough of a scholar to know this already, but he bowed his head politely. The girl stared at him, her eyes bulging. "That's why you know our names for things, like *Tanamoot* or *ard*," she continued unnecessarily, "whereas in hard-mouth Mootya, *ard* sounds like this." She threw her head back and screamed.

The circle of saarantrai, who'd been chatting together, went silent. "You're screaming at a prince of Goredd," said Ikat, crossing the lawn and taking the girl by the shoulders as if to lead her away.

"It's all right," said Kiggs, trying to smile. "We were discussing linguistics."

Ikat frowned slightly. "Prince, this is my daughter, Colibris."

"Brisi," the girl corrected, lifting her pointy chin defiantly.

It was a Porphyrian name, and she was dressed very differently from the other saarantrai. The adults wore plain tunics and trousers in noncommittal colors; they kept their hair short and practical, except for Lalo, with his long hair tied Ninysh-style.

Brisi, however, wore a diaphanous dress splashed with gaudy butterflies and birds; her hair was piled precariously on her head, in imitation of the towering coiffures fine ladies such as Camba wore. It wobbled when she moved. In fact, her screaming had sent a lock tumbling, but she seemed not to notice. It dangled, limp and forlorn, at her shoulder.

She finished serving the guests and disappeared into the shadows of the house.

Ikat began the meeting, saying (in soft-mouth Mootya), "Eskar hasn't returned. Am I correct that no one knows where she's gone?"

Around the circle, no one moved.

"You owe much to her indefatigable perseverance, Ardmagar," said Ikat. "When she arrived last winter, only Lalo would even consider leaving. We've built lives here, and we were reluctant to trust you. Your administration was harder on deviants than the three that came before."

"I regret it," said Comonot, who sat on the bench beside Ikat. "Too much time has been wasted chasing the elusive ideal of incorruptible draconic purity. The Old Ard take it to extremes, but it was always untenable. Progress—or, more prosaically, our continued survival—will require a shift in the opposite direction, toward a broader definition of dragonhood." One corner of his mouth dimpled, a strangely self-deprecating expression. "Of course, my previous attempt at dragging our people toward reform has resulted in civil war. I may not be the one to follow."

When I translated that for Kiggs, he gave a low whistle and whispered back, "Don't tell me he's learned humility!" Around us, the saarantrai muttered solemnly together; Comonot, thick hands folded in his lap, watched them with a falcon's eye.

"You've shown yourself remarkably flexible of mind, for a non-deviant," said Ikat, and Comonot bowed his head. "So many of us had given up any hope of a return that we had hardened our hearts against the desire to see our homeland again, or dismissed it as impossible. We told ourselves we fit seamlessly into Porphyrian society, that the Porphyrians accepted us fully and without reservation—"

"They certainly don't want you to leave," Comonot interjected. "It's not the Omiga Valley that's the sticking point. They're demanding near-impossible compensation for agreeing to let you go."

Ikat sat up a little straighter and her eyes narrowed. "They're not our jailers."

"No," said Comonot, "but they have an agreement with the Tanamoot, and a great reluctance to lose so many doctors, merchants, scholars—"

"To say nothing of our elevated non-citizen taxes," muttered someone.

"Many of our merchants don't wish to leave," said Ikat. "They've found a new way to accumulate a hoard, and that's enough for them, but the rest of us chafe against the restrictions. We can only transform four times a year, during the games. Bearing children is complicated, and raising them more difficult still."

"Stop talking about me, Mother," piped a shrill voice in Porphyrian, and there was Brisi, peeking out from behind a column.

Ikat ignored the interruption. "There's no chance of laying an egg, not in the time we're allowed, but human-style gestation still takes three years, by which point the baby is far too large. I had to cut Colibris out myself; she was walking within a day."

"I don't want to go to the Tanamoot!" cried Brisi, speaking over her mother. "It's not my home. I am Porphyrian, whether you admit it or not. You can't make me go. I'm an adult under Porphyrian law. I could live here on my own."

"You are not an adult," said Ikat, switching to Porphyrian. "And under Porphyrian law, even adults are subject to the head of the family."

Brisi harrumphed, turned on her heel, and stomped off. Ikat called after her, "I plan on being around for another two hundred years. You had better make peace with that notion."

Somewhere deep in the house, a door slammed. Ikat released a slow breath through flared nostrils, then said quietly, "It's hard for her. The playmates of her early childhood are not merely grown, they're grandparents. She won't reach intellectual and sexual maturity for another five years. She doesn't understand our ways, and we're a long way from understanding her."

"Bite her," said Comonot reasonably. "Right on the back of the neck."

Ikat shook her head. "The Porphyrians have laws against harming children."

"What harm?" cried Comonot. "My mother bit me every day for thirty years."

"I told you," said a male saarantras from across the circle. "They're legislating against our cultural traditions. They see barbarism in things they don't comprehend."

"But a human bite isn't safe," offered Lalo. "The skin is frail, and infection—"

I was so astonished at this turn of conversation that I'd stopped translating. Kiggs nudged me. "Why are they arguing?"

I opened my mouth, at a loss to explain, when suddenly there came a rapping at the front door. Brisi scurried out of the shadows to answer it, and moments later, tall, black-haired Eskar stepped into the garden. Everyone stared openmouthed, myself not least or last, but she didn't acknowledge our gazes or say hello. She approached one of the benches and waited silently while the saarantrai on it made room for her to sit.

The silence stretched uncomfortably. Comonot said, "You're late."

"Indeed," said Eskar, tossing her bangs out of her eyes. She looked around, taking account of who else was in the garden, and nodded terse recognition at Kiggs and me. "I'm here now. I presume we're discussing the logistics of traveling up the Omiga? Carry on."

"Where have you been?" said Comonot, skewering her with his glare. "I expected you to be here. I expected your help with planning this operation."

"I have been helping," said Eskar coldly. "I've scouted ahead, plotting our route beyond the Omiga Valley. The Old Ard's patrols are thin in that part of the Tanamoot, but they're there."

"You've learned their routes?" said Comonot.

Eskar shifted in her seat. "Some of them. But we're going to need places to conceal ourselves. I propose seizing Censor facilities on the way to the Kerama. Lab Four is easily reached if we follow the Meconi River, and—"

"Slow down," said Comonot, beetling his brows. "I have no quarrel with the Censors."

"Did you not just promise to ease up on the repression of deviants?" Ikat interjected. "The Censors are the primary enforcers of those policies."

"And if you bring these exiles home, the Censors are going to have a quarrel with you," said Eskar flatly. "The location makes strategic sense. It's poorly guarded; patrols avoid it. I used to work there and am still in contact with the quigutl in the boiler rooms."

Comonot was shaking his head. "You overstep yourself, Eskar. I need to consider all the possible—"

"It's a sound plan," said Eskar, an unexpected tension in her voice, like a bowstring strung too tight. Her eyes, two pools of blackness, met mine, and my stomach clenched. "Orma is at Lab Four."

Twenty-Two

The world went muzzy; the air was viscous around me; it was hard to think.

By the time I realized I was walking, we were nearly at the harborside, as if I had fallen asleep and the smell of fish had awakened me.

Kiggs held my hand. I stopped short and blinked at him stupidly. The street around us was dark and empty.

Thinking hurt. Memory evaporated like a dream if I grasped it too tightly.

Kiggs scrutinized my face. "How are you feeling?"

I checked, finger in the bathwater of my brain. "I—I'm not. Nothing."

"We're nearly at Naia's," he said. "Do you think you can make it?"

The Censors had been after Orma a long time. They would cut out his memories, and my beloved uncle wouldn't know me when he saw me again.

I gripped Kiggs's hand tighter. The world reeled; he was the only point standing still. He'd asked a question. I tried to remember. "Uh, I don't . . . it doesn't . . . I'm sorry."

The only light came from windows and the heartless moon, barely enough to illuminate the prince's worry. He cupped my cheek in his free hand.

I observed this from a cautious distance, the way one observes a wasp.

He pulled me eastward (I also observed). We passed Naia's building because Kiggs didn't know which one it was. I had to speak to tell him where to go (I noticed myself speaking).

Naia greeted us; Abdo (poor Abdo) lay inert in his alcove. "She's very upset," said Kiggs (referring to someone we all knew). "Her uncle was taken by the Censors."

(Why did no one remove my memories? What a mercy that would be.)

"Of course you can stay," said Naia, answering someone's question.

Then I was in a bed. Kiggs sat on the floor beside me and held my hand. Naia held a lamp.

I noted the line of demarcation between wakefulness and sleep. It was blue.

I awoke at dawn, lucid and remembering all: Eskar's report, saarantrai outrage at the Censors. The way I went blank. Kiggs . . .

Was still here. He'd fallen asleep sitting by the bed, his arms folded on top of the coverlet, his curly head within easy reach of my hand. I hesitated, then smoothed his hair out of his eyes.

He blinked awake. "How are you?" he whispered, stretching his shoulders.

"I'm not the one who slept sitting up," I said.

"Bah, I'm fine. Comonot's probably wondering where I am, though." Kiggs rubbed sleep from his eyes. "Or not. It's hard to predict."

"I'm sorry I was so—"

"You have nothing to apologize for," he said, his dark eyes serious. "I know what Orma means to you, how you've feared for him. If it's any consolation, the exiles are furious about the Censors stealing Orma away, even if he wasn't one of their own. They're all in favor of taking Lab Four on the way to the Kerama. Comonot wasn't sold, but they may not give him a choice."

It wasn't that reassuring—surely the Censors had had ample time to excise Orma's memories—but I made a heroic stab at smiling.

Kiggs gazed at me tenderly and lay a hand upon my hair. "I hate to say it, but I need to go," he said. "Are you going to be all right?"

"Oh, probably," I said, sitting up. Kiggs rose and pulled me to my feet, and we stood face to face in the semidarkness. I don't know whose arms first encircled the other, or if we came to that decision together, without speaking. We held each other close.

His beard was scratchy against my cheek. My heart beat wildly, and I realized that whatever self-control we thought we possessed had not been truly tested yet. If we were to sail home together, our resolve would soon find itself strained.

Maybe returning with Kiggs wasn't my only option, though. I had a niggling feeling that there was something else I needed to do.

A noise out in the main room interrupted that line of thinking. We moved apart guiltily; I pulled back the curtain and was astonished to see Abdo at Naia's cabinet, helping himself to yesterday's flatbread and leftover gaar, a paste of anchovies, olives, garlic, and catmint. He carried his dish to the couch, set it beside him, and began spreading gaar on the triangular pieces of bread with a spoon. He worked slowly, one-handed, but once he'd covered the bread, he made quick work of eating it. He closed his eyes and savored each bite, as if he'd never tasted anything so delicious.

I'd never seen anything so beautiful as Abdo up and awake, but I was afraid to be too hopeful. He might be himself; he might be Jannoula. I put a hand over my mouth, trying to decide what to do.

"Oh, thank Allsaints," breathed Kiggs beside me. I hadn't told him much; he and Naia must have talked more than I realized. He started to step forward, but I put up a hand and stopped him.

Abdo heard Kiggs speak or move, and his brown eyes popped open. I scanned for Jannoula's look, to no avail. It was early, and the apartment dim. Maybe she wasn't there.

Abdo prepared another piece of flatbread, and it hit me: he

was eating wrong, spreading gaar on his bread with a spoon, like a Southlander might have done. Porphyrians used flatbread to scoop up lumps of gaar.

"Prince, you need to go," I whispered, my heart heavy. "He's full of Jannoula."

Kiggs whispered back, "Surely it's possible to reason with her? Could I try?"

I stared at him hard, willing him to understand that Jannoula had just seen him emerge from my bedroom and that this was knowledge she could hold over both our heads. Kiggs may not have gleaned anything from my glare except that he needed to go. He didn't dare kiss me, of course, but he lightly touched the small of my back, then crossed the room in five swift strides. "Abdo, it cheers my heart to see you up and about," he said, pausing before the couch, and then he was gone.

I bit my lip, wishing he hadn't brought himself to Jannoula's attention. Nothing good could come of that.

Abdo ate rapturously and paid me no mind. I whispered, so as not to wake Naia, "I know you're there."

He raised his eyes to my face. *This is good,* said Jannoula through Abdo in my mind. *I am sick to death of Samsamese food.*

So she was still in Samsam? She wanted me to think so, at least. "How are you?" I said, stepping toward the middle of the room. "How's dear old Josef?"

Abdo's eyes looked at me sidelong. *Perfectly tame, which is good, since I've had to spend a lot of time in a holy trance lately while Abdo fought me.* Abdo's face wrinkled into an ugly scowl. *He's been a nuisance and a hindrance when I've had other things I wished to accomplish.*

"What other things?" I said.

Abdo shoved another piece of bread into his mouth. *You'll know when it is right for you to know. You need to redouble your efforts to gather our people. I have no connection with any of the Porphyrians now. I tried to catch the twins—they're the easiest—but they're guileless and leave me no place to hide. That horrid Zythos Mors always spots me.*

I didn't want to learn that name from Jannoula. "You mean Camba," I said coldly.

Don't tell me what I mean, she said, narrowing Abdo's dark eyes. *I mean for you to quit wasting time. Abdo heard last night that you've finally realized your noxious uncle is gone, and good riddance. The Censors are brutally pulling his mind apart right now, fiber by sticky fiber, and grinding his memories of you to dust.*

I felt like she'd knocked all the breath out of me, but I held myself together enough to notice something in her voice, an undertone of contempt, and not just for Orma. For his captors? Why would she despise the Censors? Had they stolen someone she loved, too?

That's one distraction out of the way, she was saying, *but what about this other? I'd not have pegged you as the type to take a paramour. Someone Abdo knows, too.* She eyed me shrewdly. *I'll find his name in here, don't worry.*

Abdo's face suddenly contorted in pain. He grabbed at his hair knots and pitched sideways off the couch. I caught him, preventing him from hitting his head, but he thrashed in my arms. In my mind I heard Jannoula's scream of rage.

Naia was beside us in an instant, wrapping her strong arms around him like an anchor tethering him to the earth. He struggled another moment and then went still. "Abdo!" she cried, anguished, but he raised his good hand and patted her hair.

I—I ambushed her, he said in my mind, in his own voice.

My eyes prickled with tears. *Did she seize control in your sleep again?*

I hid and lured her out, and then I struck, he said. *I'm still fighting, Phina, but I'm so tired. . . .*

He burst into tears, weeping silently into Naia's shoulder. She rocked him and whispered into his hair. Abdo's head pushed her gold-rimmed spectacles crooked, but she didn't straighten them.

He was silent several minutes. I said in a tremulous voice, "Are you still there?"

Abdo did not reply. The dark sea of struggle had closed over his head again.

Three of Abdo's aunties arrived with breakfast soon thereafter; I couldn't bring myself to eat. Naia told them Abdo had surfaced for a moment, and that raised the mood in the apartment significantly. If they couldn't bring him to Pende yet, surely it was just a matter of time.

I was not so sanguine, but I couldn't bear to dash their hopes. I went for a walk along the harbor, trying to lose myself among the milling sailors and the nets full of flopping silver fish. The sky was insultingly, offensively blue; it had no right to smile on anyone right now.

How could I travel home without knowing how Abdo's struggle had ended? I felt tempted to stay here among the Jannoula-resistant ityasaari—but that was impossible. It would mean shirking my responsibilities, and for what? I couldn't help Abdo.

I couldn't help my Jannoula-addled friends in Goredd, either. I felt singularly useless.

I walked for a couple of hours, just trying to wrestle my despair back into its box. I must have stared at the trail of inky smoke for a long time before I really saw it, bisecting the southern sky, as if something were burning at sea. The strand and docks were crowded with people trying to make out what was on fire. I picked my way through the gapers along the western breakwater and saw two ships rounding the island of Laika, one pursuing the other. It was the pursuer that burned.

Both ships flew the Samsamese tricolor flag. The world snapped into sharp focus.

The lead ship sailed at full speed toward the harbor; its pursuer slowed as the fire on its hull spread to its sails. Behind the pursuing ship, two swift Porphyrian naval sloops glided out of Laika's harbor; they flanked the burning, drifting ship easily and began rescuing sailors who had leaped into the sea to avoid the flames.

The people around me began to shout and then scream as the lead vessel neared Porphyry's harbor: it was going too fast. There wouldn't be room for it to stop once it passed the lighthouses. The crew, clearly inexperienced, lowered all sails so the ship caught no more wind; the vessel slowed, but not quickly enough. It glided between the lighthouses, veering so that it drifted sideways, and didn't stop until it crashed into a moored Porphyrian man-of-war. The crunch of wood on wood reached our ears, but slowly at this distance.

The sailors on the Porphyrian warship were clearly put out by this turn of events. They lay down planks and swarmed over, boarding the Samsamese craft.

The crew of the harbor vessel was strangely dressed. Even at this distance, they didn't look like sailors in their padded black armor. One stout, balding fellow with a long white mustache seemed oddly familiar as he argued with the captain of the Porphyrians. I was walking eastward, trying to get a better look, when it hit me: that was Sir Cuthberte, a Goreddi knight. I'd met him last winter, imprisoned at Castle Orison. What was he doing here? He was supposed to be training dracomachists at Fort Oversea.

Samsamese Fort Oversea. I quickened my step.

From the man-of-war in the harbor, a dinghy launched. Two officers with gleaming breastplates over their tunics and eight more plainly dressed sailors ferried a single knight to shore, a lanky fellow with stooped shoulders. I recognized Sir Maurizio, Sir Cuthberte's erstwhile squire. He looked as uncombed as ever and a bit green around the gills.

I rushed toward the landing area, hoping to meet the boat. Sir Maurizio spotted me in the crowd as the sailors moored the dinghy and called, "You, maidy, are a sight for seasick eyes."

I couldn't get near the disembarkation, but Sir Maurizio had a few quiet words with his Porphyrian captors, and then a sailor ushered me through the curious crowd. Maurizio, who looked exhausted up close, shook my hand and clapped me on the shoulder. "Is Prince Lucian still here? It would be just our luck to have passed him in transit, like two ships—" He paused, his tawny eyes unfocused. "Exactly like two ships."

"The prince is here," I assured him, uncertain what he knew of the ongoing negotiations.

"Good," said Maurizio, scratching his scruffy chin. "Take me to him, and to breakfast of any kind."

It wasn't up to me, however. The naval officers who'd brought Maurizio ashore were adamant that he be taken to the Vasilikon, before the Assembly of Agogoi. I was only allowed to come along because Sir Maurizio clamped his hand on my arm and wouldn't let go.

"She's my translator," he kept insisting, in perfectly serviceable Porphyrian.

"Kiggs and I were coming to you next," I said quietly to the young knight as we set off up the hill toward the Zokalaa. "Has something happened to Fort Oversea?"

Sir Maurizio sniffed and shook his head wearily. "Only the bloody Samsamese, breaking their promise to Goredd and Ninys. We were supposed to be training together for the defense of the united Southlands, but their new Regent has other ideas."

I went cold. Had Jannoula persuaded Josef to move against the knights and dracomachists? Was this on her list of things to accomplish when she wasn't fighting Abdo in his head? Maurizio seemed disinclined to go into more detail just now, surrounded by Porphyrians; I hoped I'd be allowed to hear his report to the prince.

I had seen the facade of the Vasilikon many times but had never crossed the threshold. Beyond the columned pronaia—an imposing sort of porch—we passed through heavy bronze doors into an airy foyer with windows set high in the walls. A mural on the ceiling depicted Justice, Commerce, and Philosophy having an allegorical picnic of metaphorical sardines.

At a second set of doors, a guard droned an oath at us and would not let us pass until we repeated it: *I hereby consign my lips to secrecy and my soul to Dread Necessity.*

We entered a domed chamber containing a great amphitheater. It was only partially full; all Agogoi were members of the Assembly by virtue of birth, but most had businesses and industries to run or scholarship to pursue. Only the old, the indolent, and the heads of great houses attended every day, unless some juicy controversy merited serious businesspeople skipping work.

The heads of houses were sequestered in negotiations with Comonot and Kiggs; the naval officers who'd accompanied us into the great chamber spoke quietly to an assemblywoman at the top of the room, and she dispatched a messenger into the depths of the Vasilikon.

Maurizio and I watched the Assembly while we waited for the messenger to return. They were voting on petitions from farmers up the Omiga. Each member approached the center of the amphitheater and dropped a pebble into a squat urn of Porphyrian purple marble. An old man sat upon a bench behind the urn, holding a heavy staff with what looked like a pinecone at the end; when the votes had all been cast, he upended the urn in his lap, separated white stones from red, and tallied the result in a large folio.

The messenger returned with a note dismissing the naval officers, who seemed relieved to go. The assemblywoman led us around the amphitheater and out. We followed her down vaulted corridors to a bossed door, where she left us with a guard. He administered the oath again, then opened the door for us. We emerged, blinking, into an octagonal courtyard, sunny and paved with flagstones.

The heads of great houses, eighteen matrons and patrons with gold circlets and flowing silk draperies, sat in a circle on bronze tripod stools. Many held folding fans. Speaker Melaye sat nearest the door, clutching the pinecone staff of office, and I recognized Camba's mother, Amalia Perdixis Lita. Kiggs and Comonot sat on the far side, and with them, to my surprise, was Eskar.

Speaker Melaye directed Maurizio to the center of the circle, where he stood and sweated. For a moment I wondered whether I should leave; I hadn't been sent for, and there was no stool for me. Eskar caught my eye, however, and waved me over. I skirted the perimeter to stand behind her. She turned in her seat, her sharp black eyes scanning my face, and said, "Have you recovered from your shock?"

"Yes, thank you," I whispered back, not wanting to discuss it in front of strangers. It was kind of her to ask, but also deeply odd. Had she been worried?

"Your uncle—" she began, but just then Speaker Melaye

banged her staff on the flagstones for silence, her protuberant eyes fierce.

"We will hear this knight's report," Melaye announced in Goreddi, establishing the meeting's language. Around the circle, the Agogoi fanned themselves and nodded.

Sir Maurizio bowed to Melaye, his back to us. "I need to talk to Prince Lucian Kiggs and Ardmagar Comonot alone, Your Ladyship, not speak in front of—"

"Denied," she snapped. "Your ship has entered our harbor and damaged our man-of-war. We are the city; we will hear you."

I stood behind my friends and couldn't see if Kiggs was frowning, but his tense shoulders bespoke his irritation. "It's all right, Maurizio," he said.

Maurizio turned in a confused circle, as if he feared insulting everyone by turning his back on them; he finally settled on facing Kiggs. He ran a hand through his shaggy hair and exhaled slowly. "Right. Well. Josef Apsig, Regent of Samsam, has seized the knights and dracomachists at Fort Oversea. A single shipload of us escaped; me, Sir Cuthberte, Sir Joshua, maybe three and a half dracomachia units. We were pursued here, and there are more ships coming—you may count on it."

"Josef Apsig fought the knights of three nations and won?" cried Kiggs.

"Technically, it was a bit more like persuasion, and only the knights of two nations resisted. The Ninysh might have resisted a bit harder. I don't mean to imply that they are cowards . . . ," Maurizio said, shrugging, clearly implying that the Ninysh were cowards.

Kiggs rubbed a hand down his beard; his other hand was clenched in his lap. Comonot took the opportunity to ask, "Are the dracomachia units you rescued sufficiently trained?"

"Alas, you never know for sure until they face down a real dragon," said Sir Maurizio, squinting in the sunlight and licking his dry lips. "I think most have mettle enough to bust a gasbag, as we used to say. No offense, Ardmagar."

"None taken," said the old saar.

"How many units is Samsam holding?" said Kiggs, his voice coarse.

Maurizio's throat bobbed as he swallowed. "Fifteen, Prince. Once the newest recruits are trained, it will be closer to twenty-five."

"And what the devil does Josef hope to gain by depriving Goredd of defense?" cried the prince, unable to contain his anger any longer.

Sir Maurizio shrugged his bony shoulders. "That may not be his main intention, Prince. What can one do with dracomachia units but fight dragons? Cuthberte and I believe Josef plans to have Samsam join the war, on nobody's side but Josef's own. When the Loyalists—" He cut off, shifting his gaze uncomfortably to the assembled Agogoi.

"Comonot has outlined his strategy in detail," said Speaker Melaye with surprising gentleness. "And we are all under oath here. We take that very seriously."

Maurizio grimaced. "Thank you, milady. We expect that when the war comes south, Goredd will find herself with a second front—at her back."

Murmurs rose around the courtyard; the Agogoi concealed their mouths with their fans as they whispered together. A matron in blue silk raised her fan, and Melaye pointed the staff at her. "This is worse than you let on, Ardmagar!" the woman cried. "We have no quarrel with Samsam. The policy is neutrality!"

"The priority is commerce," said Melaye. "And alas, in this dragon civil war, neutrality may prove fatal."

"Fatal to the Southlands, you mean. We have a treaty with the dragons. They would never dishonor it!" a white-bearded patron said.

"That's debatable," interjected Comonot, tenting his thick fingers. "The Old Ard have a new ideology, and it's blazingly anti-human. They consider even my Loyalists unacceptably tainted by humanity. Treaty or not, when everyone else is dead, they're going to turn their baleful eye on you."

Speaker Melaye banged her staff, and the circle all looked to her expectantly. "You didn't warn us we'd get sucked into a conflict with Samsam, Ardmagar," she said.

Comonot began to protest his lack of clairvoyance, but she held up a hand to silence him. "These knights and their ship must be gone by sunset so Samsam can't accuse us of harboring fugitives. We'll deny them that pretext for war, at least."

Kiggs raised his hand; Melaye pointed the staff at him. "Our faction requests a private consult," he said.

"Granted," said Melaye haughtily. Around the circle, the Agogoi raised their fans, speaking privately with their neighbors. My friends turned around on their stools and drew their seats closer together. I knelt and leaned in.

"If the knights are sailing back to Goredd tonight, I should be on that ship with them," said Kiggs quietly. "I'm needed at home."

"Understood," said the old saar.

"I'm not sure you do," said Kiggs. "I don't want to leave with these negotiations unresolved. We can't coordinate a military campaign with that kind of uncertainty. You have to agree on a price. I need to know you'll be going up the Omiga."

He and Comonot stared at each other for some moments.

Eskar said, "Ardmagar, stop being stubborn. Give Porphyry what it wants."

"It wants too much!" hissed Comonot.

"How much are dragons worth?" said Eskar. "Every passing day means more death, means the Old Ard and their pernicious ideology gaining ground. Bend like a willow, Ardmagar. We must learn to do this if we're to survive."

The Ardmagar turned red and his lips worked against each other. I half believed smoke might come out his ears. Somehow he swallowed it down. Our party turned their stools back around. Comonot addressed Melaye in a thin, tight voice, like a furious bassoon. "Speaker, I must get to the Kerama. I agree to your last proposal, though it was hardly more reasonable than your first. I will take every saarantras who wishes to accompany me. Your city will supply us, and we will leave as soon as all is in order."

Melaye's eyes narrowed shrewdly. "I have your word, Ardmagar, by Dread Necessity, and you have mine. We must write up our agreement and sign it." She pointed her staff at a matron, who went to the door and began giving orders to the guard outside.

Comonot bowed sharply and sat down again. "Bend like a

willow," he whispered to Eskar out of the side of his mouth. "You made it sound so simple."

"It was simple," said Eskar, unperturbed.

"Indeed. I bent and changed everything. This is going to have consequences."

A phalanx of secretaries entered the courtyard, carrying portable writing desks and piles of parchment. I leaned down level to Comonot's ear and whispered, "What did you agree to, Ardmagar?"

He rolled his eyes. "The Porphyrians are to have access to quigutl devices—not merely the right to own and use them, but the right to trade them." He shook his head. "The Southlands will never be the same. I have altered your whole world in the blink of an eye, for my own gain. I'm not easy with that."

Kiggs was getting to his feet. "Thank you even so, Ardmagar," he said, patting the old saar's broad shoulder. "We're off."

Comonot's eyes flicked from my face to the prince's. "I will see you both in Goredd, then, when I clasp your hands across the smoking ashes of my enemies."

"Isn't that what you're hoping to avoid by sneaking up the Omiga?" Kiggs said.

Comonot considered. "Yes, but I liked the sound of those words. Interesting."

Kiggs bowed. The Ardmagar grabbed his head and kissed his cheeks, performed the same awkward operation on me, and turned back to the business of formalizing his agreement. Six secretaries were poised to take dictation, making six copies at once.

We collected Maurizio and left the Vasilikon; Kiggs knew a

way out that didn't involve crossing the Assembly chamber again. When we emerged into the bustling Zokalaa, Maurizio shaded his eyes and said, "We need to leave before we're trapped here. Sunset might be too late. We load supplies and then we're off—assuming we didn't knock a big hole in the ship. I don't care to contemplate that possibility."

"Understood," said Kiggs, his face drawn. "Seraphina and I have only to fetch our things. We'll see you soon." He clapped Maurizio on the shoulder; the knight bowed and took off toward the harbor.

Kiggs ran a hand over his face and exhaled. "By St. Clare, I can't believe Eskar talked the Ardmagar into that. Those negotiations could have lasted weeks. Comonot was an immovable object against Melaye's unstoppable force." He tried to smile. "Shall we go together to gather our belongings, or shall I meet you at the harbor? The latter is faster, but the former might be pleasanter."

An idea that had almost formed earlier (had it only been that morning?) came suddenly upon me in full force, and once I had realized it, I couldn't unrealize. "I don't know how to tell you this," I half whispered, hating what I was about to say. "I can't travel back to Goredd with you."

Kiggs's brows shot up. "What?" His gaze flitted back and forth, as if he could only bear to look into one of my eyes at a time. "I thought you'd given up on gathering the Porphyrian ityasaari. And . . . and Selda misses you."

"Not just Selda," I said, reaching for his hand. He squeezed my fingers. "But Uncle Orma is . . ." My voice broke. "I might find him if I go with Comonot and Eskar. I have to try."

Emotion played across Kiggs's face like light upon water, illuminating the surface and the deeps, the known and the unknown. He closed his eyes and leaned his forehead against mine. The busy Zokalaa flowed around us; the sun inched through the sky.

"Of course you do," he said at last. "And I have to go home and help Selda, and this is how the world runs, pulling us apart over and over again."

"I'm so sorry—" I began.

"Not for loving your uncle, I hope," said Kiggs, drawing back and wiping my cheek with his thumb. "I'm not away yet. Walk with me to House Malou."

We took the hill in silence, the callous breeze cavorting between us. The doorman recognized the prince and let us in; the empty corridors echoed as we walked. Kiggs had unpacked but little, so it took only a minute to gather his belongings. I helped him carry his chest to the atrium, where he paid a scullion to haul it the rest of the way to the ship.

We lingered in the street, emptied by the midday heat. I steeled myself for the goodbye that was drawing relentlessly closer, but Kiggs said in a voice almost comically grim, "I'd like to have seen the Bibliagathon just once."

I knew of a nearby public garden with a view. I led Kiggs through the sweltering streets, up a slightly overgrown gravel path, and to the end of the garden, where the shrubbery parted and the Bibliagathon appeared below us, its dome gleaming in the noonday sun, its courtyards in cool blue shadow.

"It's as big as a cathedral," sighed the prince. "I'll have to come back. Maybe we'll come back together." He lightly brushed my hand with his fingers.

"Orma and I used to dream of that," I said. My throat tightened painfully, and I could only whisper, "Orma might not be Orma when I see him next."

Kiggs gripped my hand tightly then. "That has been happening all around you," he said quietly. "Not just to Orma. Jannoula has been altering the minds of friends. It must feel like the world is all on shifting sand."

"Promise me you won't listen to her or let her into the city," I said. "Keep her out of Goredd altogether, if you can."

"Of course," he said, raising my hand a little, clasping it between both of his. "You know I speak for Selda, too. You have two stalwart friends on guard against her. Let that comfort your heart, as mine is comforted."

I questioned with my eyes. He smiled, leaning in a little, and said, "Because I found you again. However strenuously the world pulls us apart, however long the absence, we are not changed for being dashed upon the rocks. I knew you then, I know you now, I shall know you again when you come home."

And that was the last thing he said to me before he left. I could not bear to watch him sail away. When I returned to Naia's, the emptiness in the harbor was palpable still.

ᴄᴛᴡᴇɴᴛʏ-Tʜʀᴇᴇᴄ

It would be a week before Comonot and the exiles were supplied and ready to go. I sent the Ardmagar a note that very evening, informing him that I would accompany him to the Tanamoot. I got a reply within the hour—from Eskar—inviting me to a meeting at the Vasilikon the next day to discuss the logistics and timing of the dragon exodus.

That night, however, a Samsamese armada slipped silently into position around the harbor while Porphyry slept. The barricade, seen in the morning light, comprised some twenty-five ships stretched in a line between Porphyry and the island of Laika. This was more force than a meager boatload of knights merited. The Samsamese admiral came ashore and holed up with the Assembly in the Vasilikon.

Our meeting was postponed until the following day. I spent

the unexpected free time with some of Abdo's cousins, watching the flotilla from the seawall.

The next morning, as I crossed the Zokalaa, I saw the nuncio on the steps. I worked my way through the pressing crowds in front of the Vasilikon and heard him announce: "The Samsamese demand the return of their countrymen and burned ship; Mother Porphyry happily returns them. They demand the Goreddi knights, but Mother Porphyry harbors none. Now they ask for our ityasaari."

That got my attention. I knew one person in Samsam interested in gathering ityasaari. I craned my neck, trying to see around coiled hairdos.

"Mother Porphyry denies this request!" boomed the nuncio, and the crowd cheered. "Citizens, we scorn this feeble Samsamese blockade. Our navy could crush them for their insolence, but we choose not to. The Assembly asks the citizenry for kindness and patience in these irritating times. There will be no disruption of produce from the Omiga Valley. Fisherfolk unable to work due to the blockade will be compensated. . . ."

This blockade would surely complicate Comonot's departure. The exiles were supposed to take their natural form and fly up the falls of the Omiga, but it was hard to hide two hundred dragons taking off. Word would get back to Josef, and who knew what he would do with the information?

When I reached Speaker Melaye's office, Eskar, Comonot, Ikat, and other leaders of the saarantrai had arrived, but the meeting had not yet started. I drew Comonot aside and quietly told him my concerns. He scoffed. "Regent Josef wouldn't tell the Old Ard we're coming. Why would he help them?"

"It wouldn't be to help them so much as to hurt you," I insisted. "If dragons fight each other, he loses fewer Samsamese lives per dragon death. Even Josef couldn't deny the logic of that."

"Hatred is never logical," said Comonot pompously. "He wants to fight dragons himself, not shift the war back to the mountains."

Speaker Melaye was listening in. "If the Regent hears that Porphyry is friendly with dragons," she said, "will he use that as a pretext to strike at us?"

"We'll fly by night," said Comonot, shrugging. "I'm not worried."

I worried enough for both of us.

※

It wasn't just the blockade that worried me, of course. Abdo was no better. I hated to leave, not knowing what would become of him, but there was nothing I could do for him if I stayed. There seemed to be nothing anyone could do.

Early upon the seventh morning of the blockade, a messenger brought a note from Comonot stating that we would leave at sunset. I handed the note to Naia at her accounting desk, and she straightened her spectacles to read it.

Before she could say anything, Abdo's alcove curtain was whipped aside and Abdo, breathing like he'd just run up a flight of stairs, staggered out. Naia was at his side in an instant. I hung back warily, but could tell from the way he smiled at his auntie that he was himself.

How are you feeling? I asked.

Abdo pulled out of Naia's embrace and wobbled unsteadily. *She had me trapped inside my own walls; I couldn't even sleep or wake without her say-so. But then suddenly she . . . she just left. I don't know why.* He shook his head, as though he couldn't believe it. *Her hook is still in me, and she'll attack again, I'm sure. Can you take me to Pende, quickly, before she comes back?*

A word of explanation to Naia, and we were out the door. Naia carried Abdo on her back, and we hurried toward the Zoka-laa and the temple of Chakhon.

Upon the steps of the temple, Abdo made Naia put him down. He signed as well as he could with one immobile hand; she understood him. She nodded tearfully, kissed his cheeks, and said, "Go. I'll be waiting right here."

I hesitated, wondering whether he wanted me to stay outside, too, but Abdo took my hand and dragged me in after him. We passed the cacophonous bell ropes and the great statue of Chance, did our ablutions, and ate from the loaf (I had to chance it; I was praying as fervently as anyone in the place). Abdo began pulling me across the courtyard, but a priestess—her eyes closed—stepped into our path. Abdo froze at the sight of her. She took a step toward us, unseeing, as if the god guided her feet.

Is that your mother? I asked silently.

Abdo only gave me a remorseful look.

We reached Pende's topiary garden. The priest was there, sitting cross-legged on his bench. Camba knelt on the moss in front of him; she turned irritably at the sound of our approach, but her expression softened when she saw Abdo. "By the twins," she said, getting to her feet and extending a hand to him. "It is good to see you up and about."

Even Paulos Pende could not look stern at Abdo's approach; the corners of his mouth actually twitched upward, the shadow of a smile.

Abdo kept his eyes on the ground.

"So you're back," said Pende, rubbing his wattle absently, his voice tinged with sadness. "You've pushed her aside; that took some doing." He waited, sucking gravely on his false teeth, while Abdo gave some answer in his mind. "Unhooking others is not so difficult," said Pende at last. "Unhooking yourself, as far as I know, cannot be done. If, through meditation, one could turn the mind to water, perhaps the hook might fall out on its own, but . . . it has never been tried that I know of.

"Camba," Pende said, turning toward her, "tell me what you see."

"I see the bare hook," said Camba, examining the surface of Abdo's head as if it were a map of the heavens. "The glow is faint, like a candle. She isn't present."

"Correct," said the old priest. "And praise Chance for that. She's got him on the thinnest of lines. I think you could release him, Camba. It's your first opportunity."

Camba's face held a mixture of gratitude and uncertainty; she narrowed her eyes, studying Abdo's hair knots as if looking for just the right one, and the uncertainty grew. She met my eyes briefly, and I wondered whether we harbored the same doubt: Abdo had struggled with Jannoula for weeks, so how could he be bound with the thinnest of lines?

"Father," said Camba in a hushed voice, "I'm worried that this connection is more complicated than it appears. Is it possible for Jannoula to disguise—"

"Chakhon's knees, child!" cried Pende, gripped by the sudden wrath I had seen before. "This is why I should be training Abdo, not you. He wouldn't hedge and hesitate and overthink. He would see instinctively what to do, reach in boldly, and—" The old priest gesticulated wildly, too irked to explain; Camba pursed her lips and lowered her eyes, clearly embarrassed.

"Come closer, Abdo!" cried Pende, and Abdo knelt before him. Paulos Pende placed one hand on Abdo's forehead and one at the nape of his neck, just as he'd done to Ingar, and then slowly spread his fingers, pulling Jannoula out of Abdo's mind. Once again, I saw only Pende's bony hands, which mimed crumpling something and raising it above his head. I braced myself for the thunderclap I knew would follow.

It never came. Pende lowered his hands, his eyes vague, as if he'd forgotten what he was doing. Camba and I exchanged a perplexed look. Paulos Pende gave a startled mewl like a kitten, pitched backward onto the mossy ground, and began to seize.

Camba rushed around the bench and dropped to her knees beside him. I helped her roll the priest onto his side so he wouldn't choke. I tried to unfold Pende's legs, but he thrashed and kicked uncontrollably. Abdo sat frozen, staring in horror.

It seemed to go on forever, but the mind storm, whatever caused it, finally burned itself out. Pende lay limp and unconscious, but breathing evenly.

"What happened?" I asked in a squeaky voice.

Camba shook her head; a lock of hair had come loose and curled down in front of her eyes. She didn't answer me, but muttered to herself, "No. Impossible. Not Pende."

It's my fault, said Abdo in my head. I looked up sharply; his face was gray.

"He unhooked Jannoula from your mind, and then what happened?" I asked.

Abdo's head bobbed, as if it were too heavy for his neck. *He didn't unhook her all the way. She fooled him. She's still got me.*

"Oh, Abdo," I whispered, but he wasn't finished.

He pointed a trembling finger. *And she's got him, too. She's outmaneuvered us all.*

Two novices helped Camba move Pende to his cell and lay him on his low bed; I followed. The temple sent for a physician, none other than Ikat, the leader of the exile council, mother of Brisi. She took Pende's pulse, raised his eyelids, and palpated his sacklike throat.

"His pupils don't respond to light. For someone this old, a stroke is likeliest, but we can't be sure until he wakes. I've brought analgesic powders in case he has pain," said Ikat, her calmness a balm.

As she began explaining the doses to one of the novices, Camba pulled me out of the room and closed the door.

"We are in terrible trouble," Camba said quietly, folding her arms. Another priest hurried toward Pende's cell; Camba waited until he closed the door to speak again. "If Jannoula does succeed in seizing his mind completely, she will try to use his power. None of us are safe from her then."

"She had so much trouble controlling Abdo," I whispered. "Do you really think she can bend Pende to her will?"

"It's impossible to tell, unfortunately," said Camba. "We all resist her to different degrees. Pende was good at keeping her out, but what defenses does he have once she's breached the walls? He's so old. You've seen how he can barely control his own temper."

"He's been training you to unhook her. Can you help him?"

"I don't know!" cried Camba, on the verge of tears. "I overthink everything, apparently. Anyway, you could unhook him, if only you would."

"Wh-what?" I said.

"Pende said you have more natural ability than I do, but you've tied your powers up and won't release them."

Heat rose in my chest. "You think I could unhook everyone but just . . . *won't*?"

Camba shook her head in frustration, her golden earrings jingling incongruously. "Of course not. But surely if you bound yourself, you can unbind yourself."

I wished I could, I suddenly realized. I'd imprisoned my own mind-fire in a rapidly shrinking garden; it felt more constraining every time I visited. Alas, I had no idea how to dismantle it.

I exhaled slowly, grasping at straws in my mind. "My uncle Orma is the one who taught me to keep myself contained. I leave tonight to look for him; he may have some insight into how to undo it." Assuming Orma still knew who I was. Saints' dogs. "I'll work on my own, too," I added. "I'll find the way to unbind myself."

It was all bravado; I didn't even know where to begin.

Camba nodded curtly. "You must hurry. Pende taught us meditations and tricks for resisting her. I can be a bulwark for the others—maybe I can unhook a few—but I don't know how long we'll last, especially if Jannoula has all of Paulos Pende's education and ability at her disposal. She may be capable of much more than before."

I glumly followed Camba back through the temple. Abdo was in the sanctuary, arms folded, gazing up at the statue of Great Chakhon. He turned at our approach, an unexpected spark of determination in his eyes. *I did this*, he said. *I've got to fix it.*

I knew just how he felt.

Naia took Abdo home. I lingered behind to speak with Camba, but there was little left to say. She promised to give Ingar my regards, and then she disappeared into the Zokalaa crowds, a tall figure in saffron silk.

With a heavy heart, I turned toward the harbor; I needed to fetch my things and meet Comonot and the exiles in Metasaari at sundown. Someone was shouting from the steps of the Vasilikon as I passed. I slowed, trying to see what was happening, and spied a familiar, awkward, skinny girl: Brisi, Ikat's daughter. Four other younger-looking individuals stood with her in the shade of the pronaia, possibly more children of exiled saarantrai.

Brisi flapped her arms dramatically. "Citizens of Porphyry, I have words for you!"

A crowd began to accumulate; I maneuvered nearer, scanning for saar faces I recognized, finding none. Were these hatchlings here alone?

Brisi wore an open-fronted robe tied with a sash, the sort of thing Porphyrians wore to the baths. Behind her, her comrades began removing their tunics and trousers. The whole crowd stared, but no one made a move to stop them.

"My Porphyrian family, you need to know what is happening!" cried Brisi. "As we speak, the heads of the great houses are plotting to send the exiles back to the Tanamoot. Some of us have lived here three hundred years. We are your friends and neighbors, your co-workers and business partners. We are a worthy part of this city, and we've worked hard to earn our place. Don't let them send us away!"

The crowd around me began to murmur incredulously. I couldn't tell whether they believed Brisi or not. Of course, after this evening everyone would know that most of the exiles had gone.

"Furthermore," Brisi cried, "we find ourselves suddenly in conflict with the Samsamese. Look how they have blocked our harbor. Are we going to permit this?"

The murmur changed flavor almost at once, but not the way a

Goreddi crowd's would have. In Goredd, we would have been immediately incensed at the idea of the Samsamese getting away with it. The Porphyrians, however, sounded more cautious.

"The Assembly has decided to wait it out," someone called.

"Our navy is more than a match for them, if we need to engage!" cried someone else. The crowd nodded assent.

"Our navy," scoffed Brisi, which was the wrong tone to take. Around me, people began to leave. "They can handle the Samsamese," said the young saarantras quickly, "but why should they? Why should any of our people die when we have draconian resources at our disposal, an ard under our very noses, unappreciated and unutilized?"

The crowd went silent. She couldn't possibly mean what it sounded like, I thought.

Brisi untied her robe and cast it from her, and the crowd gasped. This dragon girl, tall as an adult, still had the body of a child. Brisi threw back her head and let herself unfold, neck elongating, smooth skin curdling, wings expanding, muscles roiling along her bones. The other hatchlings followed suit, like emerging moths. A wave of sulfuric wind blasted the crowd back a few steps, but the Porphyrians did not flee.

"You will return to your saarantrai this instant!" shouted a man in soft-mouth Mootya from the back of the crowd. Saar Lalo was shoving his way forward, toward the hatchlings. "You haven't thought this through!"

I had never seen such large young dragons. Fine-boned, almost bird-like, they were full-sized. Lalo in his man-shape came up only to Brisi's shoulder. She lowered her head, eye to eye with

Lalo, and screeched in his face: "This is our city! We won't leave. We intend to help our people."

"Your *people*," cried Lalo, "need you to shrink back down!"

"No, these are all our people!" screamed Brisi, stretching her wings and testing to see if they had firmed up enough.

The five juvenile dragons bounded forward, scattering the crowd before them. Their wings beat clumsily; it took a few tries before they'd launched themselves into the air. They bobbed and tumbled, bumping into each other like bumblebees, one almost snagging a wing on the roof of Lakhis's temple. Even a few minutes' practice improved matters, however, and soon they were circling the harbor together, wheeling around the lighthouse, gaining speed.

Lalo stared after them openmouthed. Members of the Assembly poured out of the Vasilikon and streamed around him, running into the plaza, some waving their arms as if that could stop events from unfolding.

The hatchlings veered, swooped, and began setting the Samsamese ships on fire.

Not one of the twenty-five Samsamese ships escaped the flames. The four younger dragons then flew to the top of the Sisters, the double-peaked mountain that loomed over the city to the north, where I had once seen Camba hurling crates. They retained their natural forms, but whether they were threatening the city or defending it was not clear.

Only Brisi returned to the square, fluttering her wings like a clumsy hummingbird and managing to land without crushing anyone. The crowd had dwindled, but the members of the Assembly lingered in the pronaia of the Vasilikon, anger spelled as clearly as horror on their faces. Brisi did not shrink down but arched her neck and spread her wings, striking a pose before the Agogoi, as if that might impress them.

"Hatchling," called an authoritative voice in Mootya. "What have you done?"

Approaching us from the east, Ardmagar Comonot strode across the Zokalaa with an air of utter calm. He extended one hand toward Brisi, as if she were a spooked horse, and reiterated in Porphyrian for the crowd: "What have you done?"

"I burned!" cried Brisi, flapping her wings.

"But you don't burn now," said Comonot solemnly, understanding her statement differently than I had. "What does your reason tell you, hatchling?"

Brisi closed her nictitating eyelid, a veil across her confusion. "I—I don't feel it now."

"Quite correct. We all require that you shrink yourself down," said the Ardmagar. "And that your collaborators do likewise."

The young dragon did not answer, but collapsed in on herself, wings and horns and fangs telescoping inward until she had condensed into human form again. Comonot handed her her clothing, and she dressed quickly, shamefacedly, muttering, "I thought . . ."

"You felt," Comonot corrected her gently. "Very strongly, it seems."

She was feeling again, clearly; she trembled all over and could barely tie her robe. "The others were following me, Ardmagar. Let their blame be ascribed to me."

"That is not mine to grant," said Comonot. "The Assembly must try your crimes."

"The Assembly will require no deliberation on this point," said Speaker Melaye. She strode out of the crowd of Agogoi, her silken draperies billowing around her, and ascended to the top of the Vasilikon steps like an avenging ghost. "You've effectively started a war with Samsam. An act of war against the interests of the state is treason, and treason is our only capital crime."

"You can't execute her. She's a child!" cried a hoarse voice from across the Zokalaa, and we turned to see Ikat running toward us, straight from Pende's bedside. Saar Lalo helped clear her a path through the crowd. Ikat reached the steps of the Vasilikon and took the errant Brisi in her arms, scolding her. "I should have bitten you," she muttered. "I still might!"

Comonot stared in bafflement at this display of maternal anger and affection.

Speaker Melaye shook her shaved head. "This 'child' is almost sixty years old."

"I know it seems strange to you," said Ikat, stroking Brisi's hair as Brisi wept into her shoulder. "It's just as strange to me that she loves this city. Destroying the Samsamese may have been treason, but she did it for you."

"I accept my punishment!" cried Brisi, pushing her mother away. "I would rather die than go to the Tanamoot, or live with my cold, terrible dragon mind all the time."

Speaker Melaye grimaced, an unexpected spark of pity in her eyes. "Colibris, daughter of Ikat, you and your collaborators are banished from Porphyry, effective immediately. Go where you will; let us never look on you again." She turned her back on the saarantrai; the other Agogoi followed her indoors.

Brisi collapsed in tears, but Comonot was beside her in an instant, along with Ikat and Lalo, helping her to her feet, directing her steps back toward Metasaari. Comonot spotted me watching and called out, "Sunset can't come soon enough."

I waved acknowledgment and hurried to the harborside for my things.

⟨Twenty-Four⟩

At Naia's, I was surprised to find Abdo sitting on the couch, eating a dark red plum and reading. He closed the book and jumped up to greet me, looking so happy that my heart contracted painfully. "You seem more yourself," I said, my voice unsteady.

He smiled ruefully. *I have a feeling Jannoula will be occupied with Paulos Pende for a while. Surely he'll give her a good fight.*

"What were you reading?" I asked.

Abdo shrugged his narrow shoulders and shoved the last of the plum into his mouth. *An old book on meditation.* Understanding Emptiness, *by Mollox. Haven't opened it in years. Something Pende said got me thinking. I don't know. I don't want to get your hopes up.*

"Making your mind water," I said, remembering. "What does that mean?"

He shrugged again and spit the plum pit into his hand. *So you're leaving?*

I sighed. "Forgive me if I can't tell you much."

No, I understand. It's just . . . He began blinking rapidly, and then I found that my eyes, too, were stinging. Abdo wrapped his skinny arms around my middle. His head came up to my breastbone; I bent down and kissed his hair knots.

"I'm going to find a way to help you all against Jannoula," I said quietly.

He let me go and grinned impishly. *Not if I find it first.*

It felt like a thousand years since I'd seen his smile. That pure, shining distillate of happiness cut me to the heart.

My clothes didn't fit in my bag. I left my Porphyrian acquisitions with Naia, to send to Goredd, and changed back into a doublet and riding breeches. They were too warm for a Porphyrian afternoon, but I'd heard it was cold in the sky.

Abdo's family descended at dinnertime; I received seventy-two goodbye kisses. My cheeks and eyes were shining as I climbed the hill to Metasaari.

The dragon neighborhood buzzed with activity. The exiles had spent the week preparing and were ready for imminent departure. The Assembly, as promised, had supplied them, but perishable goods had been put off until the last moment. The roads were clogged with carts.

Humans arrived, too, the accumulated neighbors, co-workers, and friends of many years bearing barley bread, blankets, and tokens of memory and appreciation. Humans and saarantrai kissed each other's cheeks and promised to stay in touch.

I sighed wistfully. Would we ever see the day in Goredd?

As the sun dropped below the horizon, saarantrai began moving to the open space of Metasaari's public garden, transforming a few at a time until half a dozen magnificent dragons shaded the square, wings splayed to speed drying. The plaza could not easily hold more than that; transforming two hundred was going to take hours. Saarantrai secured bundles of supplies for these dragons to carry in their claws. The dragons' erstwhile neighbors lingered in the shadows, gaping at the display of horns and fangs.

The first of the dragons took off, massive wings laboring, blasting us with a hot sulfuric wind. He launched himself toward the ocean, the ground falling away from him, the air currents rising to catch him. We held our breath, awed; the Porphyrians began to applaud and cheer.

Comonot appeared out of nowhere and clapped me on the back. "Have you ever flown, Seraphina?"

"Only in maternal memories," I said.

"Ardmagar!" screamed a voice from across the square. Eskar, lean and fangy in her natural shape, arched her neck, and screeched again, "I wish to carry Seraphina!"

"Your carriage awaits, maidy," said the Ardmagar, taking my bag and shouldering it. "I'll make sure this comes with us." Behind him, another dragon took off.

I ran across the square, choking on the sulfurous stench as more saarantrai transformed. There were five in the sky now, dark against the deepening orange of evening, like a flock of bats. Eskar reared on her hind legs as I approached. My heart hammered in terror as she held out her forefeet, opening and closing her talons. I realized that she intended to grip me around the middle. I glanced regretfully at her spiky spine, wishing she were more horse-like in her anatomy, but I stepped forward nonetheless and let her grab me.

Her talons felt steely sharp even through the layers I'd worn in anticipation of the cold sky. I could already tell which of my ribs and axial joints would chafe. Eskar had to sprint a short distance to take off from the ground. My teeth rattled in my head as she ran, but then, with a last jarring jolt, our motion smoothed. I blinked at the retreating ground.

Fascination won out over fear; I kept my eyes open. Perhaps the diminishing city, its rooftops gently lit by the rising moon, seemed so unreal that my mind did not believe my eyes.

No, it did seem real. It felt like an enormous weight falling away from me. My eyes watered in the freezing wind.

Eskar circled toward the Sisters. I glimpsed the ancient fortress wall off which Camba had hurled glassware so long ago. From this height, the double mountain clearly stood apart from the coastal ranges. The river Omiga ran straight at its back and split in two around it. I glimpsed the terrifying falls of the western fork as we wheeled around, but Eskar followed the eastern fork up its palisaded gorge and over a series of smaller cataracts called the Stairs.

All around us other dragons flew, flapping shadows blowing brimstone wind.

We passed the curtain of the coastal ranges into the long, broad valley of the Omiga River. By the fork of the river squatted a town, Anaporphi, where the Porphyrians held their quarterly games. Its tracks and arenas were just visible in the moonlight.

We flew up the valley until midnight or so, and then landed beside a lonely stretch of river. The dragons, arriving a few at a time over several hours, shrank into their saarantrai and set up camp. We squeezed in together, five to a tent; some saar had calculated this to be the most efficient tenting ratio. Between the unaccustomed closeness, the snoring, and the aches Eskar's claws had given me, I didn't fall asleep until almost dawn. Saar Lalo shook me awake an hour later so they could dismantle the tent.

I trudged to the river to wash my scales; mist played on its face, and a grebe cried from somewhere in the reeds. The cold water dribbled down my waistband, wrenching me fully awake at last. I picked my way back to the group; they were almost ready to go, shouldering packs and tents that they'd carried up the falls in their talons.

The group had decided to walk up the valley to the next set of falls. I was glad that Eskar wouldn't have to grab me again until all my chafes had healed. Nevertheless, once I'd retrieved my bag and caught up to her, I had to ask, "Is this really the best way to travel up the valley? It's a lot slower than flying."

Eskar arched one eyebrow. "The Futile Council voted that we should walk."

"And Comonot went along with it?" I asked.

"Grudgingly," she said. "Many were refusing to come unless he let them vote. These are not the saarantrai we're used to; they're acculturated Porphyrians at some level. They care what Porphyrians think of them. And they did have a point about walking up the valley: we eat more in our natural shape, and the only game to support us here is Porphyrian livestock."

"And you didn't want to simply take it?" I said, teasing her.

She blinked at me uncomprehendingly. "I absolutely did, but I lost the vote."

The valley was a trough of verdant pastureland with mountains elbowing up rudely on either side. As we traveled, the pasture gave way to barley fields, then terraces of tea and vegetables as the valley narrowed. The cloudless sky seemed further away with each passing day, though we gained elevation. My heart was weightless for the first time in months. I thought about nothing but the road before me and the blue vault above.

On the eighth day out, the dragons turned aside from the Omiga, took their natural shapes, and flew up the thousand-foot falls of a tributary river, the Meconi, a wild straggler straight from the heart of the Tanamoot. It would be leading them home.

Eskar carried me in her talons again, but this time I wrapped myself in a blanket, padding against her unyielding claws. "Comfortable enough?" Eskar roared solicitously.

"It's sweet of you to care!" I shouted back. She snorted sulfur in my face.

The landscape above the falls was utterly different from what we'd seen below. The mountains looked raw, unfinished; the trees grew sparse and spindly. This was my first glimpse of the Tanamoot, my mother's homeland, rocky, cold, and wild.

The exiles maintained their natural shapes except for the five hatchlings, who shrank themselves back down to human form. I picked my way over to Brisi through the prickly brush and said, "Are you staying human-sized to keep me company?"

Brisi wrinkled her nose as if she thought I smelled. "We haven't had as much practice with camouflage as our elders. They think we're a liability."

I glanced around at the two hundred massive creatures, baggage strapped to their forearms, snorting and flapping and screaming. "How can they possibly camouflage all this?" I asked, shaking my head.

She blew a lock of hair out of her eyes. "In the mountains, the only thing dragons have to fear is each other. Believe me, they know how to hide." She walked pointedly away, clearly not wishing to talk to me.

The group set off on foot, to my astonishment. One would think that two hundred walking dragons would leave an enormous, easily discernible trail, but they were in their native shape now. Brisi was right: they knew how to hide in the mountains. They stepped on rocks to avoid leaving footprints in the sandy riverbank, flapping their wings to obscure what prints they did leave, and they moved with surprising stealth.

We kept to the bottom of the narrow valley, where the path was easier. Spruce forests grew a stone's throw to either side. The mountains had patches of snow on their southern faces even in high summer. The Meconi River was bitingly cold; its breath chilled the air above into wisps of mist. As we climbed, the valley widened and the Meconi subdivided into a dozen tiny streams, braiding itself among soft little islands. The trees grew shorter and thinner, as if the forest were balding. It was a land of sticks and lichen and enormous mosquitoes. The twiggy spruces cast only thin lines of shade, and the contrasting glare was headache-inducing.

The beauty of the place moved me; I loved how clean the air felt in my lungs, how far I was from everything I had ever known. People I'd hurt, people I'd failed, people who thought me a monster. Here there was no monster greater than the ragged mountains.

On the third day into dragon territory, one of our scouts gave a chirping whistle; they'd spotted a patrol in the sky. The exiles immediately folded their wings over themselves, mottled their skin, and turned into very convincing boulders.

I thought I might crawl under Eskar's wing to hide, but Brisi grabbed my arm and dragged me into a brambly bush. "In camouflage, we direct our body heat downward," she whispered angrily in my ear. "A dragon in the sky would see it otherwise. You'd bake to death under Eskar's wing."

"Thank you, then," I said, shaken. "I'm glad you know these things."

Her mouth sagged despondently. "You'd think they'd trust me to do it properly."

I could think of a reason or two the others might not trust her fully right now. She surely knew, too; she had the look of one who was beating herself up inside.

After dark, the exiles would spar with each other. Few were in fighting shape; fewer had ever been skilled enough to bring down anything more devious than an aurochs. Comonot did not seem worried. He demonstrated techniques, gave critiques, and repeated time and again, "Your minds are your surest weapons. Fight like a Porphyrian fisherman. Fight like a merchant. They'll never know what hit them."

After two weeks of walking by day and fighting by night, one evening all the adult dragons reduced themselves to human form. Lalo noticed me staring and said, "We've reached the fork of the Meconi, which means we're near Lab Four. We need to refine our next move, but two hundred dragons make for a very loud conversation."

I followed him and the other saarantrai into a narrow side valley, almost a crevasse between abutting mountains. Comonot waited at the head of it, stern Eskar beside him; the rest of the saarantrai crouched or sat on the gravelly ground. Lalo pulled me along with him, picking our way through the crowd, until we were almost at the front.

"I need volunteers to accompany Eskar to Lab Four," said the Ardmagar, cutting to the heart of the matter. "She used to work there; she believes the lab's quigutl will help our cause, but we can't risk sending everyone until she has made contact. Once we're sure of internal support, we divide our force in two. The strongest fighters storm the front gate, while the rest sneak through an escape tunnel at the back of the mountain—"

Someone raised a hand. The Ardmagar blinked irritably, then said, "Yes?"

"You seem to have made this entire plan without us," said the saar, a thickset old man. "We were promised a vote on—"

"Not on this," said the Ardmagar. A disaffected grumbling arose. Some saarantrai stood as if to walk away, but Comonot bellowed: "Stop. Sit down and listen to me."

The saarantrai sat, arms folded skeptically.

"Do you know why the Censors exist?" he said. "Because there are those who believe that without strict emotional repression, we will fall into anarchy. They think dragons will be so swayed by what they feel that they will disregard their logic, their ethics, and their duties."

At the back of the crowd, I saw Brisi squirm.

"I have been trying to understand the truth of it for more than half a year, living in human shape, walking the razor's edge of feeling," Comonot continued. "My opinion has changed over time; emotion is not always the liability I once believed it to be.

"Now we prepare to strike the Censors themselves. Not the Old Ard, but the supposedly neutral organization that enforces our repression. Like the Old Ard, the Censors want to take us backward, but I think we've come too far for that. I think you exiles—you who have lived two lives and seen both sides—are the stronger for it. You are our way forward, toward continued peace with humankind and the renewal of dragonkind.

"But I need you to show me that I'm not a fool to consider disbanding the Censors. Show me that two hundred emotional dragons can keep discipline, follow orders, and work well together. That last one—cooperation—is what our opposition lacks, and that, I think, is surely where feeling makes us stronger."

The exiles were sitting up straighter, whispering excitedly among themselves. Comonot had appealed to their emotions, of all things, and it had worked. He had a new tool at his disposal, and it was formidable indeed.

"Now," said Comonot, "who's going with Eskar to reconnoiter at Lab Four?"

Lalo, beside me, raised his hand at once.

"Lalo, son of Neelat," said the Ardmagar, scanning the crowd. "Two more."

"Seraphina must come with us," said Eskar.

"Done," said Comonot, not bothering to solicit my approval. If Eskar wanted me there, it surely had some connection with Orma. I didn't argue.

Sounds of disagreement grew at the back of the group. I looked behind me and saw Brisi arguing with her mother.

"Is there something the hatchling would like to say?" called Comonot, looking down his nose at them.

Brisi sprang to her feet, shaking off Ikat's grip. "I volunteer to go with Eskar!"

"You have caused enough trouble!" shouted her mother, tugging at Brisi's tunic.

Ardmagar Comonot exchanged a look with Eskar. She shrugged minutely. "If the hatchling wishes to redeem herself," said Eskar, "this would be a prime opportunity."

And so it was settled.

Eskar, Lalo, and Brisi unfolded themselves as the first sliver of moon rose over the distant peaks. Each time I dreaded flying a little more; each time my neck was sorer and my rib cage more bruised. Flying was fastest, even if it was harder to stay out of sight. We kept below the mountaintops, skimming the bottoms of valleys and faces of glaciers. I reached my hand down once and grabbed snow, that's how low we were. We flew until the predawn aurora was visible in the east, at which point Eskar spotted a cavern. She entered first, killed a bear she found there, and let the rest of us come in after her.

My companions ate the bear. I found I had no appetite.

We waited out the daylight. I was supposed to sleep, but the floor of the cave was rocky, and my companions, three full-sized dragons, snored, stank, and gave off terrible heat. I crouched in the cave entrance, where the air was fresher, dozing against a boulder when I wasn't working out the snore harmonics. They made a weird quintal chord, these dragons, or sometimes a diminished . . .

A change in the chord startled me awake. There were only two dragons snoring now. I looked back and saw Eskar shrinking down. She rifled through my bag without asking, took out my blanket, and wrapped it around her waist. Then she sauntered up to the cave entrance and sat a little apart from me.

"I can't speak quietly in that shape," she whispered. "I have things to tell you."

I straightened up and nodded, expecting her to delineate the plan for tonight, but instead she said, "Your uncle and I were mated."

"Indeed!" I said, embarrassed by her wording. I did not require more details along those lines. "Does that make you my aunt?" I asked, trying to joke.

She considered the question in all seriousness, staring out the cave entrance toward the glacier, and finally said, "You may call me that without inaccuracy." She was silent for several beats more, then added, with unaccustomed softness in her tone, "I never thought much of him as a dragon. He's small. A tenacious fighter, granted. A decent flier, considering his wing was once broken, but he could never have kept up with me. I'd have bitten the back of his neck and sent him on his way.

"But as a saarantras . . ." She paused, a finger to her lips. "He's something extraordinary."

I pictured my uncle's shrubby hair and beaky nose, his spectacles and false beard and angular limbs, every detail absurd and dear to me. My chin trembled.

"These human eyes seemed weak at first," said Eskar, still staring away from me, scratching her short black hair. "They detect fewer colors and have terrible resolution, but they see things dragon eyes cannot. They can see beyond surfaces. I don't understand how that's possible, but it happened incrementally as I traveled with Orma: I began to see the inside of him. His questioning and gentle nature. His conviction. I'd glimpse it in something as incongruous as his hand holding a teacup, or his eyes when he spoke of you."

She turned her needle-sharp gaze on me. "What is that inner being? That person within a person? Is that what you call the soul?"

According to Southlander theology, dragons don't have souls; she knew that. I hesitated, but surely there was no danger saying this to her now, not after what had already happened to Orma. "He had a mighty soul, my uncle. The greatest I ever knew."

"You speak as if he is dead," she said sternly.

The tears finally came; I could not reply.

She observed me closely, her dark eyes dry, her arms wrapped around her knees. "The Censors took a risk, entering Porphyry clandestinely. They were supposed to have petitioned the Assembly, and I have determined they did not. In my day, we would have run such a risk only if someone very important wanted Orma quickly. It gives me hope that this isn't the usual capture of a deviant, that they may have brought him in not for excision but for some other purpose."

The word *excision* chilled me. "What if the deed is done?" I said, drying my eyes. "Will he still be himself?"

"It depends what they take. Usually they only remove memories. Those neural pathways are largely the same whether we are in dragon or human form." She spoke as neutrally as if she were describing her breakfast. "The emotion centers of the human brain overlap with dragon flight centers; it would cripple him to remove those. They wouldn't permanently deprive him of flight, not the first time. They would remove his memories, put him on an emotional suppressant—a tincture of destultia—and give him a second chance.

"Plenty of us undergo excision at some point. Look." She bent her head forward and parted the hair behind her left ear, revealing a white stripe of scar tissue. "When I quit the Censors, they removed my memories of working there so I couldn't reveal their secrets. But I am still myself. I was not irreparably damaged."

I recoiled, horrified. "But—but you remember working for the Censors!"

Her mouth flattened. "They informed me afterward that I had been in their employ so I wouldn't reapply. But I also made myself a mind-pearl so I could remember why I quit. That was important to me."

"Why did you quit?" I asked.

"Several reasons," she said. "They would not reprimand Zeyd, the agent I authorized to test your uncle, for threatening you with harm in the course of that test."

I put a hand to my heart, touched. "You didn't even know me!"

"I didn't have to know you." Her black eyes flicked toward me. "Entrapment is an unacceptable testing practice."

So the wrong had been in attempting to trap Orma into an emotional reveal, not in dangling me over the edge of the cathedral tower. I sighed and changed the subject. "My mother left me mind-pearls. Are they difficult to make?"

Eskar shrugged. "Mothers make simple ones for their children. To encapsulate a lot of memories, and hide them well, requires outside help. There are saarantrai who specialize in clandestine meditation, but it's illegal and expensive." Her eyes unfocused. "You're wondering whether Orma did such a thing."

I held out my hand and wiggled my pinkie, showing her my

pearl ring. "He sent me this in Ninys, along with the words *The thing itself plus nothing equals everything.* I think he was trying to tell me he'd done it."

Eskar took my hand and brushed the pearl lightly with her thumb; the spark of hope in her eyes was almost unbearable. "Perhaps he was," she half whispered, "but I don't know when he could have had it done. Not while I was with him. He might have made a simple pearl on his own with a few bare facts, brief images, your name."

I took my hand back and twisted the ring on my finger.

"Mind-pearls can be difficult to retrieve if you don't know the trigger for locating and opening them," Eskar said, standing up. She hesitated, then added, "He will always be your uncle, whether he remembers he is or not."

She swooped down, kissed the top of my head lightly, and then headed toward Lalo and Brisi at the back of the cave. "Four hours until sunset," she called over her shoulder. "Sleep."

I leaned against the boulder and closed my eyes.

I only knew I'd slept because I dreamed about Abdo. He was riding in the back of a wagon with several other people, jostling and bumping over a rutted country road. The road wound into the Queenswood, which was just turning golden and autumnal. At a bend in the road, where the undergrowth was particularly dense, Abdo suddenly leaped to his feet and flipped himself out of the wagon. His companions shouted in protest, some reaching out dark hands to stop him, but he was beyond their reach, somersaulting down the hill through ferns and shrubbery until he disappeared from view.

I heard his voice: *Don't look for me.*

In the wagon, Paulos Pende stood shakily. His eyes rolled up in his head, and he fell down dead.

"Seraphina!" screamed a steam kettle, which, once I opened my eyes, turned out to be full-sized Eskar. "Ready yourself. It's time to go."

I was disoriented, and the first thing I wanted to do was look for Abdo in my head. The dream had been so vivid that I had the impression he'd really spoken to me, that it wasn't a dream at all.

Of course, his message had been that I *shouldn't* look for him. I felt my resolve tangle in knots.

In any case, there was no time. Eskar was snorting impatiently. I hastily wrapped the blanket around my ribs, and Eskar grasped me in her talons again. There wasn't much further to go; the three dragons skimmed one more valley and landed at the edge of a glacier, silver beneath the narrow moon. Ghostly wisps of steam rose from a deep crack in the ice. Eskar set me down, stuck her head into the crevasse, and flamed the ice; our companion dragons paled to blend with the glacier and spread their wings to block her light. When Eskar had widened the crack sufficiently, the others squeezed through. I would have followed on my own, but Eskar took me up protectively and carried me in. I was glad once I realized we were in a downward-sloping icy tunnel, longer than it looked; even Eskar's claws had trouble finding purchase.

We reached a flat floor at the bottom. My eyes were almost useless under the glacier; the ice was too deep for the moon to shine through, and the cavern was very dimly lit. I was more worried about the smell. A moist, clingy, sulfuric funk had hit us about halfway down the tunnel—and I mean hit, like we'd run into a brick wall of stench. My eyes watered. My nose finally gave up the game, but my throat still felt a thickness in the air and gagged in self-defense. The floor was covered in cold mush up to my ankles.

A scuttling echoed above us and a squishing below. Sparks rained in the darkness. I thought it was my eyes playing tricks, until the sparks became steady open flames at the ends of fifty long tongues, belonging to as many quigutl, the smaller, lizard-like cousins of dragons. My eyes adjusted; the cavern opened far larger than I'd realized, a cathedral of ice and stone enclosing a hulking mountain of festering muck. Quigs swarmed all over it, some with shovel blades strapped to their ventral hands.

"You're trethpassing," said a quigutl in lisping semi-Mootya, raising its spiky, lizardy head in front of us. On its hind legs, it was nearly as tall as me. Its eye cones swiveled, taking us in.

"We need to see Mitha!" screamed Eskar.

"If you know Mitha," said the quig, flaring its head spines suspiciously, "then you know Mitha doethn't work in the cesspitth."

Cesspits. That would be the mountainous muck. I wrapped an arm around my face, gagging again, and tried not to think about my boots.

A commotion arose, a stout quigutl crawling toward us over others on the dung heap. He stood up in front of us, facing his fellows, and raised his hands for silence; he had only three hands. "I am Thmatha, Mitha's cousin," he said. "I know this dragon. She saved me from Dr. Gomlann's experiment. He took my arm, but I'm alive in the pits, not pretherved in a jar." Thmatha saluted Eskar. "I will bring Mitha."

He plunged into the darkness, and we were left to wait. "Are you hungry? We've got dung," quipped one of the others.

Eskar cried, "Seraphina, get out your flute!"

She couldn't see the look I shot her in the dark; she might not have understood it if she had. "You want me to play flute. In the cesspit."

"I do!" she screamed. "The quigs will like it."

It meant taking deeper breaths than I cared to, but I tried to be a good sport and humor her. The acoustics of the dung-filled ice cave were extremely odd; my experimental warm-up notes echoed unpleasantly. There was a scuttling in the darkness; the quigs' bobbing tongue lights closed in around me. I worried that the sound had upset them, until I realized they were jabbering at me. "What'th that? Do it again. Aim it at the western wall. That should give interesting reverberationth."

I turned in the indicated direction and began to play a nursery tune, "Dance a Biddy Weasel." The quigs chattered animatedly about the wavelengths of the notes, whether one could make such an instrument from a musk ox femur, and what sort of modifications would be required if one had no lips.

I glanced at Eskar; she nodded minutely. Somehow this was part of the plan.

Thmatha returned about an hour later, evidenced by the quigs shifting their attention. He and another quigutl were ushered up to the front, and the new arrival—who I presumed was Mitha—saluted Eskar the way a saarantras would have, gesturing toward the sky. Eskar saluted back. A murmur went up; as a rule, dragons did not salute quigutl. Mitha said to Eskar, "You brought us a novelty. You were alwayth generous that way."

"It took me a long time to return!" cried Eskar. "This is meager recompense."

Mitha gave a strange double shrug with his two sets of shoulders and said, "No matter. We're ready. We've been ready for yearth. I hope this isn't all the firepower you brought with you."

Twenty-Five

I stared at Eskar, silhouetted in the feeble light: the shadow of her horns and spiky protuberances, her folded wings. She looked suddenly alien to me, full of secrets. She had not merely quit the Censors. She had not come here to see whether she could persuade the quigs to help. She'd already organized them; she'd been planning this for a long time.

There was more to her than I had guessed. For the first time it occurred to me that she was quite well suited to my uncle.

She conferred with Mitha, agreeing on what he should do and when. He replied, "All will be as you athk. We've cunningly re-wired the lab, so we need only—"

"I trust your diligence!" she screamed, apparently not caring for the details. "You have two days. These hatchlings, Seraphina and Brisi, are to assist you in your sabotage."

"Exthellent," said Mitha, swiveling his conical chameleon's eyes to look at us. "I shall keep them as thafe as my own eggth."

Eskar signaled to Lalo, who began to climb back out of the tunnel. She made as if to follow him, hesitated, and turned back to me. "Three things, Seraphina," she said, snorting acrid smoke in my face. "One: find Orma. Two: stop his excision, if possible. Three: secure yourself someplace safe during the fighting."

She turned around so rapidly the tip of her tail hit me. Mitha kept me from falling backward into the sludge, but then he kept hold of my arm and took a sniff at my wrist.

"Well, call me a thalamander: you're half human. How odd. Come on, then." He started toward a tunnel on the right-hand wall, then paused and eyed Brisi, whose wings drooped forlornly. "Shrink down, hatchling," said Mitha. "These tunnelth are too thmall for you."

Brisi blinked at him dumbly, as if the smell had paralyzed her. I touched her scaly shoulder with my hand. "Into your saarantras," I said in Porphyrian, supposing she found the quigutl accent difficult.

She shrank down, but she'd brought no clothing. Eskar hadn't warned her, maybe because Eskar would have gone naked without a second thought. I pulled a linen shirt, doublet, and breeches out of my bag, led her into the less mucky corridor, and helped her change. She found the buckles and laces of Goreddi clothing quite alarming. Mitha waited, flicking his tongue flame on and off.

When Brisi was finally dressed, Mitha rose on his hind legs and walked at my side, one of his hands touching my elbow lightly for balance. We followed the corridor to a chamber, excavated into the living rock, where quigs processed the dragon leavings. Translucent orbs set into the ceiling provided an eerie, unflickering light. "Methane and solid fuelth," said Mitha, gesturing toward pipes and tanks, gauges and kilns. "The labs run on dung. Helpth keep the facility hidden if there isn't a cess-valley nearby."

The passage narrowed again, multiple pipelines running along the wall. The flameless lanterns glowed upon the ceiling at intervals. At a nexus sat a curious conveyance, like a six-legged headless pony, wide as a bed, consisting mostly of gears and sputtering. It reminded me of Blanche's mechanical spiders, without the creepiness.

At the thought of Blanche, I felt a pang. Except for my dream of Abdo, I'd barely thought of the other ityasaari in weeks. I had shied away from my shriveled garden. It was too distressing. Soon I would find Orma and we'd work out how to free my powers, and how to free the others from Jannoula.

Assuming Orma still knew me. I shoved that fear aside.

The mechanical pony had no seats as such; quigutl don't sit like humans do. Mitha instructed us to lie on top of it on our bellies. I climbed aboard gingerly, grasping two leather loops to keep from sliding off. Brisi, beside me, gripped my arm with fingers like talons. Mitha clung to the contraption's backside, behind the rattling engine, and reached around the side to pull a lever. The headless pony clanked along, snorting steam from its bum, faster than we could walk, through passages too tight for dragons. The dim, steady ceiling lights whizzed past. I tried not to think about falling off and being trampled.

After half an hour, we reached a vaulted bay where several of these conveyances were moored, hissing and humming. Mitha helped me down; my knees were trembling.

"Lab Four," he said. "Under its own mountain. This is Quigutl Level Five, but any tunnel too thmall for a dragon is thafe. I will find you a nest. Are you hungry?"

I shook my head. Brisi gaped at him; seeing him in full light had shocked her anew. I put a hand on her shoulder, which seemed to snap her out of it. "I'm sorry," she said in Porphyrian, pinching the bridge of her nose. "I've heard of quigs from my mother, but we don't have them in Porphyry. They're so . . . ugly."

I hoped Mitha couldn't understand her. He gave no sign, and then we were interrupted by the arrival of several more quigutl. These were lab quigs, cleaner than their comrades in the pits. They came straight over, gabbling to each other, and began examining our clothes, tugging at the hem of my tunic and the cuffs of Brisi's trousers.

"Porphyrian cotton," said one knowledgeably. "That's what we're lacking, good fibrous plantth. I'm not keen on the ox hair or the bark. You see how fragile she ith?" She poked me in the face with a finger. "The bark would chafe."

"How do they do thith?" said one, fingering the key pattern along the hemline.

"It's called embroidery," I said. His eye cones swiveled quizzically, and I realized the name didn't explain anything. "You do it with a needle and floss."

The quig reached into his mouth, down into his throat pouch, and pulled out an awl. "Needle. Like thith?"

"Finer. Sharper."

"Hey," cut in another quig, who'd been sniffing me rudely. "She's a half-breed!"

The group oohed and aahed appreciatively, at which point Mitha decided the party was over and began to shoo them away. "Eskar is back," he said as he shooed. "We have forty-eight hourth. There will be plenty of time to goggle over fabric later."

"When we all go south!" cried a particularly small quig. Everyone hushed her.

"Thpread the word," said Mitha. "Quietly."

They scampered off. I exhaled; their close scrutiny had made me tense.

Mitha started up another corridor. He opened the door of an enormous room full of extremely noisy machinery; it was too loud to talk, but he made elaborate hand gestures at the quigs working inside, wordlessly communicating something. *Eskar's back*, presumably. They all seemed to understand what that meant.

"The generator," he said as he closed the door. The word meant nothing to me.

He brought Brisi and me to a quieter tunnel; the ceiling was even lower here, with hemispheric light fixtures, and we had to stoop. The walls were punctuated not with doors but with holes a foot off the ground; the air was damp and earthy. "Thith is the warren," said Mitha, indicating the whole cheese-like network of holes. He walked on four legs now, his twiggy dorsal arms folded demurely against his back, sniffing around for the right hole. I was going to have to count.

"My nest," he said, encouraging us to go inside. "You've been up all night, and I know you're not nocturnal."

Brisi and I crawled through the hole into a roughly circular room. The floor was lined with animal skins and dry leaves. There seemed to be no beds as such. Brisi slumped to the ground, exhausted. I handed her my bag to use as a pillow, and she took it gratefully. "I'll be right back," I whispered. "I need to ask Mitha something."

She uttered no protest. She may already have been asleep.

I stuck my head out of the hole and hissed, "Mitha!" He was still in sight; he stopped and waited for me to waddle to him, like a duck. I bumped my head twice, not on the low rock ceiling but on the low-hanging hemispheric lights. "Eskar has ordered me to find someone, a particular prisoner."

"We call them victimth," he said. "But yeth, I can help you look."

He led me out of the warren and up another service tunnel into a room full of . . . I guessed it was machinery. I saw a jungle of gleaming metallic vines and a peculiar slab of silvery ice nested into the facing wall. Mitha flopped onto his stomach on a quigutl stool, like a little ramp that led nowhere. From the tangle of silvery vines in front of him, Mitha pulled on a cluster of little cups and drew them toward him. Their wiry stems made them look like a bouquet of honeysuckle flowers. He stuck his claws in, one per flower, wiggled his fingers, and glowing writing appeared behind the ice.

It wasn't ice but glass. I felt a little foolish.

I'd seen written Mootya in my mother's memories—in fact, I'd seen my mother use a device called a note block. This seemed similar, but much larger.

"All right," said Mitha, squinting at the panel. "Best do this now before we reroute all the power. Which victim are we looking up?"

"My uncle Orma," I said. The word *victim* set my palms sweating. "Can you contact him with this, uh, machine?"

"No, no," said the quig. "These are medical recordth. We can determine which cell he'th in, and whether they've made a mince of him yet."

I clamped my lips tightly shut and let Mitha do whatever he was doing. His eye cones flitted back and forth as he read; impatient sparks crackled on the end of his tongue. At last he said, "He has an enormouth file, but no record of him being *here.*"

I'd braced for the worst, but this took me aback. "Could they have moved him to a different facility?"

One of Mitha's eyes swiveled toward me. "I checked. He'th not at any Centhorial facility. Is that him?" He gestured toward the panel with one of his dorsal hands.

I gasped. Orma stared out as if from a window, his brows arched in mild curiosity. "What do you mean, he's not here?" I cried. "He's right there!"

"That's a picture," said Mitha. He tapped the glass; Orma didn't blink.

If words could appear behind the glass, why not a portrait? I felt a little foolish, but it was so life-like.

Mitha was talking: "Sometimeth files are deleted for security reasonth. We'll sniff around; there may yet be something to find." Text slid up the screen; his mouth moved as he read. "Your mother was the dragon Linn, I deduce?" His fingers waggled manically in their scabbards. Two pictures of my mother, in her dragon and human forms, appeared. I pressed a hand to my mouth, not sure whether I was holding back laughter or tears.

I had never seen an image of her. She looked a lot like Orma. Prettier, maybe.

Mitha said, "She and Eskar were friendth. When Linn was compromised, Eskar wrote letterth begging her to come home and be fixed, but she would not."

"Dragons write letters?" I asked, struck by the oddity of it.

Mitha swiveled an eye cone toward me. "Your mother was in human form; she couldn't have read an aerial etching on the mountainthide. Eskar would have dictated it to one of uth. My point is, that was the beginning of the end of our Eskar's employment here. She began to doubt."

"Eskar told me she quit because Zeyd threatened my life," I said.

Mitha's head spines wobbled. "That too. Then she hired my cousin to thpy on her superiorth. He learned about the imprisoned half-human; that convinthed her to quit."

I stared at him, a knot forming in my stomach. "The imprisoned half-human?" I repeated slowly. I knew all the half-humans; only one had been imprisoned.

"The one they raised from a baby and experimented on," Mitha said simply, plucking the control cups from his fingers.

An icy certainty gripped my insides. "D-did she live in a cell with a tiny window and wear a dreadful suit of rabbit skins?"

"You know her!" said Mitha. "But don't call it dreadful in front of the otherth. We don't have good fibrous plants here in the mountainth."

I had not come looking for Jannoula's childhood. Mitha's description made me shudder, but I couldn't turn away. I had to know. I had to understand who she was and what she was doing, and here were surely answers to the questions she had always dodged.

Mitha didn't want to take me to her cell, but I insisted. He led me through the maze of service corridors, pausing only to tell the quigs we passed that Eskar was back and they had work to do. We crossed a full-sized corridor meant for dragons after Mitha made sure the coast was clear.

Our path took us through a surgery with an operation in progress, some poor saar with his brainpan open to the air. Three dragon doctors stood around the high metal table, employing mechanical arms for the actual cutting, like jointed insect legs ending in scalpels. I balked at the sight of the surgeons, but Mitha grabbed my arm with his twig-like dorsal hand and pulled me along behind the steel equipment racks. The doctors' eyes were covered with cup-like eyepieces; they could only focus on their work. Mitha signaled to the nurse quigutls, who made extra noise fetching sponges and suture thread.

I cringed and hurried quietly after Mitha.

Another service corridor brought us to a row of human-sized cells, all empty. The gray predawn light filtered through the narrow barred windows. "Not every victim cooperateth," said Mitha. "Some won't return to their natural size. They keep such mithcreants here, and they kept her at the very end."

I walked down the corridor, my heart in my throat, and opened the heavy door to Jannoula's former home. The cell was familiar to me: the dirty floor, the low bed, the cold walls. The rabbit-fur suit hung on a peg beside the door.

They had experimented on her. My stomach clenched.

No wonder she'd reacted to me the way she had. I was perhaps the first humane presence she had known. I had popped in out of nowhere and been kind to her.

And then I'd cast her out of my garden and back into this life.

My throat was almost too dry to speak. "They let her go in the end. It's too much to hope that it was an act of mercy, but . . . but why did they do it?"

"Let her go?" said Mitha. "As in releathe her to the wild? They didn't."

I frowned. "I saw her in Samsam."

He snapped his mouth open and shut, thinking. "She taught herself strategy games, and she was very good. They started asking her opinionth on various thingth."

"Strategy," I said numbly.

"General Palonn took her with him to the Battle of Homand-Eynn," said Mitha. "We made the chain for around her neck, and a better suit of musk ox hair, because they were thitting in a glacier, watching."

I was trembling uncontrollably. I sat down on her little wooden bed and held my head in my hands. "Homand-Eynn was an early defeat for the Loyalists. Comonot told me about it. The Old Ard surprised his Loyalists by hiding in a hatchery."

"Putting their own hatchlingth in danger," Mitha said, his eyes swiveling. "A gamble, but it worked. General Palonn was exceedingly pleased. He boasted to the doctors: 'You've finally created something useful: a general from a *lady*.'"

Mitha said *lady* in Goreddi, which startled me. "Did Palonn use that very word?"

"It became her nickname," said Mitha. "And she won the Old Ard more battles."

All this time we'd been assuming *lady* was a dragon name, not a word in our own language. Jannoula was the notorious General Laedi.

ᴄᐢTwenty-Six ᐢᴠ

Glisselda had to be told Jannoula was working for the Old
Ard, maybe even acting under orders in Samsam. She would
be traveling to Goredd to join the other ityasaari soon, if she
hadn't already. The Queen needed to capture her and lock her up
before she could do any more damage.

I pulled out the thnik I'd acquired in Porphyry and would
have used it at once, but Mitha cried, "They'll hear you!" He
snatched the device from my hand and tossed it down his gullet,
chain and all.

I stared at him, appalled.

Mitha made an inscrutable clicking sound in his throat; I
couldn't tell whether he was scolding or apologizing. "The Censors will detect unauthorithed transmissionth. Come. We will talk
when you have thlept."

I swayed on my feet, exhaustion finally catching me up, and

didn't have the wherewithal to protest. He led me back to the warren by a different route—no operating theaters—but when we reached his nest, it was full. About twenty quigutl lay in a heap together. "There'th room," Mitha insisted. "Pile in."

I eyed the sleeping quigs. "They won't be alarmed to see me when they wake?"

"Perhapth," was all he said before scurrying off again.

I found some edge space where I didn't touch anyone, but this part of the floor was covered in bark shavings, which poked my skin. Exhausted though I was, my nerves vibrated alertly. I thought about entering my neglected garden and sending a message through Lars again, but the last time had ended with Viridius hurt. Whom else could I contact? Who wasn't compromised by now? I lay a long time, despairing.

Sleep crept up on me like a glacier.

Sticky finger pads prodded my cheek. I sat bolt upright when I realized what they must be; half a dozen quigs scattered away from me, some up the walls and across the ceiling. I rubbed my eyes with my thumb and forefinger. The only light shone through the hole from the corridor. I could not tell what time it was.

"Mitha said to wake you," called one from the ceiling above me, defensively.

"We're collecting thnikth," said another. "You're to help uth."

"How long did I sleep?" I asked, flopping back down.

"A very long time! It's not today anymore. It's tomorrow. That

Porphyrian dragon ith already up, being helpful." They all did that peculiar mouth clap Mitha had done, and I wondered if that was quigutl laughter.

They gave me a meal of tough mountain greens and under-cooked yak; it was dreadful, but at least nothing was rotten. I followed a gang of youngsters through service tunnels so low I couldn't stand. The quigs sneaked into the personal lairs of the Censors and doctors, located thniks and thnimis (devices that also transmitted images), and squirreled them away in their mouths. Then they came back to the tunnel and regurgitated everything into a little wagon, which I wheeled past the warren into an area so tight and remote I could barely squeeze into it. A quig at that end unloaded all the devices into a storage room.

Of course, some of the devices were around the necks and wrists of Censors and doctors. Once we'd cleared out the lairs, Mitha used the interlab thnimi to broadcast his knobby face and crackling lisp to every corner of Lab Four: "Attention, Censorth! All transmitting devices must be submitted for upgrade. Compliance is mandatory, as per Censorial Order five-nine-five-oh-six dash nine."

The dragons cooperated, lining up in the oversized corridors and dropping their thniks into a mechanical wheelbarrow Mitha had set up near the chemical labs. From an air vent near the ceiling, I watched and listened to draconic small talk—who had bitten whom, how come Inna went on leave, the molecular composition of that new neurotoxin, why yaks don't get as fat as they used to. Their thniks were larger than the ones saarantrai carried, dragon bracelets that would be a heavy neck chain to a human, rings that would be bracelets. Some had thniks fastened to their heads with cobwebby filaments so that they might talk with their talons unencumbered.

I lay on my stomach in a duct. The quigutls that had jammed in on either side of me kept rubbing themselves against me like cats. After a while it was too much for me, and I hissed, "Stop that!"

"Can't," said the one nearest my face. "If they thmell you, you're dead and all Eskar's hard work is thpoiled."

It was hard to imagine that anyone capable of such tedious small talk would kill me, but four quigutl engineers had been mercilessly torched that day, one for getting too close to a Censor's person uninvited, the others for seeking out thniks hidden in the dragons' lairs. I went with Mitha's nestlings to visit them in the quigutl infirmary when our work was done. It was a brightly lit space, with several small egg-shaped pools in the floor. The injured engineers each lay in one, soaking in some viscous liquid. Brisi was helping alongside the nursing quigs, scooping up the ooze with a ladle and pouring it over tender, charred heads. The hurt quigutl seemed cheerful enough, considering that burned, blackened skin was peeling off their bodies.

"Don't worry, they're on destultia," a quig whispered in my ear. "They feel the pain, but they don't mind it anymore."

I was pondering this statement when Mitha arrived. He greeted each of his engineers in turn and then scampered up to me. He'd brought my flute from the warren; he presented it to me with a flourish of dorsal hands. "I hoped you might play a song for uth," said Mitha. He ran a hand over his eye cone. "I wrote it. I will sing, and you harmonithe."

"I like fifths!" someone piped up. "The wavelengths are integer multipleth!"

"I like tritones!" cried someone else.

Mitha coughed up an ember, spat it on the floor, and began to intone:

> O saar, beware!
> Beware the horde,
> The ones you never see.
> We build your lairth,
> Repair, invent,
> We do all this for free.
> You torch our hideth,
> You crunch our boneth,
> Kill with impunity.
> But we are not
> Tho helpless now.
> Our day cometh. We are free.

I stared dumbfounded, not merely because he'd come up with a poem that scanned and rhymed, but because the tune was so perfectly tuneless that I had no idea how to begin to play along. I couldn't just play fifths because I couldn't figure out what note he was singing. It wasn't so much a particular note as a low, throaty rumble, but then there were shrill, whistling harmonics coming through his nose. It reminded me of Brasidas's sinus-singing at the harbor market.

I worried whether the sound would carry through the tunnels, but the quigs weren't worried, and they surely knew their mountain better than I did. I decided to shrill along with him. I sent up some experimental whistles. Around me the quigs murmured; it sounded approving, but I couldn't tell for certain until they started keening along with us.

We produced the most unholy cacophony, like fighting tomcats or the blast furnaces of the Infernum. The music brought tears to my eyes, not because it was teeth-grindingly dissonant but because they were all so swept up by it. They reached for each other as they sang, with hands and tails—one wrapped around my ankle—and with their crooning notes. If I closed my eyes, I could hear what they were doing, tendrils of sound curling and responding to each other, like pea shoots spiraling around a stake. The stake was Mitha's lyrics, the one steady point of reference. This was art, quigutl art, and in some oblique fashion it was what I'd been looking for, what Dame Okra had once mocked.

I'd found my people and they weren't even mine.

It grew late. Nobody wanted to crawl back to the warrens, and quigutl etiquette apparently smiled upon sleeping wherever you happened to be. Some lay down, others piled on top of them, and everybody snored. I crawled over to where Brisi was sitting, hugging her knees. "How are you getting on?" I asked her in Porphyrian.

She shook her head slowly. "My parents said they were like rats: dirty, clever, thieving, and diseased. And I'm . . . I see there's more to them, but I'm still uncomfortable here. Why would Eskar work with them? Not for pity. She knows nothing of that."

It had made intuitive sense to me that Eskar would feel sorrow or outrage at the Censors' treatment of Jannoula, Orma, or the quigutl—but Brisi was right. Eskar hadn't felt any of that. "The thing about reason," I said slowly, thinking of Comonot's earlier explanation as I spoke, "is that there's a geometry to it. It travels in a straight line, so slightly different beginnings can lead you to wildly divergent endpoints. I think Eskar must have begun from the position that all reasoning beings are equal."

"Even if they smell?" said Brisi, yawning.

We found our own space on the floor. She quickly drifted off to sleep, but I couldn't stop thinking about Eskar's first principle. Was it provably true that reasoning beings were equal? It seemed more like a belief than a fact, even if I agreed with it. If you followed logic all the way back to its origin, did you inevitably end up at a point of illogic, an article of faith? Even an indisputable fact must be chosen as the place to start reasoning, given weight by a mind that believed in its worth.

At some point my mind gave up the fight, and by morning the quigs were all over me. I woke with someone's tail wreathing my face and someone else half burrowed under my bum, but they'd left Brisi alone. The saar-quigutl distrust went both ways.

Today Eskar was to return with Comonot and the exiles, and the quigutl levels of the lab buzzed with anticipation. Mitha ordered quigs to their posts; everyone seemed to know where to go. He took Brisi and me with him to the Electrostatics Room, as he called it, where we would be least likely to get underfoot when the fighting started. "It's going to be pitch-dark in many of the corridorth," he said, strapping a portable lamp to my wrist. It cast a ghostly bluish light. "Most backup power is already disconnected. What's left will run lightth. Even those will blink out after a while."

The Electrostatics Room had a high ceiling; Brisi and I gratefully stood upright, stretching our aching backs. The room was full of rotating machinery, so noisy that Mitha had to stand on his hind legs and shout in my ear: "That'th the generator! It makes power for the lights and machineth." He studied my face to see if I'd understood. I hadn't. He said, "You humans make fine fabric and music, eh, but you're lacking in natural philosophy. Everything is made of other, tiny things, and we make some of the smallest do work for us by bothering them with magnetth."

Mitha swiveled one eye cone, which I was beginning to understand was a quigutl wink, and said, "There are worlds within worlds, Seraphina."

He chirped to his fellows at the far end of the room, away from the generator, and grabbed Brisi and me and dragged us over. They were adjusting a large lens to focus on an image of the mountains. "The electronic eye," said Mitha, as if that explained anything.

One of his comrades pointed to a speck on the screen above the mountains. We watched it differentiate into two specks, which resolved into flying dragons. As they drew closer, the viewing angle changed, keeping the pair in sight even as they landed below the eye, on a ledge that stuck out of the mountain like a rocky lip.

I knew who they would be, but still shivered to recognize them: Eskar and Ardmagar Comonot.

A pair of enormous doors opened, sliding silently back into the mountain. A small battalion of quigutl rushed out and swarmed over the pair of them. "Sniffers," Mitha explained to Brisi and me. "To identify them with thertainty." The quigs scuttled back indoors, and soon five Censors emerged, surrounding Eskar and Comonot, who ducked their heads and submitted to bites on the neck.

The largest of the Censors spoke, his voice ringing hollowly from the little speaker by the lens. "Eskar, daughter of Askann, agent emerita first class, and Comonot, the ex-Ardmagar," he cried, circling them. "A peculiar pair to land on our doorstep. What brings you here, Agent Emerita?"

Eskar saluted the sky. "All in ard, Agent. I was recalled to active duty by the Censor Magister."

"You have the paperwork for that?"

"This assignment came under the floor." Eskar extended a wing toward Comonot. "I was uniquely positioned to capture the ex-Ardmagar."

All around me, the watching quigs quivered with excitement, whispering Eskar's name to each other. "Oh, but she is deliciously deviouth!" said one.

Only Mitha flattened his head spines in disagreement. "Not devious enough."

The head agent screamed, "You seem not to realize that we have a recent file on you, Emerita. You have been consorting with deviants in Porphyry."

Eskar did not flinch; she arced her neck scornfully. "Your agents broke the law, entering Porphyry without the Assembly's permission," she said.

Around me the younger quigutl clapped their mouths open and shut enthusiastically. Mitha flared his nostrils and smacked the most exuberant on their heads.

The senior agent arced his neck in turn. "It is also against the law to fraternize with exiles. And by 'fraternize,' I mean—"

"He knew where to find the ex-Ardmagar," Eskar interrupted. Comonot, still low to the ground, eyed her with interest; apparently her relationship with my uncle had not been explained to the general. "But of course, your agents captured Orma before he would tell me. You set me back in my investigation. I could have you fined."

They mirrored each other, arched necks and flared wings. The juxtaposition of that aggressive pose with talk of fining gave me a certain cognitive dissonance. "I was told to bring the ex-Ardmagar to the nearest Censorial facility," snarled Eskar. "I was told we were expected, and you would process my prisoner at once. This questioning is out of order."

"I outrank you. I have the right." The Censor's words came out mumbled; he was working up a flame, intending to give Eskar a hot foot at the very least. Around me, quigs squirmed anxiously. Mitha made a rumbling sound in his throat to calm them.

Never taking her eyes off the ranking agent, Eskar fiddled with a chain at her wrist as if it were a thnik. "I've signaled the Board," she screeched.

"Good. They'll send an auditor, who will affirm my right."

"No," said Eskar, almost sweetly for a dragon. "They're sending an ard."

At precisely that moment, a hundred dragons rose above the mountains behind Eskar, flying in dual wedge formations, and a loud rumbling echoed deep within the Censors' mountain, as if the earth had indigestion.

That was our signal. Mitha and his comrades swarmed the generator. I glued my gaze upon the scene in the lens, knowing it was about to disappear. For a frozen instant I saw a tableau: the four sub-agents rushing back into the lab; the head agent reaching for his neck, where his thnik should have been but wasn't; Comonot springing up, jaws wide to strike at him; and Eskar looking straight up into the electronic eye.

The picture flickered off and the lights went out. Brisi shrieked like a child.

Eskar's instructions—as per Mitha—were for the quigs to stay put, fighting only if the fighting came to them, but no sooner was the generator down than they swarmed out the door, looking for trouble. "Tho much for discipline," said Mitha, although he didn't seem particularly surprised. "Seraphina, it occurred to me that even if Orma had been here and his recordth deliberately erased, surely the Censorth would not have gone to the trouble to excise every doctor who dealt with him. One of the doctorth might know where Orma went next. I expect the medical staff will all be avoiding a firefight. We might be able to corner one in the operating theater. Would you like to try?"

I could not imagine how a quigutl, a human, and a . . . Brisi were going to corner a full-sized dragon, but surely doctors could be reasoned with, and might answer our questions. It was better than sitting here uselessly. I said, "Lead on, friend."

Mitha scampered out of the room and up the service corridor. I grabbed Brisi's elbow and dragged her along; she had a strange expression on her face, as if she were listening hard. All around us, draconic screams reverberated through the living rock. Brisi quivered—though with excitement or fear, I couldn't tell.

Mitha darted up a dark side corridor, so narrow my elbows brushed the walls, and pulled a lever to open a thick stone door. We were immediately blown back by terrible heat, blinded by a cascade of fire in front of us. I choked, barely able to breathe, as if the dragon fire had burned the life-giving air. Mitha pushed me back, crying, "Wrong way! I didn't think they'd be fighting in this corridor yet."

But I couldn't move. Behind me Brisi was pushing the other direction, wriggling, squirming past me; she shoved me hard into the rock wall in her haste to get by. She stopped in the doorway and stripped off her clothes. Her silhouette stood out starkly against the firefight behind her. She was all skinny arms and legs, and then she was more. She elongated and uncoiled into a terrible spiky shadow and leaped without hesitation into the fray.

I cried out, afraid for her, but Mitha was pulling the lever, closing the door. Tongues of flame licked around its edges, then were extinguished as it tightly closed. "Well, good," said Mitha, a slight tremor in his voice. "She belongs there. It is right. Come—I've thought of a better route."

He led me through some extremely tight tunnels; I crawled on elbows and belly and tried not to imagine getting stuck. At last we popped out of a trapdoor into an operating room, empty but for the hulking metal tables and surgical arms; they cast malevolent shadows in the light of my wrist lamp. A pool of silver blood glinted on the floor.

A dragon screamed in the surgery next door. Mitha scampered ahead, but I was loath to approach. I crept up to the enormous doorway and peeked into a room eerily illuminated from all angles by quigutl wrist lanterns. In the center was a full-sized dragon, its eyes wild. It snatched up a quig in its jaws and shook it like a terrier, snapping the smaller lizard's neck. Two dead quigutl lay sprawled across a large metal table nearby, silver blood dripping off their dangling legs and congealing on the stone floor.

Around the dragon, on the walls and ceiling, under the cabinets and the sinister-looking surgical machinery, dozens of quigutl swarmed. The dragon tossed the dead one into the air and snapped at another; it dodged out of reach under the metal table.

"Dr. Fila!" cried Mitha. He'd reached the middle of the room, brandishing a dragon-sized scalpel in each of his four hands. They were like swords to a quig.

The dragon doctor turned, quigutl gore hanging from his teeth.

"Remember when you neutered my brother?" said Mitha,

waving his surgical tools. "Remember when you removed my mother'th voice box?"

The doctor spat fire. Mitha dodged; the flame hit an operating table and sent it flying. I ducked back, terrified.

"Remember the acclaim you received for the machine my uncle built?" called another quigutl from behind the dragon. "Remember how you don't remember we exist until something breakth or you decide to break one of uth?"

From all around the room, the quigs began to croon Mitha's song: *But we are not so helpless now. . . .*

Mitha did a waggling dance around the room, avoiding Dr. Fila's jaws. The dragon doctor kept his wings folded; there wasn't room to spread them without getting entangled in wires and dangling instruments. Mitha capered upon a metal table; the doctor struck, missed, and bit the table. The clang reverberated sympathetically up my spine, setting my teeth on edge. For a moment the doctor seemed disoriented.

The quigs all pounced at once.

They moved so fast I saw nothing but streaks of light, the wrist lamps writing danger in the air. Within seconds they'd bound Dr. Fila with thin, strong flesh-flensing wire, shutting his jaw so he couldn't flame and immobilizing his limbs.

Once they had him tied up, they did not taunt or harm him; they scurried about the room, mopping up blood, righting toppled equipment, and—absurdly, to my mind—making repairs. They removed the bodies of their fallen kin.

I approached cautiously. The constant movement of their

lights made it difficult to navigate the maze of broken metal and glass; the room reeked of quig breath and sulfur. The dragon fixed his shiny black eyes on me. Smoke leaked from his nostrils.

Mitha looked up from scooping broken beakers into his mouth and waved at me. He gestured toward a metal basin full of water. I handed it to him and he spat melted glass into the water, which cooled and hardened into a long, transparent noodle. Mitha ran his tongue over his lips, scouring them with its ignited end, and then said, "Shall we question thith fellow?"

"Will he be in any mood to answer?" I said, sounding more flippant than I felt. I was still shaken. "They've wired his jaw shut."

The dragon's head was on the floor. Mitha clocked him on the nose with the basin, then climbed up and sat among the spikes with a scalpel aimed at the doctor's eye. "We're going to unfasten your jaw," the quigutl explained. "You will answer Seraphina's questionth nicely. If you make any threatening move, I will pull out your eyeball, climb into the hole, and eat your brainth. My mate will lay eggth in your sinuseth."

"Enough, Mitha," I said. Mitha chirped, and one of his fellows began working on the wires around Dr. Fila's jaw, loosening them until the dragon could form understandable words through clenched teeth.

"Seraphina," he said thickly. "I know your name. I have a message for you."

Fear bloomed over my heart like frost. "From whom?"

"Your sister half-human. General Laedi," he snarled. "She has your uncle. We sent him south to her. You are to return to Goredd at once. She is done humoring you."

"Did you excise his memories before you sent him south?" I asked, my voice low and fearful.

Dr. Fila snorted. "Would he be a lure to you if we had? It's you she wants, Seraphina. If she had known the mad lengths you'd go to in order to find him, she never would have had us bring him here. She'd have kept him at her side from the start."

Mitha, for reasons known only to him, hit Dr. Fila again with the basin and knocked him out cold.

ᖪTwenty-Seven᛫

Within the hour the lab had surrendered to Comonot and his exiles.

Eskar explained it to me later: the stronger fighters, storming the gates, had drawn the best of the Censors' guard to the main entrance. The weaker fighters, sneaking into the escape tunnel, had relied on stealth and deviousness, ambushing Censors and scientists one by one. They'd reached the heart of the mountain virtually unopposed, and the Censors had had no choice but to admit defeat.

Well, most decided they had no choice. The Censors were not untainted by the new ideology Comonot and Eskar had observed. Five Censors fought to the death and took three exiles with them, injuring four more. Others seemed to subscribe to the extreme anti-human ideology but couldn't quite make up their minds to die for it. They were herded down into holding cells deep underground, where they would have ample time to reconsider their political affiliation.

I was still with Dr. Fila when two exiles came to collect him; I followed them through twisting, darkened hallways to an enormous atrium at the heart of the mountain. Here, at least, light trickled in through several small windows in the ceiling, so far away they looked like buttonholes. Hundreds of dragons milled around the atrium, patching each other up and inventorying supplies. Dr. Fila, who still seemed woozy from his encounter with Mitha, was sent across the room to line up with scientists, technicians, and a dozen deviants from the holding cells.

"You are called upon to aid your Ardmagar," Saar Lalo was screeching at them. "The world is changing; you may yet change with it."

The quigs restored power to the ceiling lights, to my immeasurable relief. It surely reduced my chances of being trampled in that room full of milling dragons.

I needed to find Comonot. Orma had been sent back to Goredd, so that was where I needed to go; I only hoped the Ardmagar could spare someone to carry me south. As I searched for him, I passed Brisi and the four Porphyrian hatchlings. They'd shrunk into their saarantrai again and were excitedly recounting their first dragon battle to each other. "I bit a scientist right in the rostral protuberance," boasted one.

"Oh, that's nothing," said Brisi. "I torched an auditor's cloacal vent."

I asked after Comonot everywhere, but only Ikat, who was patiently instructing quigs in the application of cobwebby bandaging, had noted where they'd gone. "Eskar took him up the north passage to the Censors' archives."

She indicated a wide ascending corridor, so steep it was like climbing a mountain itself. I was sweating and breathless by the time I reached a cavernous archival chamber, and then was utterly appalled by the sight of the Ardmagar—wearing his humanity and nothing else—dancing around in the middle of the floor. Behind him, in her natural shape, Eskar operated a viewing machine similar to the one Mitha had used, but scaled to dragons. Two other full-sized dragons lurked in a corner of the room: an exceedingly antique specimen, his eyes filmed over by cataracts and with strange wart-like growths on his snout, and a smaller hatchling, his head spines sharp and gleaming. The oldster leaned heavily on the young one, like an aged grandfather being helped about by his grandson.

Ardmagar Comonot caught sight of me and bounded over. I tried not to stare, but he was blubbery around the middle. "Seraphina!" he cried, and for a horrifying moment I thought he was going to hug me. "We did it! The lab is ours, and soon every Censorial secret will be, too."

"You're in your saarantras," I said, aiming my eyes at the distant stony ceiling.

He actually laughed, which drew my gaze, and I saw him ripple all over like a bowl of aspic. "I wanted to feel it," he said. "Triumph, right? I like this one. It's inspiring."

"I need to talk to you," I said.

"Soon," he said, holding up a hand. "Eskar is looking something up. She has made an extraordinary claim, based on a snippet of information stashed in a mind-pearl, and I require correspondingly extraordinary proof."

Across the room Eskar waved a wing in acknowledgment.

"What did she claim?" I asked, suspecting I knew. "Was it that the Censors secretly imprisoned a half-dragon here and experimented on her?"

"How would you have heard about it?" asked Comonot. Eskar arched her spined neck to look back at me.

I darted my gaze toward the two unfamiliar dragons in the corner. I didn't like to talk about this in front of strangers. "The quigutl told me she was Eskar's reason for leaving, although Eskar herself neglected to mention it."

Eskar's third eyelid fluttered in confusion. "I didn't think it relevant."

"She's been planning this subterfuge for years," said Comonot admiringly. "She quit the Censors because of a reasoned, moral objection." I forgot I shouldn't look at him; he winked appallingly. "Oh, you humans may prefer *empathy* and *mercy*, but that's like intuiting the answer to an equation: you still have to go back and work the problem to be certain you were right. We can come to genuinely moral conclusions by our own paths."

Across the chamber, the ancient dragon harrumphed, coughed up an enormous gobbet of phlegm, and spit it into a corner, where it smoldered. He wheezed as he spoke. "You'll find its records under Experiment 723a . . . but I could find it faster . . . if you'd let me use my own machine. . . ."

"And erase anything else?" cried Eskar. "I don't think so."

"Routine maintenance," screeched the old archivist, whining

like a broken bagpipe. "Everything I erase is stored in my mind. I never forget."

Eskar had called up the correct file on the reader and was skimming it rapidly, emitting impatient puffs of smoke from her flared nostrils. "Yes, this is it!" she cried at last. "General Palonn's niece, born of his sister Abind, who died. The creature was locked up for twenty-seven years and used as a research subject."

Comonot stood very still now, with his arms folded. "And for this action, which I agree is questionable, you think we should disband the Censors entirely?"

"She was intelligent, and intelligence has value," said Eskar. "It's the same principle you applied to humanity. A sound principle, Ardmagar, but it needs to be expanded, not contracted."

"A ludicrous principle," screeched an unfamiliar voice, and we all turned to look at the hatchling supporting the old archivist. He bared his teeth. "Other creatures may be intelligent, but only dragons are truly logical. Logic is pure and incorruptible. By engaging with non-dragon intelligences, dragons may be corrupted until they are no longer dragons. Consorting with humans degrades us; we must burn the corruption out of our own."

His words made me shudder. I glanced at Comonot, as if he might have shared my sentiment, but he was staring intently at the youngster, clearly interested. "That's it," he said, nodding firmly. "That's the new logic: I'm not a dragon in your estimation, and it's worth your life to put an end to mine. Now I've heard it stated plainly. But where did it come from?"

"From that *thing*," grunted the elder archivist, dribbling from a corner of his mouth. "Experiment 723a. You considered it intelligent, Eskar? It was too intelligent by half."

I couldn't keep quiet any longer. "Her name is Jannoula. She's been helping them strategize. Remember telling me about General Laedi, Comonot? That's her."

"They're taking advice from a half-dragon when there are perfectly whole dragons they don't consider dragons at all?" said the Ardmagar, raising his bushy brows.

"Laedi is useful—for now," screeched the archivist's young assistant. "Don't imagine we'll let her live once the civil strife is over."

"She has a talent for persuasion," I said to Comonot. "She's in the Southlands now, pursuing the Old Ard's ends. She had Orma sent back to Goredd."

"The Censors tortured her!" cried Eskar, pulling the control cups off her claws. "They made a monster."

"A monster who does our bidding," sneered the younger dragon.

Eskar gave him a withering look down her snout. "You hope."

Eskar may have been baiting him, but she'd raised a crucial point. It wasn't obvious that the Old Ard could rely on Jannoula. She hated dragons; I remembered how contemptuously she had spoken of them, how upset she'd been about Orma and me being friendly. She had talked her way out of prison at last, I suspected; the Old Ard believed they were using her, and she let them believe that.

Eskar had succeeded in provoking the youngster. Wisps of

smoke leaked from his nostrils and he quivered all over, itching to fight her but unable to lunge because he was propping up the aged archivist. "You are a blot on draconic purity, Eskar. We know all about you, how you lived with a deviant in Porphyry and loved him, how you are afflicted with a creeping sympathy for quigs. We will burn out this cancer, to our last breath. It doesn't matter how many of us die: two pure dragons are all we need to renew the race to its former—"

He cut off with a squawk. The elderly archivist, sudden as a snake, had clamped his crusty jaws upon the back of the youngster's neck, just below his head. The hatchling's jaws opened and shut reflexively, and his eyes rolled. The archivist held on until the younger dragon lost consciousness; when he let go, the hatchling's head flopped to the floor, bounced once, and lolled grotesquely.

"I'd have bitten him sooner," creaked the old dragon, "but I have trouble with my eyes. I had only one chance to hit that nerve, and I had to get it right." The archivist limped closer to the unconscious hatchling and leaned against him; he sagged distressingly without support.

The Ardmagar saluted the sky. "All in ard. I take it you don't subscribe to this new philosophy?"

"I am too old for philosophy," squawked the archivist. "And the half-human didn't have to work as hard as all that. All it did was hold a mirror to our biases and say, 'Look how right you already are!'"

"Those disgruntled generals had been plotting against you for decades, Ardmagar. Things might never have gone beyond scheming and spying if the half-human hadn't goaded them into action.

Its uncle, General Palonn, visited once a year, but Experiment 723a didn't require much time. 'Comonot is impure, Uncle. You could set things right. If you had a spy in Goredd, he could put an end to this foolish treaty in one blow.'"

"She knew about Imlann?" I blurted, appalled by the idea that my grandfather's attack on Comonot and the Queen last midwinter had been due to Jannoula's influence.

The ancient dragon bared his broken fangs disdainfully. "Not by name, but the half-human was an uncanny guesser. It inferred that the generals must have a spy. Only I considered its intuitions dangerous; no one else took the creature seriously."

The archivist coughed, a sound like crashing boulders. "And thus have we sullied our own nest. Only I am old and farsighted enough to see how the parts constitute the whole, to read the words etched into this mountainside. We Censors have enforced a species-wide amnesia, thinking to protect and preserve dragonkind, but it makes us vulnerable to flatterers and blind to lateral thinking. I may be the last dragon living who remembers the Great Mistake; those who overruled me by keeping this half-human alive are doing their best to repeat it."

Eskar, who had been listening with interest, lowered her head submissively. "Teacher, what is this Great Mistake you mention? My memories from my time here were excised."

"You wouldn't remember it in any case; you would never have been told about it. I speak now only because it is clear that the Ardmagar intends to disband the Censors." The archivist blinked his rheumy eyes, avoiding the Ardmagar's gaze. "Nearly seven hundred years ago, my grandfather's generation undertook a secret experiment. They captured human women and bred with them on purpose to see what would happen."

My breath caught in my chest. Here was the experiment Orma had long wondered about. What's more, its timing was roughly that of the Age of Saints. More corroboration for Orma's theory about the Saints being half-dragons? "H-how many half-dragons did they breed?" I asked, my voice thin and small in the vast chamber.

"Four hundred twenty-one *half-humans*!" cried the archivist, testily correcting my terminology. Of course he knew the exact number; he was a dragon. I, alas, did not know how many Southlander Saints there were. One for every day of the year, at least.

That had been my sticking point with Uncle Orma's thesis: interbreeding on such a scale had seemed unthinkable. If the Saints had been part of a deliberate draconic experiment, though, suddenly their existence made a lot more sense.

"Only the Ardmagar Tomba and his top generals knew about it," the old archivist continued. "These half-humans had capabilities mere dragons did not. They were to be a race of weapon-creatures to wipe humanity out of the Southlands once and for all.

"Tomba and the others failed to consider that half-humans might take the humans' side," wheezed the archivist, his wings shaking with palsy. "They turned their minds against us, invented the martial art to fight us. War against humans was never the same again."

That martial art was the dracomachia. I was convinced now beyond all doubts: Orma had been right.

The archivist snorted and spat on the floor again. "My

grandfather bred three half-humans himself, and he helped found the Censors after dragonkind's ignominious defeat. There was to be no more interbreeding. We Censors were charged with ensuring that the Great Mistake never happened again."

"By suppressing all memory of it?" I cried.

"And by policing those undraconic inclinations that might lead someone like yourself to come into existence. Clearly we have failed in our mandate," he snarled, his milky eyes squinting, as if that might help him see me. "I smell what you are, you *thing*. You also should have been eradicated. I would kill you right now, if not for Comonot and this fearsome female."

"Do you hold my treaty to blame?" said Comonot, eyeing the older dragon warily.

The archivist flapped his spindly wings once, a species of shrug. "If our task had been to hold the plates of the world in place, we would have known it was doomed from the start. Perhaps our ideal, too, was futile. Some things you only see after the fact."

He began coughing again and couldn't seem to stop.

Eskar rushed to the archivist, knocked him onto his side, and jumped on top of him. "She's trying to clear his airways by forcing his diaphragm to contract," said Comonot at my shoulder. "Don't be frightened. It's very effective."

I drew him away from the violence in the corner. "Ardmagar, I need to go home. I've learned that Jannoula—General Laedi, Experiment 723a—will be traveling to Goredd next. Could you warn the Queen? I haven't been able to contact her because the quigs took my thnik."

"Of course," said Comonot, his gaze still drifting toward Eskar. "I'll tell Queen Glisselda about Jannoula, and that you're on your way."

"Can you spare Eskar to fly me?"

Comonot drew back, giving himself a triple chin, and frowned. "Absolutely not. I need Eskar here. We have two more labs to capture on the way to the Kerama. The hatchlings can take you."

I bowed. It would have to do. At least I'd be going home.

Comonot's eyes had locked on Eskar again. She was still jumping on the archivist, even though he'd already coughed up a ball of yak skin and a small boulder. "Do you suppose," said Comonot, leaning in confidentially, "Eskar would consent to be mated?"

I choked. The Ardmagar slapped me on the back. "I know about your uncle," he said. "That gave me the idea. Eskar exemplifies what I want for our people: the reexamination of assumptions, the flexibility needed to choose unorthodox options."

"She chose Orma," I said throatily, still coughing.

"Nothing stops her from choosing me as well." The old saarantras gave me a sly sidelong look. "Sometimes our reason will lead us to the same morality as your empathy and feeling, and sometimes it won't. I find that . . ." His mouth formed not-quite words, waiting for his mind to catch up. "Exhilarating?" he offered at last.

I wasn't sure about that, but then I was going home, and that was exhilarating enough for me.

I returned to the atrium, where the former exiles had built an enormous fire and, like true Porphyrians, were preparing a celebratory feast. Cooking was not a draconic art, by any stretch; dragons wolfed down their prey, warm and bloody, like all good predators. The exiles still relished grabbing a felldeer by the throat and shaking it until its neck snapped; I'd witnessed this many times on our journey. It wasn't raw that bothered them so much as bland.

One of the things Porphyry had agreed to supply, and which the exiles had carried uncomplainingly, were sacks of pepper, cardamom, and ginger. They used these spices now to exquisitely season their roasted yaks.

Comonot arrived just as everything was ready. We feasted long into the night. I slept by Eskar, who'd been told I was going. "You should have asked me first," she muttered, a sulfuric scolding. "I could have persuaded Comonot to let me go."

She didn't say so, but I suspected she would have stayed in Goredd until she found Orma. I rather doubted Comonot's chances with her.

I was impatient to get going, but another half day passed before the Porphyrian hatchlings were ready to leave. "We had to make preparations," Brisi—in her saarantras—explained, leading me by the hand to a smaller chamber off the main atrium.

I gasped in astonishment. The hatchlings had built a basket of woven wire and wood. "Do you like it?" said Brisi, bouncing on her toes. "You looked so miserable when Eskar carried you. Now you can sit properly. It's an aerial palanquin."

I helped them move it into the atrium, where the hatchlings

unfolded in a clutter of extending wings. Quigs scrambled to unlock and open a mechanical door in the ceiling. It let in an unexpected shaft of brilliant moonlight; I'd lost track of night and day down here. Grasping my basket with her front claws, Brisi flew me to the height of the mountain and out into the open sky. The other four hatchlings flew circles around us.

The palanquin was ingenious, but Brisi was not the strong, smooth flier Eskar was. I experienced every wing beat as a terrifying drop followed by a stomach-lurching heave. I was sick over a glacier. Brisi watched with interest and screeched, "A thousand years from now, that will still be there, frozen in the ice. Unless a quig eats it."

We flew until dawn, hid and rested, and took off again in the late afternoon. Days passed in this pattern. The hatchlings carried me in turns, but none had Eskar's wingspan. My stomach acclimated, but then I would toss and turn when it was time to sleep, unaccustomed to the stillness of the ground.

The hatchlings, to my surprise, seemed to have a clear idea of how to get to Goredd. I asked Brisi about this one morning when we stopped to rest. "Maternal memories," she screeched. "I've always had them, but they didn't fit in my head properly. They make sense for the first time, in context."

We passed encampments, glacial plains filled with dragons of the Old Ard. My entourage took care not to fly too near, and kept a sharp eye out for scouts. It was easier to evade the eyes of other dragons than I would have guessed. Some instinct, or perhaps maternal memory, prompted my entourage to use the landscape to full advantage, skimming valley bottoms and ducking up ravines. Often the clouds hung low, a white ocean between grim island mountaintops, and the hatchlings used this for camouflage. More than once, they landed and held still, disguised as rocks or snow (after stowing my basket and me in the twiggy taiga or under a glacier).

On the sixth night, however, we crossed a ridge and found ourselves above a "vulture valley"—a draconic cesspit. An enormous old male had been resting on the ground, concealed by the ridge; he spotted us overhead and flew to intercept us, screaming, "Land and be identified!"

The hatchlings had strict instructions to comply with all such demands. Per Comonot's orders, they were to land on the nearest snowy peak and explain that I was another dangerous deviant (like Orma, I supposed) to be delivered to General Laedi.

My entourage had other ideas. Brisi plunged into a sudden nosedive straight toward a knife-like ridge; her quick movement triggered the old male's prey drive, and he barreled after her. Icy wind bit my cheeks; I could not catch the air to breathe. The earth spun and tilted sickeningly as Brisi stretched her wings. My sight blurred; my ears rang; my head snapped back painfully.

She circled back up toward her fellows. The bright spots in my vision cleared, and I saw that the others had stretched a net of chains between two of them. They flew at the old saar's face; he was focused on Brisi and couldn't dodge in time. Claws and horns entangled, he thrashed and bucked, pulling the net out of the hatchlings' grip. They screamed in dismay, but the net did its job.

The hostile dragon was too tangled up to fly. He careened out of the sky and hit the sharp, rocky ridge at a horrifying angle. He died instantly, his neck broken.

The hatchlings, alarmed, buzzed around him like bees. They'd only meant to entangle him so they could escape, but there was no undoing what had happened. After a hurried discussion, they carried his body in the net to a more secluded ravine, where flames wouldn't be a beacon to our enemies, and burned him according to Porphyrian funereal custom. Brisi spoke words I didn't know, until I realized it was her native tongue in a dragon's voice, a hard-mouthed Porphyrian. I understood just enough to discern prayers to her gods, Lakhis and Chakhon.

Giving the unknown dragon a funeral had struck the hatchlings as the fitting and proper thing to do. I marveled at this. Comonot had been loath to give the Porphyrians quigutl devices, but he'd utterly failed to foresee the Porphyrian innovations the exiles would bring with them: voting, cuisine, and now funeral rites. The world was changing indeed.

It was nearly dawn, so we found ourselves a different secluded gully to sleep in. As I tried to get comfortable on the rocky ground, I said to the hatchlings, "It was clever to bring a chain net, and to know how to use it. Dragons are famously bad at working together, but you made it look natural."

Brisi examined her talons, a coy gesture a human girl might have made, but completely bizarre in a dragon. "We learned to use nets from the fishermen back home."

Around us the others softly murmured, "Porphyry!" like another prayer.

Three nights later, Brisi pointed out the slender Acata River, which Comonot said was the border of Loyalist-held territory. Within an hour, we were found: the Loyalists, expecting our arrival, had sent a small battalion—a flight of thirteen dragons—to keep an eye out for us. The hatchlings screamed Comonot's watchword, but the Loyalist dragons still nipped at their wings and tails, herding us south to a sloping valley above the tree line, where their ard was stationed.

General Zira was a canny old female, small but with great presence. Something in her gaze must have reminded the hatchlings of their own mothers; they flattened themselves submissively. "I've received word from the Ardmagar!" Zira screamed. "Seraphina is to be transported to Lavondaville; one of my ard is to take her." Around me, the Porphyrian dragons began to protest. Zira shrilled over them: "The hatchlings are to remain here. The Ardmagar hopes I can make decent, disciplined fighters of you."

"We're already fighters!" cried Brisi, clutching my basket to her. "The Ardmagar gave us this duty. Completing it is surely discipline."

Zira, unimpressed by this argument, agreed to a compromise: Brisi would finish the journey with an experienced guide, while her comrades remained with the Loyalists.

We slept that day and left at first dark. Lavondaville was a single, long night's flight away, due south. Brisi muttered incessantly that it was not so hard to find and she didn't need help. Our guide, a spiny male called Fasha, had recently returned to the front from the city garrison at Lavondaville; he led in stoic silence. We passed Dewcomb's Outpost, the northernmost Goreddi settlement, and soared over the rolling hills of the Queenswood. Then, just as the sun poked its bright nose over the eastern ranges, I saw my city. The walls held new constructions—trebuchets, ballistae, and other machines of Lars's devising—but I knew the silhouettes of the rooftops, knew the castle and cathedral tower. This was my home, however far afield I roamed. I choked up to see it again.

"Can I set you in that clearing?" Brisi screamed, circling a relatively treeless spot at the southern edge of the Queenswood. She was proposing to dump me in the swamp. I'd be soaked and muddy by the time I waded home.

I cried, "Not here! Castle Orison."

Saar Fasha heard our conversation and shrieked, "No dragons may land on the castle." It seemed a very sensible rule, honestly, and I wondered what had happened to make it necessary. Fasha led us west around the city, across the Mews River, and south toward an armed encampment on the plain.

At first I wasn't sure whose army it was, but then I saw the Goreddi green and violet flying from one of the larger tents. These were our knights, it looked like, the ones who'd escaped Fort Oversea with Sir Maurizio.

The night watchmen, who'd been playing cards and watching the sunrise, cried out at our approach and scrambled into a more defensive stance, polearms at the ready. A skinny fellow—Sir Maurizio himself—emerged from one of the largest tents in just his breeches, blinking and scratching his shaggy head. As we drew closer, he spotted me, waved enthusiastically, and tugged a shirt on over his head.

We set down in a nearby beet field. Brisi miscalculated the softness of the ground and had to flap her wings like a humming-bird to avoid crushing my litter into the dirt. Sir Maurizio struggled against the hot headwind but was soon at my side, reaching out to untangle me from the basket.

He helped me get clear of the flapping wings, then turned and saluted the two dragons, shouting, "Thank you, Saar Fasha and Saar Other-Dragon-I-Don't-Know!"

"Colibris!" screamed Brisi, arching her neck proudly. "A Porphyrian dragon. Witness how I am not as useless as you supposed!"

That last comment was directed at Saar Fasha, I assumed. He took off again at once, without a word; Brisi had to scramble to catch up. Once in the air, she flew impertinent circles around his head like a crow harassing an eagle, and I couldn't help smiling. That hatchling was going to find her own way.

Around camp, dracomachists had emerged from their tents in defensive stances, as if they slept with their polearms at hand; they now relaxed and stretched and went looking for breakfast. Sir Maurizio led me to one of the command tents—distinguishable by its stripes and by the fact that an adult could stand upright inside—just as a young man came barreling out, still buttoning his scarlet doublet, and nearly crashed into us.

It was Prince Lucian Kiggs. "Seraphina!" he cried, clasping my hands impulsively and letting them go almost as fast. He'd kept the beard, to my absurd delight.

"She fell from the sky like a comet," said Maurizio, grinning roguishly. "Is Sir Cuthberte decent? In body, I mean. His mind is always in doubt."

"These walls are quite thin, you know," called a grumpy voice, only slightly muffled by the canvas. "And of course I am. I was up before all you laggards."

"Good morning, Prince Lucian," I said, my voice husky with exhaustion and disuse. "I need to speak with the Queen at once, and then I should like to sleep. I've been nocturnal for the past week; I'm up past my bedtime."

The smiles around me had all evaporated; Kiggs and Maurizio exchanged a glance I couldn't interpret. I was suddenly struck by the strangeness of Kiggs camping out with the knights. "What is it?" I said quietly. "What's happened?"

Kiggs's mouth puckered as if he tasted bitter bile. "I can't take you to the Queen. She's forbidden me to set foot in the city."

"What?" I said. "I don't understand."

Kiggs shook his head, too angry to speak. Maurizio stepped in. "We arrived two weeks ago; Jannoula arrived three days before we did."

I inhaled sharply, my heart sinking like a stone. "Saints' dogs!"

"The guards at the gates had orders to seize her on sight, but she persuaded them not to, or so I'm told," said Sir Maurizio. "Lars of Apsig, who was overseeing construction on the city walls, supposedly smuggled Jannoula into the palace."

"She's wormed her way into my home," said Kiggs, worry written plainly in his eyes, "and has clearly influenced Selda—"

"We don't know that yet," said Maurizio.

"The worst of it," said a portly old man with a drooping white mustache, opening the tent flap behind Kiggs, "is that Jannoula's proclaimed herself a Saint, and instead of sensibly throwing her out on her ear, the city can't seem to get enough of her."

I met Sir Cuthberte's sad gaze; he held the tent flap wider. "Come in, all of you. Seraphina hasn't told her news yet. I suspect we'll want to be sitting down."

Twenty-Eight

Sir Cuthberte Pettybone hobbled into the dim command tent and sat gingerly on a three-legged folding stool. Sir Maurizio motioned us toward places on the floor beside a large map covered in little figurines. The morning sun shone through tiny holes in the canvas ceiling.

"You'll forgive an old man taking the only chair, Prince, Seraphina," said Sir Cuthberte, rubbing his knees as if they ached. Besides his long white mustache, what hair he still possessed stuck out behind each ear like a pale, tufty bird's nest. "It's hardly courteous, but I am not as spry as I once was."

"Liar," said Sir Maurizio. "We know you're saving it up for the dragons, going to kill them with courtesy." Sir Cuthberte cough-laughed.

My eyes adjusted, and I noticed that the markers on the map

weren't figurines as such, but stones, clumps of sod, and a handful of broad beans. The map was a charcoal sketch on a blanket.

"The Old Ard are rocks. Our side—Goreddi and Loyalist, and the Ninysh, if they ever get here—are clods, which I thought apropos," explained Maurizio, noticing where I gazed. "The beans are the Samsamese. Our scouts report that they're coming from the south-southwest, and that they're delicious in stew."

Sir Cuthberte struggled with a smile under his mustache. "Forgive our squire, Seraphina. You recall what a dedicated nuisance he is."

"That's *Sir* Dedicated Nuisance now," said Maurizio, sniffing in mock offense.

"The Samsamese look close," I said. "How long until they get here?"

"They could be here in a week," said Maurizio.

"And how long until the Loyalists feint south?" I asked. The map, for all that it was cartoonish and covered in clods, made this looming campaign feel suddenly real.

"General Zira's current estimate, based on Comonot's progress reports, is three weeks," said Sir Maurizio. "He's just taken Lab Six, if that means anything to anyone, and he wants to connect with more Loyalist enclaves before he enters the capital."

I gaped at Maurizio. "So we could be fighting the Samsamese before the Old Ard even get here?"

"Could be," he said. "We're not entirely sure what the Regent thinks he's doing."

"When the Samsamese took Fort Oversea," said Sir Cuthberte

grimly, "I said to myself that Josef must be itching to fight dragons. I didn't see how he was going to persuade the Ninysh and Goreddi dracomachists to cooperate with him." From inside his tabard he untucked a silver chain holding a pendant in the shape of a dragon's head. "You remember Sir Karal, my comrade-in-arms?"

"Of course," I said. Karal had been imprisoned with Cuthberte when I'd interviewed them about a rogue dragon. He'd been much surlier than Cuthberte.

"You recall what a skeptical old nut he was. He never would have agreed to Samsamese treachery." Cuthberte waved the dragon-head thnik. "I can speak to him with this. For a few days after our escape, he was plotting and scheming, looking for a way to free the lot of them from Samsamese tyranny. Then something happened."

I had a terrible feeling I knew what it was.

"The knights and dracomachists were visited by 'a living Saint,'" said Cuthberte bitterly. "Sir Karal told me—joyfully!—that he'd seen the light of Heaven in her, that it was lucky he hadn't escaped with the rest of us, or he'd have missed his higher purpose."

"And what is that higher purpose?" I asked, dreading the answer.

"To kill dragons," said Sir Cuthberte, glaring under his brows like a formidable owl. "All dragons, even Goredd's allies."

I tried to make sense of this. If Jannoula was General Laedi, working for the Old Ard, why would she raise an army of Samsamese to fight against the dragons? Did she think they'd kill more Loyalists than Old Ard dragons, or that they'd fight Goredd, too, and weaken us? It reminded me of the Old Ard victories she'd plotted, where so many dragons had died on both sides that *victory* was hardly the word for it. Did she consider those losses worth it?

The Old Ard seemed to, with their new logic. I felt like I had all the pieces in front of me and couldn't put them together.

"Anders saw the light of Heaven, too," Kiggs was saying. "Phina should hear his story."

Maurizio unfolded his lanky frame and left the tent. He soon returned, leading a callow young dracomachist with a shock of straw-like hair. The fellow had been apprehended in the middle of breakfast; his upper lip was foamy with goat's milk. He wiped it on his sleeve.

"Squire Anders," said Sir Cuthberte sternly, drawing his frosty brows down. "This is Seraphina. She wishes to hear about your meeting with the Queen."

"I delivered your missive, as per your command," said young Anders, standing stiffly at attention. "An' I made sure the Queen read it and all. She threw it in the fire and said under no circumstances is Prince Lucian to set foot in the city, and that he could obey his Queen for once in his life, the villain." The squire paled and nodded courtesy at the prince. "Begging your pardon, Your Highness."

Kiggs gave a desultory nod and gestured for him to continue.

"What happened as you were leaving?" Sir Cuthberte prompted.

Anders's expression softened and his gaze grew distant. "Ah, that's when I saw the living Saint, sir, coming in as I were leaving. She knew my name an' touched my chin an' said, 'Count yourself among the blessed, and take my word to your squadmates.' And then she . . . she . . ."

"Tell the rest," said Sir Cuthberte.

Anders kicked at the ground with his toe. "No one believes me. If you've brought me in so this maidy can laugh at me, I don't—"

"No, no," said Sir Maurizio gently, clapping the squire's shoulder. "She's well brought up; she'll wait until you've gone."

"Well," said Anders, peeking shyly at me, "then I saw the light of Heaven. I swear by St. Prue, it were all around her, glowing like a Speculus lantern, or the moon, or . . . or like the heart of the whole world."

I didn't laugh. I felt a terrible sadness, and I wasn't sure why. Maybe because Jannoula was preying on the gullible; maybe because even the gullible could see this light that I could not.

"Thank you, Anders, that's all," Sir Maurizio said, letting the lad out. The tent flap swung behind him, and Maurizio sat back down.

Kiggs met my eyes, a quiet outrage in his. "How are people taken in by this?" He didn't say it out loud, but I suspected there was another question behind the first: *Do you think Glisselda has been fooled as well?*

"I warned the Queen about it," I said, trying to reassure him. "It's the ityasaari mind-fire, the stuff they weave St. Abaster's Trap with." I waved a hand around my head, as if I had this unseen corona. "Jannoula can make hers visible to humans. That's how she could influence Josef even though he hates and fears half-dragons."

Kiggs slapped his thigh. "I knew there had to be a trick to it! She's no more Saint than you are."

His words hit me hard; he was right in more senses than he knew, but I couldn't tell him about Orma's theory, St. Yirtrudis's testament, or the Great Mistake. Not now, in front of everyone. I didn't know how the knights would take it.

I wasn't sure how Kiggs would take it, either. He'd be interested, I had no doubt, but he was more religious than I was. Would it also be upsetting?

Kiggs, who was studying my expression, said gently, "There was something you needed to tell Selda. What was it?"

I took a deep breath and dove in. "I learned some things about Jannoula at Lab Four. Her uncle, General Palonn—is that a name you're familiar with?"

Sir Cuthberte nodded solemnly. "He's the Old Ard's most aggressive general. Likely to be the next Ardmagar, if and when they finish the current one off."

I grimaced. "Palonn gave Jannoula to the Censors as an infant, and they experimented on her." There was a sharp intake of breath around the tent. I continued: "The Old Ard learned she was a talented strategist. They nicknamed her General Laedi."

"The butcher of Homand-Eynn?" said Sir Cuthberte incredulously.

"And she's in the palace with Selda!" cried Kiggs, who seemed ready to leap up and storm the gates of Lavondaville himself.

Sir Maurizio was shaking his head, coming up with an argument of his own. "I can't make it make sense," he said, scratching his shaggy head. "If Jannoula is working for the enemy, and she's the strategist you claim, why would she goad the Samsamese into biting her masters in the arse?"

"I don't know," I said. "The Old Ard believe she's acting in their interests, but they also plan to kill her when she stops being useful. She's astute enough to realize this, I should think. Might she be taking countermeasures to save herself?" It still didn't add up. "We need to learn her true purpose, and how much influence she has over Queen Glisselda."

"If the Queen won't let her own fiancé into the city, I'd guess Jannoula has far more influence than she should," said Sir Cuthberte grimly. "We can't have Jannoula running Goredd's war, whatever the devil she's up to."

We were all agreed, but our best course of action was unclear. The knights halfheartedly suggested marching into the city and seizing Jannoula, but it seemed foolish to provoke a fight with the city garrison on the eve of an actual war. All our troops needed to conserve their resources for the fight ahead, not go around injuring each other.

"No military action," I said. I looked to Kiggs as I spoke, hoping he at least would understand. "I feel partly responsible for Jannoula. If there's any way to save her, I have to try that first."

Kiggs's gaze was gentle and humane. I could not hold it; I looked at my hands.

"You've got guilt," he said, his voice like an audible pat on the head, a palpable comfort. "Guilt and I are old friends. It's the gadfly that stings all night, the never-ending banquet. It's what you feel when you rush back home to your fiancée, intending to tell her all that's in your heart, but she won't even see you."

I was slightly shocked that he would speak so plainly in front of the knights, but they seemed to have gleaned nothing from his speech. He leaned forward, elbows on his knees, and said, "What would you have us do, Phina?"

I frowned, staring at the rustic battle map. The Ninysh, Goreddi, and Loyalist clods were scattered about, indistinguishable from one another.

"Sneak me into the palace," I said slowly. "She has wanted nothing more than for me to join her Heaven on earth. I'll join her; I'll be her friend, as close as I can, until I understand what she's about and how to stop her. I'll disentangle Glisselda from her influence." Around the map the three men nodded. We put our heads together and planned.

I'd been nocturnal so long that by noon I was no longer functioning well. They let me nap in a command tent; the field cot felt like the comfiest bed I'd ever known.

I awoke midafternoon to the sound of dracomachists training in a nearby pasture, but didn't get up right away. Before I entered Lavondaville, I needed as much information as I could gather about the Ninysh ityasaari, Lars, and Jannoula. Had she finally gotten her hooks into Blanche and Nedouard? What was she doing with them?

I steadied my breathing, spoke the ritual words, and entered my . . . well, I still thought of it as a garden, no matter how it had withered and shrunk. The place hadn't changed since the day I'd called each avatar by name. The sky still sagged, propped up by Jannoula's cottage and the trees of Pandowdy's swamp. The denizens lay in a line on the lawn, inert as dolls. Tending the garden took no time now; I walked in and counted.

I located doll-Nedouard. If Jannoula had gotten her hook in him, she could easily find out that I'd looked in on him. I would have to be careful not to reveal anything sensitive. I didn't think she could tell where I was, but she'd guess I was near. The visit itself would raise her suspicions. I didn't see what choice I had, however; I couldn't go in guessing.

I took doll-Nedouard's tiny hands in mine and braced myself for the terrifying vortex of consciousness, but the vision didn't suck me under quite like it usually did. It felt distant and false, like I was peering through a spyglass.

My vision-eye hovered at ceiling level, looking down; that was normal, at least. I saw a narrow, whitewashed room with simple wooden furniture. The beaked plague doctor, below me, fetched a kettle from the hearth, its handle wrapped in a handkerchief against the heat. He poured steaming water into a pewter basin on the table, and then unbuttoned his shirt. His caved-in chest and bony shoulders were paved with silver dragon scales. He wrung out a cloth, wincing as it scalded his fingers, and began to clean his scales.

I watched him some moments, pondering the paradox of reaching inward to look outward. I spoke to Nedouard in my head: *Good afternoon, friend.*

"I thought I felt you watching," he said, wringing out his

washcloth gingerly. "I must admit, I prefer your approach to hers. It's less intrusive."

I didn't have to ask whom I was being contrasted with. *Jannoula got to you at last. I'm so sorry. How did it happen?*

The old doctor dabbed at his shoulder; steam rose off his speckled back. "Blanche was hit first. She tried to fight, which caused her terrible pain. She raided my store of poppy tears, wanting to die, but missed the dose and became very ill.

"So I said, 'Blanche, I can give you a more effective poison, if that's what you want, or you can stop fighting Jannoula for now, and I'll help you find another way out.'"

I shuddered at his matter-of-factness, but Nedouard merely opened the unguent pot beside the pewter basin, took up a horse-hair paintbrush, and began slathering salve onto his scales.

Surely I would know if Blanche had died. Surely the bit of mind-fire I had taken into my garden would dissipate.

Nedouard continued, "Blanche took my advice, for what it was worth, and when the Saint—as Jannoula calls herself—came knocking on my door, I welcomed her in."

Why would you do that? I asked, horrified.

He was silent for a moment as he oiled his scales. "I'd hoped," he said at last, buttoning his shirt, "that I might find a way to free Blanche from the inside, but I don't have the requisite mental abilities. The best I can say for myself is that I'm so boring and cooperative that Jannoula pays little attention to me. There are plenty of others drawing her energies elsewhere."

He pulled a leather satchel from under the table. "I can't free anyone with my mind, but I still have some hope of influencing her. Maybe she can be reasoned with, talked into releasing everyone. To that end, I've been studying her mental state. I've never met anyone like her. She's missing some basic qualities—empathy, caring—but she mirrors them to manipulate people. I'd hoped to find a way toward rehabilitating her, but she's so broken. . . ." He shrugged bleakly.

You don't think she can be? I asked. I did not even want to entertain that idea; if she couldn't be saved, then my guilt was preserved for the ages, like an ant in amber.

"That's not exactly it," he said. "It's that the more hurt she causes, the less I want to save her. Some days I argue with myself about the true meaning of my physician's oath. Is a net good near enough to no harm?"

He had been rummaging in his bag as he spoke. He pulled out a vial and swirled its oily contents meaningfully. "Can I bring myself to poison her? So far the answer is no, but it's my conscience in the balance against Blanche's ceaseless pain, Dame Okra's truncated personality, and the comatose old priest.

"When Jannoula made Gianni throw Camba down the stairs, I was close to killing her," he whispered. "So close. I wish I weren't such a coward."

I could barely find my voice. *Did you say Camba?*

He apprehended my tone at once. "Oh, Seraphina," he said, his shoulders slumping sorrowfully. "You wouldn't have heard. The Porphyrians are all here. Everyone but Abdo."

ᴄᴛwenty-Nineᴏ

This news upset me so much that I dropped his tiny avatar like a hot ember and the vision winked out. I was on my knees in the mud of my minuscule garden, gasping for breath.

The Porphyrians hadn't intended to come. They would have resisted. I felt sick, thinking how Jannoula must have accomplished this.

But why wouldn't Abdo be here, and did "comatose old priest" refer to Paulos Pende? The dream came back to me, wherein I thought I'd seen Abdo dive from a wagon and Pende fall down dead. Had it been more vision than dream? I wasn't sure whether to seek out the answer with eagerness or dread.

I would surely attract Jannoula's notice, but I had to look in on everyone. I had to see for myself where everyone was and what Jannoula had done to them. I started with the white-haired Porphyrian singer, stubby-limbed Brasidas, taking up his avatar and letting my eye look out upon the world. He was in a place I recognized from my student days, the Odeon of St. Ida's Conservatory, giving a public performance. The seats were packed with astonished townspeople; his eerie voice filled the domed hall.

I lingered a moment, entranced by the beauty of his singing, then recalled that he was not the only one I needed to check on. I forced myself onward and found Phloxia the lawyer in St. Loola's Square, standing on the base of the statue and speaking in a thunderous voice. Her crowd was even bigger than Brasidas's. The sinking sun tinted her face an orangey bronze.

"You are right to wonder, Lavondaville!" she cried, her enormous mouth wobbling. "If the Saints were half-dragons, why did they write such fiery polemics against dragons and half-dragons alike? Why didn't they tell us what they were?"

Around her the crowd murmured, echoing her questions, their faces intent.

"The Saints did not record their origins because they were afraid," Phloxia announced. "They were strangers in this land. Goredd appreciated their help, but memory is short and suspicion runs deep. Who among you has not felt bias in your hearts toward those who were different? The Saints bore the burden of human prejudice every day.

"They forbade interbreeding because they did not want another generation of ityasaari to suffer as they had suffered. They were trying to take mercy on the future, but we see now that this was an overreaction. Half-dragons are not the monsters you were led to believe, but Heaven's own children."

Phloxia's speech was as enthralling as Brasidas's music. She must have been formidable in the Porphyrian courts of law. But where had she learned Southlander theology, and what was she doing? Preaching? Was this how Jannoula made converts?

As I began to withdraw from the vision, something across the square caught my eye: a three-story mural, unfinished but recognizable, of St. Jannoula herself. The eyes, in particular, were huge, green, and so kindly the heart within me melted a little. The painter was nowhere to be seen, but I had no doubt whatsoever who she was.

Then I was off again, after Mina the winged warrior. She was drilling with the city garrison, instructing them in the use of two swords. She whirled, a silvery cyclone of death, a mesmerizing dance of pain, another half-dragon showing what marvels our kind were capable of. Jannoula had a finger in every pie she could think of, it seemed.

I looked upon Lars and found him on the city wall, supervising the fine-tuning of a trebuchet. Blanche was with him, a cord tied from her waist to his like an umbilical cord. Was it to keep her from harming herself? My heart ached for her.

I checked in on Gaios next and found him walking down Castle Hill toward St. Gobnait's cathedral with his sister, Gelina, Gianni Patto, and Jannoula. All four wore funereal white, and only then did I realize that the others had been wearing white as well. Was this Jannoula's chosen color? She hadn't been raised Goreddi; it would hold no morose associations for her.

Citizens waving flags and flowers had gathered along both sides of the street as if this were a daily parade route. Gaios and Gelina smiled gloriously, waving at the gawking crowds, walking with the confidence of strength, the beauty of youth and athleticism. Hulking, claw-footed Gianni, whose pale hair had begun to grow back like a corona, slumped along at the back, keeping the crowds from coming too close. He looked thoroughly spooked by the cheering citizenry, and I felt a pang of pity.

Between the twins, basking in their glow, walked Jannoula. She spread her arms as if to embrace the entire city. She mimed pulling the people's love toward herself, crushing it to her breast, washing it over her head. She looked like she was swimming slowly through the air.

I had kept quiet, careful not to draw Gaios's attention, but he must have felt me holding his hand in my mind. He swatted at the air as if he were bothered by bees. Jannoula looked at him and narrowed her green eyes.

I let him go. I'd seen enough.

I took the hands of Camba's little avatar and braced myself for whatever might come.

From the ceiling of a palace corridor, I saw Ingar. His square spectacles gleamed; his round face beamed with the same vague cheer as when I'd first met him, under the influence of a Saint. He shuffled slowly up the airy corridor, pushing a wheeled chair.

I did not immediately recognize the tall Porphyrian in the chair, but it was Camba. Her hair had been shaved off—a punishment inflicted by Jannoula, I assumed. She was dressed in a plain white surplice that fit her poorly, and both her ankles were bandaged.

Gianni had thrown her down the stairs, Nedouard had said.

Camba raised one hand, and Ingar stopped the chair, still smiling vapidly. She looked around and behind, craning her long neck, but they were alone in the hallway.

Camba half whispered, "Guaiong."

Instantly Ingar's countenance changed, congealing and sharpening into the expression he'd worn in Porphyry. He glanced around, leaned forward, placed his hands on Camba's shoulders, and said quietly: "What is it, friend? Are you in pain? Is she hurting you again?"

Camba's head was as bald as Ingar's now; her brown ears, stripped of ornaments, were perforated with a line of tiny holes. She reached up and grasped Ingar's pale hands tightly. "Seraphina is looking upon me in her mind. You remember what Pende said: she has a bit of our light. I want her to see that we're still fighting, that we haven't given up."

Ingar smiled wryly at Camba, his eyes full of sadness, kindness, and something more. "I'm not sure my pathetic attempt at a mind-pearl counts as fighting," he said. "I don't know how many times it will work. If you can hear me, Seraphina, come back soon."

I spoke to Camba at last: *I hear you. I'm coming.*

Camba closed her dusky eyes; Ingar pressed his cheek against her head, his face slowly slipping into forgetfulness again.

I left them, already strategizing. His attempted mind-pearl seemed to restore him to himself for a short time. Camba clearly thought it might be helpful; there must be something we could do with it.

I'd left Abdo for last because I was scared to look for him. Maybe he was simply back in Porphyry; maybe he'd succeeded in making his mind water, as per his meditation book, and Jannoula could not compel him to move.

Or maybe he was dead. But surely not. Surely I would know.

His avatar, to my great surprise, wasn't with the other grotesques. I looked under the sundial and the loaf-like shrubberies (lifting them out of the ground entirely, and setting them gingerly down), turned over the big leaves at the edge of Pandowdy's swamp, and found him at last lying half submerged in a mud puddle, stiff as a stick and small as my pinkie. I took his tiny hands between my finger and thumb.

Then I was in the world, my vision-eye hovering in the evening sky above a wood. I knew this place: the edge of the Queenswood. The city shimmered to the southwest, torches illuminating the construction on the walls. Below me a road wound north toward Dewcomb's Outpost, the mountains, General Zira's encampment. I hovered at the point where forest met fens. Even in the twilight, the changing trees glowed gold. Leaves spun and danced on the breeze like pale nocturnal butterflies.

I saw no Abdo. I drifted lower, scanning the border between wood and wetland. The road bisected it at a right angle, and here at this almost-crossroads stood a little tumbledown shrine.

I approached the lonely shrine with my vision-eye. Inside, in the near dark, a small stone statue, roughly human-shaped, stood on a plinth. It had no features to speak of, no face, no hands. It wore a red apron edged in gold, the fabric faded and fraying.

Beneath the statue hung a plaque with an inscription:

When he lived, he killed and lied,
This Saint who lies submerged.
The ages passed, the monster died;
I ripen, I emerge.

I could not read the name of the Saint; it was obscured by moss.

In the darkest corner of the shrine, so still he might have been a second statue, Abdo sat cross-legged, his hands upon his knees and his eyes closed. Someone—woodcutters? travelers?—had taken him for a meditating pilgrim and left him bread and a dish of fruit and a cup of water. I nearly wept with relief; I wished I had arms to embrace him with.

Of course, that would have disturbed him. Even my gazing at him might break his concentration. But what was he doing? Disconnecting himself? Could Jannoula move him when he was like this? He'd been moved here from Porphyry, somehow, but he wasn't in the city with the others.

I recalled the vision-dream again. Maybe Abdo had found a way to show me he'd escaped. But could he move without drawing her attention? Could he stop concentrating long enough to eat that bread and fruit? Did he ever sleep?

I wished I could have checked on Pende, but I had unfastened his mind-fire from my garden.

I will find the way to help you, friend, I whispered, terrified of distracting him, but needing to let him know that I saw him.

I may have imagined it, but the corner of his mouth quirked slightly into the shadow of a smile.

If the sun was setting over the marshland north of the city, it was setting on our camp. It was high time I got out of bed. Kiggs and I would be heading out once the moon set. I stretched stiff limbs, emerged from the tent, and went in search of the prince. I could hear dracomachists training in a field, so I turned that way.

And stopped short. A dragon sat in the field, his scales rusty in the sunset. I had spent the last month among full-sized dragons, and still the sight of one so close to my home struck fear into my bones.

This one only feigned hostility, taking on the new dracomachists six at a time. He feinted right and dodged left, evading fighters' bristling polearms, then spit fire—a small jet, nothing like what he could have done. Fighters cartwheeled out of the way, evading the burn. The dragon extended his wings and beat them furiously; it was hard to take off flat-footed, but there was no way for him to get a running start with so many sharp implements aimed at his chest. He couldn't take off vertically, either: one crafty dracomachist had sneaked up and pinned down his tail.

The other dracomachists stood around the field, watching. Sir Joshua Pender, whom I'd first met as Sir Maurizio's fellow squire, paced back and forth, lecturing on what they were seeing, the mistakes being made. Prince Lucian Kiggs and Sir Maurizio leaned against the low stone boundary of the field, talking quietly. I approached them.

"I'm not glad of this war—far from it," Maurizio was saying, "but still I am deeply moved, watching this. I've practiced this art since I was a child, and I took it on faith that the moves had purpose and were worth preserving." He shook his head, awed. "Until Solann volunteered, I'd never seen our dracomachia used against a real dragon. I feel vaguely bad about finding it so beautiful."

I'd reached the wall. Kiggs turned to look at me. "Did you get some rest?"

"Not enough," I said, rubbing my forehead. "Did you know the Porphyrian ityasaari are here?"

His brows shot up. "I never saw them arrive. But does this mean . . . Jannoula succeeded in bringing all the half-dragons together?"

I thought "succeeded" was an uncharitable way of putting it, considering that I was the one who'd failed. I squinted against the sunset's glare. "She dragged them here against their wills, but not quite all of them. She doesn't have Abdo."

Jannoula hadn't brought Pandowdy in, either, now that I thought about it. Maybe she'd found him as repulsive as I had, or maybe she couldn't move him. How was a limbless slug to get to Lavondaville under its own power?

Sir Maurizio was unbuckling a weapon from his waist; he wrapped the straps around the scabbard and handed the whole thing over to me. I drew the unassuming antler hilt, revealing a wickedly sharp dagger.

"What's this for?" I asked.

"Just in case," said Maurizio, keeping his gaze affixed to the dracomachists in the distance. "I'm a military man, raised by knights since I was seven years old. I realize this tends to bias me toward a certain kind of solution, but I want you to have the option."

"The option to kill her?" I asked, trying to hand the dagger back.

Sir Maurizio didn't take it. He pointed up the meadow at a pair of dracomachists near the wall who were hitting each other with their fireproof gauntlets instead of listening to Sir Joshua's lesson. "See those two?" said Sir Maurizio. "The tall one's Bran; his brother's farm was near our cave. The short one, Edgar, is really a lass. There are several female dracomachists here. We let them imagine they've fooled us; we can't afford to turn able-bodied recruits away. Edgar is Sir Cuthberte's grandniece, or some such. I've known her since she was a baby."

I watched them horse around. They were no older than me.

"These are the people who will be dying," said Maurizio quietly. "Make sure you weigh them on the scale of your considerations, won't you? And keep your options open. That's all I ask."

There was nothing to do but nod solemnly and promise I would try.

⨏Thirty

I didn't take the dagger with me. I let it fall behind some baggage in the command tent when no one was looking. It had a distinctive enough handle that there would be no doubt whose it was; I hoped he would forgive me.

Sir Cuthberte gave Kiggs and me a set of matched thniks so we could communicate from different parts of the castle. The sun set early, even so soon after the equinox, but Kiggs insisted upon waiting until the moon's slender sickle followed suit. I watched it and wondered who would be harvesting in this upcoming season of war.

When the darkness had deepened to the prince's satisfaction, we set off for Lavondaville, cutting across flax fields on an ancient peasants' right-of-way. Torches gleamed along the city walls as work crews continued building Lars's war machines into the night.

Lars was under Jannoula's sway, but his work carried on. An

agent of the Old Ard wouldn't have wanted Goredd so well defended, surely?

We intended to sneak into the castle through the northwest sally port, where we'd fought my grandfather, the dragon Imlann, at midwinter. I would check in with Glisselda to gauge how much influence this self-styled Saint had over her, then take my place among Jannoula's ityasaari. Kiggs was coming to aid and support me, but until we knew why Glisselda had refused him entry to the city, he was to stay concealed and spy from the shadows.

As we walked through dark fields, I spoke to him quietly about Jannoula, trying to prepare him: "She awed Anders in only a few minutes; she's had access to Glisselda for weeks. Don't be surprised if your cousin has been persuaded completely."

He shook his head stubbornly. "You don't know Selda like I do. She acts like this wee, delicate girl-child, but she's tough as a weed. She knew not to trust Jannoula. I won't believe it until I see it, and maybe not even then."

"Jannoula has Josef eating out of her hand," I said. "She's persuaded dragons to an extreme ideology. Don't underestimate her."

We'd reached the Mews River bridge; the sound of arguing farmers carried over the water. Kiggs led us upstream to a skiff and poled across without getting us too soaked. The frogs of autumn croaked grumpily and plopped off the bank as we landed.

"What is this 'mind-fire,' exactly, and how was Jannoula able to show Anders hers?" said Kiggs when we were safely out of earshot.

I took a deep breath and told him what little I knew: how all ityasaari seemed to have mind-fire, but only some could see it; how Jannoula could manipulate it, planting her hooks in ityasaari or revealing her light to humans; how I had taken a bit of each ityasaari into myself—Abdo could see the threads leading into me—but nobody seemed able to see my light at all.

"I presume my garden walls block my light somehow, but it's a bit of a paradox," I concluded. "Because where is my light, exactly? Inside the garden?" I made a circle with my hands, miming the walls. "It can't be. Abdo said my garden looks like a cellar. Pende didn't see my light there. My mind-fire, like most of my mind, is on the other side of the garden wall, I think. But if it's outside the wall, why can't anyone see it? Is there a second wall somewhere? A wall I didn't consciously build?"

We'd arrived at the base of the scrubby hill leading up to the sally port. The Queen's Guard kept a stable nearby; a lantern hung in the window, its light like a piercing cry. We crept around so no one would detect our presence, then climbed a ways in silence.

When we reached the shrubbery that concealed the cave entrance, Kiggs finally spoke. "You know, all this talk of walls, and of inside and outside, reminds me of the story of the inside-out house."

"Inside the outhouse?" I asked, not trying to be funny, but sincerely having no idea what he was talking about.

He paused inside the cave, feeling around for the lanterns that would light our way. This was going to be a short trip if he couldn't find them. "The inside-out house," he repeated. "It's a Pau-Henoa tale, a really obscure one, from pagan antiquity."

"My papa wasn't much for stories, unless they were legal precedents," I said. "Anne-Marie is Ninysh and never cared for Goredd's trickster rabbit."

A soft clicking sound was Kiggs lighting the lantern with flint and steel. A yellow glow illuminated his face from below before going out. He adjusted the wick. "Well," he said, rapping out some more sparks, "the story goes like this. Once upon a time, a greedy fellow named Dowl wanted to own everything in the world. The law in those days said that if something was in your house, you owned it."

"So my father would have liked this story," I said.

The lantern flame finally held; Kiggs smiled eerily. "Dowl cleverly decided to build an inside-out house. It was just an ordinary house, but he claimed that the space inside was really outside, and the entire world, including everyone else's houses, was on the inside. He was a bit of a magician, so when he spoke the words, they bent the way he wanted and became true. The entire universe was 'inside' his house and belonged to him.

"Now, as you can imagine, not everyone was pleased with this arrangement, but the law was the law, and what were they to do? The only space 'outside' of Dowl's house was no bigger than a one-room shack."

"I see where this is going," I said as Kiggs lit the second lantern from the first. "One day Pau-Henoa, the rabbit trickster, came along."

"Of course he did," said Kiggs, handing me the lantern. We set off walking again, up the cave-like tunnel toward the locked doors of Castle Orison. "The story is much more complicated and hilarious than I can remember, unfortunately, but the upshot is that Pau-Henoa persuaded Dowl that most of what he had 'inside' his house was junk. The mountains were broken; the oceans smelled; vermin were everywhere. Dowl began to throw things away, pitching them 'outside.' The one-room shack expanded and expanded until everything we see today—the whole universe— was 'outside' Dowl's house."

I laughed, picturing the universe bounded by the walls of a house, and Dowl all by himself on the other side of those walls— the "inside."

"Inside Dowl's house is nothing now," said Kiggs in a half whisper, as if this were a ghost story. "Nothing but a desperate, empty longing."

It was a place that wasn't a place, an inside that surrounded the outside. I said, "What made you think to tell me all this?"

We'd reached the first of three locked doors; he pulled a key out of his sleeve and waggled it at me. "The paradox of your garden. The garden wall is an inside-out house. The space you think of as 'inside' your garden isn't; it's outside. Your wider mind, including your mind-fire, is actually inside the house, perfectly contained."

When I tried to picture it, my thoughts got tied in knots, but one fact stood out to me: the entire point of the wall had been to contain my mind, to prevent it from reaching out to other ityasaari. Of course my mind-fire had to be inside the wall.

Kiggs locked the door behind us, his eyes twinkling in the lantern light. "It just struck me as a way of thinking about it. There is no literal garden, one presumes, and no physical wall." He took my arm. "I cannot quite believe how merry I feel," he said, still explaining. "It is a joy and an infinite relief to take action at last— any action. I have felt stymied and incapable, Seraphina, but now here we are walking toward a mystery, just like old times." He squeezed my arm. "I could tell you a dozen stories."

Around us the darkness hovered tenderly. We passed through it.

Kiggs knew the castle inside and out. It was riddled with hidden passages, but they weren't contiguous. We couldn't get all the way to Glisselda's suite without crossing empty rooms or, worse, public corridors. I followed Kiggs, hushing when he signaled, removing my boots and carrying them. We sneaked through the boudoirs of sleeping courtiers, and one room where they weren't sleeping but were eminently distracted.

We finally reached a narrow passage that ran the length of the royal family's quarters. Kiggs touched a panel door wistfully as he passed, and I wondered whether that led to his own rooms. About twenty yards along, he paused at another door and pressed a finger to his lips. I nodded understanding. He beckoned me closer and whispered, "She will be surprised to see you, of course. Try to wake her gently. There will be a bodyguard in the antechamber and two more guards in the hallway."

Kiggs released the spring latch mechanism, but the door did not swing inward. He handed me his lantern to hold and tried the latch again. He gave up on mechanical finesse and pushed the door with both hands, then with his back and legs. It wouldn't budge.

"There's something in the way of this door," he said, no longer whispering. "A trunk, or a bookcase. Something heavy, as if she's deliberately blocked it." He gave it one last exasperated shove. "So much for speaking with her tonight, before Jannoula knows you're here."

"Could I go in through a window?" I said. His expression told me this was impossible. "How about the front door?" The impossibility in his expression deepened, which perversely amused me. "You've seen me bluff guards before. What's the worst that could happen?"

"They arrest you and throw you in the donjon."

"Which would bring me to Glisselda's attention," I said. "Not the entrance I planned, but I'll work with whatever I get."

He sighed, poor, long-suffering prince, but led me through the door we'd passed earlier and into a well-furnished suite. He didn't confirm that these were his rooms, and there weren't enough books for me to say with certainty—but then, his workspace was up in the East Tower. He wouldn't have done much here but sleep.

At the door to the main corridor, he took the lanterns back and whispered, "The corridor does a dogleg, so they won't see you emerge from this room. Peek around and choose your moment. You've got your thnik?"

I jabbed a finger at him. This one was a ring.

"I noticed you left the dagger behind," he said quietly. "I

considered bringing it, but decided you were making a principled choice. I hope we don't regret that."

I swiftly kissed the edge of his beard. That probably didn't assuage his worry, but it raised my courage. I stepped outside, and he silently closed the door behind me.

I crept up on Glisselda's guards, who sat facing each other on stools, engrossed in a card game. They did not see me until I was directly in front of her door. "Hoy, maidy, how'd you get up here?" said the taller guard, craning his neck to peer down the corridor, as if there might be more of me coming.

"I'm one of the ityasaari," I said, raising my doublet sleeve enough to show a couple of scales. "St. Jannoula sent me with a message for the Queen."

"It couldn't wait till morning?" said the other guard, older but shorter, with a helmet like an overturned basin. He folded and unfolded his hand of cards. "Her Majesty is very particular about her sleep. Hand it over and we'll see she gets it in the morning."

"I'm to tell her in person," I said. "It's important."

The men looked at each other and rolled their eyes. "St. Jannoula herself, by the Queen's order, don't see her in person after hours," said the taller guard, stretching his legs forward so they were blocking the door. "Even if we let you by, which we won't, you'd still have to talk your way past her bodyguard, Alberdt. There's no doing that."

"Why not?" I drew myself up as if I were equal to any Alberdt under the sun.

"Because he's deaf," said the older guard, reordering his cards by suit. "Only responds to finger signs. Dunno about you, but I only know this one."

His gesture asked me, unsubtly, to leave. I gave meager courtesy, turned on my heel, and walked up the hallway with what dignity I could muster. Once past the dogleg, I ducked quickly into Kiggs's suite and bolted the door—and none too soon. I heard them stomp past once, twice, thrice, trying doors, trying to work out where I'd gone.

"I take it that didn't work," whispered Kiggs. "Now what?"

It occurred to me that we might stay in this suite until morning; I suspect it occurred to Kiggs as well. If so, we each rejected the notion on our own, without any discussion. He led me back to the secret passage.

"It will be harder to move around undetected during the day," Kiggs whispered as we left his rooms. "I think we should get down to the council chamber while we can, and wait for the morning council meeting. Would that suit you as an arena for your return?"

It was as good as anything I could think of. Kiggs led the way, sticking to hidden passages as much as possible, watching for guards in the open hallways.

We reached the council chamber without incident; it was shaped like the quire of a cathedral, with rows of tiered seats facing each other across a central aisle. At the head of the room was a dais with a throne for the Queen. Beyond it, green and violet banners draped the wall behind a large wooden crest of our national emblem, the prancing Pau-Henoa. Kiggs counted off curtains and behind the third from the left found a notch in the wall, which proved to be a door. He worked the trick latch, and we slipped through into a narrow room, furnished only with a long wooden bench.

"In the old days, when the council consisted of unruly knights and warlords, our queens kept armed men concealed here, just in case," said Kiggs, setting down his lantern. "Now it's a forgotten space."

We tried the bench, found it uncomfortably narrow, and resituated ourselves on the floor, with our backs to the council chamber wall.

"Sleep if you can," said Kiggs. "You'll need all your wits if you mean to spring out at the council in the morning."

He sat so close that his arm was touching mine; I was wide awake. Cautiously, I tilted my head until it rested on his shoulder, expecting him to shrug me away. He didn't.

He leaned his head against mine.

"You haven't mentioned Orma once since you returned," Kiggs said softly. "I haven't wanted to ask, for fear of upsetting you."

"He wasn't at Lab Four." My voice creaked as I spoke. I inhaled sharply through my nose, trying to hold down my feelings; I didn't want to cry, not now. "I don't know the state of his mind. The Censors sent him here, at Jannoula's request, so I presume she knows where he is. I mean to ask her."

"I'm so sorry," said Kiggs, his voice like sunlight. "How awful not to know."

I closed my eyes. "I try not to think about it much."

There was a long pause; the sound of his breathing soothed

me somewhat. "Do you know what some theologians believe about that story I told you? The inside-out house?" he said at last.

"I thought it was a pagan tale, predating the Saints," I said.

"Yes, but some religious thinkers—the ones I like best—believe the pagan ancients were wise, that they caught glimpses of greater truths. They take Dowl's house, the emptiness surrounding the fullness of the universe, as a metaphor for the Infernum. Hell is nothingness."

I frowned. "According to your earlier analogy, that's my mind, friend."

He chuckled into my hair, enjoying this. I loved him terribly just then, how he puzzled through obscure scholarship and reveled in ideas, never mind that he'd called my mind hell. The idea was the thing; he would entertain all comers.

"So if the Infernum is an empty interior, what's Heaven in their conception?" I asked, nudging him.

"A second inside-out house, inside—or rather, 'outside'—the first," he said. "If you cross its threshold, you realize our world, for all its wonder, has been but a shadow, another kind of emptiness. Heaven is more than this."

I snorted, unable to contain the urge to argue. "Might there not be another inside-out house in Heaven, and on and on in infinite regression?"

He laughed. "I can barely get my head around one," he admitted. "In any case, it's just a metaphor."

I smiled in the darkness. There was nothing "just" about metaphors, I was beginning to think; they followed me everywhere, illuminating and failing and illuminating again.

"I have missed you so much," I said, overcome. "I could spend eternity here at your shoulder, listening to you muse about whatever takes your fancy."

He kissed my forehead, and then he kissed my mouth. I kissed him back with an unanticipated urgency, thirsty for him, dizzy with him, filled with light. One of his hands lost itself in my hair; the other found itself at the hem of my doublet, fingering the linen shirt at my waist.

Alas, I was a dragon at my center, encircled in silver scales. That touch started me thinking, and thinking was the beginning of the end.

I spoke into the space between kisses—"Kiggs"—but then another kiss pulled me under. I wanted nothing but to forget all my promises and drown in him, but I couldn't let myself. "Lucian," I said more determinedly, taking his face in my hands.

"Sweet Heavenly Home," he gasped. He opened his deep brown eyes and leaned his forehead against mine. His breath was warm. "I'm sorry, I know, we can't."

"Not like *this*," I said, my heart still racing. "Not without discussing or deciding."

Kiggs wrapped his arms around me, as if to still my trembling, or anchor me to the earth; I buried my face in his shoulder. I could have wept. I hurt all over like one suffering terrible insomnia, when the body aches with longing for sleep.

Somehow we both did find our portion of sleep there in each other's arms.

๑Thirty-One๑

I awoke, with my cheek against his shoulder and a terrible crick in my neck, to the sound of voices in the council chamber. The drapes filtered light greenly through a lattice in the door; we could see nothing but could hear everything clearly. The councilors, a couple of dozen ministers and nobles, filed into the room beyond and found their seats. A trumpet fanfare goaded everyone into standing for Queen Glisselda's entry.

Kiggs shifted from floor to bench and leaned his elbows on his knees, listening.

Glisselda spoke in a voice subdued and mild: "Blessed, would you kindly open this session with a prayer?"

Blessed? Kiggs and I exchanged a glance.

"I am humbled and honored, Majesty," said a contralto voice. It was Jannoula's. Kiggs raised his eyebrows inquiringly, and I nodded. He twitched restlessly, as if fighting the urge to rush out and put an end to this false-Saint nonsense right now. I touched his arm to still him; he covered my hand with his own.

"Hark, ye lovely Saints above," Jannoula began, in an unwieldy imitation of ecclesiastical language. "Gaze on us beneficently, and bless your Goreddi children and your worthy ityasaari successors. Give unto us the strength and courage it will take to fight the beast, thine unrighteous enemy, and bring us bold allies in our time of need."

It was time. I nodded to Kiggs, who opened the door. I silently slipped through the curtains and stepped onto the dais beside the golden throne. Jannoula stood a few steps in front of the Queen. The ministers and courtiers of the Queen's council had bowed their heads in prayer, as had the dozen ityasaari to the left of the aisle. They did not notice me.

I glanced over at the throne, looked again, stared. I had not recognized Glisselda. The full crown, not her usual diadem, was perched on her head, and in her pale hands she bore the orb and scepter, emblems of queenship that her grandmother had rarely brought out of storage, considering them an unbecoming ostentation. Queen Glisselda wore a stiff golden cape edged with ermine, prickly lace at the neckline, and a silk gown, embroidered gold on gold. Her fair hair seemed frozen in corkscrew curls; her face, already pale, had been whitened with cosmetics, her lips stained pomegranate red.

The lively, intelligent girl I knew was almost invisible under all that pomp. The blue eyes were familiar, but they pierced me with a terrible coldness.

We'd wondered how much influence Jannoula had gained over the Queen; the answer was visible in this change, I had no doubt.

I tore my gaze away from the glittering Queen. Jannoula, dressed in crisp white linen, stood before me with her head bowed. Her brown hair came to a point at the nape of her neck.

"Does Heaven ever grant you the bold allies you pray for, Jannoula?" I said, loud enough for the whole room to hear.

She whirled to face me, mouth agape and green eyes startled. "Y-you're here," she stammered. "I knew you would come."

She hadn't known; I'd caught her flat-footed. I found a small satisfaction in that.

"My Queen!" cried Jannoula, turning to Glisselda. "Look who's come."

Glisselda looked past us as if we weren't there, but Jannoula didn't seem to care. She turned back toward me, her hands tucked into the broad sleeves of her pale gown. "I knew you would return to me of your own accord, Seraphina," she said ingenuously, surely playing to her audience. "Do you regret forsaking your dearest sister?"

It was a ludicrous, deplorable act, and yet even I wasn't immune to it. She'd asked the one question that would hurt me. "I do," I said, swallowing hard. Alas, it was true.

Was it possible for me to test the degree to which Queen and council were being manipulated by Jannoula? I wanted to shock them, and I wanted Kiggs to hear the reaction, too, from his hiding place. I cleared my throat and tugged at the hem of my doublet, buying time as I considered what to try. "I rushed back from

Lab Four because I feared for you, sister," I said slowly. "I heard news that worried me."

Jannoula's lips parted; she looked convincingly innocent. "What was it?"

"The dragons claim you work for them, that you devised the Old Ard's strategies and advised their generals. They nicknamed you General Lady," I said, surreptitiously observing the room. The half-dragons did not react to the news, but many council members were whispering among themselves, looking disturbed. Glisselda remained impassive.

I held my breath, imagining Kiggs holding his, too. Would Queen and council question Jannoula about this alarming information? Were they so besotted with her that they'd excuse her every transgression?

"Blessed Jannoula," said the Queen, her high voice piercing the councilors' growing grumble. "Seraphina implies that you're the Tanamoot's spy."

For the briefest instant, Jannoula met my gaze with steely coldness, but then her green eyes widened. "Your Majesty," she said warmly, "it pains me to say that Seraphina's charge is true, if incomplete and imperfectly understood. Dragons held me prisoner my entire life. My mother, the dragon Abind, returned pregnant to the Tanamoot and died in childbirth. My uncle, General Palonn, donated me to Lab Four as an infant."

I expected her to show her scarred forearms again, the way she had in Samsam, but she was unlacing her bodice, baring the middle of her torso. The council gasped in horror; she turned to face the Queen, who neither flinched nor looked away. A long, purpled scar ran down Jannoula's body, from her breastbone to somewhere below her navel.

"They opened me up," she said, her eyes locked on me, as she refastened her gown. "They filled my blood with poisons, taught me physics and languages, ran me through mazes, determined how long I can last without food or warmth. I died twice; they brought me back to life with lightning.

"When my mother birthed me, I wept. When I was reborn, I raged. My third awakening made me realize I was meant to be in this world. I could not leave until I had discovered my purpose and fulfilled it."

She turned with a graceful whirl of skirts, like a dancer, clasped her hands to her heart, and continued: "One day, one of my kind—our own St. Seraphina—found me and gave me hope. I learned I had a people."

I glanced out at the ityasaari: Dame Okra, Phloxia, Lars, Ingar, Od Fredricka, Brasidas, the twins. They smiled; I couldn't bear to look.

"From that day forth," Jannoula was saying, "all my energies focused on escape. If that meant convincing my uncle to trust me by devising strategies for the Old Ard, then that's what I did. I won them victories, yes, but each came at terrible cost. I saw to that."

I had noted this before. I hoped Kiggs was paying attention.

"My only purpose, my single-minded goal," said Jannoula, her voice high and clear, "was to come to Goredd, the home of my dearest sister. I would have moved Heaven to do it."

There wasn't a dry eye among the councilors, old and young

alike. The Queen dabbed subtly at her own with a lace-edged handkerchief; the ityasaari wept openly. Jannoula stepped toward me, took my hand in her cold fingers, and raised it triumphantly, as if we were dear friends reunited at last; only I could feel how hard she clenched my hand.

"O brethren!" she cried. "Let this be a day of rejoicing."

And with that, still clamping my hand like a crab, she strode up the carpet toward the far end of the chamber, dragging me with her. Behind us the council broke out in heartfelt applause. Jannoula waved without turning around and said nothing more until we were out in the corridor, walking swiftly through the palace.

She flung my hand away. "What was that?" she said through her teeth. "An attempt to discredit me? A little something you thought everyone should know?"

"I really do want to help you," I said. I meant it, though probably not the way she hoped. "I saw your old cell at Lab Four, your fur suit on the peg behind the door. I know what they did to you." The thought of the place made my throat tighten. "The dragons told me you were still theirs, though."

She stopped short. "I am not theirs. I have never been theirs," she snarled. "The unbearable arrogance of dragons! They will learn soon enough."

"Will they, indeed?" I said. "How do you intend to teach them?"

She spread her arms. "Look around you. Find one thing I've sabotaged. The Goreddi war effort is the stronger for my presence, I promise you. Lars and Blanche are perfecting the war engines; Mina is teaching new sword techniques; my artists are inspiring the people. St. Abaster's Trap was full of holes; I've fixed it. Goredd needed me, and I am here."

"And Orma?" I said. "I was promised he'd be here."

Her expression darkened. "You'll see him when I decide you may."

"You underestimate my stubbornness," I said.

Jannoula leaned into my face, lowering her voice to a vicious whisper: "You overestimate my patience. Let me make one thing clear: I could dismantle you before the whole world. I could persuade any of those simpering courtiers to knife you, or each other, or themselves. Bear that in mind."

I raised my hands, conceding, and she nodded grimly. "Come on," she said, not reaching for my hand again. "I'll show you the Garden of the Blessed."

The Ard Tower, where Glisselda and I had waited for Eskar, was now home to the collected ityasaari. It loomed, dramatically tall, at the western end of the palace complex; the belfry at its top, bell-free for many years, had once warned the citizens of Lavondaville that it was time to take to the tunnels under the city.

"You can see the entire Mews Valley from the top," Jannoula said as we traversed one last courtyard, crisscrossed with red euonymus hedges. "It will be the perfect place from which to spring St. Abaster's Trap."

Lars and Abdo had bowled me over with Abaster's Trap when

it was just the two of them creating it. Jannoula had many more ityasaari at her disposal. That was a lot of power available to someone I didn't trust.

Jannoula gazed at the crown of the tower, shading her eyes with one hand. "You realize that we, too, are Saints, as surely as St. Abaster himself."

"I don't believe that," I said.

"Ingar brought me the testament of St. Yirtrudis; I read his translation, but I'd already gleaned that we ityasaari were Saints. It's in my gift to apprehend these things."

"The Saints were half-dragons. It doesn't follow that all half-dragons are Saints."

"Does it not?" she said, a smile playing on her narrow lips. "Do I not reveal the light of Heaven to humankind? Are we not all ablaze with soul-light? All of us but you."

I studied her fine-boned face, trying to gauge how much she believed and how much was cynical pretense. She seemed sincere, which only made me more skeptical.

"Even with your stunted soul," said Jannoula, "it's still right that you're here, Seraphina. This is to be the genesis of a new world, a new age of Saints, an era of peace. We will make ourselves a place of safety, and no one will ever harm us again."

That, or something like it, had been my dream, too. I felt a little queasy.

"You will be my deputy," she said, taking my arm, smiling as if this were the coziest thing in the world. "We all have jobs to do."

"And everyone's happy with this?" I asked, observing her

shrewdly. "St. Pende's been incapacitated, you broke St. Camba's ankles, and St. Blanche wants to die."

"Unavoidable casualties," she snapped. "Everyone's mind works differently. I haven't found the easy way into them yet."

"You lost St. Abdo altogether," I said, goading her. I couldn't stop myself.

"You've heard a lot of interesting things." Her smile was brittle, her eyes hard. "From whom? I wonder. You needn't worry about any of them."

"I do worry," I said quietly.

"Well then, perhaps that can be your job," she said.

Along the western edge of the courtyard, workmen smoothed sand, laying a new flagstone path. "We're calling that the Pilgrim's Way," she said. "It leads into the city, open and unobstructed for any who wish to approach us devotionally."

We met townsfolk coming out of the tower, old crones, little girls, young wives of good households with servants in tow. At the sight of Jannoula, they pressed hands to their hearts and gave full courtesy. Two girls, maybe five years old, bumped each other as they curtsied, fell down, and burst into giggles. Jannoula pulled them to their feet, saying, "Stand, little birds, and Heaven smile on you." Their mother, blushing, thanked Blessed Jannoula and led the giggling sisters away.

Was Jannoula showing them her mind-fire? I wished I could tell when she did it.

Jannoula lingered at the tower door, watching them go. "They come to cook for us and do our laundry. They bring fresh flowers, hang draperies, and sweep our floors."

"How did you merit so much devotion so quickly?" I asked, making no attempt to keep the sarcasm out of my voice.

"I show them Heaven," said Jannoula, without a trace of irony. "People are so desperate for light."

She opened the tower door and mounted the spiral stairs. The walls were freshly whitewashed, the steps painted blue and gold. On the first floor, a short hallway spiked off from the stairwell; we didn't go down it. We paused at the second floor, which comprised a single large room. The vaults of the ceiling were supported by a fat column in the center, like a date tree. Slim arrow loops had been converted to glass windows; a fire roared in the hearth. A lectern at the far end faced rows of stools, arrayed like pews in a chapel. Townswomen dusted the recesses of the vaulted ceiling with rags on long poles, polished the plank floor, and hung garlands of hedge laurel.

Jannoula pulled me back into the stairwell, leading me up two more stories to the fourth floor, where a short hallway ended in four blue doors. She opened one, revealing a wedge-shaped room. "I'll have your things brought up from your old suite," she said, leaning in so close she could have kissed me. "Yours is the most coveted room, of course. Directly next to mine."

By afternoon, eager pilgrims had spirited my possessions—instruments, clothing, books—from my old suite to the Garden of the Blessed. I hovered, supervising, wincing as they banged my spinet on the spiral stairs. The instrument barely fit beside the narrow bed; I stowed my flute and oud under it. Most of my books were left behind, but I was told I could use Ingar's library, imported all the way from Samsam, which took up the entire sixth floor. I jammed my sheet music into the crowded chest alongside the new gowns Jannoula had insisted I have, all crisp white linen.

My door hinges shrieked like the restless ghosts of cats. Floorboards grumbled crankily wherever I stepped. With Jannoula next door, sneaking out would be difficult; speaking with Kiggs on my thnik would require circumspection. The walls were thick stone, but rafters rested in open notches below the ceiling. All speech risked being overheard.

I wanted so badly to contact the prince, to learn what he'd done after the council meeting and what he was doing now. Would he try to see Glisselda? There were other ways he could help me; he could spy in the city at large and come to understand the general attitude toward these upstart Saints. If the city was still preparing wholeheartedly for war, what did the people believe about this era of peace Jannoula had told me she was ushering in?

Or he could find my uncle. I had no intention of waiting on Jannoula's whim.

Jannoula had tasks to attend to, as did most of the ityasaari. I checked every room, starting at the top, and learned that none of the doors locked. I found no one but cooking, cleaning pilgrims, until I reached the bottom floor. In a whitewashed room with a sooty hearth and a shuttered arrow-loop window, Paulos Pende lay upon the narrow bed, Camba in her wheeled chair at his side.

Pende's eyes were open, but he seemed not to see me. The right side of his face sagged as if it had melted. Camba held his gnarled, arthritic hand.

She smiled sadly at the sight of me. "You came. I'm sorry I can't stand to greet you. I am not quite as you remember." She touched her shaved head self-consciously. "I'm in mourning until we are returned to ourselves."

I closed the door behind me, crossed the plank floor, and kissed her cheeks. "I'm relieved to see Pende lives, but so very sorry you were dragged here. What happened?"

Camba's eyes were dark and solemn. "Poor Pende. He could not resist her long; he had the skill, but not the strength. Jannoula made a puppet of him. He lay hands on us, as he used to do to pull out her hooks, but now he was putting the hooks in. If anyone refused the touch, he threatened to harm himself." Camba looked at the old priest with tenderness and sorrow. "In brief moments, when he was himself, he begged me not to acquiesce, to let her kill him. But he is my spiritual father. I couldn't let it happen."

The door opened behind me and I startled, but it was only Ingar, carrying an armload of wood and kindling. He bobbed his head at me and began with hazy cheerfulness to build a fire.

Camba watched him, her eyes distant. "Once she caught us, she sent us to the harbor by night. We stole a fishing boat and were halfway across the gulf before anyone missed us, I imagine."

"She couldn't possess all of you at once," I said, as if I could change what had happened by pointing out that it couldn't have.

"She didn't have to," said Camba. "Some have no defenses once she's in. The twins, Phloxia, Mina. It's like she turns a compass in their heads, and suddenly north is south and west is east, and they are easily led in any direction. Brasidas can partition his mind and keep her away from the vital parts, but he's an old man. What can he do against Mina and her swords? What can I do?"

That was a bleak question. We sat silently, watching Ingar prod the nascent fire.

"When we were nearly here," Camba began again, her voice almost inaudible, "Abdo dove out of the wagon into the Queenswood. I expected Jannoula to force him back, or to send Mina after him, but suddenly Pende was on his feet screaming, fighting her in his head. We felt it; I don't know how. He sent his fire back at her, and it scorched us all." She stroked the old man's gnarled hand.

"It broke him," I said, my voice hushed and awed. He'd given everything he had.

"But Abdo escaped," Camba said, holding up a finger. "I draw strength from that. There are ways to fight back, and she can't anticipate everything. Our differences work to our advantage."

The fire crackled. Ingar stepped back from it, looking lost. Camba called his name softly; he came to her and sat on the floor at her feet, leaning his head on her knee.

"When I looked in on you yesterday, I saw . . . what you wanted me to see." I didn't like to say *mind-pearl* within Ingar's hearing; he might report everything we were saying to Jannoula. "What can you tell me about that?"

Camba's dark, solemn eyes told me she understood. "It was his idea to try it. He pulled everything important into one corner of his mind, sealed it off so she can't get it, and let her have the rest. He knew he couldn't keep her out altogether, that she would pour into her old pathways like molten silver into an empty ants' nest. I'm surprised it works as well as it does, but I don't know how long he can keep it up."

"We will talk more about this later," I said. *In private,* I wanted to add, but didn't. Camba was sharp enough to glean what I meant. "There must be some way we can use ... all the things we've learned."

Nedouard would help us, too, but I didn't dare mention him now. Mine was the only mind secure enough to hold all the pieces; alas, that meant I was going to have to puzzle them together on my own.

Camba opened her mouth to speak, but at that moment we heard footsteps across the ceiling, as if a herd of merry cattle had come prancing in. The ityasaari were back; I could not linger here. I kissed her cheeks again and went up to meet the others.

Devoted townswomen had set up a long supper table in the chapel on the second floor, and the ityasaari were busily seating themselves around it. I stood in the doorway a moment, watching my fellow half-dragons with a lump in my throat.

Ingar came upstairs behind me and said, "Excuse me." I was in his way. I tried to back out of the room, but Dame Okra spotted me and was at my side in an instant, embracing me and crying,

"Home at last, dear girl!" Winged Mina and shark-toothed Phloxia kissed my cheeks; Gaios and Gelina led me to the table. I sat by blind Brasidas, who squeezed my fingers and whispered, "Did you bring your flute?" Od Fredricka brought me a bowl of lentil soup from the townwomen's cauldron by the fire; Nedouard, apparently anxious not to seem too glad to see me, nodded his beaked head minutely. Lars smiled with heartbreaking warmth; pale Blanche, still tied to Lars by a cord around her waist, kept her eyes on the table, picked at a scale on her cheek, and did not smile. Gianni Patto sat upon the woodpile by the hearth, a loaf in each hand, and roared, "Fee-nah!" with his mouth full of chewed-up bread.

"It's good to see you all," I said, and that was the truth, but it was also terrible. I did not know how to contain such a contradiction inside myself.

Phloxia led us in prayer, and then they had a dozen questions for me at once. I fielded them as noncommittally as I could, trying to feel out which of them were not so enamored of Jannoula. No one stood out in that regard—not even Nedouard—but maybe they were being cautious. I would give them time.

For my part, I had just one question: "Where's Jannoula?"

"She never eats dinner with us," said Dame Okra, waving a dismissive hand.

"She sees her spiritual advisor in the evenings," said Lars earnestly. "Even the very great need their confidants. No one can bear everything alone."

"I see," I said, and let the subject drop for now. I would find out who that was. I hardly dared hope it was Orma—the idea of him being anyone's spiritual anything was laughable—and yet . . . I had to be sure.

As I was getting ready for bed, a dog-eared sheaf of bound pages was shoved under my door by an unseen hand. I picked it up and turned it over. Jannoula had written in blocky letters on the front: *St. Yirtrudis's testament, translation by St. Ingar. For Saints only. Read it. Understand who you are.*

"At your command, Blessed," I muttered. I wasn't sleepy anyway. I settled in for a long night's read.

ᴄ∿Thirty-Two∿ᴐ

Once upon a time, the dragons made a Great Mistake. Unintended births of a few half-humans had revealed a peculiar quality when the two species mixed. Ityasaari minds seemed to leak out into the world, to tap into some vein of influence inaccessible to others. These mental powers fascinated dragonkind, and they believed that such abilities, if harnessed, might change the course of their ceaseless war with the Southlands. They deliberately bred more than four hundred half-humans.

That was not their Mistake, although they will ever insist it was.

The Mistake was in showing no kindness to the ityasaari, no empathy or recognition. The ityasaari were tools of conquest, and nothing more.

Until the day my brother Abaster said enough.

I stayed up all night reading. When my lamp ran out of oil, I went down to the chapel, stoked the embers of the great hearth, and read by firelight until my eyes watered and my head ached. I went out to the courtyard at first light and read by the rising sun.

Those ityasaari—the generation of Saints—had turned against their dragon masters in spectacular fashion, fighting their way out of the Tanamoot, coming south and teaching humanity to fight. When dragonkind faced the dracomachia for the first time, they'd seen nothing like it. It devastated their numbers, and they retreated to lick their wounds and repopulate the Tanamoot.

The people of Goredd, Ninys, and Samsam were pagans in those days, worshiping an assortment of local nature gods. To the Southlanders, the half-dragons, even the most deformed, looked like living manifestations of these spirits. This made some ityasaari uncomfortable, but Abaster—always ready to claim the mantle of leader—gathered them together and said, "Brethren, are the humans wrong? We who have touched the World-Mind know we are more than this crumbling flesh. There is a Place beyond places, a Moment outside of time, a Realm of infinite peace. If we don't tell humankind about it, who else can?"

So they let themselves be worshiped, and they wrote down laws and precepts and mystical epic poetry, and they spoke to the people of the light they had seen, how the world was merely shadows cast by that light, and they called the light Heaven. And everything worked out beautifully, until some acquired a taste for power and began to quarrel with the rest.

Ah, that light I couldn't see. It was everywhere, apparently.

I stumbled back to bed for a few hours' sleep and dreamed of the War of the Saints (something I'd never heard of before reading Yirtrudis's testament). My stomach woke me at midday. I reluctantly donned a white gown and went downstairs, but the only person I saw was a gnarled old woman sweeping the chapel. "Where is everyone?" I asked her.

She said, "Go outside and look up. I'll not watch today, as a penance on myself."

Her words gave me pause. "What will I see?"

Her small black eyes, sharp as a mouse's, gleamed as she said, "The light."

I rushed out to the courtyard. The lawn was covered in townspeople and castle guards, all looking toward the top of the Ard Tower expectantly. If I shaded my eyes, I could make out the silhouettes of ityasaari at the top; Gianni Patto's height made him the most visible, but I recognized Mina's wings and the matched outlines of Gaios and Gelina. They appeared to be holding hands in a circle.

Camba couldn't climb the tower on her own with two broken ankles; had they carried her up, or was she shut up in her room?

Around me people began to gasp. Some fell on their knees and bowed their heads; others clasped their hands to their hearts and gazed rapturously. From where I stood, nothing seemed to have changed. I whispered to the young woman beside me, who watched the sky calmly, "What is happening, exactly?"

"You're disrupting my prayer," she snapped, but then she

seemed to take stock of my white gown. "Oh, forgive me—I didn't know you. You're the Counter-Saint, the one who can't see Heaven, aren't you? Blessed preached about you yesterday afternoon."

Heat flared in my chest. While I'd supervised the moving of my things, Jannoula had apparently been spinning myths about me. I'd read the testament; the original "Counter-Saint" was Pandowdy, leader of the insurrection against Abaster, buried alive for his trouble. What could Jannoula possibly mean, calling me that? Nothing good.

"She said you're a necessary piece of Heaven's plan," said the young woman hastily, as if all my mortification were visible in my face. "Everything contains its opposite. That keeps the world in balance."

I swallowed my irritation and said, "So what do you see up there?"

"A golden light." She turned her brown eyes skyward again. "They can concentrate it into a fiery orb, like a second sun, or spread it across the sky like a magnificent dome, enclosing our whole city in glory and keeping the dragons out."

St. Yirtrudis claimed that Abaster had had this power, strong enough to defend a city on his own. Of course, cities were smaller in those days. Now that I knew what the people around me saw, it was less mysterious that Jannoula could have struck belief into so many hearts so quickly. It was hard to deny your own eyes.

It occurred to me that now, while Jannoula and the ityasaari were occupied, I might check in on Kiggs without fear of being overheard. I rushed to my room, leaving the door open a crack so I could hear the others coming back down, and settled on the bed with the thnik Sir Cuthberte had given me. It chirped several times before I heard Kiggs whisper loudly, "Hold on. I'm in a crowd."

I waited, wondering how he could be in a crowd. I'd assumed he was still in the castle, hiding. At last his voice crackled, "All right, I've ducked into the cathedral."

"You're in the city?"

"I felt stymied in the castle," he said. "Out here, I'm checking on the readiness of the garrisons, supplies, wall defenses. Whatever she's up to, Jannoula seems not to have disrupted our war preparations. That's good news."

"How are you checking these things without being seen?" I asked.

"Oh, I'm being seen. I make sure it's only by officers loyal to me. I told them that business about my not being allowed into the city is a strategic ruse so I can check on certain individuals secretly." There was a pause, and I could almost hear him grinning. "You're not the only one who can bluff her way out of trouble, you know."

I bluffed my way into trouble just as often, but I didn't argue. "Are you seeing this, uh, improved St. Abaster's Trap?"

"Isn't it astonishing?" he cried. "Back when it was just Lars and Abdo, with Dame Okra tossing teacups, I never would have guessed how powerful and beautiful it would eventually become. Selda and I had hoped it might be one defense among many, but I think this could keep the city safe, and everyone in it."

"Yes," I said miserably. "Perhaps it could."

"Can they make it without Jannoula?" he asked.

"I don't know," I said.

"Because we need this," said Kiggs. "Unless you find evidence that she's sabotaging the war effort or betraying us to the Old Ard, I hate to say it, but her Saint act can wait to be debunked. There will be time to free the other ityasaari from her grasp after all Goredd is free from war."

"I suppose," I said, my voice weak.

"Goredd must come first," he said. "I have to say, though, this is the most astonishing thing I have ever seen." He spoke as if he'd positioned himself at a door or window of the cathedral in order to keep watching the sky.

"I can't actually see it," I said, irritation creeping into my voice.

"Can dragons see it, or not? I should ask the garrison here. You know what it reminds me of? The words of St. Eustace: 'Heaven is a Golden House—'"

I didn't want to hear it. I said, "As you check on war preparations, would you keep an ear out for news of Uncle Orma? Comonot's garrison or the scholars in Quighole might have seen or smelled him."

"Of course, of course," said Kiggs distractedly, and I felt that he had ceased to listen, all his attention transfixed by the golden sky.

I returned to the chapel. When the ityasaari finished practicing St. Abaster's Trap, they came down from the tower, laughing and chattering. It seemed Camba had not participated, but it took me a few minutes to notice that Lars and Blanche were missing.

On the stairs, Lars began shouting for help.

"Blue St. Prue!" said Dame Okra, pushing past me. Lars staggered through the doorway, Blanche over his shoulder. Dame Okra helped him carry Blanche into the chapel and lay her down before the hearth. Blanche was not unconscious, as I'd supposed, but weeping silently. She wrapped her arms around her head and curled into a ball.

A rope still connected her to Lars.

"Not again!" cried Nedouard. He was at Blanche's side in an instant, taking one of her slender hands and feeling her pulse. Single scales dotted her skin like scabs; bruises purpled her throat.

"Sorry," sobbed Blanche. "S-sorry."

"She waited until you'd gone downstairs," said Lars miserably, his gray eyes rimmed in red. "Wrappedt the rope around her neck and jumpedt. She almost took me with her this time."

"We can't keep forcing her to participate!" Nedouard cried incautiously. "The mind-threading hurts her. It's cruel."

Padding footsteps on the spiral staircase paused. I glanced back and saw Jannoula watching us narrowly. She turned away from Blanche's misery and continued down the stairs without a word. In that moment I hated her.

Nedouard got Blanche untied; I helped him take her to her room. We tucked her, still weeping, into her narrow bed. I turned to go, but the doctor gripped my arm fiercely and whispered, "Don't let the light in the sky fool you. *This* is Jannoula's true handiwork. We submit, or she breaks us."

I clasped his hand, my heart hurting. "We will find the way out of this."

Jannoula had called me her Counter-Saint; it was time to start countering.

I quickly learned the routines of the Sainted ityasaari: they woke at dawn for prayers in the chapel, followed by morning council, St. Abaster's Trap, and lunch. In the afternoon, they went their separate ways for various tasks—preaching, painting, performing, reaching out to the populace—and then they took their evening meal together, spent a quiet hour in the chapel, and went to bed.

Jannoula was absent every evening; I tried to follow her once, but Gianni Patto apparently had orders to keep an eye on me. He planted himself in my way, idly scratching his dagger-like claws in the dirt. I gathered my nerve and attempted to step around him, but he grabbed my arm with one enormous hand and hauled me back inside.

I attempted to find ways to speak with Glisselda. The Queen had seemed to swallow uncritically Jannoula's explanation of her association with the Old Ard, but that didn't mean she couldn't be reasoned with. Surely I could find a way to talk to her, to loosen Jannoula's grip without appearing to do so.

Alas, I could never find an opportunity to speak with Glisselda alone. Jannoula was always present before and after council, and in the afternoons, when Her Blessedness went to preach at the cathedral, she assigned Dame Okra to escort me everywhere. Try as I might, I couldn't give the old ambassadress the slip; she was on me like a tick. I succeeded exactly once in arranging a meeting in the Queen's study. Glisselda looked up eagerly from her desk when I entered, but the moment she saw Dame Okra, her expression fell closed. We spent an awkward half hour, sipping tea and speaking of nothing. Dame Okra watched hawkishly, and a wiry, gray-haired guardsman, Glisselda's deaf bodyguard, lurked in the corner like a statue. I hinted that Glisselda might order Dame Okra away—she was still Queen, after all—but the only person who picked up on the hint was Dame Okra herself, who was cross with me for the rest of the day.

Cross, but no less present.

I tried to sneak out to see Glisselda at night. I would surely do better at bluffing the guards this time; I'd say Jannoula required the Queen's presence in the Ard Tower, and then I'd escort Glisselda there, giving us a chance to speak privately. Alas, I never made it out of the Ard Tower. When I opened the front door, there was Gianni Patto, curled up in the courtyard, blocking my only way out.

But then, what would Glisselda have said if I'd spoken to her? The same things Kiggs was telling me every evening over the thnik, that Goredd needed St. Abaster's Trap and the ityasaari could wait to be freed until the war was over?

A week passed, and then another. The Samsamese army, which had been only a week's march away, kept its distance for now. The Loyalists were to feint south in just six days. I felt like I'd accomplished nothing.

Since Jannoula was out every evening, my one consolation was that it was easier to speak with Kiggs than I'd initially feared. One evening, he had surprising news: "I see Jannoula, about a block ahead of me, on the river road. Do you want me to learn where she goes?"

"If you can follow without her seeing you," I said, sitting up in bed, as if I might add my alertness to his.

It was some moments before his voice crackled again: "We're turning south with the river. She's got a following, people drifting out of taverns and alleys. They're like gulls behind a fishing boat. And you know what? She lets them touch her and smiles at every one. For all that she's an egotist, she seems a kindly one."

"She's not a kindly one," I snapped. She had an allure even when she wasn't speaking or glowing with mind-fire.

He chuckled infuriatingly, and for a while there was nothing but the sound of his footsteps. He reported crossing Cathedral Bridge. "She's heading for the seminary gate," he said. "If she enters, it may be difficult to follow her inside."

"Don't follow her inside. That's all the information I needed," I said. I would go to St. Gobnait's Seminary and see for myself as soon as I could. I could lose an ityasaari chaperone in town; this was my city.

Kiggs stayed quiet a long time. I stared at the thnik ring, one finger over from Orma's pearl ring, wondering whether to call his name. Suddenly he said, "That wasn't difficult. A prince of the realm can still go wherever he needs to."

"You followed her in?" I said, shocked.

"Don't worry," he said. "The door monk believed I was here to guard Jannoula. Why would he ask her about me when she already knows I'm coming?"

I frowned, disliking the risk he was taking, but there was nothing I could do.

"Whoops," he said.

"What is it?" I whispered, my heart in my throat.

"It's fine," he said. "I thought she went down this corridor, but it's a dead end. . . ."

He trailed off, which frightened me more than anything he could have said. I was about to call his name, but luckily I hesitated.

"You were following me," said Jannoula's contralto voice. She sounded amused.

I bit my lips shut. His thnik was still on; if I spoke, she'd hear me. Kiggs said, "You're mistaken." His voice was muffled, as if he'd concealed the device in his fist.

"Am I? You're not here to chasten me for my impiety? Don't look so sheepish—I know skepticism when I see it, and it's nothing to be ashamed of. It's a relief, oddly, to meet someone who doubts." She sighed, like one who bears an impossible weight of duty. "Here, at last, is a person I can't disappoint."

Kiggs laughed; my stomach turned over.

She'd read him quickly and taken exactly the right tack: humility, doubt, and obligation. He was cautious, but she could use caution. All she needed was an angle.

The prince's thnik buzzed once and clicked off.

ᴄ᷈Thirty-Three᷈᷈

Jannoula brought Kiggs back with her from the seminary, and
he was seamlessly reintegrated into castle life, as far as I could
tell. If Glisselda was angry with him for disobeying her orders and
entering the city, I presume Jannoula smoothed things over between them. The details didn't reach me; I could only observe
from a distance. Kiggs attended council, made plans for the defense of the city, toured the walls, and drilled with the Queen's
Guard.

Kiggs was easier to approach than Glisselda. Two days after
Jannoula had apprehended him, I spotted him striding purposefully across Stone Court with three others of his regiment. I called
after him and he waited for me, letting the others walk ahead
toward the barbican gate. I was a little out of breath when I
reached him, but I had to know: "Did you see her spiritual advisor? Was it Orma?"

He shrugged, turning the helmet he carried in his hands. "I didn't see him, Phina. But you know, even if it is Orma, she may have a very good reason for keeping you from him. She's not quite the madwoman you always made her out to be. She's got a remarkable mind, and if she has some rough edges, well, she can be reasoned with—"

I turned away, unwilling to hear more. Jannoula's glamour had clearly affected him; I could no longer feel safe speaking to him openly. That was one more ally gone.

Jannoula did not gloat about Kiggs, which of course raised my suspicions. She would not have forgotten seeing him, through Abdo's eyes, coming out of my room in Porphyry. She knew Queen Glisselda had ordered him to stay away. I had wondered whether the two things were connected, whether Jannoula had told Glisselda what she'd seen in Porphyry, and Glisselda hadn't wanted to see Kiggs as a result.

That didn't add up, though. Glisselda was not herself, but she should have been furious with me as well as Kiggs, if she'd really found out the truth. I felt certain Jannoula was saving it for a special occasion.

Time passed relentlessly. My anxiety grew. I wanted to stop her before the war came south so that we'd have time to determine whether the other ityasaari could make St. Abaster's Trap without her. Kiggs had said we needed this trap, and I agreed; it would not do to hobble Goredd's defenses, but that meant incapacitating Jannoula in some way that was reversible, in case we found the other ityasaari couldn't make the trap without her. That ruled out killing or poisoning Jannoula. Camba, Nedouard, and I, conferring in hasty whispers when we could, had come up with no better way to stop her.

Astonishingly, the solution came to me from St. Yirtrudis's testament. I'd read it three times through by now and had grown quite fond of my secret patroness and her lover, the Counter-Saint, monstrous Pandowdy. The first time through, I had pictured him as a big, horrible swamp slug—I couldn't help it—and had found their romance off-putting. The second time through, however, I paid attention to Yirtrudis's descriptions of him. Pandowdy was no slug. He was tall and fearsome (I pictured him as a younger, handsomer Gianni Patto, with nicer teeth). He was a mighty fighter, a berserker who'd killed dragons with his bare hands. After the dragons were defeated, he'd been lost and out of place, prone to rages. Only Yirtrudis seemed to see a man and not a monster. Under her tutelage, he learned to control himself; together they'd founded a school of meditation.

Yirtrudis's envious brother, Abaster, who had already murdered three other Saints for daring to contradict his doctrines, had had Pandowdy buried alive. *My brother has undone the best of our generation,* Yirtrudis wrote, *because Pandowdy would not call the World-Light "Heaven." When Abaster is through with us, there will be no more room for interpretation. He will have pruned our myriad beautiful visions down to one.*

Mention of the World-Light gave me chills. I suspected I couldn't have called it Heaven, either. I rather liked this Pandowdy.

Only on my third read-through did I realize that Pandowdy had once wrecked St. Abaster's Trap. There was a single sentence about it, easy to gloss over: *Pandowdy became a mirror, reflecting the fire back at Abaster until he was so burned we could not rouse him for three days.*

It was the last night before the Loyalists' retreat; we had only one day left to try something before the barrier would be in active use against enemy dragons. I met with Camba and showed her the passage. She was sitting up in bed, Ingar curled at the other end like a big, dreamy cat. "What does that mean," I asked, "and is it something we can do?"

"It's possible to reflect her mind-fire," said Camba thoughtfully, sitting up straighter. "I tried something like that once, on an intuition. I stood at the end of the line during St. Abaster's Trap and pushed the fire back at her with all my will. It stung her like a bee." Camba rubbed her leg absently. "She was furious. That's when she made Gianni throw me down the stairs."

I winced. "It didn't incapacitate her, though?"

Camba shook her head. "It hurt enough that she doesn't let me participate in the trap anymore. I can't even climb the tower. Also, she takes a precaution: she stands in the middle of the line instead of at the end. If anyone reflects fire back at her, it will roll past and carry on down the line. If both ends reflected it at the same time, though, perhaps she would be caught between two waves."

"Was it hard to reflect the fire?"

"You must be consciously present," said Camba, making a bowl of her hands, as if that were where awareness might be centered. "You have to time it so that just as it reaches you, you harden against it."

"I can't participate in St. Abaster's Trap because I've bound myself up. You can't participate. There's only one of us who might be able to help," I said, thinking of Nedouard, "and I don't know if his mind is strong enough."

"Ingar would help," said Camba. Ingar lolled at the end of the bed, humming tunelessly. "We would need to explain the plan when he's lucid, so he understands. You could trigger his mind-pearl at the last moment."

That would require me to go to the top of the tower while they practiced, and Jannoula had never yet let me do that. Surely I could bluff her; to my surprise, I rather looked forward to trying.

"Won't Jannoula learn the triggering word if I say it aloud?" I asked.

Camba scoffed. "It's subtly pronounced, and he only wakes if you speak it exactly right. Ingar has a finely tuned ear for language, even in this state."

The word was *guaiong*, antique Zibou for "oyster"—Ingar's little play on the idea of mind-pearls, I supposed. I practiced saying it, under Camba's patient tutelage; there were entirely too many vowels. It took a quarter of an hour, but I finally resurrected Ingar's will consistently. He understood the plan and approved. I practiced a few times more, until a dire headache overtook him and we had to quit. He lay with his head on Camba's lap, and she rubbed his forehead.

Camba's eyes held a cautious hope. "If this succeeds, I will try to unhook Jannoula from the others," she said softly. "I can't reach out to them without opening the door that would let her fully into my mind. I've tried it; even when she was sleeping, she noticed immediately. I can't help anyone else when I'm fighting for sovereignty of my own mind. If she were incapacitated, though, I could surely free the others."

"What about yourself?"

Camba shook her head. "I don't know. Pende always said it's impossible to free yourself, but perhaps it depends on how inert she is."

I nodded slowly, wondering if there was a way to keep Jannoula incapacitated. Nedouard might have some drug that would do the trick. I would talk to him next.

I left Camba's and crept through the sleeping tower to Nedouard's room on the fifth floor. He was awake. I entered silently, closed the door behind me, and whispered in the old doctor's ear, "I have a plan for tomorrow."

"Don't tell me too much." His beak made his whisper a challenge to understand. "I've evaded her interest so far, but she could pry anything out of me if she wished."

I told him what he was to do, and no more. He scratched his ear uncertainly. "I'm not sure I can do what you ask," he said. "Is that really all it takes to reflect the fire? I simply will myself to be a mirror?"

"Yes," I said firmly, hoping it was true, trying not to let him see my doubts.

"Pray it works," said Nedouard. I kissed his cheek in parting, trying to reassure him, though I no longer had any notion whom or what to pray to.

Goredd's last peaceful morning dawned drizzly and gray. I stumbled down to breakfast, having barely slept, but before I could sit, Jannoula was at my elbow. "Today's the day," she said breathily in my ear. "You're coming with me."

"Coming where?" I said, instantly wary, but she only smiled in answer and steered me out of the tower, across the puddle-flecked courtyard, and into the palace proper. Down some corridors, up some stairs, and into the royal family's wing of the palace we went, stopping before a familiar door. The guards grunted and nodded, barely looking at us.

I entered the airy gold-and-blue sitting room. The table still stood before the tall windows, where once they'd fed Queen Lavonda her breakfast, and seated there were two of my dearest friends. Kiggs was on his feet at once, his face disconcertingly clean-shaven and his dark eyes twinkling; Glisselda, dressed for council in her stiffest brocades, smiled radiantly and cried, "Surprise!"

Her expression took me aback more than the word; she hadn't looked so merry in nine months. I smiled back, momentarily forgetting the Saint at my elbow.

"We've got council in half an hour, but we hoped you'd take breakfast with us," said Kiggs solemnly, tugging at the hem of his scarlet doublet. "Blessed Jannoula said it's your birthday in two days, but we'll be too preoccupied to celebrate properly then."

My smile hardened. Truth from Jannoula made me just as suspicious as lies. Kiggs stepped up to lead me to the table; I let him take my arm, but kept one eye on Jannoula. She grinned like a fiend. She was up to something, but I did not discern what until I had a chance to really look at our breakfast. Amid a surprisingly simple spread of tea, rolls, and cheese sat a marzipan torte covered with plump blackberries.

That torte was the only thing I remembered about my twelfth birthday; I'd shared the taste with Jannoula. The sight of it brought a flood of memories: how she'd run rampant in my head; how she'd stolen, twisted, and lied; how Orma had saved me.

I glared at Jannoula; she smirked back.

"Blessed Jannoula told us you love blackberries," said Glisselda.

"She's too kind," I managed to say.

Kiggs, to my right, handed me a flat parcel wrapped in linen, no bigger than the palm of my hand. "The thought is going to have to count for rather a lot, I fear," he said. I tucked the gift into my sleeve; if Jannoula had picked it out, too, I didn't want the royal cousins to see my expression when I opened it.

This was all her doing, some game she was playing with me, I was sure. The worst part, almost, was that Kiggs and Glisselda seemed perfectly themselves. I couldn't see how far Jannoula had influenced them. No doubt it would be a nasty surprise when it surfaced, like finding a spider in your slipper. I couldn't relax; that was when she'd hit me hardest.

Here I was with my two dearest friends, and I felt completely alone. To my left, Jannoula's smile turned feline.

"I am grateful that there was time for this before the war comes to us," she said, taking a knife to the torte at once, not bothering with the breakfast foods. "It is such a privilege to have gotten to know Your Majesties over these few weeks. We have much in common, and not merely that we all love Seraphina." Jannoula patted my wrist with one hand, licking marzipan off her other thumb. "Although of course we do. Seraphina is very dear. She's why we're here this morning."

Jannoula transferred a large piece of torte to her plate. "I feel especially blessed to have spent time with you this week, Prince Lucian," she said, waving the tines of her fork at Kiggs. "What a joy it was to discuss theology and ethics with you, to learn that you value truth above all else. I admire that deeply."

Kiggs, gazing at her rapturously from across the table, actually blushed. Was she glowing at him, too, or was flattery enough?

"Honesty is the cornerstone of friendship, don't you think?" said Jannoula, looking at me and licking her blackberry-stained lips. "These two, of course, go well beyond friends. They're cousins, raised together like siblings, and they'll soon be married. It was their grandmother's dearest wish."

Kiggs became very busy slicing more cheese; Glisselda examined the bottom of her teacup. I watched Jannoula narrowly, still not gleaning her purpose.

"I think we four friends should strive to have no secrets from each other," Jannoula said, and suddenly I understood the point of this charade.

In Porphyry, she'd seen Kiggs coming out of my room. She was going to extort some concession from me. I kicked her under the table. "We're done," I said through clenched teeth. "We can discuss what you—"

"You see," said Jannoula, ignoring my kicks, "an awkward

indiscretion has come to my attention. It would be best to clear the air so we can trust each other as we should."

"Stop," I snarled. "You win, but let's talk about it in—"

"*Someone* has fallen in love with Seraphina," she said, smiling awfully. "Confess—it's good for the soul—and then we can all discuss it, openly and honestly."

Kiggs clapped a hand to his mouth; he looked green. Glisselda, across the table from me, looked worse. She'd gone deathly white, and she swayed dizzily, as if she might fall out of her chair.

We had hurt her. She shouldn't have had to learn the truth this way.

She pushed back from the table and fled deeper into her suite. Kiggs exchanged a glance with me, then rushed after her.

Jannoula shoved an enormous chunk of marzipan into her mouth and grinned.

"Why would you do that?" I cried, furious with her.

"For your birthday," she said with her mouth full, a wicked spark in her eyes. "My gift to you: an understanding that everything you love is mine. Mine to spoil, mine to bestow." She plucked blackberries off the torte, piling them in her left hand, and then rose to go. "Come, we've got a busy day ahead of us."

"You have caused my friends Heaven knows what heartache!" I cried. "I'm not walking away from them like a villain."

Jannoula clamped a hand on my arm and pulled me to my feet. She was stronger than she looked. "The amusing thing is," she said, exhaling damp blackberry breath in my face, "you don't know the half of it. I know them better than you do. I know so many things you can't even imagine, Seraphina. I know the Loyalists will arrive sooner than anyone realizes, and that I could make St. Abaster's Trap all by myself."

Her words struck fear into my heart. This talk of making the trap by herself . . . had she learned what we were planning? I couldn't tell. She made sure to leave plenty of doubt.

She marched me back to the Ard Tower. I didn't resist—there wasn't time. Jannoula swept me upstairs to the chapel, where the ityasaari lingered over their porridge.

"Forgive me for interrupting your meal, brethren," cried Jannoula, "but it's time! The Loyalists approach, and the Old Ard will be close on their tails. St. Abaster's Trap must be put to its holy purpose. Today the world will witness what the minds of the blessed can do."

The others leaped to their feet, muttering enthusiastically, and filed up the spiral stair. Camba wasn't with them; she took her meals in her room because she couldn't climb the stairs. She wouldn't know things were moving forward earlier than expected. It was hard to feel for her mind-fire in my garden without calming my mind first, but sometimes desperation did the trick. *Camba,* I thought at her, *be ready to start unhooking people if Jannoula falls.*

Jannoula grabbed my arm again, and I jumped. "Come watch us. Even one who insists on walking this world alone must be awed by what we can accomplish together."

She'd anticipated my request. That could not be good. I followed her up the stairs, my heart sinking into my shoes.

The others were already gathered on the roof, twelve ityasaari: Nedouard, Blanche, Lars, Mina, Phloxia, Od Fredricka, Brasidas,

Gaios, Gelina, Gianni Patto, Dame Okra, and Ingar. The rain clouds had parted, and the sunlight made their white garments gleam like a beacon, like the ard fires of old. They stood in a semicircle before the low balustrade wall. Blanche was tied to Lars with a rope too short to wrap around her neck, safe against her will.

If our plan worked, Blanche might soon be free. I hoped for it fervently.

They joined hands in a horseshoe, open toward the northern mountains, Ingar at one end and Nedouard at the other. I lingered to one side. Jannoula joined the very center of the line, her mouth bowed upward into a hard little smile. She began a ritual chant from St. Yirtrudis's testament, what the Saints of old had recited when they strung their minds with St. Abaster's: *We are one mind, mind within mind, mind beyond mind, warp and weft of the greater mind.*

I edged up to Ingar and quietly said, "Guaiong."

Ingar came to himself, eyelids fluttering open, and nodded at me. He remembered what to do. At the other end of the chain, Nedouard nodded back.

Jannoula closed her eyes. I could almost follow her mind-fire traveling down the line, each ityasaari gasping in turn, expressions melting into something ecstatic—except for Blanche, who whimpered in pain.

Ingar and Nedouard tensed their shoulders as if bracing for a blow, ready to cast their wills against Jannoula's. I pressed my hands together, praying to no one in particular. This had to work.

Jannoula opened one eye and looked at me, a slow-motion

wink in reverse. She grinned with perfect feline malice, threw her head back, and cried out. I thought—hoped—she had been hit with reflected fire, but then Nedouard and Ingar screamed and fell to their knees, writhing in agony.

"I can be a mirror, too," said Jannoula. "And Nedouard can be my spy without even knowing it."

Nedouard rolled around, weeping and flailing; Ingar clutched his head in torment.

"Stop!" I shouted. "Don't punish them. It was my idea."

"Oh, I'm punishing you, too," she said. Nedouard and Ingar screamed louder. Tears sprang to my eyes; I could not bear this.

Jannoula stood between Od Fredricka and Brasidas. She stepped out of line and joined their hands together behind her, like latching a door. I backed away from her without looking, remembered how high we were, and sank to my knees dizzily. Jannoula hauled me to my feet. The world reeled.

"Look!" she cried, forcing me up to the low retaining wall, pointing at a dark line rising above the peaks like a storm front. There were more dragons than I had ever seen at one time, Comonot's Loyalists making their strategic retreat.

"Now look here," she commanded, wheeling me around to face the southwest. Past our encamped knights, past our baronets and their bivouacked armies, past the colorful force arrived this week from Ninys, columns of dark-uniformed troops crossed the horizon.

"The Samsamese," I croaked. "Whose side will they take?"

She shrugged. "Who can say?"

"Surely you can. You maneuvered them here."

Jannoula laughed. "That's the beauty of it. I genuinely don't know. Perhaps Josef will sit and watch. Perhaps some of the Goreddi and Ninysh knights he pressed into service will turn on him. That would be interesting, wouldn't it?

"You haven't even seen the Old Ard yet. The sky will be full of fire." She raised her pointed chin into the wind, like she was posing for a portrait. "Of course, there might have been more, but a third of the Old Ard's forces went back to the Kerama to intercept Comonot."

That news arrived like a punch in the face. I had thought myself such a skeptic, the only one who knew what she really was, but I'd believed her when she said she wasn't working for the Old Ard.

She gazed at me coolly. "Oh, come now, don't sulk. Comonot has a chance. He's taken four labs, gaining momentum and support as he goes; he's persuaded backwater settlements to join him, and every quig in the Tanamoot is his friend." Her face puckered when she said *quig*, as if she could smell one. "At least, that's the last we've heard. The Queen's only communication link to him has been mysteriously severed."

I suspected this was not so mysterious, at least to Jannoula.

"Anyway, it seemed unsporting that he should walk into the capital virtually unopposed," she said. "No one would die. Peace might break out before I wished it to."

"You've bent this entire war to your own ends," I croaked. "You shaped this new ideology of draconic purity so they wouldn't mind sacrificing themselves."

"Oh, it's not new." The wind made her short brown hair stand up on her head. "It just needed refinement so they wouldn't mind fighting to the death. After all, a pure dragon should not care about dying. Caring is an emotion; emotions are human and corrupt. A dragon who cares is not a dragon."

"*You* don't care," I said. "I've felt so much guilt for having abandoned you to them. So much pity and remorse. But you just want dragons to die."

"Not just dragons," she said, her eyes diamond-sharp. "Humans are no better. My mother left me the memory of my human father and my violent conception. She wanted me to understand human nature. She was a bell-exempt student, walking home at night; he was a rapist. I had nightmares about it when I was small, but now I've visited the alley where it happened. I understand what a fool she was. She should have killed him then and there, the treaty be damned. He was a monster; she was not monster enough."

"I'm so sorry," I half whispered, as if my pity could make any difference now.

Jannoula scoffed. "We are Saints, Seraphina. It is our right to decide who dies, our privilege to move pieces across the chessboard of history." She gestured as if she were crashing two stones together, or two skulls. "We may break this world as we see fit."

Her face had become a mask. "This is my war. All sides will destroy each other, and those who survive will be ours. We shall rule them with justice and mercy, and we shall finally be free. I have ordained it."

The first wave of Loyalists had reached us; they screamed by overhead. Jannoula smirked and reached over Ingar's twitching body for Dame Okra's hand. Jannoula threw back her head, and the force of her will rippled down the chain. I could not see the light they made, but I didn't have to.

Dragons began falling out of the sky.

Thirty-Four

I'd been adamantly opposed to killing Jannoula; that seemed naive now. In a surge of desperation, I rushed her, trying to catch her off balance and disrupt the trap somehow.

Without even opening her eyes, she blocked me with the collective mind-fire and slammed me back against the parapet like some irritating insect.

Gianni Patto, grinning toothily, broke the line and approached me with his big hands extended. I'd hit my head; I couldn't dodge. He tossed me over his shoulder, which stabbed me painfully in the stomach. For a moment, the world seemed to stand still while I saw everything: the blue slate rooftops of Castle Orison, armies crawling across the plain, dragons drifting in the air around us like autumn leaves on a pond. Jannoula laughing.

Then Gianni hauled me down the tower, skittered across the flagstone courtyard on his big chicken feet, and lumbered into the palace. He hit my head on a door frame coming in, and then on another at my final destination, some disused suite on the third floor facing south. He dumped me unceremoniously on the bare wooden floor and banged the door shut behind me.

I scrambled to my feet and tested the door. It wasn't locked. I opened it a crack, only to see Gianni Patto sitting on the floor outside. He turned his big ugly pumpkin head to grin at me, and I slammed the door in his face.

I took stock of where I was. There was a broad bed with no linens, tall windows with no drapes, empty shelves, an empty cedar chest, an empty fireplace. The suite had only two rooms, the smaller of which, a dressing room, had south- and west-facing windows.

There were no sheets or drapes I could use to climb out a window, and no hidden doors, but I could watch the war from here. Jannoula had thought of everything.

The battle was unfolding before my eyes. The Loyalists flew past the city, doubled back sharply, and clashed with the Old Ard in the overcast sky. The Old Ard had been so close on the Loyalists' tails that I hadn't distinguished the two waves until the Loyalists turned. Dragons grappled and flamed above the city. St. Abaster's Trap brought down dozens from both sides.

Dropping our allies was no accident. Jannoula knew what she was doing.

On the plain, Samsam hit Goredd's flank; Josef had apparently decided to punish us. The knights left the Samsamese to the Ninysh and Goreddi foot soldiers; their job was to engage the dragons. During the Age of Saints, they'd had ways to fight dragons in the sky—missiles and wings—but these arts had been lost to the ages, or had died with the banishment of our knights. Nine months had not been long enough to revive them. The dragons of the Old Ard stayed high and focused intently on the Loyalists, out of range of our dracomachists for now.

What was happening to Comonot in the north? Had he already struck at the Kerama, only to find it held more strongly than anticipated? I dreaded to think what the result would be if he was defeated.

Jannoula had played all sides against one another. I should have killed her weeks ago. I'd had abundant time and opportunity.

I'd been so certain I could find another way.

If only I could have unbound my own mind-fire, surely I could have made a difference. I flopped onto the bare bed, meditated until I found the garden gate, said the ritual words, and entered. My garden, once so full of life and promise, looked like nothing more than a weed-strewn lawn around the Wee Cottage, with a swamp at one edge of it. There was a rail fence around the whole thing—that was absurd. I might have kicked a rail fence over in the real world, but this one had me bound up tightly. I circled the perimeter—a five-minute walk, if that—and even came up with a silly ritual chant: *Unbind, unbind, dissolve, dissolve.* Nothing happened.

I looked at my garden denizens, scattered across the lawn like twigs. The little Abdo twig was upright. Maybe it was a sign. I took his tiny hands and whirled out into a vision.

He was still at that roadside shrine, surviving on offerings. In fact, he seemed to have acquired a following; someone had put a knit cap on his head, and there were scraps of parchment tucked into his tunic. Those would be prayers and intercessions. Someone who could meditate as long as he had must have Heaven's favor.

Abdo had evaded Jannoula for weeks now. If I escaped, the two of us together could figure out how to release each other and fight back.

I returned to my garden, and it occurred to me that there might be a way to walk through my wider mind along the other side of the wall. I'd never tried to see my garden from there; generally the gate just appeared, as if out of a fog. I stepped out and turned to face it. Spreading to either side were the high, crenellated battlements of a castle. This was what held me in, not the rail fence.

I wasn't going to tumble this wall by walking around it, although I did try. It was all I could think to do.

A knock at the door yanked me out of my head abruptly. I flailed around the bed, disoriented. The room was dark; night had fallen without my noticing.

I felt my way to the door, opened it, and then stood there blinking at lamplight from the hallway. A shadowy figure loomed before me, lit from behind so I couldn't see who it was. There were two palace guards behind him, and Gianni Patto was nowhere to be seen.

"Why are you sitting in the dark?" said a familiar basso voice, and I thought my heart would break.

Now that my eyes were adjusting, I recognized the beaky nose and piercing eyes. He wasn't wearing his false beard, and his shrubby hair had been trimmed in some kind of monk's tonsure—in fact, he was wearing the mustard-colored habit of St. Gobnait's Order. "Orma," I managed to whisper.

He glanced behind him as if he were concerned the guards had heard me. They just looked bored. Orma cleared his throat. "Brother Norman," he said. "I was sent with a message." He held out a folded parchment letter, sealed with wax.

"W-won't you come in for a moment?" I said. "And bring a lamp, uh, please. I have no light in here."

Orma cocked his head to one side, considering. I could have wept at that dear, familiar quirk. The scruffy guards seemed amused. One took a lantern down from its wall niche and passed it to Orma. "Take your time in there, Brother," he said with a wink.

"Take all night," said the other, waggling his bushy brows.

Orma, looking perplexed by the innuendo, followed me into the room and closed the door behind us. He set the lantern upon the cedar chest at the end of the bed, and I saw, behind his right ear, the telltale excision scar. I did weep then. I turned my back to him and broke the seal on the letter, sniffling and trying to keep my breath even, wiping my eyes on my linen sleeve. I held the letter so it caught the light, and read in Jannoula's blocky hand:

I almost forgot that I had another birthday present for you. Well, not exactly for you. Everything you love is mine. That's how it has to be. Who has hurt me more than you? Who showed me loving kindness, let me dream of freedom, only to snatch it all away? This monster helped, of course, but he's just an empty shell now. I can't hollow you out the same way, but you're going to wish I could.

I crumpled up her letter and threw it as hard as I could across the room. Orma, who had placed himself near the door, standing with hands folded, said placidly, "I take it there's no reply?"

There was no point asking if he remembered me; he clearly did not. I said, "Are you the one Jannoula visits at the seminary? Her spiritual advisor?"

"It would be inaccurate to call me an advisor," he said, looking mildly puzzled. "She comes to the seminary to dictate her memoirs to me. Her handwriting is terrible."

So I'd been right about one thing. It was cold comfort. "But why are you at the seminary to begin with? You're not a monk. I know you're a saarantras."

He ran his tongue over his teeth. "And how do you know that?"

"I used to know you," I said, my heart pounding. Was it wise to talk to an excision victim about the things he couldn't remember? I nervously twisted his ring on my pinkie, and then suddenly it hit me: What if the ring he'd sent me was the trigger for his mind-pearl? I hardly dared hope. I held out my finger and waggled the pearl ring at him.

He stared blankly at my hand, then at my face. Nothing changed in his expression.

"You may be mistaken," he said. "The human mind produces an astonishing variety of false memories—"

"You were excised!" I cried, furious and frustrated. "You've got the scar. I'm one of the things they took from you." I racked my memory for anything else Eskar or the exiles had told me about excision. "Do you take destultia?"

He recoiled a little from my vehemence. "Yes, but again, you are mistaken. I have a heart condition called pyrocardia. When I am full-sized, my heart overheats until it catches fire inside me. Human form is safer, but I still could suffer an infarction. I was prescribed destultia, and they excised my memories of catching fire, because those are traumatic."

"You used to be a musicologist," I said. "Do you remember none of that?"

He shrugged. "I study monastic history. You have clearly confused me with someone else." He paused, as if this conversation were too boring to sustain. "If that's all, I should be getting back."

And then he was gone. He took the lantern. I was too shattered to protest.

I fell asleep at some point. Another knock dragged me from my dreams. I buried my face in the feather mattress. The knocking continued. I had no idea what time it was, only that I was furious and exhausted. I pulled myself out of bed and threw open the door. The leering guards from earlier had been replaced by a gray-haired, wiry man in the Queen's livery, with pox-scarred cheeks and a large jaw. Illuminated from below by a lantern, he looked sinister. He held out a scrap of palimpsest. I took it with trembling fingers.

This is Alberdt. You can trust him, I read in Glisselda's graceful writing.

He was the Queen's deaf bodyguard, who'd lurked behind her during that awkward tea in her study. His eyes were kind, like Nedouard's. Still, when he gestured for me to follow, I balked. This had to be a trick. Glisselda wouldn't want to see me, not after that disastrous breakfast. Jannoula was making more mischief at my expense.

It was better to be out of confinement, however. There might be some opportunity for escape. Reluctantly I came out of the room and closed the door.

Alberdt carried a bulky satchel, which he handed to me; the hilt of a short sword protruded from the top. He led me up a northerly corridor. Along one wall was an alcove containing a statue of Queen Rhademunde. Alberdt sidled up to the old Queen and reached behind her. A narrow panel to the left opened soundlessly; Alberdt waggled his grizzled brows at me. Together we plunged into the dark, secret guts of the castle.

This passage comprised nothing but a spiral stair. We descended for many stories, finally emerging in a vaulted passageway, the castle's subbasement. At the bottom of the stairs, the young Queen waited with a lantern, a dark cloak thrown over her long chemise.

Her face had been scrubbed pink, and her eyes were rimmed in red, as if she had been weeping. Her hair was in a simple plait for sleep, though various golden curls had escaped. We stared at each other a long moment, my face burning with shame. She was surely furious with me; I didn't know what to say.

She signed at Alberdt before speaking to me; he answered her in kind, saluted, and climbed back up the stairs. "He's been so helpful," she said, turning toward me and smiling wanly. "He's not immune to Jannoula's glamour—none of us are—but it's harder to manipulate where she can't communicate. She hasn't bothered to learn his finger speech, thank Allsaints in Heaven."

Glisselda paused, the lantern light illuminating her from below like a statue in the cathedral. I was seized with guilt. "I am so very sorry—" I began.

She held up a hand to stop me. "Don't. Lucian confessed all. I don't mind about that—he's like my own brother—but I need to know, do you love him?"

"Yes," I half whispered, terrified to admit this to her even now.

"Then there is nothing else to say," she said, her smile turned sad. "Lucian wins. Long live Lucian."

I stared at her in bafflement. She sighed loudly. "I *was* angry—but it was all to the good. It has been so hard to resist her, Phina. I put on masks and erected walls, but still there were cracks for her influence to shine through. Anger, though, dispelled the mists from my mind and let me see Jannoula's cruelty clearly for once, which is a rare and beautiful blessing. Then last evening she had Orma brought in, and I saw what she's done to him," said Glisselda, tears in her voice. "Oh, Phina, how I hurt for you.

"That's why I'm here now. I'm releasing you. You, in turn, must find some way to help us from outside."

Outside the walls. The castle walls were easier to breach than the ones in my mind, it seemed.

She offered me her arm, and together we walked through twisting passages, north and west, toward the sally port.

"Alberdt is upstairs guarding your empty room," she said. "Other guards will take his place, but I'll have him deliver your meals. I don't know how long we can keep this up—days, at most—so you need to act quickly. Free us from her. This war is bad enough on its own, but she has made everything worse."

"She told the Old Ard about Comonot's gambit," I said as we reached the first locked door of the sally port. "They've sent reinforcements to the Kerama."

Glisselda, fumbling with her key, emitted a sour laugh. "And she's sabotaged the communication box in my study, I suspect. We haven't had contact with the Ardmagar in days. I will try to reach him through General Zira, but it may already be too late."

We passed silently through the network of caves, the cool, damp breath of the predawn hours on our cheeks; she was escorting me all the way out. When we reached the cave mouth, I faced her and said, "Thank you. And I'm still sorry."

"Feh," she said, waving off my apology. "Just remember, Seraphina, as if it could change anything: it was me who rescued you, not Lucian. That silly boy is upstairs, convinced that he has resisted Jannoula's charms and that he can save her—and you, and everyone—if he can make her see reason. She uses our best qualities against us."

"Which of your qualities has she used against you?" I asked quietly.

She lowered her gaze. "My heart, alas. She talks about you, and tells me how sad she is that you despise her, and then I pity her, because it would be a terrible thing to lose your . . . I mean . . ."

Her cheeks had gone very pink. I waited for her to gather herself.

"Bah!" said Glisselda, stamping her foot. "You and Lucian are so very smart, but you walk around with your eyes closed."

Glisselda rose on her toes and kissed me on the mouth.

And then I understood why she'd been the first to flee the breakfast table; why she cared more about whether I loved Lucian than whether Lucian loved me; why she'd always been so happy to hear from me, whatever else was happening. I understood something about myself as well, even if I didn't have the will to examine it just then.

I managed merely an "Oh."

"Oh, indeed," she said. Her face in the twilight looked unexpectedly old. She valiantly tried to smile. "Go now, and stay safe. Lucian would never forgive me if I sent you out to be killed. He has his faults—like not obeying my simple request to stay out of the city—but he would've insisted on accompanying you into the unknown."

"You could come," I said, and meant it.

She laughed in earnest then, like welcome rain. "No, I could not. You've witnessed the full extent of my stupid bravery. But please, if there's to be peace in our time, bring yourself back whole."

She retreated into darkness. I turned to face the slate-blue world. Abdo was out there somewhere. We'd find the way to free my mind-fire. In any case, he was my last, best hope.

I hefted my baggage and picked my way down the rocky, weedy slope.

Thirty-Five

The sun was rapidly rising. I needed cover or I'd soon be visible to the city walls, to sharp-eyed dragons in the sky, and to Jannoula up in the Ard Tower. I doubled my pace down the scrubby hill, then across two low-lying pastures, scattering sleepy sheep before me. Over one last stone wall, across a culvert, the wetlands began, full of dense foliage to conceal me.

I sat in the shadow of an orange beesuckle to see what Alberdt and Glisselda had packed in the satchel. Besides the sword, there was bread and cheese, a pair of sturdy boots, and a change of clothes. I put on the boots at once, then devoured the food. I'd eaten nothing since breakfast in Glisselda's suite the day before, and not much then.

As I chewed, I considered. I wasn't confident that Glisselda's subterfuge would last long; the guards would notice they were watching an empty room, or Jannoula would try to throw Orma in my face again. Jannoula could trace any ityasaari's mind-fire to my head and speak to me in my garden—she'd done it through Gianni and through Abdo. I didn't think she would be able to find me that way, but I wasn't completely certain. If their lines of mind-fire came out of my head like snakes—to which Abdo had so charmingly compared them—could she see them? Could she follow them back to me?

It hit me: What if the way to unbind myself was to release everyone from my garden? The garden hadn't started shrinking until I'd unbuttoned Gianni Patto. That might be a clue. If the wall was no longer necessary, might it disappear?

Unfastening Gianni and Pende had hurt terribly. I curled into a ball, steeling myself. I had to do this all at once, like jumping into icy water, or I would lose my nerve.

Lars Brasidas Mina Okra Gaios Od Fredricka Phloxia Ingar Gelina Nedouard Blanche Pandowdy Camba. One after the other, in rapid succession, I unfastened the ityasaari from my mind.

And then, lastly—O Heaven, it would shatter me—*Abdo.*

I flopped back on the damp ground, my arms wrapped around my head, sobbing and retching, grief clamping my heart, my lungs full of needles. I had never felt so empty or alone, all the way to my core. The hole must collapse. I would cave in on myself.

Dragons were already engaging in the pink morning sky overhead. The screams of generals rousing their troops echoed off the walls of the city. I felt dark shadows cross my eyelids.

I opened my eyes just as the invisible hand of St. Abaster's Trap began batting dragons aside. They fell like birds hitting a window.

The trap was still invisible to me. I had not found the way to release my mind-fire. I had pulled myself to pieces for nothing.

The city blocked my view of the armies on the ground, but I saw endless sky battles as I crossed the swamp toward Abdo's shrine. Dragons swooped and circled, flamed and grappled, trying to drop their enemies out of the sky or bite off their heads. Through a blaze of autumn leaves, I saw dragons skim along the city wall, setting soldiers and war engines on fire, only to be slammed by St. Abaster's Trap.

I kept moving, staying under foliage. Around midday, I flopped down upon a mossy hillock under a willow and let myself rest. The percussive thud of scaly bodies hitting the swampland woke me again and again; only the dampness of their landing place prevented their setting the wetland on fire. Smoke curled above the Queenswood, which was drier. In the late afternoon, I awoke when the fighting changed timbre. I squinted at the bright sky. Above me, five young dragons had taken on a much larger specimen.

With a net. The Porphyrian five were alive and biting.

Only when darkness fell did the cries abate and the dragons regroup at their own camps. I wondered how the human armies had fared, how many dead they would gather, a bitter harvest off the plains.

Crossing the wetland at night was perilous business. I mentally thanked Alberdt for the sturdy boots, because I was often up to my knees in muck. My white gown, though I hoisted it up, grew sodden around the hem. I finally called a halt on higher ground and dug through my bag for something drier to wear. I changed into a tunic and trousers and launched myself at the swamp once more.

The northern road ran upon a levee. I scrambled up the embankment eagerly when I found it, glad the going would be easier now. I was almost there. The moon rose, coating my path with silver. I saw the tumbledown shrine at last, and my heart swelled.

I reached the lean-to, sweating despite the chill. I paused near the odd statue, the human figure without features or hands, like a gingerbread man. Its decorative apron fluttered in the breeze. My eyes adjusted to the darkness, but I couldn't make out anyone in the shadows. "Abdo?" I asked the inky blackness behind the statue, but there was no answer. I knelt, not believing my eyes, and felt around for him. I found his plate and cup, both empty, but no Abdo.

He'd been here just last night. Where could he have gone? Had he finally freed himself of Jannoula and could now move without fear of drawing her attention? That was glorious news, if so, but unfortunate for me. I'd lost my last ally, and I had unfastened him from my mind. How was I to find him?

The irretrievable aloneness settled upon me again.

I don't know how long I stared at the darkness, or what deep well of stubbornness I drew from to get myself back on my feet, but eventually I wiped my eyes and dusted myself off. The moon had shifted and now shone through a hole in the roof, illuminating the statue's bald crown. I remembered the odd inscription and knelt, looking for it again.

When he lived, he killed and lied,
This Saint who lies submerged.
The ages passed, the monster died;
I ripen, I emerge.

Saint who lies submerged . . . the monster . . . I went cold. I
hadn't known the fate of St. Pandowdy when I'd read that inscription before. What other Saint had been buried alive? Who
else had been described as monstrous? Had he been buried in this
very swamp, the one I'd been trudging through all day?

My Pandowdy—the giant slug from my garden—lived in a
swamp. I'd dismissed the name as a coincidence.

I brushed lichen off the bottom of the inscription, trying to
make out the name to be sure. I traced the *P* with my finger, and
the *A*, all the way to *Y.* There could no longer be any doubt.

Was there some connection between St. Pandowdy and the
scaly swamp slug of my visions? They couldn't be the same being.
Yirtrudis's beloved had not been so grotesquely inhuman. But . . .
could he have survived being buried? Might he have changed over
time? *I emerge* made me think of a cocoon; what if I'd been seeing
some kind of chrysalis?

It was a mad idea. He'd be seven hundred years old.

But if Pandowdy was nearby, in whatever form—worm or cocoon, monster or ancient Saint—was there any chance he could
help? Maybe Abdo had glimpsed his mind-fire out there in the
swamp and gone looking for him.

Maybe I could follow. I was at a dead end otherwise.

Abdo must have left signs. I hoped I hadn't spoiled them

already by barging in here. I retraced my steps, examining the moonlit road, but saw no tracks. I picked through the tall grass behind the shrine, discerning nothing. The mud had been churned up, but a wild pig might have done that. I was about to give up when my gaze drifted across a fetid pool and I saw them: footprints on the far bank. There were only two, but they were indisputably human and exactly the right size.

They pointed straight into the heart of the fen.

I plunged in after him. I didn't see what choice I had.

I was an inexperienced tracker, but Abdo hadn't been trying to hide. I found a few more footprints and some bent foliage, but after an hour I was guessing, walking forward on faith alone. He had to be ahead; he had no reason to hare off randomly. That conviction carried me a long way, up until I stepped onto a patch of moss and found myself sunk up to my thighs in a black lake.

My boots were rapidly filling up. I scrabbled through the weeds and hauled myself onto the muddy bank, leaving an enormous hole in the frogbit and algae veiling the water's face, the greenery I'd mistaken for moss. Looking at it now, the lake was obvious; only water was that flat. I'd grown tired and unobservant.

It was also obvious, as I scanned the water, that Abdo hadn't fallen into it. There were no Abdo-sized holes in the smooth green surface. He'd have gone around ... if he'd come this way at all. I emptied my boots, shaking them ferociously in my frustration.

The chorus of autumn frogs, which I had barely been aware of, stopped peeping. The whole world seemed to hold its breath. Something was near, but it wasn't Abdo.

The green surface of the lake roiled as dark water churned beneath it.

I scrambled away from the edge just as a scaly, featureless thing broke the surface, a tarnished sliver slug wreathed in slick waterweeds.

A short, strangled laugh bleated out of me. "Pandowdy, I presume."

Seraphina, the creature rumbled back in a voice like distant thunder. My frantic heart nearly stopped.

"How do you know my name?" I asked hoarsely.

The same way you know me. I have seen you, a patch of darkness against the colors of the world, he said. I felt his voice through the soles of my feet and up my spine, as if the very earth had muttered, and yet I had a feeling it was also in my head. *You keep yourself to yourself. I do not judge you. Sometimes it's the only way.*

I couldn't be the only one he was aware of. "What about Abdo?" I asked. "Has he come past?"

He was looking for me. He's here, said the earth, vibrating meaning through my feet.

I glanced around. Abdo was certainly not here, but then the creature seemed to have no eyes. He saw mind-fire—or the lack of it—but how? With his mind? Maybe it was hard to judge distances.

"You aren't . . . St. Pandowdy from the Age of Saints?" I asked, still looking around in case Abdo stepped out from behind a shrub.

Am I not? The ground pulsed rhythmically. Was he laughing? *Some have called me Saint. My mother called me All Ugly. I have lain here for centuries.*

A breeze rustled the yellowing witch hazel leaves above me and chilled me through my wet clothes. This creature was truly ancient; it was difficult to fathom. I managed to say, "I need your help."

I don't think so, he rumbled.

"Pandowdy!" I cried, for he seemed about to submerge. "A lot of people and dragons are going to die. Jannoula wants—"

I know what Jannoula wants, he said, lolling in the water. *But how do you think I can help, Seraphina? Shall I come to your city and kill her?*

I didn't see how he could do that—he seemed to have no limbs—but he was a living Saint from the Age of Saints. That had to be worth something.

He was answering his own question: *Humans, dragons, Saints. Geologic eras. They come and go. I am done with killing. Time does the job for me.*

"I don't need a killer," I said, thinking quickly. "But maybe an ally, a voice of authority. Someone to convince the armies to stand down until Jannoula can be . . ."

I see, he growled. *You've come for the peacemaking Saint, not the murderous monster. Alas, that works no better: I never asked to be a*

Saint. I was never good at it. Do you really suppose anyone would believe I—all gruff and muddy—was anything special? That they'd listen?

"I don't know what else to try," I said, my voice heavy with frustration. "I can't seem to release my powers, and I can't stop Jannoula alone."

The breeze carried a tang of smoke from the Queenswood. The monster bobbed in his pond like some moldy tortoise. *You're right,* he said at last, *you can't do it alone, which is why it's peculiar that you take such pains to be alone. Your fortress is cleverly constructed, but you have outgrown it. When I grow too large, I shed my skin. This is why I have lived so long, Seraphina. I'm still growing.*

"So you're not going to help," I said, unable to keep the bitterness from my voice.

I already have, he said. *You seem not to have noticed.*

A pearlescent gray was growing in the sky behind the mountains. Another day of fighting would soon begin. I tried one last tack despairingly: "St. Yirtrudis is my psalter Saint. I've read her testament; I know what you were to each other. If ever you loved her, I beg you in her name—"

He thrashed in the water, emitting a rumble so low it was not a sound but an earthquake. The ground bucked, yanking my feet from under me, and I landed hard on my hip in the mud.

I told you, he roared, *I am no Saint!*

"You're a monster, retired from killing," I said waspishly. "I know."

You do not know. You cannot begin to know, he thundered. His voice seemed to echo off the very mountains, and yet I was sure it sounded only in my head. *When you have lain in mud for six hundred years, perhaps you can claim something resembling knowledge.*

I pushed myself back to standing, my breath hard and ragged. I had nothing else to say to the creature. My impious father might have shrugged and knowingly asked when the Saints ever lifted a finger for anybody.

This one wouldn't even consent to be a monster.

I had to find a way to be monster enough for both of us.

I walked away from him, despairing and out of ideas. I'd lost Abdo's trail, the armies would be awake and at each other's throats again soon, and I was wet and miserable. The last was the only one I could do anything about at the moment. I found a fallen log to sit on and opened the satchel Alberdt had sent with me to see if he'd thought to pack dry stockings.

He hadn't. Instead, I found a little parcel wrapped in cloth, the birthday present Kiggs had handed me what seemed like an age ago. It must have fallen out of the sleeve of my white gown when I'd changed clothes.

It was my birthday, I realized with a start. I unwrapped the gift with trembling fingers. He'd said the thought would have to count, but at first I couldn't tell what he'd been thinking. The prince had given me a gilt-framed round mirror the size of my palm. What was I to do with this? Check my teeth for spinach?

The frame had words engraved in it. The moon was sinking

behind the western hills, stealing my light away, but I finally discerned *Seraphina* along the top, and *I see you* along the bottom. *I see you.*

I laughed and then I wept. I could barely see myself in this tiny mirror, my mind-fire was shut off from the rest of the world, and Jannoula had taken everything I hoped for and twisted it to her own purposes. It was all wrong, all backward, and I couldn't even see my way clear of it to . . .

An idea was beginning to form. It was all backward: Saint, Counter-Saint. Was there a way to reflect her light back at her?

I fished in my bag for the gown I'd changed out of. Its hem was filthy, but it would look sufficiently white in the morning twilight. I pulled it out hand over hand and then drew out the sword. It wasn't a very long sword, but it was going to have to do.

I had exactly one idea, and it involved reaching the center of the battlefield before either side struck. With the sword in one hand and the damp, clingy gown in the other, I walked and then ran. I'm no runner, but months of riding and travel had increased my endurance. Once I came to the road, it was smooth going, my squelching boots notwithstanding.

It was also downhill. That helped.

I was racing the sun, which crawled relentlessly toward the door of dawn. I passed trampled farmland, burned-out barns; I prayed the farmers had reached the city and the tunnels safely. A flock of renegade sheep flowed across the road ahead of me, turned south so they blocked my way, then north so they ran right at me. I let them rush around me, a fleecy river, then kept on my way.

To my left, smoke rose from the city, and its walls were scorched and cracked in places. I saw movement on the walls as fresh soldiers replaced the night guard. I wondered if any of them saw me running.

I could see the camps now, the armies beginning to stir. To the north, in the Queenswood, the Old Ard camped. The Loyalists were south, out of sight from here, behind some low hills, so that they might strike from unexpected angles. Our knights and the ragtag infantries of Ninys and Goredd were spread across the south, and to the west were the Samsamese. The Ninysh had thrown up hasty earthworks against the Samsamese—yesterday, presumably, while I wandered the swamp. The dirt walls would shunt the Samsamese north, making it easier for them to engage with the Old Ard than with the Goreddis.

My road led into the middle of everything. I was practically falling over my feet by this point. I let myself walk the last half mile, past torn-up fields and pasture churned to mud, tying the gown's long sleeves to the sword as I went.

The gown and sword, a makeshift flag, caught the breeze when I raised it above my head. It flapped behind me, and the first rays of sun, cutting underneath a heavy brow of cloud, shone on the fabric and made the white linen glow. It was my flag of surrender.

There was movement in the camps, a stirring that I hoped was a question: Which side had sent me out, and why?

One by one, the camps sent representatives to parley. Sir Maurizio did not immediately recognize me; he paused when he realized whom he was walking toward, but then put his head down and picked his way doggedly across the blackened field. Not far behind him, a familiar blond beard bobbed: it belonged to Captain Moy, who'd escorted me through Ninys. The Old Ard sent a general, shrunk into his saarantras, who introduced himself as General Palonn; I knew him as Jannoula's uncle, the one who'd put her at the mercies of the Censors. The Loyalists sent General Zira, whose saarantras was a thickset, energetic woman. Neither Palonn nor Zira had bothered lightening their skin for the likes of me. The Regent of Samsam, Josef erstwhile Earl of Apsig, sauntered up last with apparent unconcern, his helmet under his arm and his fair hair tossing in the breeze.

"Whose envoy are you, then?" he sneered. "Blessed Jannoula would not have sent you. She warned me that you were not to be trusted."

"She was right: I am absolutely not to be trusted," I said, barely glancing at him. No one had yet appeared upon the city walls.

Josef puffed up indignantly, but it was hard to quarrel when I'd agreed with him.

If I was to reflect Jannoula's fire, I had to attract her attention, but I still saw no sign of her atop the Ard Tower. I stalled. "My friends, I am here to discuss the treachery of a certain half-dragon called Jannoula—"

"A half-dragon like yourself?" said General Zira, as abrupt and intimidating in her saarantras as in her natural form. "Like the half-dragons who have been indiscriminately knocking my Loyalists out of the sky?"

"A corrupt, unnatural being," purred General Palonn. "We know her. We intend to kill her when this is all over, you may be sure of that. She fooled us for a time, but it has become clear that she's playing both sides."

"Yes," I said. "She has lied to all sides, bent this war to her own purposes with her formidable powers of persuasion—"

"The person who persuaded Ninys to help Goredd was you," said Captain Moy, looking at me sidelong and tugging on his long blond beard. "We know nothing of this Jannoula."

"And who was supposed to kill her if there was no other way to stop her?" said Sir Maurizio, holding up an antler-handled dagger. "I think we're owed an explanation for this."

"I have your explanation," said Josef snidely. "Seraphina is a deceitful snake."

I had completely lost control of this parley, but I couldn't let myself get upset, not even at Josef. Persuading them wasn't the point—although it was galling that there seemed to be so many good reasons to blame me for everything. I said, "Jannoula doesn't care who wins, only that we lose as many good people and dragons as possible."

"The only good dragon—" Josef cut off sharply and clutched at his heart, eyes wide. I followed his gaze toward the city and saw her, our Jannoula, striding out along the battlements. A stray sunbeam had cut through the clouds and illuminated her blinding white gown, almost as if she'd planned it. The other ityasaari followed behind her, as many as could stand, like a line of doves.

All eyes turned toward her. She took the hand of the half-dragon next to her to make the chain, and they raised hands together as if in victory. Josef fell to his knees. *Santi Merdi!* cried Moy, and Maurizio gasped, and even the two dragon generals looked stunned. "Can you identify the source of that light?" Zira asked, almost inaudibly.

So dragons could see it, too. I really was alone in my incapacity.

Here was my chance, though. She'd come out to show everyone the light—or Heaven, or whatever dragons took her mind-fire to be. I willed myself to reflect it back at her. Nothing seemed to happen. Nedouard and Ingar had been able to reflect by willing it, but then they'd been threaded directly to her mind. I would find the way. I had tucked the little mirror into my sleeve; I gripped it now to give me strength, and threw everything I had at Jannoula.

I make my will a mirror, I chanted to myself. *I make my wall a silver sphere.*

I glanced up; nothing had changed, except that Jannoula was looking at me. I don't know what I must have looked like to her. Nothing reflected or gleamed.

I had been a fool to think this could work. On the battlements, Jannoula crashed her fists together like she'd done during our talk on the tower. She was out of her mind, and I'd been out of my mind to imagine I could counter her.

I froze. *Out of my mind.*

Go into the cottage, go out of my mind. Those had been my ritual words when I fortified the Wee Cottage and banished her from my garden. Might I have inadvertently created yet another inside-out house? What if that door led out of my self-constructed fortress and into the world? The egress might have been right in front of me all along.

I closed my eyes and found my shriveled garden at once. I

filled it like I filled my own skin. The cottage door loomed before me; its padlock crumbled to dust in my fist. I took a terrified breath, opened the door, and stepped through.

I was a thousand feet tall, a towering blaze, a column of fire extending to the sky. I saw everything: the limp, slender river; the trampled plains and rusty mountains; the war camps, full of beings who shone like stars; the city ablaze with humans and my kind. Even the dragons were lit up like bonfires. I saw cows and dogs and every squirrel in the forest. Did life glow like that? Had it always?

It was profoundly, unsettlingly right. I'd been dealing in shadows before.

Surfaces were no obstacle. I could discern Glisselda in the city, could see right to the heart of her. I saw Josquin in Segosh and Rodya and Hanse with the Samsamese, saw Orma in the seminary and Camba in the tower. Comonot, Eskar, and Mitha gleamed in the Tanamoot—how was it possible? Kiggs was with the city garrison, and I felt a pang for him, but not only for him. For the whole shining world.

Jannoula on the walls shone differently. She did not blaze forth from a single incandescent core; at her center was a deep, hollow emptiness, like a hole in the world.

I remembered that emptiness. I'd seen it firsthand.

Humans and dragons—everyone she had touched with word or deed—were linked to Jannoula with shining filaments. Some threads stretched to the Tanamoot. To my new eyes, she was a spider in a vast web; Abdo had described Blanche's mind-fire filaments that way, yet this network was vaster, and the connections seemed to draw light toward Jannoula. The half-dragons, lined up beside her on the city wall, were more than simply hooked. They were grappled to her with bright bands as strong as iron.

It was in service of the void at her heart, this light being drawn from all directions. What she gave was nothing compared to what she took. That dread, sad emptiness drew me; if I looked too long, I feared, I might fall in.

She saw me, knew me, reached for me with tentacles of fire. I was already fire, but still they seared and burned and tore. She struck again, but I could not bear to strike back, not when she had such a hole at her heart.

Not when I suspected I'd helped create it.

She lashed and flailed; I bore her agony, took the pain into myself and diffused it. However much I absorbed, she had more for me. I began to weaken under her onslaught.

I see you, Phina! cried a familiar voice, and then another mind unfurled in the Queenswood: Abdo. He'd been invisible to me; now his mind bloomed and cavorted.

I've been trying to do this! he cried. *That old grump under the swamp would not advise me, but I see what you've done.*

I could have wept with relief, I was so glad to see him. But how could I hear him? *I let you go,* I said.

His entire being smiled fire. *You did. But I did not let go of you.*

He reached toward me, across miles, with a jet of flame; I reached and felt my strength renewed. *Can we free everyone?* he asked.

We began, tentatively, with the spider filaments closest to us; it was hard to direct our fire to such a fine task. The threads severed easily, glowing ends floating away in the bright air, but they were myriad, a dense netting all around us. The more lines we broke, the more we saw.

We should free the ityasaari, said Abdo. *Some might be able to help us.*

Jannoula heard us. Were our very minds open to the air now? "Keep back!" she shouted. "I will walk them off this wall!"

Abdo ignored her and reached toward the city with a fist of fire.

An ityasaari pitched off the battlements, screaming as he fell. Abdo and I reached convulsively to catch him, but he fell through our immaterial hands and shattered on the ground.

It was Nedouard. His light went out.

The loss reverberated through my being. All the light was my light.

Even the eerie glow in the north.

It was enormous.

I see you! I cried, addressing that glow. The earth shook, the tremor lasting seconds, then minutes. Pieces broke off the walls; trebuchets tumbled end over end; cauldrons of pyria burst into geysers of flame. My body fell down, and my mind reached out, despairing, for the people of my city and the ityasaari on the wall.

Jannoula held the ityasaari back from the edge; the tremor wasn't her doing.

Behind the city something rose, its life so unbearably bright that I narrowed my mind's eye and used my human eyes. It was a walking mountain covered in dirt and scrubby trees, black ooze pouring off it. As it walked around the city, pieces of swampland starting to cake off, it began to look like a monstrous man. The city walls came up to his waist; he moved like he'd forgotten how, or had rusted during his years underground. He seemed to be made of metal.

No, not metal. Silver scales.

He steadied himself with one great hand against the city wall. He had told me he'd never stopped growing. He'd meant it literally. What had I been addressing all these years? His finger?

Pandowdy was vast; his mind-fire was vaster. "You let yourself out, Seraphina," he roared in a voice like the world breaking. I was dimly aware of people around me covering their ears and buckling under the weight of sound; he wasn't just speaking in my mind anymore.

"You too," I said. "You're not what I thought you were."

His eyes, rimmed in mud, blinked slowly, and the lower half of his face split horizontally, revealing a gaping maw, a terrifying smile. "Neither are you. That's why I've come. I observe that you are stuck," said Pandowdy, leaning against the buckling wall. "You've worked out the mind, but sometimes what you need is matter."

Jannoula ran back and forth on the battlements, crying to the bombardiers to fire on Pandowdy. Some did. Pandowdy shook pyria off himself; the trebuchet stones bounced away harmlessly.

He reached a gargantuan hand across and plucked Jannoula off the battlements. She screamed. Someone lunged after her, jabbing Pandowdy's hand with a spear. It glanced off the giant's scaly finger; the spearman tumbled over the edge of the wall.

It was Lars.

Pandowdy caught him in his other hand and set him gently on the ground. Jannoula still flailed, shrieking. The other ityasaari shuffled toward the edge of the wall, ready to fling themselves uselessly against the giant.

"Pandowdy!" I cried.

"Do not be afraid, little sister," he said. The ground vibrated with his voice.

He brought his hand across and broke the shining filaments, like a gardener pinching off buds. He released the ityasaari, the soldiers on the wall, the councilors at court, the Regent of Samsam, the generals of the Old Ard both here and in the Tanamoot. He moved to break Abdo's tether, but Abdo gestured for him to wait, then reached inside and unhooked himself. Pandowdy nodded respectfully.

The Saint—for I was convinced he was a Saint, indeed, whatever the rest of us might have been—now had a fistful of dangling mind-fire threads. "She is broken, this one, in her mind and heart," he said, carefully scooping up the blazing filaments and packing them back into Jannoula. "You must learn to fill yourself with yourself, Blessed."

"D-don't break her any further," I pleaded, feeling responsible.

He gave me a sidelong look, and for a moment I thought he was angry. But he said, "Would you break a mirror, Seraphina, because you fear to look into it?"

"What will you do with her?"

He held her up in the sunlight, as if examining her for cracks. "She's interested in the Saint trade," he rumbled. "After nearly seven hundred years, I may finally have worked out how to be one. I have the next millennium free. I'll see what can be done."

He moved as if to walk away, but an outcry rose all around, from the Samsamese behind me, the Goreddi and Ninysh soldiers to the south, the entire city: "St. Pandowdy!" They'd heard me call his name, I imagined, but how were they concluding he was a Saint? What did they see, what did they make of all this mind-fire?

Pandowdy paused and looked at the tiny people surrounding him, his aspect deeply weary. "I'm not carrying away all your problems, Seraphina," he boomed. "Only the smallest. This"—he gestured to the armies around us—"is for you to sort out."

"I understand," I said, my voice sounding smaller in my own ears. I was fading back into my body; I struggled against it. "How do I maintain this fire?" I cried.

"No one can live like this all the time, inside out," Pandowdy said over his mountainous shoulder. "It's too much, even for me."

"I don't want to stop seeing!"

He laughed; the earth laughed under our feet. "You won't. You'll return to it, and you'll measure the world by a different scale now. But you can't stay. Release it, good heart. Give it back to the world. There will be more."

He turned on his enormous heel, tearing a divot out of the pasture where he stood, and in four strides he was around the end of the city and heading north into the hills. He waded through the Queenswood, over the first of the foothills, and was gone.

I looked back at the conflagration called Abdo. We agreed without speaking and collapsed into ourselves again, the mind-fire exploding outward in a shock of rightness and love and memory. It rippled through the world in a great wave, rattling the bones of knowledge, shaking the heart of complacency, echoing in a hundred thousand skulls.

I found myself on my back in the dirt, sick and dizzy. I raised my head in time to see the gates of the city open and a golden-haired Queen on a red horse come galloping toward me through the crystalline sunlight.

And then there was, blissfully, nothing.

Thirty-Six

My first impression upon waking was that I had ended up in Heaven. I was cradled in a cloud. A sweet autumnal breeze wafted gauzy curtains like the gossamer wings of the blessed. Sunlight gilded all it touched; the Golden House was made of sun. Everything made sense now.

This was not my room, not any of my rooms. I raised my head with difficulty, for it was very heavy, and saw Kiggs sitting with his back to me, writing at a desk.

Oh, good—he was dead, too. It wasn't just me.

"She stirs!" he cried, hearing my suspiration, or the clouds creaking under me. He rushed to my side, flopped onto the golden expanse of nebulous bed beside me, and lay propped up on his elbows. He pushed my hair (a storm cloud) out of my face. He smiled, and his eyes were stars.

"Before you ask: you've been out a whole day." He rested his chin in his hand, pressing at his cheek as if to stop himself from foolishly grinning. He couldn't stop. He gave it up. "I was worried," he said. "We all were. There was this giant Saint, and fire, and you were . . ." He spread his hands as if trying to encompass the unfathomable scale of it. "How did you do all that?"

I shook my head, which was full of suns, flashing and jangling and making it hard to answer. Maybe this wasn't Heaven, but I was no longer of this world. Or else I was the world. Maybe the distinction was pointless.

I closed my eyes to quiet the intensity around me. The world was no longer on fire, but there was an echo of fire in everything. A memory of fire. It was still too much. I felt everything.

"The war . . . ," I began in a voice like autumn leaves.

"Peace has broken out," Kiggs proclaimed. "Glisselda has negotiated terms with all sides. The Regent of Samsam is heading home, tail between his legs; the Loyalists and the Old Ard are still here, patching broken wings and shattered trust, but they'll soon depart as well. General Zira reports that Comonot muscled through in the Kerama, but we don't have all the details yet."

Kiggs leaned in until I could feel his breath in my ear. "When St. Pandowdy picked Jannoula up, I felt it. Like sorrow or release, or like I loved her for just a moment and wanted her to be well. I wanted the world to be well. It was the most extraordinary thing. And then before you collapsed, it came over me again, this burst of . . . what?"

He was incandescent even with my eyes closed, too bright to look at. I reached out and touched his face. He took my hand and kissed the palm.

I gasped. I was like an open wound; I felt everything tenfold.

"I don't know what to call any of it," I said, trying to catch my breath.

He laughed, like sunlight on water. "Jannoula glowed, but then St. Pandowdy—and you—"

"And Abdo," I said. He would not have known he was seeing Abdo.

Kiggs would insist on asking me to answer the unanswerable. "I want to understand what I saw. I want to know—"

"If I'm a Saint?" I asked.

He said softly, "That wasn't my question, no, but feel free to answer that."

I squeezed my eyes more tightly shut. I had been waking slowly into myself again, but that question accelerated the process, made me harshly aware of my physical form. My sleep chemise— who'd dressed me?—was stiff and my scales itchy; I had blisters between my toes; my mouth was unpleasantly dry, and I could really have stood a trip to the garderobe. Every prosaic ache and quirk and failing rushed to my notice at once. I put a hand over my eyes. "Pandowdy may be a Saint, whatever else is true."

"Agreed," said Kiggs.

"I saw everything, Kiggs. I held the whole world in my mind at once"—I didn't hold it now; I could feel it still trickling away— "but don't . . . I can't call myself a Saint."

"Fair enough," he said. "Maybe that question isn't for you to answer."

I rolled onto my side, facing him, still not opening my eyes. "But there was something . . . extraordinary. I was more than me, and the world was more than the world. How do I reconcile my-self with that, Kiggs?" I asked, my voice cracking under the weight of new distress.

"With what, love?" he asked.

I took his face in my hands; it was terribly urgent that he understand. "How am I to fit back into myself after this?"

He laughed softly. "Haven't you always been more than your-self? Haven't we all? We are none of us just one thing."

He was right, of course. I opened my eyes at last and exam-ined the beautiful surface of him. His teeth were slightly crooked; that was the only difference between them and diamonds.

His face was too smooth. "You disappeared your beard," I muttered.

His brows arched in surprise. "So you did like it. Glisselda didn't see how that was possible."

"Glisselda!" I said, pulling my hands away from his face. "How is she?"

He nodded, firmly affirmative. "She's Queen," he said wryly, "and then some. Like none we have ever witnessed before." He smiled. "She and I have talked, and confessed our hearts' trans-gressions, and I believe we understand each other. What's left to say should perhaps be said with you present, as it pertains to you also."

My head lolled toward him, then sank deep into a pillow. He lay his head beside mine and brushed my cheek with a finger. I rippled like the ocean.

"All will be well," he said.

He was right; I had seen it. All was well—or could be, if we worked to make it so. We were the fingers of the world, putting itself to rights.

I had no chance to explain this because he kissed me.

Who can say how long that lasted? I had learned to step outside of time.

By evening I had ebbed entirely into myself again. Life still glowed around me—the ityasaari blazed like torches—but I no longer saw everything at once. *No one can live like this all the time,* Pandowdy had said. It was a relief in a way. There were mundane things that needed my attention.

We ityasaari sat up with St. Eustace for Nedouard that night. A private wake at the seminary was followed by his interment beneath St. Gobnait's at dawn. Only the ityasaari, Prince Lucian Kiggs, and Queen Glisselda attended; he'd had no family in Ninys to track down.

Dame Okra Carmine, his ambassadress, made sure he had the proper Ninysh touches: spruce wreaths at his head and feet, pine-flavored pastries, and sweet Segoshi raisin wine. She wept harder than anyone, ashamed of all she had done and been. I didn't see how to reassure her; my forgiveness—or Blanche's—could not make a dent in her guilt.

Nedouard was interred in a wall niche in the cathedral's catacombs. I wept for the kindly, unfortunate doctor. He'd asked me a question once: *Are we irretrievably broken?* I hadn't known the answer, but I thought I knew it now. After most of the others had filed out of the crypt, I whispered to his grave plaque: "Never beyond repair, good heart."

Blanche, kneeling in prayer nearby, heard me. She stood, brushing the dust of centuries off her dark blue gown (we were none of us wearing white, I noticed, though this was a funeral). She took my arm and silently accompanied me out of the catacombs.

We caught up with the others climbing the hill to Castle Orison. A quilt of cloud shrouded the sun, and the breeze blew chill; the rains of late autumn would set in soon. As we trudged along, an unexpected shouting arose behind us, a voice that was simultaneously familiar and unfamiliar: "Phina! Prince Lucian!"

The street was full of people following us while trying to appear like they weren't. Kiggs stepped up beside me and pointed. "That's not . . . is it?"

"It is!" came another shout. Abdo ducked out from behind a cartload of firewood and charged up the hill toward us.

"You can hear him?" I asked Kiggs.

"How can I not? He's shouting."

"And I will shout again!" cried Abdo. "I can't stop shouting!"

He was completely filthy, as befitted a lad who'd spent weeks camping out in a shrine and trekking across swampland. His hair was tangled, full of moss and twigs. The cleanest thing about him was his grin, which was enormous and gleamed like the moon.

"Hello, everyone!" he shouted without moving his lips. The other half-dragons' mouths already hung open; there were only eyes left to bug out, which they did alarmingly.

"How are you doing thet?" said Lars.

Abdo did a little waggling dance, sticking his tongue out and making antlers of his hands, the whole and the broken. "I figured it out! My mind is as large as the entire world. I could speak to everyone at once, if I wished. It's not talking, exactly, but it sounds the same, doesn't it?"

He was using his mind-fire—the way everyone had heard me say Pandowdy's name—to make a sound heard with the ears and the mind and the heart all at once.

Lars said, "It wouldt be less eerie if you move your lips and pretendt the sound comes from your face."

"Oh!" said Abdo, contorting his lips. "I'm out of practice."

He was moving his mouth in the wrong ways at the wrong time, clearly faking. It was hard to watch. "You could practice in front of the glass," I suggested.

He shrugged, grinning, too delighted with himself to take it as criticism. He bounced around us, greeting each half-dragon in turn. He hugged Camba, in her wheeled chair, and laughed when she told him he needed a bath. Blanche, who still clung to my arm, watched him in wonderment, a smile slowly creeping across her lips.

The ityasaari did not care to spend one more night in the Garden of the Blessed, and neither did I. I had everything moved back to my old suite as soon as possible.

Blanche, Od Fredricka, and Gianni Patto took up residence at Dame Okra's large ambassadorial residence in town while she made arrangements for them to return to Ninys. "They're going to need protections and assurances, to say nothing of support," she explained, bustling about officiously, when I visited her at home. "Count Pesavolta isn't certain he wants them, said they're 'disruptive' and 'polarizing.' Well, I expect I can hammer some certainty into him."

"They're welcome to remain in Goredd," I said. "The Queen said—"

"I know," she said, her froggy face puckering sadly. "But you must understand, now they associate Goredd with . . . well, with that time. You can't blame them."

I didn't, but I wished things were different.

Lars stayed at the palace for now, although he did not return to Viridius. The old man used me as a go-between. I told Lars that Viridius forgave him and wanted him back, but Lars just smiled sadly and said, "I cannot yet forgive myself." He drifted through the palace like a ghost.

News reached us that Porphyry had dissuaded further Samsamese aggression with a decisive naval victory. The Porphyrian ityasaari wanted to set out for home before winter made the roads difficult. Gaios, Gelina, and Mina spoke of taking off on new journeys after escorting the others back. They were only waiting for Camba and Pende to be well enough to travel.

Camba was healing; she began to take her first hobbling steps around the palace gardens with a cane. Pende, alas, was not so fortunate. I had been hoping against all reason that Jannoula's departure might bring about some kind of recovery for the old priest, but he still lay inertly, his condition unchanged.

Ingar brought him outside into the wan autumn sunshine to watch Camba practice walking. The old man stared at nothing, his wattled chin sunk to his chest.

I was helping Camba keep her balance while Ingar adjusted Pende's lap blanket. "I feel terrible about Paulos Pende," I said quietly, adjusting my arm around Camba's waist. "If I could have unbound myself sooner, maybe—"

"I also tend to blame myself first," said Camba. Her head was still shaved for mourning, though she'd rehung her golden earrings. "The world is seldom so simple that it hinges on us alone. Pende played his own part. He told you your mind was bound and that it was a problem, but did he make even the slightest attempt to help you?"

"He doesn't deserve this," I said, unsure where her argument was leading.

"Of course not," said Camba. "And neither do you deserve all the blame. Sometimes everyone does their best and things still end up wrong."

While I considered this, Ingar approached us, smiling widely. I ceded my place to him. "I think we can keep the old man comfortable as we travel," said Ingar. "There are carriages designed for invalids, with good springs so they don't jostle too much. I'll take Phloxia to procure one; if there was ever anyone born to deal with merchants, it's her."

I noticed the pronouns. "You're going back to Porphyry, Ingar?"

"I didn't get enough time at the library," he said, kissing Camba on the cheek. Camba kissed his bald head.

"Your own library is here now," I said, surprised that I wanted him to stay.

His eyes softened apologetically. "I've read all the books in *my* library."

"Of course," I said. "How silly of me."

I embraced them both together. Camba held on to me for a long time.

"You will come to us in Porphyry again," she said. "There will always be a place for you in our garden."

"Thank you, sister," I said, my voice constricting.

The Porphyrians were ready to leave within three days. It hurt to let them go, but it hurt the most with Abdo.

The boy, bless him, had not stopped talking since he arrived, but at least he'd finally worked out how to whisper. It hadn't been trivial; he could broadcast his voice to the entire city if he wished. We had all been subjected to random bursts of Abdo's spooky, disembodied voice. Speaking softly, or to just a few people at once, took more finesse.

On Abdo's last evening, I joined him, Kiggs, and Selda in a small parlor in the royal family's wing of the palace. Abdo seemed finally to have realized he was leaving, and was quieter than usual. "You're welcome to stay," said the Queen gently. "We have plenty of good uses we could put you to. Maybe even devious uses."

Abdo shook his head. "I have to get home." He looked at his fingers, the strong and the still, twisting in his lap. "I need to make up with my mother. When I saw . . ." He paused, as if looking for the words. "What was it like for you, Phina, when you opened your mind wide and saw everything?"

Blood rose to my cheeks. I hadn't discussed it, except for what I'd told Kiggs (which seemed a bit embarrassing now). I didn't feel capable of talking about it. "There was a great brightness and, um . . . Imagine what it would look like if you could see music, or thought."

Glisselda's gaze grew distant, as if she were trying to picture it; Kiggs leaned forward, elbows on his knees, and asked, "Was it Heaven?"

That question took me aback, but Abdo answered it: "That's how your Saints interpreted it. It looked like our gods, to me—not literally, not the way they're depicted in statues, but the vibrant space between them, where Necessity is Chance and Chance flows into Necessity. The world is as it must be, and as it happens to be, and those are the same thing, connected and right, and you understand and love all of it, because you are all of it and all of it is you."

"In love with all the world," said Kiggs, quoting Pontheus.

That was exactly what I'd felt—it almost brought tears to my eyes to remember—but Abdo's eloquent explanation still didn't capture it. You couldn't put words on something like that. Heaven, gods—these were concepts far too small.

I said, "So what happens when you make up with your priestess mother? Will you join the temple you once scorned?" It sounded harsh when I said it aloud, but I did not see how Abdo was going to fit everything he had experienced into the confines of a temple.

But then, I was managing to fit into myself.

"Something like that," Abdo said, smiling.

"I think that's very admirable," said Glisselda, raising her chin and giving me a stern look. "If your priesthood is anything like ours, Abdo, they need good-hearted people like you. You're going to help your city."

I couldn't tell whether I thought that was a bad idea or whether I was just going to miss him terribly.

Abdo took his leave soon after, bowing to Glisselda and shaking Kiggs's hand. They wished him a safe journey. When he came to say goodbye to me, tears welled in my eyes. I hugged him a long time in silence, and he said to my mind alone: *I won't be far from you, Phina madamina. You don't go through what we've been through together and not leave some of yourself behind.*

I kissed his forehead and let him go.

Blanche, with quigutl assistance, restored Glisselda's communication box, and we finally heard from Ardmagar Comonot. He'd reached the Kerama, but not without difficulty. "We were outnumbered two to one," he said, "but you would not believe how those exiles fought. They were impassioned. I've never seen the like. And to some degree, we got lucky. I made it to the Keramaseye—the great amphitheater in the sky, where the Ker meets—and took up the Opal of Office. All around us, the fighting died as the Old Ard saw what I had done, and they remembered there was more to being dragons than their pernicious anti-human ideology: there are traditions, and protocols, and the correct order of things. And the correct order of succession is that

I may defend myself, with law or with talons. No more cowardly backstabbing or costly war."

He had ended the war; Kiggs and Glisselda congratulated him heartily. There were still months, or perhaps years, of debate and negotiation ahead—whether to disband the Censors altogether, how to integrate the exiles, whether the Ardmagar should be elected and be subject to term limits—but Comonot seemed to relish the prospect. "It doesn't matter how long it takes. We're debating instead of biting each other's throats out, and that is entirely for the good."

I told him about Orma's condition, and he grew quiet. "Eskar may have insights into what the mind-pearl trigger could be," he said at last. "It will be several months before she can travel, however. She's imparting memories to her egg-to-be, but once she's laid it, she can leave it in a hatchery."

Glisselda met my eyes with a quizzical look, not sure how to respond to this news. "I'm so pleased for you, Ardmagar," I said, although I was a little disheartened for my uncle.

"Don't congratulate me yet," said the old saar gruffly. "I see how these Porphyrian-born hatchlings carry on. There really is more to this than neck-biting, I fear. And, Seraphina," he added, "I heard your tone just then, and recognized how it contradicted your words. That's how astute and sensitive my experience has made me."

I rolled my eyes for the benefit of the royal cousins. "And?" I said.

"And you needn't fear for your uncle," he said. "Eskar has done her service to the Tanamoot, and she'll be at his side again, first opportunity she has. Once I would have judged her harshly for it and sent her to be pulled apart. Now I only marvel at the capaciousness of her heart."

Kiggs and Glisselda were married before the end of the year.

The three of us agreed it should happen. Consensus came surprisingly easily, although I think we each had different reasons. Glisselda couldn't bear the thought of marrying anyone else; if she had to marry someone, let it be the dear old friend who knew her better than anyone and would keep their partnership strictly political. Kiggs, for his part, felt practically married already—to Goredd. It was his grandmother's wish that the cousins should rule together, there was duty and honor involved, and I was able to convince him that I didn't mind.

And as strange as it may sound, I didn't. We three knew what we were to each other; we would plan and negotiate and build our own way forward, and it was nobody's business but ours.

Glisselda was still a consummate traditionalist in her own way; the wedding had to have the proper nightfest, cathedral service, wedding journey, and all. It was to be Goredd's wedding, the opening salvo of the new reign of peace.

A nightfest is exactly what it sounds like: it lasts all night. First came feasting, then entertainments, then dancing (once dinner was sufficiently digested), then more entertainments, then strategic napping (followed by vehement denials of napping), and finally the service at St. Gobnait's cathedral just as the sun was coming up.

I organized the entertainments, of course. It was both strange and comforting to fall back into that work. I performed on flute and oud over the course of the evening, and danced twice, unobtrusively, with my prince.

What I didn't anticipate was the awed silences. The way people paid special attention when I played, watched me dancing, gathered in a silent circle around me while I took my refreshment, and sneaked tugs at my gown.

These people had seen something. Even in the tunnels, I'd heard, they'd been able to see Pandowdy's light and feel the rumble of his voice. A stone had been cast, and we'd only just begun to see its ripples.

I shared a carriage to the cathedral with Dame Okra. "You're awfully sanguine," she said, watching me with carefully affected casualness. "You weren't overrun, so you won't know this, but Jannoula's mind leaked into ours sometimes. She knew what the prince was to you."

"Do all the ityasaari know?" I said, less alarmed than she probably hoped.

She shrugged, a smirk on her froggy face. "Possibly. I just have one question: What will you do about the fact that Queen Glisselda will be expected to produce an heir?"

Absurdly, I found her nastiness—the sheer normalcy of it—reassuring. I said, "We shall have long meetings where Kiggs agonizes and Glisselda teases him. That's the pattern so far."

"And you?" she said, leering. "What do you do?"

"I do what I have always done," I said, suddenly realizing the truth of it. "I reach across and bring the worlds together."

Nothing was just one thing; there were worlds within worlds. Those of us who trod the line between were blessed and burdened with both.

I stepped from the carriage into sunlight, into the crowd, smiling. I walked myself into the world.

ᴄ∩Ɛpilogueᴜ

My new suite had belonged to Selda's mother, Princess Dionne. The bedroom had been entirely refurbished, but I hadn't let them touch the sitting room; I liked the dark paneling and heavy carven furniture. Selda had insisted I take the harpsichord that once graced the south solar, and I couldn't resist. It fit awkwardly in the room, but what else was I to do with all this space?

I was at the instrument that rainy afternoon when a page boy showed him in. I didn't look up; this was going to take all my courage, and I needed a little more music to get there. He wouldn't mind my being rude.

He seated himself near the door to wait me out. I had been playing one of Viridius's fantasias, but I switched smoothly to my mother's composition, a fugue she'd written in honor of her brother. I loved it beyond all reckoning. It captured him perfectly: the solidity of the bass notes, the rationality of the middle ranges, and then the occasional, unexpected twinkle in the treble. Stillness and motion and a touch of sorrow—my mother's sorrow. She had missed him.

I missed him, too, but I could bear this. I took a deep breath.

I rolled the last arpeggios and then turned to face him. Orma still wore the mustard-colored habit of St. Gobnait's Order. I twisted his ring on my finger, hoping I'd deduced its meaning correctly, that he'd really made a mind-pearl.

Finding it would be a challenge.

He was looking not at me but at the coffered ceiling, his mouth open slightly. I said, "Brother Norman?"

He startled. "I interrupt your practice," he said.

That had been intentional. I said, "Did you recognize that song?"

He goggled at me, apparently trying to parse the surprising question. That was how it had to be from now on, if we were to find the untidy edges of any remaining memories. We would have to take them by surprise.

"I don't know," he said at last.

I took anything other than a negative answer as encouraging. "Did you like it?" I pressed.

He looked blank. "The abbot said you need an amanuensis and wish to interview me, but I have no interest in the position. I suspect you would like to continue your earlier line of inquiry, but that will be fruitless. I have no memory of you before Jannoula brought me here. I only want to finish my studies and go back—"

"Are you really so interested in monastic history?" I asked.

Wintry rain lashed the windows. Orma pushed up his spectacles; his throat bobbed as he swallowed. "No," he said at last. "But the destultia I take for my heart is an emotional suppressant. I'm not interested in anything, per se."

"It leaves you unable to fly when you are full-sized." I'd been reading up.

He nodded. "That's why we don't all take it as a matter of course."

"Do you remember what it's like to fly?"

He raised his dark, inscrutable eyes to mine. "How could I not? If they cut that out of me, they'd have to take too much. I'd have no memory . . . left. . . ." His gaze grew distant for a moment.

"There are pieces missing," I said. "You've noticed."

He fingered the scar on his scalp. "I hadn't, until you suggested it. I would chalk it up to diagnosis bias, but . . ." His expression was like a closed curtain. "There are a few things that don't make sense."

There was some inherent trait in him, some tendency to question, that had gotten him into as much trouble as emotions, if not more. Surely I could revive that curiosity if I prodded. "That song I was playing? You taught me that. You were my teacher."

His eyes were obscured behind the glare off his glasses. The wind rattled the windows.

"Come work with me," I said. "You can be weaned off the destultia; I know the trick of it. We will rediscover what they've stolen." I held out my hand and waggled the ring at him. "I think you made yourself a mind-pearl before you were caught."

He tented his long fingers. "If you're wrong, if I really do have pyrocardia, I will very likely die."

"Ye-es," I said slowly, wondering whether pyrocardia was something the Censors might have given him somehow, as a surprise present. I'd have to ask Eskar when she arrived. "I suppose you might die. But are you finding monastic history a very compelling reason to live?"

"I'm not human," he said. "I don't require a reason to live. Living is my default condition."

I couldn't help it; I laughed, and tears welled in my eyes. That answer was so quintessentially Orma, distilled to his elemental Orma-ness.

He watched me laugh as if I were an inexplicably noisy bird. "I'm not convinced this is worth your time or mine," he said.

My heart contracted painfully. "Don't you ever wish you could fly again?"

He shrugged. "If it means dying in flames, my wishes are irrelevant."

I took that as a definite yes. "You used to fly with your mind. Metaphorically. You used to be interested in everything. You asked inconvenient questions all the time." My voice broke; I cleared my throat.

He stared at me but said nothing.

My heart sank. "Aren't you curious, even a little?"

"No," he said.

He rose as if to go. I stood, too, and paced toward the windows, despairing. I couldn't make him stop taking destultia, or force him to be my friend. He could walk out of the room and refuse to see me again, and there was nothing I could do about it.

From behind me came the sound of a bench scraping on the floor, and then a few tentative notes on the harpsichord, like a child might make, cautiously approaching the instrument for the first time.

I kept my eyes on the rivulets running down the glass.

There was a chord, and then another, and then a small explosion of sparkly notes—the opening strains of Viridius's *Suite Infanta*.

I turned sharply, my heart in my throat. Orma's eyes were closed. He played the first three lines, then faltered and stopped.

He opened his eyes and looked into mine.

"One thing they can't remove without damaging other systems is muscle memory," he said quietly. "My hands did that. What was it?"

"A fantasia you used to play," I said.

He nodded slowly. "I'm still not curious. But . . ." He stared at the rain. "I begin to wish I *could* be."

I gestured to him to move over on the bench. He made room for me, and we sat together the rest of that afternoon, not talking, but letting our hands walk over the keys and remember.

Acknowledgments

This book was a beast to write. The following people ensured I was not eaten:

Arwen Brenneman and Rebecca Sherman, whom I can never thank enough; Phoebe North and the Glassboard Gang; Naithan Bossé and Earle Peach, who got me thinking about harmonics at just the right moment; Inchoiring Minds and Madrigalians; Becca, who showed me the taiga; Tamora Pierce, who knows about battling Grendels; Rose Curtin and Steph Sinclair, consultants to the clueless; Iarla Ó Lionáird; Jacob Arcadelt; Josquin des Prez; Bessie, my trusty bike; and my mother, who's always happy to talk about art.

I gratefully acknowledge the late Douglas Adams, to whom I owe the idea of an inside-out house, and Pink Floyd, to whom there are more sly allusions in this book than I can count.

Finally, thanks to Jim, Dan, Mallory, and the fabulous folks at Random House, who have been unflaggingly supportive and kind. And to Scott, Byron, and Úna, my heart and home.

Cast of Characters

At Castle Orison

Seraphina Dombegh—our charming heroine, often called Phina, half-dragon

Queen Lavonda—ill and abdicated

Rufus, Dionne, and Laurel—Lavonda's unlucky children, all dead

Queen Glisselda—plucky new head of state

Prince Lucian Kiggs—Glisselda's cousin and fiancé

Viridius—court composer, Seraphina's erstwhile employer

Lars—designer of trebuchets, lover of loud music, half-dragon

Abdo—dancer and scamp, possible property of a god, half-dragon

Tython—Abdo's pious grandfather

Dame Okra Carmine—undiplomatic Ninysh ambassador, half-dragon

Alberdt—resistant guardsman

dozy page boy—sleeping on the job

In Ninys

Josquin—Dame Okra's distant cousin, a chin-bearded herald

Captain Moy—leader of the Eight, the authoritative chin beard

Nan—Moy's doughty daughter

Des Osho—the Eight, Phina's armed escort through Ninys

Nedouard Basimo—kleptomaniac plague doctor, half-dragon

Blanche—reclusive hermit, fond of spiders, half-dragon

Od Fredricka des Uurne—muralist with a chip on her shoulder, half-dragon

Gianni Patto—claw-footed bogeyman of the Ninysh mountains, half-dragon

Count Pesavolta—ruler of Ninys and reluctant funder of quests

In Samsam

Hanse—terse old huntsman who escorts Phina through Samsam

Rodya—unwashed young bravo, the other escort

Josef, Earl of Apsig—Lars's half brother, disdainer of dragon-kind, up to no good

Jannoula—banished from Phina's mind, half-dragon

Ingar, Earl of Gasten—lover of books, learner of languages, disciple of Jannoula, half-dragon

In Porphyry

Naia—Abdo's favorite auntie

Paulos Pende—elderly priest with a powerful mind, leader of the half-dragons, or ityasaari, in Porphyry

Zythia Perdixis Camba—statuesque lady, unexpectedly familiar, ityasaari

Amalia Perdixis Lita—Camba's aged mother, Agogoi

Mina—winged officer of the law, ityasaari

Brasidas—blind market singer, ityasaari

Phloxia—shark-toothed lawyer (literally), ityasaari

Gaios and Gelina—handsome fleet-footed twins, ityasaari

Draconic Friends and Foes

Ardmagar Comonot—deposed leader of dragonkind, bothering the Queen

Orma—Phina's uncle, on the run

Eskar—former undersecretary of the dragon embassy; running with Orma, or pursuing her own plans?

Ikat—physician, civic leader of the dragon exiles in Porphyry

Colibris—Ikat's daughter, forever young

Lalo—exiled saarantras, eager to go home

Mitha—quigutl of Lab Four, friend to Eskar, insurrectionist and folksinger

General Zira—prominent Loyalist general

General Palonn—prominent general for the Old Ard

General Laedi—new strategist for the Old Ard, the butcher of Homand-Eynn

Noble Knights

Sir Cuthberte Pettybone—knight of Phina's acquaintance, too old for war, too young to die

Sir Maurizio Foughfaugh—erstwhile squire of Phina's acquaintance, still a dedicated nuisance

Sir Joshua Pender—training the next generation of dracomachists

Squire Anders—the next generation, easily dazzled

Glossary

Agogoi—founding families of Porphyry, now make up the ruling Assembly

Allsaints—all the Saints in Heaven. Not a deity, exactly; more like a collective

ard—Mootya for "order, correctness"; may also denote a battalion of dragons

Ardmagar—title held by the leader of dragonkind; translates roughly to "supreme general"

aurochs—large, wild cattlebeast, extinct in our world; existed in Europe until the Renaissance

Bibliagathon—great library of Porphyry

Blystane—capital of Samsam

Castle Orison—Goreddi seat of government, in Lavondaville

Censors—extra-governmental dragon agency charged with maintaining draconic purity

Chakhon—Porphyrian god of chance, sometimes called Merry Chance

Comonot's Treaty—established peace between Goredd and dragonkind

destultia—draconic drug; an emotional suppressant, analgesic, and pyrocardia cure

Donques—village in the Ninysh alps

doublet—short, fitted, and often padded man's jacket

dracomachia—martial art for fighting dragons; invented by St. Ogdo

excision—surgical removal of memories from deviant dragons, performed at the discretion of the Censors

Fnark—Samsamese village, site of St. Abaster's shrine

gaar—Porphyrian anchovy paste, more delicious than it sounds

Goredd—Seraphina's homeland, one of the Southlands (adjective form: Goreddi)

Heaven—Southlanders' afterlife, as outlined by the Saints in scripture

Homand-Eynn—site of a terrible Loyalist defeat

houppelande—robe of rich material with voluminous sleeves, usually worn belted; women's are floor-length; a man's might be cut at the knee

ityasaari—half-dragon (Porphyrian)

Ker—council of dragon generals that advises the Ardmagar

Kerama—capital of the Tanamoot

Lab Four—secret Censorial facility in the Tanamoot

Laika—island near Porphyry where the Porphyrian navy moors

Lakhis—Porphyrian goddess of necessity, sometimes called Dread Necessity

Lavondaville—Seraphina's hometown and the largest city in Goredd, named for Queen Lavonda, who made peace with dragonkind forty years ago

Loyalists—dragons who take Comonot's side in the civil war

Meconi—river leading from the Omiga Valley to the interior of the Tanamoot

Metasaari—Porphyrian neighborhood, home to exiled saarantrai

Montesanti—monastery of St. Abaster's Order in Ninys

Mootya—language of dragons, rendered in sounds a human mouth can make

Ninys—country southeast of Goredd, one of the Southlands (adjective form: Ninysh)

Old Ard—dragons opposed to Comonot and his Loyalists

Omiga—principal river of Porphyry

oud—lute-like instrument, often played with a pick, or plectrum

palasho—palace (Ninysh)

Pinabra—vast pine forest in southeast Ninys

Porphyry—small city-state at the mouth of the Omiga River, northwest of the Southlands; originally a colony of dark-skinned people from even further north; may also refer to its territories along the Omiga River

psalter—book of devotional poetry, usually illustrated; in Goreddi psalters, there's a poem for each of the major Saints

pyria—sticky, flammable substance used in dracomachia for setting dragons on fire; also called St. Ogdo's fire

pyrocardia—deadly heart condition in dragons

Quighole—dragon and quigutl ghetto in Lavondaville

quigutl—small, flightless subspecies of dragon with a set of dexterous arms in place of wings; do the dirty, fussy jobs that dragons can't or won't

saar—Porphyrian for "dragon"; often used by Goreddis as a short form of *saarantras*

saarantras—Porphyrian for "dragon in human form" (plural form: saarantrai)

St. Abaster—defender of the faith; hates dragons, but loves smiting; revered in Samsam, but popping up all over

St. Capiti—representing the life of the mind; Phina's substitute patroness

St. Clare—patroness of the perceptive

St. Fionnuala—Lady of Waters; called Fionani in Ninys

St. Gobnait—patroness to the diligent and persistent; cathedral in Lavondaville named for her

St. Ida—patroness of musicians and performers; music conservatory in Lavondaville named for her

St. Ogdo—founder of dracomachia; patron of knights and of all Goredd

St. Pandowdy—lost Saint

St. Tarkus—another one

St. Willibald—patron of markets and news; called Wilibaio in Ninys and Villibaltus in Samsam

St. Yirtrudis—the heretic; Phina's true patroness; author of an interesting testament

Samsam—rain-soaked country south of Goredd, one of the Southlands (adjective form: Samsamese)

Segosh—capital of Ninys, center of art and culture (adjective form: Segoshi)

shawm—oboe-like instrument

skittle-pin—small pin used in lawn or table bowling

Skondia—Porphyrian harborside neighborhood

Southlands—Goredd, Ninys, and Samsam together

Tanamoot—dragons' vast country north of the Southlands, wild and mountainous

Vasilikon—Porphyrian seat of government

Zokalaa—great square of central Porphyry